FALLING IN LOVE
ON THE FRONT LINES

"I just don't want to get too close to anyone over here. You understand?"

"Not really."

Tyler groaned. "Listen, men and women get together over here for all sorts of reasons. When it's over, there's a lot of heartbreak because what they thought they had was created by the circumstances, by the war. And that's if both of them make it *through* the year. That's if one of them doesn't get *killed.*"

Jennifer felt as if she were falling into the depths of his soul through the blue windows of his eyes. He was serious about what he was telling her, she understood his concerns, but the more she stared, the deeper she tumbled.

"I just want to get to know you a little, that's all." Even as she uttered the words, she knew they were a lie.

"Maybe," he said with emphasis she couldn't possibly misinterpret, "that wouldn't be enough for *me.*"

SING
TO
ME,
SAIGON

Kathryn
Jensen

POCKET BOOKS

New York   London   Toronto   Sydney   Tokyo   Singapore

This book is a work of fiction. Names, characters, places and incidents either are products of the author's imagination or are used fictitiously. Any resemblance to actual events or locales or persons, living or dead, is entirely coincidental.

POCKET BOOKS, a division of Simon & Schuster Inc.
1230 Avenue of the Americas, New York, NY 10020

Copyright © 1994 by Kathryn Jensen

ISBN: 978-1-4767-2810-0

First Pocket Books printing May 1994

10 9 8 7 6 5 4 3 2 1

POCKET and colophon are registered trademarks of Simon & Schuster Inc.

Cover art by Gregg Gulbronson

Printed in the U.S.A.

*Dedicated to the memory of
Theresa Paula Coyne Jensen.
You gave me the strength
you never knew you had.*

ACKNOWLEDGMENTS

I am indebted to these individuals and organizations for their generously offered expertise and advice: Mr. Armando Framarini and Sgt. Billy Jamison of the U.S. Army Ordnance Museum, Aberdeen Proving Ground; 1776th Security Police Squadron-Training Section, Andrews Air Force Base; Richard Lane at Fort George Meade; JoAnn Tater; and, with regret that I cannot give credit where it is due, those individuals who prefer to remain anonymous but graciously shared their Nam memories.

My heartfelt thanks to Bill Pearce for his gentle but insightful critical read of the manuscript.

Finally, for her loving help in creating this book, from concept to printed page, I offer my gratitude to Linda Hayes—indispensable agent as well as cherished friend.

Sing to me, Saigon
And I will sing
      to you
Of loyalties
      and loves,
Bravery
      and beasts,
Beauty
      and war's
Last harsh caress.
Whose touch will linger
Forever on my flesh
And in my Heart.

SING
TO
ME,
SAIGON

1

Marblehead, Massachusetts—1966

The limestone cliffs ringing the harbor glared a clean gray-white in the July sunlight. When she'd been very little, Jennifer Lynn used to believe that a particularly industrious team of maids periodically scrubbed them down. The image made perfect sense to a child who was accustomed to seeing everything else in her life scrupulously washed, waxed, buffed, and polished by a fleet of servants.

It had been disappointing, even unsettling to discover that the beauty of the cliffs had nothing to do with human effort. Anything so wonderful oughtn't to be left to nature's whim. Such lack of control frightened her—until she learned to appreciate the element of chance, the dizzy, delicious exhilaration of risk.

Risk! The word's mere mention sent chills up and down her spine.

Whitecaps nipped at the bow of the sturdy launch in which Jennifer and her best friend, Francie, rode. They scuttled between other boats, dropping off an elderly man and his wife at their majestic Westsail, stopping once more to unload a young couple at their trim little Flicka. All the while, Jennifer thought about risks—the risks of love, of war, of money.

Jennifer leaned back against the shellacked oak rail, shook out her blond pageboy, and with it any deep thoughts. Today was too perfect to be serious—besides, she wasn't dressed for it.

She wore a halter top—white cotton with tiny navy-blue anchors hand-embroidered by a Palm Beach seamstress along the neckline and below her breasts—and tight white canvas short-shorts. She stretched out her slim eighteen-year-old body, clasping her hands behind her head and arching her back as she shut her eyes against the glare of the sun. Opening her mouth, she tasted the salt spray kicked back by the powerful twin Mercury outboard motors, then squinted slightly, just enough to observe the expression on Francie's face.

"Is he watching?" Jennifer whispered.

"Like a hawk."

"Stop grinning," she said, hissing. "You'll spoil everything."

The pixyish redhead covered her lips with one hand. "I can't help it. Oh, my God! Here he comes. He's going to attack you. I just knew you'd gone too far this time."

The balding man in traditional yachtsman's white duck slacks and navy-blue blazer had stood up from his bench along the gunwale. He moved silently across the boat and settled himself on the empty bench seat next to Jennifer.

After a moment, he asked, "Don't I know you, young lady?"

What a gem! Jennifer blinked in the sunlight, observing him. His face was red. Not from sunburn, she was sure. He had watched her outrageous performance clandestinely at first, from beneath the brim of his cute little admiral's cap. Seeing the fellow's interest in her, the launch jockey, Mark, had bet Jennifer a keg that she couldn't get him to come on to her before they dropped him at his sloop.

The seduction had been working quite well. The man, who resembled a dried-up prune of a bank manager, had wiped his palms on his pant legs, then removed his jaunty cap and dabbed at his forehead with his blazer sleeve, although the ocean breeze was brisk and cool. His eyes hadn't left Jennifer's long, smooth legs for a full three minutes. Now she could tell he was silently practicing his speech. He looked uneasily at Francie, as if her presence made him especially cautious of what he was about to say.

Say it, Jennifer thought. *Say it!*

She shaded her eyes with one hand and gazed up at him limpidly from her half-prone position. "Know me?" She sighed. "I suppose it's possible. Perhaps Palm Beach? Or the Hamptons? We have places there."

"No-o-o," he said after consideration. "Ummm . . . I was just going to remark that you seem awfully young to be . . . well . . ." He dropped his eyes, found his pipe in one pocket and brought it out to play with nervously.

Jennifer leaned closer, breathed softly into his ear, and said, "To be what?"

Startled, he pulled back, scowling at her. Then recollection dawned in the doughy creases around his eyes. "Maxwell Swanson. You are Max's little girl!"

Oh, Christ! she thought.

He grinned triumphantly and slid a healthy two feet away from her. "My . . . well, you have filled—um, grown up. Quite a young lady. Heard you were at Miss Porter's."

Jennifer caught a smirk on Mark's suntanned face. *Make it a case?* he mouthed, upping the ante.

She wrinkled her nose at him. *You're on!*

"I've graduated," she said. The chic boarding school in Farmington, Connecticut was, thankfully, in her past. At last she had her longed-for freedom.

Three other passengers rode the launch while Mark steered it across the harbor. They pretended to be just now noticing the new house being constructed at the far end of the cliff. Pointing to it. Discussing a flaw in style. Jennifer knew they disapproved of her flirting. But they didn't understand her game.

"Well," he continued, "it's been years since I saw you . . .

3

or you saw me for that matter. Time does fly, heh?" He chuckled. "I'm Franklin Robarge. Your father and I are old friends . . . or business associates, really."

"Really," Jennifer said, folding her arms over her chest.

This could drag on forever and get nowhere at all. It wasn't fair! Mark probably knew the guy, had him pegged for a local, not some New Yorker renting for the summer. But what the hell, Mark didn't know everything!

"And do you and Daddy share the same taste in fashion?" she asked impishly, drawing a deep breath. Her halter top swelled.

Robarge coughed, reaching for his tobacco pouch. "I . . . I don't know, actually."

Jennifer noticed how his eyes tended to drift toward her breasts. Aha! A slim ray of hope.

"Daddy doesn't like miniskirts, or short-shorts. Says they're unladylike. I think I look very much like a lady."

"Oh, yes." Cough. Chuckle. "Can't mistake you for much else." Robarge fell silent. He concentrated on ramming his pipe full of tobacco leaves. Pinch, stuff, stuff. Pinch, stuff, stuff. "Is your father still in electronics?" he asked finally.

She'd lost; he was changing the subject.

"Yes." She sighed.

Electronics were making Max Swanson richer by the minute, even as they sat here. He could shut himself up in his study for weeks, doing nothing at all, and keep on getting richer. He could take a month, or two, sail around the world. Swanson Limited would continue raking in the bucks. But he didn't sit and he didn't sail. He "pressed on," like the enormous perpetual motion pendulum she'd watched end-lessly as a child at the Boston Museum of Science. Nothing stopped him. Nothing swayed him from his self-ordained path.

However, that wasn't what most bothered her about her father. What really got to her was that he fully intended to control *her* life, just as he controlled her mother's and sister's.

First he'd enrolled her in Miss Porter's, because that was where little Gloria Vanderbilt and so many of the North

Shore's feminine elite had been educated. Then there had been "coming out" at a lavish, outdated ceremony at the Ritz-Carlton. She'd been accepted at Radcliffe, which was where she'd go in the fall—unless she could think of a way to get out of it. Her parents recommended that Jennifer follow a liberal arts course in order to "round out" her preparation for life. But everyone knew that was just another way of saying she needn't be prepared to *do* anything with her life. She'd marry one of the many young men she'd waltzed with as a deb. It didn't matter if she finished college, or what she chose to major in while there. The important thing was making connections, dressing right, attending the proper schools, knowing the appropriate phrases to drop. When an Auchincloss or Kennedy or du Pont was in the room—and her parents entertained often at Swanson House on the cliff—she could almost guarantee Max and Patricia were drooling into their port.

But she'd made up her mind two years ago that she wasn't going to let them turn *her* into another boring, hypochondriac ex-deb matron of society like her sister. Sarah was perfectly miserable.

In theory, Jennifer's friends agreed with her philosophy. None of them enjoyed being boxed in. But then, they reasoned, what use was there fighting family? Once you'd fulfilled your basic obligations, you could use your inheritance however you liked. Jennifer thought her friends were blind. Most of them got too caught up in playing a role, with no chance to be themselves. Life was just too, too dull and predictable.

Jennifer caught Robarge watching her again. When she met his eyes, he looked away quickly.

"Ho, Mr. Robarge," said Mark with overdone gusto. "Your stop." He winked at Jennifer. *Time's up.*

She fumed as Robarge stood and hefted a canvas bag full of gear.

"Tough luck," murmured Francie. "But you had to strike out, sooner or later."

Jennifer looked at her friend, then Mark. Robarge was stepping onto his boat. She rolled her eyes to the cloudless blue sky. *Not fair!* she thought. Mark had cheated, but he'd claim victory. Tonight on the rocky beach around the bonfire, all of her friends would sit guzzling beer she had bought, and Mark would remind them of her failure—her first in a long series of carefully choreographed seductions.

Inside her, a tiny spark, nourished by defeat, grew to a flame. What had begun as a game now had became a question of honor! That unscrupulous Mark. She wouldn't let him get away with it.

Jennifer shot up off the bench and moved on seaworthy bare feet across the damp floorboards of the launch to the steps and Robarge. She grabbed him by the vent in his blazer.

He turned with a startled jerk. "What is it, Miss Swanson?" he asked with some irritation.

She fluttered her long, pale lashes at him. "Are you all alone today . . . sailing?" she asked, with a suggestive tilt to her hips.

One foot still on the launch, the other on his own deck, Robarge balanced between the two boats as they bumped together, bobbing unevenly over the wave tops. "Yes, for the time being . . ."

She pulled herself up beside him, and, holding her breasts close to his lapel for Mark's benefit, she whispered into the man's ear. When Robarge drew back, he was smiling with obvious anticipation.

"No, I insist! Come aboard. Glad to have you, dear!" He offered his hand to help her over the side to the polished oak floorboards of the sleek yacht.

When Mark pushed off, he cast Jennifer a baleful look. She stood smugly on Robarge's deck, her arm laced through the crook of his elbow. While everyone on the launch was still watching, she rose on tiptoe and pecked him on the cheek.

"You're a dear," she whispered.

Mark bought the keg. He had served up a couple rounds by the time Jennifer arrived on the moonlit beach, and the

6

lobsters, clams, and corn-on-the-cob were steaming and done.

Jennifer plopped down on the sand beside him and rested her head on his shoulder. "Am I the best, or am I the best?"

"Get lost," he grumbled.

"Come on." She patted his hand. "A kiss for the loser."

He brushed her off. She reached for his paper cup, but he drained it in two gulps, ignoring her. The salt air had turned wheaty with the smell of beer. "The Sounds of Silence" played on a transistor radio. Clusters of teenagers discussed a civil rights march planned for somewhere in Alabama . . . or Vietnam. Always Vietnam these days.

"Spoilsport," she scoffed, then got to her feet and dusted the sand off the seat of her pants.

She found Francie snuggled up with a guy she'd met last October at a Phillips–Exeter dance.

"They all make me ill," Jennifer moaned.

"What's wrong now?" Francie asked.

"All of you. You talk a great line about being rebels, making changes in the world. But do you *do* anything? I'm the only one who accepts a challenge."

Francie giggled. 'Most of us are a little more cautious."

Francie's date started to open his mouth, but Jennifer jumped in before he could say anything.

"Take Craig here, he marches at protests against the war now and then. You both get all puffy with pride every time he ends up in jail for a few hours."

"Greg," he corrected.

Jennifer shook her head. "See. All he can think of is . . . get the name right. For the papers, so he can needle his old man. Do you think that's going to do any good?"

Two other couples moved over to listen in on the conversation. "Maybe you can take on Johnson's entire cabinet," suggested one boy.

They all hooted. "Sure, Jenny. Screw them all. Maybe you can stop the war that way."

"Well, I sure as hell can't do worse than you with your silly rallies and petitions, now can I?" she demanded.

"Have a drag," offered a sandy-haired boy she didn't recognize. He laid a hand on her hip and grinned lewdly. She figured he'd crashed the party and had been treated to a recital of her exploits.

"Sure," she said with a sweet smile. But, as soon as he handed her the marijuana joint, she walked away, puffing it down to a glowing spot in the night.

"Hey! You totaled it!" he yelled after her.

She ignored him and plodded on alone down the stone-strewn beach. Francie caught up with her. They walked together in silence.

After a while, Jennifer asked, "What's Mark so pissed off about?"

Francie shrugged. "I think he likes you. Maybe he doesn't appreciate you coming on to every guy the way you do."

"Then he shouldn't make bets."

"You don't have to take him up on them."

"Oh, yes, I do," said Jennifer.

Francie sighed. "What you need is one really super guy."

"You sound like my parents."

Francie laughed. "They don't talk like that."

"Same concept. Get married, join the Corinthian Yacht Club, perform charitable acts, raise a family . . ."

Francie threw up her hands and turned to walk backward, facing her friend. "Are you trying to fix it so that can't happen? I mean, none of *our* men will dare consider you proper wife material. Their families would be scandalized."

"Honestly?" Jennifer beamed.

Francie shook her head. "You're impossible."

The night deepened, and the only sound that competed with the gentle slush of the waves on the beach was the chug-chug-a-chug of a few outboards coming in late after a day of sport fishing.

At last Francie said, "You didn't get laid, did you?"

"No."

"You tricked Mark."

"So."

"What did you tell Robarge to make him let you go with him?"

"I said that my daddy's boat was just outside the harbor, off Brown Island, and I wanted to join him, but I had no way out. He offered to take me."

Francie grinned in the dark. "Serves Mark right."

Jennifer threw an arm around her friend's shoulder and steered her back toward the bonfire. "I thought so."

They eventually rejoined the group. Mark sat on the far side of the circle, looking sullen. But after a few minutes he came around and wordlessly handed Jennifer her guitar.

She looked up at him and wondered if she should tell him about Robarge. No, it would spoil the fun . . . the only fun she ever had, the one thing that separated her from the rest of them, aside from her music. And that didn't even count when you stopped to think of it, because she sang only what they asked for, to please them.

"Which one?" she asked, grasping the neck of the guitar and flipping the strap over her head.

" 'Blowin' in the Wind,' " shouted someone.

She nodded and strummed the guitar, adjusting the screws for pitch.

As a hush fell over the beach and the strings vibrated beneath her fingers, she began in a sweet lyric soprano that chilled the nerves and made couples move closer in the orange glow of the firelight. Dylan's words quivered and drifted from her lips, the shape and tone of each as pure as early morning mist over the Atlantic.

Jennifer knew she did not sound like a rock singer. Her voice was really all wrong. But if the notes she produced had been visible—light instead of sound—they would have sparkled in the firelight and danced across the wave tops like skipping stones. During the time it took her to finish the song, she was elsewhere, more than herself, taking into her soul a world full of mournful, weary, war-sick women warning their governments to stop fighting before it was too late. And she could almost believe that there was a chance people might listen. But when the silvery tones faded from her lips, she realized how deceptive music could be. She didn't care about the war. It wasn't real to her.

As she sang another song, then another, she dwelled on

her own futile rebellion. Maybe she was more of a fool than all of her friends combined. Didn't she cheat at every corner? Even in her famous seductions. For she'd escaped every one untarnished. The game for her was snagging her prey. After that, she lost all interest.

It wasn't that she was afraid of sex. But her friends did it, and they smoked pot and drank beer and talked nonsense about righting the world—joining the Peace Corps, going to law school to serve their country, or taking a bus (the ultimate sacrifice) to march in Birmingham. They were such fakes.

Maybe, by not doing it with guys, that was another way of rebelling. Or maybe she should just give in and go along with them. Because what did it matter when everything was said and done? She was a North Shore Swanson. Her life was charted. All that was required was to drift along with the current.

2

On Newbury Street, that November, someone had erected a brightly painted booth. A poster was pasted over one end. It was a picture of a hawk-faced Uncle Sam, garbed in his garish ensemble of red, white, and blue, pointing at passersby.

The tiny plywood structure looked outrageously out of place, situated as it was alongside the fashionable shops of Burberry's, F.A.O. Schwarz, and Brooks Brothers (where all Miss Porter's girls stocked up on mountains of pale pastel cardigans, which they counted and competed with to see who had the most).

As Jennifer and Francie were walking past, two girls emerged from the booth. They wore starched white caps and uniforms. They were giggling and hugging each other with mutual delight.

Jennifer was intrigued by their simple joy as she and Francie strolled behind them down the sidewalk. They looked so happy! How could anyone be that ecstatic? She watched as the pair crossed the street, holding hands like schoolgirls, swinging arms, laughing. They turned down a side street toward the historic, treed Fenway and stopped into a bar.

"Come on," she said, grabbing Francie by the hand.

"Where are we going?"

"I'm thirsty."

"Good. I'm hungry. Let's grab a cab. Lunch at *Anthony's?*"

"No," said Jennifer. "Right here will be fine."

Francie grumbled as they crossed the street, coming to a dead halt a couple feet in front of the bar. "I don't think I could actually eat anything in *there.*"

The place was little more than a dingy, back-street hole in the wall. "Just a drink, then. We'll go for lunch later."

"This doesn't have anything to do with those two nurses, does it?" asked Francie suspiciously. "I hate it when you start up conversations with total strangers."

"How else am I going to find out about the real world?"

In Farmington they were *never* allowed out on their own. No movies. No unchaperoned weekend shopping sprees. Holidays were brief respites from school, but just as sheltered. Only this summer, before leaving for college, had she been allowed to wander through Marblehead and into Boston—so long as she stayed with Francie. Francie Trent was known to be "level-headed."

"I only want to find out what they're celebrating."

Francie thrust her nose into the air. "They've just passed their little practical exams undoubtedly. How to empty a bedpan. *Re-al-ly,* Jennifer. I don't like—"

Jennifer got behind her friend and shoved her through the grimy doorway.

She'd never been in a place like this before. The interior was deliciously dark. The two nurses sat at a table in a rear corner; as if they were regulars.

Jennifer liked the smells: whiskey and damp wood. Francie wrinkled her nose.

Jennifer laughed. This was real! This was human. She doubted a place like this existed in Marblehead.

Jennifer wove between the tables. Behind her, Francie

scuffled along in little rabbit steps. A few men at the bar turned, curiously watching their progress.

Sitting down at the table nearest the nurses', Jennifer listened in shamelessly. They were talking about Vietnam, but not in the way her friends talked about it.

"This is *so* fantastic!" the blond one cried. "We'll both be going to the Ninety-fifth Evac, for sure, *together!*" They squealed.

When the waitress came over, the nurses calmed down long enough to order.

Jennifer whispered to Francie, "They're *going* to Vietnam! Can you believe it? I didn't think women were allowed."

"And they're happy?"

Jennifer was fascinated.

"Order me something," she told Francie and rose from the table.

Francie clutched at her sleeve, but Jennifer shook her off. "They won't serve us; we're not twenty-one," she called out.

Jennifer groaned. At home it was perfectly acceptable to have an aperitif. Servants never asked for identification.

"Ginger ale, then. I don't care." Feeling more nervous than she let on, she approached the young women. "Hi!" she said.

They looked up.

The blond one had short, permed hair and wore owlishly mod eyeglasses. She raised a hand. "Hi."

Jennifer sat down. "I overheard. You're going abroad? Overseas, I mean," she quickly corrected herself.

"Yeah. Vietnam." The petite brunette giggled. "I wasn't sure we could pull it off. But we did it."

"Oh," Jennifer said.

What was drawing these two girls to a country that her friends were pulling strings to avoid? Most had educational deferments. But if those ran out—as it was rumored that they would next year—they could join the National Guard or Peace Corps. Some even talked of fleeing to Canada, if necessary.

She supposed she should congratulate the nurses, since they seemed so pleased with themselves.

"Well, that's great." She waved Francie over, but her friend turned her head away, intentionally ignoring her. "Have you been trying very long to get over there?"

"Not trying so much as hoping," the blonde replied, suddenly solemn. Their beers arrived, as well as Jennifer's drink. They all took sips. "We just graduated and don't have any experience. You know, in a hospital except as students. So, it seemed like a long shot."

"But the army badly needs nurses," said the other. "There aren't enough to take care of our soldiers."

"There are that many wounded?" Jennifer asked. From the accounts she'd read in the *Globe,* she knew Americans were being hurt and sent home. Some died. But the numbers didn't seem all that terrible when you considered it was a war, declared or not.

"Oh, yes," said the blonde. "The casualties have to be very high. Otherwise, they wouldn't have taken us."

Jennifer nodded. She doubted her friends ever talked like these girls. The words nonintervention or deferment hadn't been mentioned once. "Why do you want to go there?" she asked curiously.

The two nurses looked at each other. "Well," the owl said, in a very patient tone as if her motives should have been evident, "if we stay in Boston, see, we'll get minimum starting pay and barely have enough to live on. We'll pull the worst shifts, with all the drudge duties. But in Nam with the army, you make grade real fast, and the money's fab."

"And you feel needed," her sidekick added quietly. "I mean, we went to school to learn how to take care of hurt and sick people. So, here we'd be changing bed linens and giving massages. There we'll be saving lives!" She seemed to glow from deep inside—a little brunette light bulb looking for a corner in which to shine. Jennifer envied her skill and her bravery.

She listened to them go on about their plans: when they'd leave, what they'd pack. They argued good-naturedly about where they'd spend their R-and-R—Tokyo, Hawaii, or stateside. The travel didn't impress Jennifer. After all, she'd had plenty of chaperoned trips to Europe. What struck her as especially wonderful was that people were depending on these young women to come and help them. No one had ever depended upon her. No one *needed* her. She was just another deb, with nowhere to end up but in an "appropriate" marriage.

Jennifer wished the nurses good luck and returned to Francie, who refused to talk to her. The redhead with her bouffant do and pale, freckled turned-up nose silently drank her Coke, eyes glued to the door and the street beyond.

Jennifer paid Francie no attention. Her mind was buzzing. Life seemed to have taken on an entirely different color. Maybe possibilities *were* open to her after all!

"Ready to go?" Jennifer asked, jumping up.

Francie gave her an acrimonious glare.

"Let's get a move on," Jennifer prodded.

"You mean," Francie purred, "you don't want to hang around for another drink in this spiffy establishment?"

"Come on." Jennifer laughed, pulling Francie up and out of her chair.

Outside, Jennifer led Francie up Newbury Street, then stopped in front of the red, white, and blue booth. Two men and a woman, all in crisp, official-looking army uniforms, lounged against a makeshift desk.

"Jennifer," Francie warned, tensing beside her. "No. Absolutely not. You can't be thinking what I think you are. Your mother will never speak to me again if I let—"

"Don't worry," Jennifer said. "I just want to ask a few questions."

"Well, that's just fine," Francie huffed. "I thought we came to Boston to shop. I'm going on to Brooks Brothers, with or without you!"

Jennifer examined her friend's expression. Once faced with the loss of an audience, Jennifer was obviously expected to give up. But this time was different. This wasn't a prank. What she was about to do could have real consequences in her own life and the lives of people she hadn't even met yet.

"I'll join you at *Anthony's* in an hour," she said quietly but firmly.

A few minutes later, Jennifer swallowed the lump in her throat as she watched her best friend climb into a taxi, which immediately disappeared into the Boston midtown traffic.

She edged her way up to the booth and began flipping through a brochure. The conversation behind the coffee-ringed counter ceased.

"May I help you?" the woman asked.

Jennifer looked up. The two male officers were checking her out. One smiled at the other—the way men did when they sized her up. *Delectable but probably jail bait*, their expressions said. They turned away.

"Is this where I sign up for Vietnam?" Jennifer asked in a rush of breath.

The woman straightened. Her skeptical gray eyes took in Jennifer's mandarin-collared brocade coat, its mini length, perfectly matching the skirt underneath, her plum calfskin Capezzio flats.

"You're a nurse?"

"Well, no," Jennifer admitted. She chafed her hands together. As soon as the sun slipped behind clouds, the air grew chill. Or was it the woman's tone? "But I'm sure I can learn very fast. And . . . and there must be lots of other jobs I could do there . . . to help out."

The words had a nice flavor as they slipped over her tongue. Mother never helped out; she organized. Chaired committees. Helping out was for suburban housewives.

The woman was shaking her head. "I'm afraid not, miss. What we need are nurses."

"Are *you* a nurse?" asked Jennifer.

"No, I'm in recruiting."

"Oh. But, if I signed on with the army, then I'd get training, right?"

The woman nodded. "But not nursing school, dear."

"Well, after I had some training—like with clerical things—" She was unsure of the correct terms. "—I could go to Vietnam."

"It's unlikely. Do your parents know you've come down here?"

"I'm as old as those nurses you just signed up," she retorted, offended. "I didn't see their parents."

"Miss, I'm sorry. Nurses are what we need. I don't know what you're trying to run away from, but I think there must be other solutions."

Jennifer stood riveted to the same spot for several minutes, feeling her cheeks flush red hot. She'd never been turned down before, for anything. It had always been so easy to get whatever she wanted. And now somebody was saying she wasn't good enough!

After what seemed an eternity, she spun away. She was halfway down the block when a voice called her back.

"Miss. Miss, wait a minute."

Jennifer stopped. She stood stiffly in the middle of the sidewalk, her fists clenched at her sides, her eyes brimming with tears she refused to let fall. What she absolutely didn't want now were consoling words. But when the woman motioned for her to come back, she obeyed.

"If you're really interested in jobs in Vietnam, I could put your name on a mailing list. Sometimes the government or private agencies . . ." The woman's voice was kind as she explained various options. "Why don't you fill out this information sheet—about your education and interests. If something comes up . . ."

Jennifer smiled. "Thank you," she said, picking up a pen.

It was not until the following March, during spring break from Radcliffe, that the letter arrived. Miriam, who served their meals, had placed it beside Jennifer's plate before lunch. The postmark read Los Angeles. Across the table from her mother, Jennifer opened the unimpressive-looking envelope without expectations.

The words slowly sunk in, like syrup over pancakes,

sweetening a gray day she'd expected to be ordinary. Her hands shaking, she refolded the letter and slipped it back into its envelope.

"I'm going to New York," she told her mother, all in one breath.

Patricia Swanson looked up over her half lenses from the far end of the mahogany clawfoot table. "Invitation from a school chum for the holidays?"

Jennifer hesitated. Any other time, she'd have told her mother the truth, if only to see the marble-smooth contours of her face change shape. They rarely did.

But this was too important for the truth.

"Yes," she lied. "I'd like to pop down tomorrow."

Her mother glanced down at her list again.

Jennifer couldn't recall a time when Patricia Swanson didn't have one sort or another of a list in hand. She was an absolute genius at making them. Once completed, she'd divide each large list into separate little ones that she'd then pass out to people who'd take care of accomplishing each task.

Jennifer felt a wave of sadness. Imagine, going through life without ever taking one of those jobs for herself. At the end of it all, what could her mother say she'd done with her own hands, her own body and soul? She'd made lists.

"I think it would be good to spend some time away," Patricia murmured without looking up. "You'll be home by the twenty-eighth? Sarah and her boys will be here for a visit."

"Absolutely," Jennifer promised.

"Have Marguerite make your reservations." She frowned at the gold pen in her hand. "Do you need help drawing up a packing agenda?"

"No," Jennifer said, softly.

She stood up and walked around the long table. In an uncharacteristic gesture of intimacy Jennifer kissed her mother gently on top of her soft, amber-waved coif. She left the room, aware that the woman's puzzled gaze followed her up the winding staircase to her bedroom.

* * *

18

Beside the revolving door of the Manhattan skyscraper was a copper plaque listing the building's occupants. *U.S. Armed Forces Radio* was the last name. Jennifer lugged her guitar case into the cold, gray granite lobby. Slinging her purse and the alligator attaché case that contained her music over the other shoulder, she hobbled to the elevator.

The thirteenth-floor receptionist made her wait in a room with twenty-two other girls. About half of them had long hair, curled up in crisp rolls at the feathery tips. The rest wore brief bobs, longer in the front so that the ends curved under at the jawline. A few had brought guitars, but most just held music folders in their laps.

The letter hadn't explained much about the position that she was applying for. The job required a young woman, aged sixteen to nineteen with a pleasant speaking voice. Previous experience as a model, actress, or singer would be helpful. Flexibility was a must, as travel overseas for one year would be necessary.

She idly flipped through the various magazines, none of which were her mother's standby, *Town and Country*. One girl left the room, a few minutes later recrossing the lobby on her way out. Another name was called by the receptionist. The room grew less crowded.

When it was Jennifer's turn, she walked through the door and down a corridor, following a girl who consulted a clipboard. After several twists along the route, Jennifer was directed into a studio with a glass-windowed booth.

"Have you done radio before?"

"No," Jennifer said, "but I learn—"

"Never mind. Just watch the red light. When it goes on, read into that microphone. Don't get too close, or you'll buzz. About six inches is right. Here's the script. Put on your earphones. Good luck." And she was gone.

Jennifer sat in a plastic swivel chair and stared at the insides of the booth. It was about half the size of her closet at home. The little room she was in was brightly lit, the space beyond almost totally dark. On the far side of the glass, she could dimly make out a half-dozen faces, but no expressions.

The light flashed on. Startled, Jennifer glanced down at the papers in her hand. The top page seemed to be a weather report. Clipping the earphones into place, she began reading the words with as much authority as possible, trying to imitate the meteorologist on WBZ-TV.

"That's fine," a phantom voice interrupted through the earphones before she'd finished. "Go on to the next page."

She bent back a sheet and scanned. This appeared to be a one-way conversation—a girl talking to her boyfriend, only he wasn't answering.

She started to read, imagining herself gabbing with her friends about the topics written into her script. She seriously doubted that anyone she knew—if suddenly dropped into a jungle on the other side of the world—would care about the most recent motion picture releases. Or sharing hamburgers and vanilla milk shakes at Dairy Queen. Or going to a Jimi Hendrix concert.

Something wasn't right. She stopped abruptly.

"You're doing swell, miss," said a man's voice. "Is something wrong?"

She shook her head. Then nodded. All wrong.

"This is what you want some girl to read to soldiers in Vietnam?"

"Right."

"Well, it's . . . it's *cruel.*"

The microphone on the other side of the partition was muffled, as if someone had covered it with a hand. Apparently, a discussion was taking place in response to her comment.

"Explain, please," a woman's voice requested after a while.

"Well," Jennifer began nervously, squinting at the shadowy figures past the glass. "These are young guys, lots of them teenagers like me, right? And they're away from home. Some of them don't want to be where they are."

"True."

"How long are they supposed to stay over there?" she asked.

"A year. Longer if they volunteer for another tour."

She could swear that last voice belonged to a soldier. It was sharp and official and guarded.

Jennifer took a deep breath. "Well, here I am telling them the weather, which they can probably see for themselves since they're outside a lot. Then I start talking to them about the stuff at home they're *missing*. It sounds like I'm over here, having a great old time for myself, and they're . . . well, where they are, thousands of miles away, able only to dream about this stuff. If they aren't already homesick, they will be by the time I finish."

"She's got a point," someone muttered.

"What would *you* say to them?" asked the woman's voice. "If you were there, Jennifer."

She thought a minute. She thought about all her friends who had their families and prep school chums and sailing mates. How would Mark or one of the other guys feel if he were cut off from all that? Banished to a war-torn foreign country with only strangers for companionship?

"I'd be their girl," she said simply.

A few voices tittered.

"One girl to satisfy thousands of GIs. Good trick if you can pull it off."

"Show us," said the woman.

The request seemed to float around in her brain for a long time before she reacted to it. Then Jennifer laid down the script and closed her eyes.

Although she'd suggested the idea, she had no precise idea what she'd meant by it. She imagined a boy her own age, like one of those she'd seen in newspaper photos.

He wore fatigues and leaned on a barbed-wire and sand-bag guard post. His face was sweaty and dirty. A distant, lonely look lurked in his eyes. He cradled an M-16 over his chest and he stood ankle-deep in muck. He probably didn't come from a family like the Swansons of Marblehead, but he didn't want to be where he was any more than her friends wanted to take his place.

"Hi, honey," she began in a low, intimate tone. She wouldn't use a name. She leaned closer to the mike. "Glad I caught you tonight. Just had to talk to you for a little while. I brought a couple new records. Would you like to hear them?" She paused as if listening for an answer. "I've got the Beach Boys, and one from last year—Petula Clark singing 'Downtown.' And another one by the Beatles, it's called 'Ticket to Ride.' Then there's a favorite of yours, 'House of the Rising Sun.' If you have the time to just hold me a little while and listen, it'd be great."

She paused.

There was silence from the other side of the glass wall.

"Then, you'd play the records?" a man's voice asked.

Jennifer nodded, knowing they could see her. She went on chatting for a while, flirting a little, sounding cuddly and content to be with her one special guy.

As she continued, she came to a strange realization. She had at least one thing in common with the boys she was talking to. She didn't have anyone special now, and guessed she never really had. They might have a girl waiting back home. But a girl at that distance might as well not exist. So long as she, Jennifer Swanson, had no one special, she could make each one of them her lover, over the airwaves.

As she spoke, Jennifer silently unfastened the clasps on her guitar case and took out the instrument. She began to strum softly in the background, then wove into "Blowin' in the Wind." She braced the guitar on her knee and sung into its smooth, curved shape. Forgetting about the microphone and the people on the other side of the glass. Letting the soft phrases fill the little booth. She could hear her own voice in the earphones, and she perfected a note, drawing it out to make it sound just right, light but firm, sure of itself in her crystal-clear soprano. A certain breathiness and intimacy slipped into her song. She was singing for somebody out there she'd never seen before, but who meant *everything* to her. It felt like the most romantic thing she'd ever done.

At the end, she strummed the last chord and let it fade.

After a few seconds, the woman's voice came again. "Thank you, dear. We'll give you a call in a few days."

A call. Not a contract. Not a job. Jennifer's heart sank. They didn't want her.

Feeling numb under a crushing sense of defeat, Jennifer

packed up her guitar. No one met her outside the booth. She trudged back down the long corridor alone, passed the next interviewee, as she, in turn, followed the girl with the clipboard.

Jennifer was furious with herself. She hadn't given them what they wanted. She'd argued against their plan—that was stupid. Whether they were wrong or right, they had a specific type of person and show in mind.

Jennifer returned to the Stanhope, near the Metropolitan Museum of Art, where she'd registered the night before. Within an hour, she was packed. She summoned the porter to come for her bags.

Jennifer was crossing the ornate lobby when the concierge waved her down. "Miss Swanson! A gentleman has been looking for you."

She turned to see a tall, distinguished-looking man in a navy-blue suit with a striped tie. He stepped quickly around the concierge.

"My name is Freck, Joseph Freck."

As she shook his hand, she squinted up at him. He was in his fifties, she guessed, and had gray hair fringing his temples. Prominent, hawkish nose. Heavy black eyebrows, although his eyes were blue.

"So?"

"I heard your audition today. You have a most remarkable voice, Miss Swanson. And your résumé was quite interesting. We don't get too many society gals."

Straightening her shoulders, she looked him unflinchingly in the eye. He was making fun of her. "Not quite what you had in mind, am I?"

"No. But then again, we weren't absolutely sure of what we did want. About half of the interviewers hated your little act."

She shrugged, but the pain of rejection was acute. She wished she could just lose this guy and crawl onto her plane without having to speak to another soul.

"But," he continued, "I, personally, thought you were marvelous."

She shot him a cool look from beneath her blond lashes.

23

Evidently, he was trying to pick her up. *She* more than anyone should be able to recognize the signs.

"I'm going to miss my flight," she said sharply.

He frowned, glancing around the lobby. "Please. Give me ten minutes. Have a drink with me in the hotel café. There is something very important I must say to you."

"All right," Jennifer agreed reluctantly. "Ten minutes."

They found an empty table and ordered martinis. No one asked for her ID. Jennifer lit up a Camel for effect. She imagined that smoking made her look more worldly. She only smoked in public. Freck observed her in silence until the drinks arrived.

After they'd each taken a sip, he began. "I fought in World War Two, in Italy. I was in the infantry. There was some young woman who did an Armed Forces Radio show. She was all that kept me going some nights . . . those nights we could pull in the signal from London. She was an American girl, not a Brit."

Jennifer listened, suddenly more interested.

"I agree with you," Freck said. "We don't need weather forecasts. We need to give those boys something to hold on to until they get home. I can imagine them wanting to hold on to the girl behind your voice. And, if they ever *saw* you . . ."

Jennifer looked into the pale blue eyes of Joseph Freck. The warmth and frankness in his voice robbed his speech of all offense. She appealed to him, yes. But he wasn't hitting on her—not for himself anyway. She listened, intrigued, as he described how the radio show might be reworked.

"We could call it, "A Night with Jenny." You'd spin records, sing to the guys, play your guitar. And just talk to them, the way you did in the booth." He stopped, watching her eyes for any positive reaction. "We already have other shows taped in this country and broadcast on some three hundred stations in the Armed Forces Radio Network. But what we want is a girl right over there with our boys—doing a show just for them." He paused to study her expression. "You'd be in a major city, broadcasting from a studio, nowhere near the action. Perfectly safe."

Jennifer snuffed out her cigarette in the crystal ashtray and drew her tongue between her lips. For some reason, possibly because he'd mentioned safety, she now wondered about the risk involved.

"There might be a little problem. My parents . . ." If she wanted to, she knew she could use them as her excuse not to go. Although she was old enough to just take off wherever she wanted, it was conceivable that she might wish their blessing. However, Freck had made this job sound every bit as important as nursing soldiers back to health. She took a deep breath and decided. "I want to go. I want the job."

"Good," he said, and knocked back the last of his martini. A calculating twinkle shone from the recesses of his eyes, so that for a moment they lost their almost boyish innocence. "Don't worry about your parents. I'll take care of them."

3

For the next few weeks, Jennifer was floating on air. She returned to Radcliffe, sitting in her classes, fantasizing about Saigon, the people she'd meet there, having her very own radio show!

She didn't tell her parents about her plans.

But as time drew near to her departure date in late April, she knew she could no longer put off the inevitable. She told her father that she'd withdrawn from Radcliffe and would be leaving for Asia within a week.

Max Swanson flatly refused to allow his daughter to leave the country. He wired the dean, requesting that Jennifer be reinstated.

Frantic, Jennifer telephoned Freck at a Washington, D.C., number he'd given her. She was afraid that her father would do something crude, like have the police waiting for her at the airport to drag her home if she tried to leave without his permission. She feared he might use his connections to cause Armed Forces Radio to withdraw their offer. Freck, however, seemed unconcerned, reassuring her that her father was merely reacting to the fear of change. All men hated change. He would take care of everything.

On the following Saturday, Freck called from Boston. He spoke briefly with her father. Max agreed to see him, but only to put "this nonsense" to rest.

Jennifer paced her room, overcome by a feeling of dread. No one, to her knowledge, had ever gone head-to-head with her father and come out on top. When she heard a car pull up in the drive below her window, she dashed down the stairs and intercepted her father.

"Daddy!" Jennifer cried, chasing him across the oak parquet floor of the vestibule. "Try to be good."

"I don't know what you mean, Jennifer Lynn," he muttered, waving off Carlton when the butler started toward the door. Max's shoulders, in the black Milanese tailored suit, were as rigid as his face.

"I *mean,*" she said with emphasis, "you tend to get very bullish. You tend to . . . to intimidate people, you know."

"Do I?"

Jennifer caught up, stepping between him and the door as the chimes rang for the third time. She was afraid her father wouldn't let Freck stay even long enough to deliver his argument on her behalf.

"Daddy, wait," she pleaded, looking up into his stern gray eyes.

She realized that she'd placed a hand on his chest, as if to physically restrain him. Touching was unheard of in the Swanson family. A dry peck on the cheek was the limit of affection, and all that she remembered of familial intimacy from her earliest childhood. She quickly withdrew her fingertips.

"Please. Listen to Mr. Freck. This is important to me, Daddy. I need to do this . . . for me."

For a moment her father's glance settled over her up-turned face. A subtle softness entered the gray eyes, and he blinked.

"I will listen," he said stiffly. "I always listen, Jennifer Lynn. A man doesn't come as far as I have in business without hearing what people have to say. But that's *all* I've promised. Do you understand?"

She nodded, stepped aside, and her father swung wide the front door.

A huge stranger in black chauffeur's uniform filled the opening. "The Swanson residence?" he demanded in a pinched, superior tone. "Mr. Joseph Freck is expected."

For one of the very few times in his life, Max Swanson seemed to have no idea what to say.

Covering her lips with one hand to stifle a giggle, Jennifer watched, fascinated.

"Yes," her father replied. "Yes, I'm Maxwell Swanson."

The chauffeur gave a curt nod and spun on his heel. A moment later he'd swung open a rear door of the limousine.

Jennifer could see Freck's hawk nose appear from behind a newspaper. Without rushing, he folded the pages and laid them on the deep blue, crushed-velvet seat beside him. He uncoiled from the vehicle.

With a flash of appreciation, she recognized how cleverly he'd taken the upper hand. Freck was no longer a lowly personnel recruiter for the government, come begging. He was a visiting dignitary. But her amusement was short-lived.

Freck's manner with her father, once they were all three settled in her father's study, became that of one business man discussing a merger with another. An apprehensive chill settled in her veins.

Sadly, Jennifer watched her father's face as he listened to Freck. If he refused to let her go with this man, it was not because he loved her and feared for her safety, or longed to have her near him. It was because Max Swanson felt it was his social obligation to refuse. His peers would never let *their* eighteen-year-old daughters fly off to a war-torn nation halfway around the world. Neither would they allow them to take on a "job." A suitable, carefully chosen position, perhaps. Unpaid, of course. Something genteel and worthy and for the good of the less fortunate.

But perhaps the fact that she'd be aiding in the war effort (which was patriotic), and helping the soldiers (they certainly were less fortunate if they'd been unable to buy their way out of the army) would sway her father. She glanced from

28

one man to the other, still hopeful. She sat quietly, trusting Freck to do as he'd promised.

The government recruiter cradled his thin, panted knee with both hands and leaned back into the leather chair on the opposite side of her father's desk as he continued speaking in a calm, instructional voice.

"Our central broadcasting station is in Saigon. It's not far from the U.S. Embassy. Security is very tight."

"Where would I live?" Jennifer asked, unable to keep silent any longer.

"You'd have an apartment in the American compound with the diplomatic corps and senior military officers." He turned back to Max. "I assure you, sir, no hardship or danger would be involved." Freck smiled reassuringly. "I have three grown daughters of my own. I would, without hesitation, allow any one or all of them to accept this post."

Max considered the other man. "I've told Jennifer that I don't wish her to go. That still holds, Mr. Freck."

Jennifer felt as if she'd been holding her breath for the past fifteen minutes. Now she released it with a groan of disgust and jumped up off her chair.

"Daddy! This is *so* unfair. You have to give me a chance to—"

Max held up a hand. "Enough." He pulled a stack of papers toward him across the desk top, his signal that the interview was ended.

Jennifer slumped back into her seat, deflated, limp. But Freck didn't move and his glance moved dispassionately around the dim room.

Jennifer had always been in awe of her father's study, but she could tell that Freck was not in the least intimidated by the dark Edwardian furnishings and towering glass-fronted bookcases. She wondered if he had a room like this of his own, somewhere.

Jennifer stood up uneasily between the two seated men. One was studying a contract, the other seemed unaware that he was supposed to slip meekly away.

There was a noise at the door. Patricia Swanson entered the room.

"Oh." She smiled, looking momentarily confused. "I thought I'd missed you, Mr. Freck. My husband said you wouldn't be staying long."

Freck appeared not to be offended. He rose and gestured to a seat beside his. "We've just been chatting. Please join us."

Max looked up from his contract with irritation.

"I had just finished telling your husband a little about Jennifer's living arrangements. Her social life," Freck said, "would be of interest to you. Ambassador Elsworth Bunker entertains innumerable dignitaries and diplomats. As a resident of the embassy, Jennifer would be a regular guest at all functions." He paused, his clear blue eyes giving Patricia a meaningful look that said *You and I understand one another. I'm handing your daughter a plum. Don't let her pass it up.* He continued slowly. "Social contacts from my own youth have remained important throughout my adult life. Don't you find that so, Mrs. Swanson?"

Her mother lit up like a candle. "I expect, now that you mention it, there would be a concentration of people with excellent backgrounds . . . serving as advisors, and . . . such—" She waved one hand to fill in the void. Jennifer suspected that Patricia had no idea what she was saying. Politics and the military would be out of her realm.

Jennifer forced herself not to bounce on her seat. A spark of hope crackled inside of her. Freck was doing it. He was charming her mother. If he could convince her . . .

"Precisely." Freck smiled coolly. "Aside from the society of New York or D.C., you simply don't find yourself in that sort of milieu in this country. Jennifer would have only the one year to take advantage of her situation, unless she chose to stay on. But one year away from family and friends seems long enough in all fairness. On the other hand, she will have developed contacts with some of the future leaders of our world."

"Well," her mother said, laughing, glancing pointedly at Jennifer, "now that's not to be taken lightly, is it?" But her smile wavered as it collided with her husband's remote scowl.

"The fact remains," Max Swanson grumbled, "Jennifer would be a disk jockey on a radio station in Asia. A *disk jockey,* Patricia. That's not the future I'd planned for *my* daughter."

Patricia's cheeks flushed. She dropped her eyes and Jennifer actually felt sorry for her.

"Daddy," she murmured. "It's just for a year. Please."

"And what about college?" he demanded.

"I'll start all over again as soon as I come back. And I'll be better able to concentrate by then. I'll have learned all sorts of things about the world." She paused to study her father's expression. It hadn't softened in the least. "This means so much to me, Daddy," she said carefully, praying he'd listen to her just this once.

For a fraction of a second, Jennifer's eyes locked with her father's. She could read no emotion behind their cold gray surface.

Abruptly, Max stood up from behind his desk. "I don't like being put into a corner, Mr. Freck," he said dangerously. "It seems that Jennifer is set on taking this ludicrous trip, and my wife has been seduced into thinking you're offering a novel brand of finishing school."

Jennifer's mouth dropped open. She glanced at her mother in time to see the pink flush deepen and creep up her cheeks and into her blond hairline.

Freck remained seated, meeting her father's dead gray eyes with equanimity over folded hands. "She is your daughter. Of course, I would not presume to make such an important decision for you on her behalf. I can only give you my word that she will be safe, and her future can only benefit from her year away from home. The final decision must be yours—"

"No!" Max interrupted sharply. "The final decision is hers."

Jennifer felt herself shrinking into the tapestry cushion of her chair as her father turned to look down at her. She was supposed to refuse Freck's offer. No other decision would satisfy.

Her throat constricted. She couldn't get a single word out.

"Mr. Freck," Patricia said, "perhaps Jennifer is a bit young to be put in this sort of situation. Maybe in a year or two, once she's—"

"Wait!" Jennifer shouted.

Her parents stared at her.

"Daddy said it was my decision. I've decided. I'm going. That's the end of it."

She met her father's eyes levelly, something she'd rarely dared to do. "I love you, Daddy . . . and Mother." Her voice was suddenly shaky at having to manage the strange words. "But I need to do this. I don't know why, but I must."

Patricia dropped her glance to her lap. Max Swanson's gaze hardened, as if his daughter's admission of love were a sign of weakness.

"Go!" he barked. 'But you'll be doing this on your own, Jennifer Lynn. Don't wire home for money or consolation when you find the romance of this little adventure wearing thin. Maybe a shot of reality is what you need. For once in your life perhaps you'll appreciate—" He stopped himself, spun around, and walked out of the room.

Patricia hurriedly excused herself and followed.

Her heart swelling in her throat, Jennifer looked at Freck. He winked, letting her know he shared her victory.

She didn't feel entirely victorious.

On a cold, rainy April day, one of the Swanson maids helped Jennifer pack two large trunks and three suitcases with clothing.

Patricia had instructed the servant to be certain her daughter had ample gowns—both cocktail and ball length—and Oscar de la Rentas took up a lot of space. There was no getting around that!

Then there were shoes—fifteen pairs, carefully chosen to coordinate with as many outfits as possible—including two pairs of evening slippers by Vivier. Every one was individually tissue-wrapped to avoid soiling expensive fabrics.

Next, at Freck's suggestion, light-weight garments suitable for tropical weather were pulled from the walk-in closet.

Jennifer took this to mean cruise wear. Since she already owned a substantial collection of fashionable white pants and flowered tops with matching jackets and floppy brimmed hats to ward off the sun, very little new clothing of this sort needed to be purchased. She had, however, driven into Boston to pick up one pair of Bass hiking boots. And she'd mail-ordered sensible khaki pants and a matching blouse, in case she got a chance to tour some of the countryside outside of Saigon.

The morning of her departure, her father left early for his office. She'd spoken barely five words to him since the day of Freck's visit. When she telephoned him in Boston to say goodbye, Max's secretary informed her that he was in a meeting. He'd left explicit instructions that he was not to be disturbed.

Patricia had a tea at three, for which she'd be late if she accompanied her daughter to Logan Airport to await her flight. They'd given each other a quick, embarrassed hug at the front door. Francie had left the day before with her boyfriend, headed for a rally in Washington, D.C.

Jennifer watched through the taxi's window as the white clapboard mansion on the cliffs of Marblehead shrank to the tune of crunching gravel. The trunks had been sent on ahead in another cab, since there wasn't room in one for everything. Jennifer consoled herself on the long, lonely drive with the fact that at least she was prepared sartorially for any eventuality.

On the flight to San Francisco, she deliberately sat apart from most of the other passengers, overcome by the realization that her life had taken a fresh turn. She was following her heart, her own intuitive sense of destiny for the first time in her life. She savored every second of her newfound freedom.

Jennifer smiled, watching the clouds float past her window while she sipped Coke from a plastic tumbler and munched on salted nuts. Although she'd flown with her parents many times, she'd never traveled alone.

Her father had stuck by his declaration that she was financially on her own. He had offered her no emergency money nor credit cards. Patricia and her daughter had always kept personal accounts at all the better stores in Boston, New York, and Palm Beach. A simple signature was all that had been necessary for Jennifer to walk away with armloads of clothes.

Freck had arranged the flight. Transportation to Vietnam, within the country, and back again, would be taken care of by the government. Her accommodations within the American compound in Saigon were gratis. All she needed to worry about was food. And her salary, although modest, would more than cover that since, Freck assured her, food was cheap and there were many fine restaurants throughout the city.

At last Jennifer tired of staring out the window and daydreaming. She opened her slim leather attaché case and pulled out a briefing folder that had arrived by special post earlier that week. It was crammed with exotic photos, official-looking background notes on the culture and history of the Vietnamese people, practical points on health care. It was like the glossy brochures one got from a travel agent. Reading the pages each night in bed had added to her anticipation, though she grew puzzled.

After all, there was supposed to be a war going on over there. Soldiers were fighting somewhere in those lush jungles that peeked out between her fingertips. Still, she supposed Freck was just being sensible about what he sent to her parents' home. The more exciting information was bound to be waiting for her at Travis Air Force Base in California. That was where she'd be boarding another jet for the second leg of her journey.

When Jennifer at last arrived in San Francisco, a female army officer was waiting for her at the end of the disembarkation tunnel. She was short, efficient-looking, with tidily cropped hair tucked up under a uniform cap.

"I'm Lieutenant Sally Nelson," she said pleasantly, holding out her hand in greeting.

Jennifer shook it. "I'm glad to meet you, Sally. Are you going along with me?"

Sally laughed and shook her head. "No. I'm stateside public relations."

"Then you've never been to Vietnam?" Jennifer was disappointed. She didn't mind traveling alone. But she'd looked forward to meeting somebody who had an intimate knowledge of the country. There were so many questions she was dying to ask!

"No, I've never been there. But I might someday."

Sally didn't sound very interested in the prospect, Jennifer thought.

At Travis Air Force Base, the two women unloaded Jennifer's luggage from the van Sally had driven. The lieutenant flagged down a couple of enlisted men who helped them with the trunks, which now seemed embarrassingly large and heavy.

"I hope I didn't overpack," Jennifer said, sighing as they stood back and watched the soldiers drag her trunks through the glass doors.

"Well," Sally said, "you will be gone for a year."

A doubtful note in the woman's voice snagged Jennifer's attention.

"Do most of your personnel stay just one year?" she asked.

Sally shrugged, hefted two Louis Vuitton suitcases, and started walking.

Jennifer picked up the third and her guitar case.

"They tell me a year is a long time over there," Sally began again without prompting. "Most people find it more than enough time."

"Oh." Jennifer thought for a moment. "I hope Saigon isn't too awfully metropolitan."

"Hmm?"

They'd marched themselves into a throng of GIs who seemed unwilling to clear a path. No one even bothered to salute Sally, the way Jennifer had seen people do in the movies. Sally swung one suitcase in front of her and pushed straight through, looking like a little snowplow scattering soldiers left and right.

"I mean," Jennifer said, gasping, trying to keep up with her, "there wouldn't be any real adventure to going there if Saigon was like New York, or London, or anything."

Sally laughed. "I don't think there's much chance of that."

She checked Jennifer's luggage at a long counter and handed the claims stubs to her. Then she led her down a hallway to a waiting room. A plate-glass window overlooked the airfield.

"Look," she said, turning to face Jennifer, "I have to leave now. You'll be fine here. That's your plane. See it there? Across the tarmac?"

A Pan Am 707 was being refueled some distance from the terminal. Jennifer nodded.

"I have to pick up a girls' band and deliver them for this same flight. You have no idea what a hassle that's going to be. Amps. Guitars. Drums, even." She rolled her eyes. "Just sit tight and listen for your boarding time." She shot a hurried glance at her Timex watch. "Dammit! Only an hour and I've got to go all the way across town."

Sally spun to leave, but Jennifer thrust out a hand to stop her.

"I suppose I'm a bit confused," she admitted. "But I'd thought perhaps I'd get a briefing, or . . . or some instruction before I went over."

Sally stared at her woodenly.

"I mean, I don't know anything really about my job."

"Oh, that." Sally laughed, shaking her head. "Don't worry about that, honey. Just smile. They'll all love you!"

And off she ran, zigzagging across the waiting area between GIs.

Smile? Jennifer mused. *What the hell does smiling have to do with radio?*

With a queasy feeling in her stomach, she sat down on a molded fiberglass seat. A bright pink wad of gum was visible under the front edge. She moved her legs to avoid it.

The only luggage she'd held on to were her purse and guitar. She kept them close to her. Purse on her lap. Guitar on the floor, touching her ankle. For some reason she wanted the comfort of her music as close to her as possible.

The plane was supposed to land at Tan Son Nhut Airfield, near Saigon. Someone would meet her there and take her to the American compound where she'd have her own apartment. That was all she knew.

She had two thousand dollars in American money that she had split three ways—between her purse and her shoe and her guitar case. It was her own money, a small portion of her grandmother's trust fund for her—an account naming her parents as custodians and requiring their signatures for withdrawals until she turned twenty-one. Her mother had signed for it and told her it was all her father would allow.

Jennifer had assured her that, under the circumstances, the money would easily last the full year—although two thousand dollars was her normal allowance for just two months.

At first, she sat looking out the window, hoping some of the soldiers would come over to talk. Then, as she watched them fidgeting with their duffel bags, puffing on cigarettes, cursing tensely at each other, or standing alone and trying to look aloof and inconspicuous in their shaved heads, she became wary of them.

They didn't look friendly. They didn't appear to want to talk to anyone. Just dissolve into themselves and shut out the outside world. Suddenly, she realized how very frightened they all were.

And at that same moment, Jennifer wondered why *she* wasn't afraid of going to Vietnam. And if she should be.

4

Melantha Benning planted her six-foot-two frame in the middle of the waiting room and looked around. The young black woman wore a U.S. Army nurse's uniform: crisp, olive-drab skirt cut to the knees—longer than was fashionable on the street—and a fitted jacket. A second lieutenant's butter bar was pinned on each of her shoulders. Her cap rode the crest of her Afro like a proud ship.

Surveying the scene with her usual street wariness, she took in the sea of uniforms. It looked as if she might be the only woman on the flight, but that didn't bother her.

More than half of the boys in the room were *brothers.* Their coffee-colored skin stood out against the minty green-white glare of the lounge walls and contrasted with the pale faces of the white soldiers.

It was true—must have been true—what Curtis had written home in his letters. The black man was Washington's favored front-line soldier. For years, the government had struggled to find a solution to the race situation. Maybe Vietnam was their answer: a lot fewer came home than went over there.

Melantha stared at one group of men in fatigues. That tall,

bony one might have been Curtis. He had the same jutting chin and smooth brown skull peeking through his stubble of shaved hair. But her baby brother had already been in Vietnam three months.

Because she was an officer she was not supposed to fraternize with grunts. Enlisted men. But Melantha tended to pay attention to rules when they suited her. She walked over to the four men.

They stiffened when they saw her coming, their eyes glazing over. One dropped a joint on the linoleum and snuffed it out under the heel of his boot.

She smelled the sweet marijuana-laced air hovering around them. "Waste of a smoke," Melantha observed dryly. She looked up at the one that reminded her of Curtis. "Where you headed, Private?"

"Nam," he said dejectedly.

Grumbling, the man standing beside him lit up again. She nodded at him. "You, too?"

"Same for all of us, girl." He passed along the glowing roach. "Bound for glory," he laughed, a humorless hack ending with yellow smoke seething between his crooked teeth.

The soldier on her left had been watching her critically. "You're on the boss man's side," he accused maliciously, flicking a brown finger at her gold bar, his stubby nail clicking against metal. "Why not get lost, sis-tah?"

Unintimidated, Melantha glared down on him from her extra three inches. She didn't flinch at the snarl on his lip. Curtis did the same thing, acting tough when he was terrified.

She remembered sitting with him on their concrete stoop on 7th Street the day after he received his draft notice. Melantha had tried to talk Curtis out of going. "Go back to school," she told him. "They can't take you then. That'll give you more than another year. By then this war stuff will probably be over." Curtis tucked his long knees up under his chin. "Hell. School, that's the most degrading place there is."

"Just 'cause you don't make honors," she began, sitting down beside him, "it doesn't mean you . . ."

He laughed, throwing his head back. "Honors? You're talking pure nonsense, girl. I can't even *read*—and you're talkin' A's and B's and stupidity like that."

She leaned back against the hard edge of the step above her. "I'm no smarter than you, Curt, but I did it. You can, too."

"Shit." His eyes roamed the street restlessly.

"What about Amelia?"

His shoulders tensed. He shrugged, as if trying to toss a weight off of them. "What about her?"

"You and she are getting married, right?"

His roving glance fixed on a metro bus as it wheezed to a stop near the corner. "S'pose."

Melantha struck him hard in the ribs with her elbow. "Suppose? *Suppose!*" she wailed at him, grabbing his arm. "What you talking about? She's counting on you, Curt! She's gonna have a baby."

"I know that, Mel." He shook her off roughly and stood up. "Don't you think I know that!"

Jamming his fists into his pockets, he stalked up and down the cracked cement sidewalk littered with cigarette butts and paper and chunks of amber glass. Before Momma died, leaving Mel to care for her little brother, she'd swept the stoop and strip of sidewalk in front of their apartment every morning. Mel still did it most days, but this morning she'd been too worried about Curtis.

Melantha bit her bottom lip, watching her brother pace. He was working himself up again to do something he'd be sorry for. She'd seen him go through the same motions before. He'd knocked off a liquor store when he was fourteen, and he and a couple friends made summer money hustling tourists around the Lincoln Memorial when they were sixteen—picking pockets, stealing purses, selling stuff to one tourist they'd stolen from another. But Amelia had kept him straight. Loved him up and made sure he stayed away from his old crowd. But once she had gotten pregnant,

Curtis changed. He still saw her, wanting to know how she was feeling, and walking her to her prenatal appointments at the clinic. But his restless, grim moods had become worse.

Melantha sighed. She pushed up off the stoop and stepped in front of Curtis, blocking his wild pacing.

"You're all she's got, Curt. Don't do this to her."

His lip curled in a snarl, and his brown hand snapped up to shove her aside. She stood her ground and, eventually, his fist fell back to his side. Curtis's narrow, dark face puckered up. Tears washed down his cheeks.

"Ain't that just the point?" he moaned.

She looked at him, stumped.

"What point, Curt?" she asked softly.

"Me!" he shouted, jabbing a thumb at the center of his chest. *"I* am all the woman's got!"

"Oh, Curt." Melantha pulled her little brother tenderly into her strong arms and held him while cars clanked past them on the rutted street. A cold, winter Washington rain started to fall. "You are plenty. You are a *good* man."

"But," he ground out, trying to stem bitter tears she could hear clogging his throat, "I can't make a dime, have to live with my sister or else be on the street. What the hell am I gonna do with a wife and kid? Damn it, Mel, she'd be better off without me."

"No," she said firmly. "She loves you. And things'll get better."

"Seems like my only choice is the army," he said.

"Oh, Curtis, you fool!" She pounded him on the chest with her fists. "You'll get yourself killed!"

He pretended to crumble under her attack. Then he bobbed and wove like a prizefighter. Fancy footwork. Fake jabs. "Not me, Mel. I got the speed. The reflexes. Stay low, keep moving. That's my motto!"

"Bullets are faster." But she couldn't help smiling at his act.

"Well, maybe Mr. Uncle Sam'll turn me into a mean, lean, fighting machine. All you commies, watch out! Curtis is on the way!"

She reached out and grabbed one of his hands. "Don't go," she pleaded. "I promised Mama I'd look after you. How can I do that if you're halfway 'round the world?"

He pushed her away, then kissed her on the forehead. "Least they gotta pay me if they take me. And I hear from the brothers that's been there you make out real nice money-wise. Amelia and me will do fine, sister."

Remembering that day, Melantha looked at the men in fatigues who were waiting for their flight. She could see a little bit of Curtis in each one of them. The stiff back, expecting insult. The flexed knees, ready to run—or swagger. The nervous eyes, taking in any motion. They still didn't trust her.

But the guy who'd told her to leave was still glaring at her in challenge.

She turned to face him. "I'm a nurse," she told him in a deceptively mild tone. "You might need me someday. Don't push it, brother."

He squinted at her. "You are a nurse," he repeated. "Like in a fuckin' hospital?"

"That's right."

"Hey, man, leave her alone," the soldier with the joint said. He shifted uneasily as an MP looked their way.

The grunt who wanted to argue laughed. "She's a bigger fool than all of us, you know? Nobody drafted her. She *volunteered!* And she could have had a sweet job in some doctor's office. Shit!"

Mel sidestepped and threw her long arm around the man's shoulders in a companionable gesture. But she wasn't smiling.

Startled, he shot a puzzled glance around the circle— before he felt the tip of the blade through her jacket pocket.

"Say, lady . . . sir . . ." He flinched and tried to back away, but her arm locked him in place.

Melantha's body was strong and hard like a man's, and her height made her even more intimidating when she was angry. And she got angry when someone tried to mess with her—or someone she cared about. Unleashed, her temper was even worse than Curtis's.

She slipped the point of the scalpel, resting in her hidden right hand, a fraction deeper through her jacket lining, a bit farther into the fabric of his coarse fatigue shirt.

"You kiss your mama with that mouth?" she asked pleasantly.

He nodded, then shook his head, unsure of what she wanted to hear. The others watched curiously, unaware of the blade.

"You got a filthy mouth, boy," Melantha scolded him. "Your manners aren't real pretty, either. I don't give a damn about whether or not you respect me as a woman or a U.S. Army officer, or any of that crap. But I worked my ass off to get to be a nurse. You or nobody else is gonna rub my face in it, hear?"

She was still talking softly, her face emotionless. But he was listening intently.

He nodded, looking pale.

"Otherwise, you and me, we'll play doctor. I only watched surgery, but I wonder what doin' it feels like."

His knees buckled, and he started to go down. Melantha caught him and eased back on the scalpel. She smiled before releasing him.

"S-sorry," he said, gasping.

He shot a glance at the others, making sure no one noticed the tiny red splotch just above his belt on his uniform shirt, clamping his elbow over it.

"Didn't know you were so serious about your work . . . ma'am," he apologized again.

"Well," she said with a stiff smile, "I am. I'm a damn fine nurse."

When her flight was called, Jennifer picked up her guitar case and purse and strode quickly to the gate. Nobody else was in a rush. She ended up close to the front of the line.

Some of the soldiers had arrived late and were kissing goodbye their girlfriends, wives, mothers and fathers, or little children. There was a lot of noise and confusion and high emotion. Travel orders were being checked a final time

43

by a sergeant just before the airline representative collected boarding passes.

When the sergeant studied the papers Jennifer had been sent, he smiled at her. "Part of the band?" he asked. "Where are the other girls?"

She shook her head. "No. I'm going over to do a radio show."

"Really?" he asked.

"Yeah."

"Well, they'll have you traveling all over with the band anyway. So it won't make any difference. Or else," he gave her a once-over, "maybe they'll give you your own road-show, honey."

She laughed. "No, no," she began, "I'm just going to Saigon. I doubt if I'll get a chance to . . ."

But he initialed her papers and quickly reached for the soldier's orders behind her. The line crawled forward.

Jennifer stepped outside into the nippy breeze coming off San Francisco Bay. The plane was across the field a ways. There hadn't been room for it to pull up to one of the connecting corridors. Now that she was down on the same level with the jet, it looked much bigger.

After a surprisingly long hike, Jennifer reached the metal stairs. She started up the steep incline. Her guitar case was awkward and cumbersome. It banged against the railing and she tripped. Catching her balance, she continued upward toward the silver cigar-shaped fuselage, painfully aware that soldiers carrying twice as much were waiting restlessly behind her. The case banged again.

"Sorry," she mumbled nervously.

"Help you with that?" A Midwestern accent.

She turned on the step to see a boy who looked too young to be wearing a uniform. He was nearly a foot taller than she, capless, his dark brown hair shaved wide around the ears, but allowed to grow out thickly on top. Worn fatigues conformed to his body like a protective layer of army-drab skin.

"Thanks," she murmured, as he shifted his duffel bag and reached for her case.

44

Their fingers brushed in the transfer. Jennifer felt him flinch, as if the touch had physically hurt.

As she continued climbing, she wondered if he was bashful around girls. Something about him—his manner, the way he hadn't avoided her eye—made her dismiss that possibility. She was aware of him, very close behind her. Aware of the motion of his body—controlled, strong, precise. At the top of the stairs, she turned to retrieve her guitar.

"I'll take it to your seat for you," he told her stiffly, his blue eyes snapping.

No, she thought again, *not bashful.*

She stepped into the cabin, which was already filling up with cigarette smoke. Beneath the tang of tobacco, the compartment smelled of insecticide and stale air.

"Where are you sitting?" he asked.

"Oh, I don't know, I . . . ." She glanced at her pass, for the first time realizing that no seat had been indicated.

"Wherever you like, princess," he said gruffly.

She glared at him for a second, annoyed at his tone. His eyes were as thick and hard as plate glass, throwing back her image and allowing nothing behind them to show. They frightened her, but at the same time were enigmatically intriguing.

"Right here," she said hastily, pointing to the first pair of seats she spotted.

He stepped forward, swung the case over his head and shoved it onto the rack above her seat. "Have a nice flight," he said wryly. Then he dropped back a half-dozen rows before heaving his duffel bag onto a stack of others that were accumulating in a space where several seats had been removed. Without giving her another glance, he lit a cigarette and sat down beside another GI.

Jennifer looked down the length of the compartment that seethed with a turmoil of too many men jammed into too little space. Street jargon slammed against her ears. A soldier bumped into her, knocking her sideways so that she was forced to sit immediately or be trampled.

She cast the Midwestern boy an inviting glance between the seats. He ignored her, staring out a window. Why did she feel drawn to him when he so clearly wanted nothing to do with her? Francie would say it was the challenge. Jennifer wasn't sure.

The girls' band never made the flight. Six hours later, the overcrowded jet landed in Hawaii.

As soon as the plane rolled to a stop, Jennifer stood up and stretched along with everyone else.

The intercom buzzed on, and the pilot spoke: "We're not here to go to the beach, boys and girls. No one leaves the plane. This is just a refueling stop."

A groan went up through the compartment.

"How much longer are they planning on keeping us shut up in this sardine can?" somebody demanded.

Shocked, Jennifer pricked up her ears. It sounded like a woman's voice. Except that the words had been spoken without any force, and they'd carried easily above the din. She turned, searching faces. Halfway down the aisle sat a tall, black woman in an officer's uniform.

If she'd known there was another female passenger, she might have tried to sit with her. Having someone to talk to would make the time go faster.

Jennifer rubbed the small of her back, bent forward at the waist, and shook out her hair for a long, luxurious moment. When she stood up, it seemed half the men on the plane were watching her as if they hadn't noticed her before, as if they had never in fact seen a woman in their lives. It occurred to her that most of them had been numb to their surroundings when they'd boarded the plane in San Francisco. By now the reality of what was happening to them had sunk in, and they were alert, taking in everything. Especially a slender blonde in a bright yellow miniskirt.

"Hi," she said, smiling brightly.

"Hi," a chorus of GIs returned with enthusiasm.

She felt their eyes burning up her long legs to the brief hem of her skirt, blatantly inspecting her breasts, getting lost in her tangled blond hair.

"Oh, my," Jennifer murmured. And she drew the tip of her tongue over a lip that had suddenly gone bone dry.

Between the bodies of the standing men, she could make out the dark oval face of the woman officer. Their eyes met for a moment, then the black woman laughed and, shaking her head, looked away.

Jennifer's touch of nervousness metamorphosed into aggravation. She didn't like the way she'd been sized up and dismissed. Not only had the woman been rude, she'd declared in that one expressive second that Jennifer Lynn Swanson, whom she didn't even know, was a nobody.

Jennifer had been ogled and chased by boys and grown men, she'd been jealously imitated and had her downfall plotted by her girlfriends, she'd been the cause of petty scandal along the staid North Shore. But she'd *never* been treated as if she didn't matter, as if she didn't even exist!

Squaring her shoulders, Jennifer marched down the aisle of the jet, pushing herself between GIs. She stopped beside the black officer's seat.

"I thought I was the only woman on board," she said evenly.

The woman didn't answer.

Jennifer was determined. She'd coaxed the soldier who'd been sitting next to her into divulging his name and where his family lived, but he hadn't wanted to talk any more and had dozed off to sleep. After spending the long flight from Boston on her own, and having no one to talk to all the way to Hawaii, she wanted some company. She was, she decided, going to *get* some company—one way or another!

"Maybe," she continued with forced pleasantness, "we could arrange with some of the other passengers to trade seats. We could sit together and chat. There's still a lot of time left before we reach Saigon." She paused when she still got no reaction. "I think one of the stewardesses said we'd be refueling again in the Philippines."

Brown eyes swiveled to callously survey her.

Jennifer blinked, puzzled. Here she was being nice to someone and the woman was looking at her as if she were dirt.

They studied each other.

"All right," the officer agreed finally, in that same deep voice that sounded as if it would cut through steel walls. She stood up . . . and up . . . and up. An Amazon!

Feeling a little overwhelmed, Jennifer turned around and quickly led her new companion back to their seats. The boy who'd been sitting beside her had gone into the bathroom as soon as they'd landed. A minute later, when he returned, Jennifer said quickly, "I wonder if you wouldn't mind swapping seats, so we—"

"Leave your gear here, soldier," the black officer ordered. "There's an empty seat about fifteen rows back on the left."

"Yes, ma'am," he said tightly.

Jennifer sighed. "We really should have asked if he minded."

"Let me guess. *Baw-stun?*"

Jennifer grinned at the fake New England accent. "Close. Marblehead, that's north of Boston."

A slow nod, eyes never leaving Jennifer's face.

"My name's Jennifer Swanson," she said, holding out her hand.

"Melantha Benning."

"Are you a nurse?" Jennifer asked.

"Yes."

"Oh." Jennifer cleared her throat. She felt as if she were being tested, and she was failing without knowing why. "I wanted to be a nurse, but—"

"No, you didn't," Melantha broke in.

"I beg your pardon?" Jennifer could feel the plane begin to taxi across the airfield again.

"You don't want to be a nurse, girl, any more than I want to be hooker on N Street."

Jennifer crossed her legs and thrust her hips straight back into her chair. Maybe sitting with this woman was a mistake. "If I say I wanted to be a nurse, I mean it," she said stubbornly.

"Oh, right." Melantha laughed. "Little blondie in starched white polyester, sashaying between rows of beds. A captive audience. Wall-to-wall men. Hah!"

Jennifer was horrified. "It's not like that at all!"

"Sugar, I've seen it before. You have no idea what you're talking about. You'd last ten minutes in an emergency room. Vietnam is one enormous ER, only without the equipment."

"How do you know?" Jennifer asked. "Have you been there before?"

Melantha looked out the window. "No. I've never been."

"So, how do you know so much?"

"My brother writes home." Actually, he dictated letters to a buddy who could write.

Jennifer watched the strong dark features as Melantha's glance pivoted back to her. Behind those eyes, a soft light flickered. "You're going over there to be with him?" Jennifer guessed.

Melantha blinked once.

She had spoken to only a few black people before. They were servants or the few token minority students she'd met at Radcliffe. Miss Porter's didn't have any minorities. Years ago, when she'd asked her father why, he'd told her that their parents couldn't afford the tuition. But she'd always wondered if that were true.

Jennifer was intrigued by this woman. She looked like such a tough, no-nonsense woman.

"Do you think you'll be stationed near your brother?" she asked.

"I don't know. I'll ask to be. Maybe Curtis and me can get leave at the same time." She turned and looked straight at Jennifer. "So, what are you doing here?"

Jennifer gently kicked her guitar case with one toe. She'd brought it down from the shelf thinking she'd play a couple songs, but the landing had interrupted her.

"I'm working for Armed Forces Radio," she explained. "I'll have a show, spin records, and maybe sing a little."

Melantha's wide lips edged up almost into a smile. Since that was the most positive reaction she'd gotten thus far, Jennifer described something about her background and the little bit she knew about her job.

"You're probably right," she finished, "I'd have made a rotten nurse. But I can sing, and I wanted to help, so . . . here I am."

The other woman looked amazed. "Just like that? You left your cozy New England mansion? I'll bet your mama and papa just about shit bricks!"

Jennifer blushed and giggled. The vivid image was too close to the truth. "They weren't terribly thrilled," she admitted.

For the first time, Melantha gave her a genuine smile. "You're braver than most everyone on this plane," she said.

Jennifer gasped. "Oh, no!"

"Absolutely," Melantha insisted. "Most of these boys, they're goin' nowhere fast. Just plain kids is all they are. They've never had much at home, so they're not giving anything up. You've had it all."

"But I don't feel as if I've had *anything.*" Jennifer caught her lip between her teeth. That sounded terrible—the typical spoiled debutante. "I mean. I don't feel as if I'm losing anything by choosing to go over, because I haven't really done anything on my own. And until I do, well, it won't actually be *mine.*"

Melantha considered this in silence. Then as the plane leveled off for its next leg of the journey, she leaned back against the seat and shut her eyes.

After a couple of minutes, Jennifer was sure the nurse was asleep. Feeling vaguely rejected, she faced forward and gently traced the stitching on her guitar case with one finger.

"Can you play that thing?" Melantha asked without opening her eyes.

"Um-hum."

"Sing something, Jennifer Lynn." Melantha's lips lifted in a teasing smile. "Something they play in *Baw-stun.*"

5

Jennifer tuned her guitar to the notes in her head, one string at a time. E-A-D-G-B-E. The soft pads of the fingers on her left hand felt for the cool metal frets. Resting back against the gauze doily over her seat cushion, she closed her eyes and listened as the strings sang to her. She felt their vibrations as she plucked each one in its turn with the gently curved nails of her right hand. Until each note was right, she wouldn't sing a note.

Jennifer didn't feel self-conscious about the prospect of singing in front of Melantha and the soldiers. When she sang, she drifted worlds away in her mind. Each tone and variation of it was a separate stop along a beautiful journey. Nothing else existed.

That was the way it had been since she'd first picked up Francie's guitar when she was ten years old. Some children possess an imaginary companion. Some create fantasy worlds with dolls, miniature cars, plastic ponies, and shoebox houses. Jennifer had had her guitar.

The jet glided away from the islands of Hawaii in a smooth, long arc across the Pacific. Jennifer's light strums accompanied the sensation of being airborne. She opened her eyes slowly and smiled to see Melantha watching her hands as if mesmerized by their motion.

"What should I sing?" Jennifer asked, as she always did.

"Know any B.B. King?"

"Who?"

Melantha laughed at her. "Never mind, sorority girl." She unbuckled and turned around to kneel on her seat. "Any requests?" she bellowed out.

"She any good?" It was a black voice, with the same chip-on-the-shoulder defensiveness Jennifer had at first sensed in the nurse's speech.

"She's good," Melantha said, surprising Jennifer since she hadn't heard her sing a note. "Listen, if you don't ask for something decent, she'll likely start in on some Annette Funicello crap. Come on. I ain't sitting next to no teeny-bopper whining at me all the way to Saigon."

"She know any Dylan?"

"How about the Stones?"

"Make it Motown or nothin'," grumbled a deep bass voice.

Jennifer laughed, shaking her head. "Quite a variety of tastes. I'm not sure I can manage this."

Melantha's brown eyes—alive with warmth and spirit—fixed on her reassuringly. And suddenly Jennifer felt a little uncomfortable, as if this woman was making too much of her. She glanced down at the strings beneath her fingertips with an uncharacteristic attack of shyness.

Melantha plopped herself back down on her seat. "Why don't you just pick something fun?"

"Aw, come on. She can't play!" someone called out.

Laughter and talk resumed. They'd dismissed her.

Jennifer felt a scorching flush creep across her cheeks. She'd never let anyone get the better of her before. *And it's not going to happen now!* she decided. She willed away the butterflies in her stomach and struck a chord.

A huge hand immediately clamped over the neck of her guitar, choking off the notes.

Jennifer looked up at an enormous, heavy-set figure looming over her—a white soldier who looked like a corn-fed Iowa farmboy. However, his eyes were bloodshot, and he hadn't recently shaven. He yanked the guitar out of her lap.

"Hey!" she protested.

Bracing one foot on the arm of her seat, he boosted the polished willow-wood body to his knee, whammed the flat of his hand against the strings, then broke into a wild rock riff.

Hoots of approval filled the cabin.

"Right on!" he answered the appreciative crowd. "Let's party!"

Jennifer was mortified. If they didn't want to hear her music, that was fine. But they hadn't even given her a chance. And this soldier had no right to borrow her guitar without even asking.

He was banging its delicate body with cruel abandon, his big, clumsy fingers missing strings and scraping the pretty hand-painted rosette around the sound hole. But his enthusiasm seemed to be appreciated. Men in the front half of the plane sang along and stomped their boots.

Jennifer jumped to her feet, terrified that at any second the soldier's huge hands would crush her precious guitar. "Give it back!" she demanded.

Her voice was lost in the clamor of his rough strums and wailing Mick Jagger impersonation, singing "I Can't Get No Satisfaction."

Melantha stood up, pushing Jennifer not very softly back into her seat. She wrapped her ample hand around the boy's wrist, stopping the music.

"Give Princess back her instrument," she said in a low voice.

"Hey-ya, Duke. *I* gotta instrument for Princess!" somebody shouted.

The entire cabin broke up. Jennifer, who'd never blushed in her life, turned scarlet red.

But Melantha didn't even flinch. "I said, give it back to her, grunt."

"Or, what?" the boy snarled, giving Melantha a shove with his elbow that dislodged her hand from his wrist.

Jennifer thought she saw the black woman's eyes flash toward the luggage rack over her earlier seat. But all Jennifer could see there was a folded uniform jacket. "Listen, bitch," the soldier continued, "they may be able to fly me halfway 'round the world to fight in some rice paddy. But I ain't takin' no damn orders from no woman!"

"Cool it, Duke!" a voice warned. "She's an officer. She can get you in trouble."

"I'm really, really afraid." Duke sneered, swerving away, carrying the guitar with him toward his seat.

Jennifer shot Melantha a horrified look. She'd rather lose every piece of Vuitton luggage, her gowns, and custom-made shoes than be parted from her guitar. Before Melantha could stop her, she leapt from her seat in pursuit of the soldier. Snatching up a paperback book that lay open on someone's lap, she heaved it at Duke's back.

It hit him squarely between the shoulder blades and fell with a hollow smack in the aisle.

Duke stopped, slowly turning around to face her, a look of disbelief in his pink eyes. Had he been drinking? she wondered suddenly. He wasn't exactly focusing on her.

"You shouldn't ha' done that, little girl," he ground out. With surprising agility, he lurched at her.

Jennifer ducked but didn't manage to avoid his big hand. It snapped out and gathered a fistful of her blouse and the white, lacy slip underneath, jerking her up close to his face. The entire plane, so full of boisterous soldiers one minute, was now absolutely silent. Standing at the far end of the center aisle, the two stewardesses appeared unsure of what to do. No one moved or, it seemed, breathed.

Jennifer squeezed her eyes shut to try to clear her throbbing head. A second later, she became vaguely aware of a sudden motion nearby. Then she felt her captor go rigid.

When Jennifer's lids snapped open, she glimpsed a slender leather thong drawn tightly around the boy's throat. His Adam's apple spasmed just above it. His eyes looked glazed, confused.

"Let her go," a man's quiet voice commanded.

Immediately, the hand gripping Jennifer's blouse relaxed. It rose in the air, fingers spread wide open as if displaying their innocence.

"Hey, man—" the farmboy croaked.

Jennifer grabbed her guitar, backing away quickly with it, shaking her clothing back into the general area it belonged. She couldn't make out who stood behind Duke, holding the noose, but she sensed that whoever it was had some experience doing what he was doing at the moment— forcibly dragging a man backward by his neck.

"Sit," the voice ordered.

Duke descended abruptly into a seat.

Standing close beside the armrest was the soldier who'd helped her up the stairs with her guitar. He didn't look very big next to Duke—a good eighty pounds lighter—but he glared down on the other man with a deadly expression. Slowly, he let up some of the pressure on the thong.

"See if you can sober him up," he suggested to the men nearby. "If he stays drunk, he'll just get into more trouble and end up in the can before he gets his orders."

The tension in the other soldiers' faces around her seemed to fade. They'd been ready to take sides, she realized. Jennifer was horrified that she'd been the cause of such a scene. And she'd come here to try to help!

Her eyes drifted thankfully to the tough, young soldier. But he looked quickly away.

At last, he fully released the thong. Duke momentarily tensed, but looked too exhausted to exert himself now.

As Jennifer shakily walked back to her seat, she sensed angry vibrations emanating from the men on either side of the aisle. She realized they resented her presence. She was an intruder, a reminder of men like her father who'd put these boys on this plane, of girls who'd kissed them goodbye, of friends who'd never be standing at their side in battle. She wanted to say something to make them understand that she was one of *them*. But was she? *She* wouldn't be trekking across a field, afraid that the next fall of her boot would trigger a mine.

Her eyes met those of a relieved Melantha, then drifted back toward the young man who'd rescued her. Grateful, she wanted to thank him, but he'd already sat down. To reach him, she'd have to pass by Duke, and she didn't want to make things worse than she already had.

Mel tugged at her blouse sleeve. "He was drunk," she said. "He didn't know what he was doing."

"Sure. It's all right."

Mel faced the back of the plane. "Hey, you!" she shouted. "One in my seat. Throw me my jacket. I'm cold."

The soldier pulled Mel's coat out of the overhead storage bin. It was handed from man to man until it reached her.

She checked inside one of the pockets. Seeming satisfied, she put it on and sat down. "My good-luck charm," she said solemnly, patting her pocket. "We won't be having no more difficulties."

Jennifer had no idea what she was talking about. But a rabbit's foot or four-leaf-clover didn't seem powerful enough medicine to combat another assault from Duke. She started to put away her guitar.

Mel laid her hand on Jennifer's arm. "Whatcha doin'?"

"I can't very well sing now," Jennifer said with a tight laugh.

"Why not?"

"Do you want a brawl at thirty thousand feet?"

Mel shook her head and smiled. "They're all quiet now and thinking about what almost happened. Doesn't make anyone happy, seeing people run up against each other that way." She paused, watching Jennifer's expression. "Some of these boys won't go home, Jennifer Lynn. Whether they're black or white, or how much money their daddy makes, or if they're from Rhode Island or Tennessee won't make any difference. Sing 'em a song."

Jennifer let out a long, slow breath. She looked at Mel for several minutes. Finally she shrugged. *After all,* she thought, *this is why I'm here.*

Tucking the guitar into her lap, she crossed her legs on the scratchy cushion and looped a strand of blond hair behind one ear. She plucked softly, beginning one of her favorites: "The Sounds of Silence."

Her soft soprano and the sadness that filled her heart when she thought about the distrust and violence she'd just witnessed lent a second melancholy overtone to the Simon and Garfunkel song. This time nobody throughout the compartment interrupted by so much as a cough or a whisper.

She drew out the final note, clear and soft and perfect at the end. Her guitar strings vibrated long after her voice faded, a final reminder of the song. Still, no one spoke. A few men shifted in their seats.

"That was real nice," Melantha said at last.

Jennifer smiled at her. She felt looser, having gotten through one song. Her hands had shaken at first. Now they rested lightly on the smooth varnished wood of her instrument: her companion. Although no one else complimented her, she could sense waves of approval from the boys and men around her.

"Maybe a change of pace," she murmured, beginning again, this time with a folk-rock strum. She flashed Mel a grin.

By the time she got to Sonny Bono's second chorus in "I Got You, Babe," a few male voices (some of them heartbreakingly off-key) were softly echoing her. And when Jennifer finished her third song, a smattering of applause drifted through the jet's cabin.

She felt more important in that moment than she had on the evening when she'd stood in the Ritz-Carlton ballroom in her white organdy gown, being presented to Boston society.

"Hell, Duke," a voice rang out, "she can sing better 'an you!"

There was a nervous burst of laughter. Jennifer turned around to face the farmboy-soldier. He glanced at her sheepishly from beneath heavy lids. Briefly, their eyes locked, and he nodded at her with grudging respect. "Yer just saying that 'cause she's prettier."

There was an explosion of guffaws. Everyone seemed relieved.

After that, all the tension evaporated from the smoke-filled cabin. A couple dozen of the boys hastily moved up toward the front so that they could see Jennifer, as well as hear her. But there wasn't really enough room for anyone to get comfortable. One soldier dragged two enormous duffle bags from the pile. He placed them close together in the aisle and patted their olive canvas surface.

Jennifer sat on the makeshift stage facing the rear of the plane as more of her audience found places on the floor or perched on the backs of seats—despite the stewardesses' attempts to keep everyone in their own seats and to clear a passageway down the aisle.

Jennifer sang for nearly three hours, one song after another without taking a break. She felt terrible when she didn't know one they requested, but she was content to be here with them. She could feel their need for love and softness in their young lives that had suddenly become frightening and unpredictable. Finally, she had to stop. Her throat had closed up tight and dry. She wasn't used to singing so long at one time.

Melantha brought her a can of Coke that one of the stewardesses had hoarded away when the beverage supply ran out. She popped open the top and handed it to Jennifer.

"You should sing professionally," she said.

Jennifer sputtered on the tepid soda. "No."

"Why not?"

"My voice."

"It's beautiful."

"That's just it," Jennifer said, lowering the soda can after a very long drink. "It's too . . . well, *perfect* sounds egocentric. But that's sort of the way it is. No character. All note and tone. Now, Dylan—"

"Sounds like a gravel pit with a head cold," Melantha finished for her.

Jennifer laughed. "But he's wonderful. He sounds so worldly. So right for his music."

"But that's not your kind of music," Melantha said thoughtfully.

"I like it," Jennifer objected.

"I didn't mean that. I meant, it's not right for—" She laid her head on one side, studying Jennifer. "I don't know. Your voice sounds like it's trying to escape those songs you were singing. And you're holding it back so it won't."

Jennifer shrugged. "I've never really thought of it that way." She settled back into her seat, suddenly tired. Checking the diamond Piaget watch on her slender wrist, she was surprised to find it was three A.M., East Coast time. She hadn't set her watch back.

Mel talked for a while about her neighborhood in Washington, then fell silent. Behind her, Jennifer could hear cards shuffling, pages of books turning, snores and muffled recitals of family trees. She curled up and slid into a deep sleep.

Jennifer did not even stir when the plane refueled in the Philippines. Mel shook her awake hours later as the jet took a sudden dip over the South China Sea. Gripping the arms of her seat, Jennifer swallowed to force her ears to pop.

"What's going on?" she said, gasping, still foggy from sleep.

"Routine procedure, I guess," Mel said grimly. "The pilot just made an announcement that we are entering the free-fire zone around Saigon."

Jennifer tensed. "Is there a chance of the plane being hit?"

Mel reached across the aisle and nudged a soldier. "Do the commercial planes get hit?" she asked.

"Naw. Not much anyway. Our howitzers are constantly sending outgoing to keep the VC from moving up artillery. Not many incoming shells get through."

Mel nodded as if satisfied.

"Not *many?*" Jennifer murmured to herself. As far as she knew, it only took one to down an airliner. She felt queasy.

Their jet didn't even circle the field once. It came in steep and ran at the tarmac like a charging bull, its engines raging and fighting the drag of the wing flaps. She glanced back at the stewardesses who had strapped themselves into seats at the rear of the plane. They were talking casually as if used to such daredevil landings.

Jennifer's stomach definitely was not. It cringed at the base of her spine, and she was unable to get her fingers unclenched from the folds of her skirt until the jet came to a complete stop.

They landed at Tan Son Nhut Airbase, west of Saigon, at noon on May 17, 1967.

"What now?" she asked Mel.

"Hey, I'm new in town, too."

Jennifer smiled at her. They were all new in town.

Before they were allowed to leave the jet, a stocky sergeant with a bushy mustache and swollen eyelids came aboard and told them to all sit back down. He gave them a fifteen-minute briefing on the location of bunkers around the airfield. If there was a mortar attack while they were walking between the plane and the in-processing station, they were supposed to run straight for a bunker.

Jennifer listened without fully believing what she was hearing. Howitzers . . . rockets . . . mortars . . . incoming . . . outgoing . . . bunkers . . . direct hits—and she'd only just landed! This was *not* the country she'd envisioned while studying her pretty brochures.

Even before the cabin door opened to allow the sergeant to enter, Jennifer had been aware of the heat. It radiated through the square pane of glass next to Melantha's seat and made it hard to concentrate on the sergeant's directions.

Now, as a sudden flurry of activity overtook the compartment, Jennifer stared out the window: her first view of Vietnam. Blurry heat waves rose from the surface of flat, sun-baked runways and hovered under the metal bodies of parked planes, as if forming the big birds' nests. Low military buildings had taped-up windows. There were dusty-looking palm trees and miles of tall wire fences topped by barbed coils of concertina wire.

On board the plane, soldiers were sorting out duffel bags, bumming cigarettes, returning borrowed *Life* and *Playboy* magazines and packs of Bicycle Brand playing cards. She felt useless in the middle of their activity. She desperately wanted to travel back a few hours and relive those moments, thirty-thousand feet over the Pacific, when she'd cradled each of these boys safely in her songs.

In her seat, Jennifer blinked sadly as she watched them file past. A few called out goodbye or "see ya round." Some just smiled shyly as they sidled down the narrow space between seats, hefting their belongings on one shoulder. She felt she couldn't trust her voice to answer. All she could manage was a dim smile as she raised one hand sadly in farewell.

Mel poked at her arm. "You waitin' to sweep the floor?"

Jennifer grimaced and stood up. "I just feel terrible," she murmured.

"Huh?"

"I may never see any of them again."

Mel shook her head. "Girl, like I said, you'd make a rotten nurse." The officer strode down the aisle to retrieve her own bag as the last few men squeezed past her, heading for the door.

Jennifer felt something brush against her arm. She spun around and faced the young man who'd tamed Duke. For the first time, she noticed he wore sergeant's stripes.

"So long," he said in a low voice, but his eyes weren't anywhere close to a smile.

She nodded at him, undone by his sweet, boyish face. It contrasted so with the tough expression on his lips, the rock-hard set of his shoulders, and the worldly blue glint in his eyes. His lethal leather thong was now wrapped around his wrist, barely visible beneath the cuff of his fatigues.

He started past her.

"Wait!" She gripped his arm so fiercely he was forced to stop or drag her down the aisle with him. Her glance caught on the name patch stitched over his left breast pocket. "Sergeant Tyler," she said. "Thank you for helping me out."

To her surprise, his rich blue eyes hardened, glittering threateningly at her. She felt him tense beneath her fingertips.

Jennifer's first impulse was to cringe away, letting go of his arm as if it were hot metal. But, inexplicably, she fought losing contact with the young soldier.

"You don't like me, do you?" she asked impulsively.

"No, ma'am, I don't."

Ma'am, she thought ruefully. They were probably the same age! "What have I done to you?"

"It's what you won't do for any of us," he snapped.

"Princess, we better go," Mel called from the cabin doorway, concern edging her deep voice.

"I'll be along. You go ahead," she said, waving the other woman away, her attention riveted on the soldier. "I don't understand," she told him.

In a quick move he broke her hold then seized her by the shoulders and pulled her within inches of his chest. "What the hell *are* you?" he demanded, his eyes flashing. "A tease, is that it? Or Little Miss Benevolence, come to shower her smile and songs on the unfortunate American GI."

Jennifer struggled against his grip.

"I'm not a tease!" she shouted. *Not now, anyway. Maybe once I was, but not now!*

"Then you're another bloody good Samaritan! Just what the world needs!" His face pressed down so close to hers that she could see the tiny beginnings of beard poking up through each follicle.

"If you want to label me, that's what I am—someone who wants to help."

"So . . ." Tyler's voice lowered. "So, you'll put in your generous two bits for a couple days, a week or two maybe. Then you'll fly home full of self-congratulation. Any idea how that makes the boys who don't have any choice but to stay feel?"

Jennifer fought the desire to go limp beneath the pressure of his rebuke. She'd never experienced such a potent anger in a man before. Her father's rages had been nothing in comparison to this.

"I . . . I'm not like that," she stammered in protest.

"Sure." Abruptly, his grip released.

She stood swaying in one spot, feeling the heat on her flesh where his wide fingers had dug in. She made herself straighten up and shot him a look that let him know she'd accepted his challenge.

"I'm going to be around for a whole year, Tyler. Just like you." She tossed her hair in a pale veil over one shoulder. "Maybe we'll even take the same plane home."

For a fraction of a second, his eyes locked with hers. They were questioning, demanding, unsure. This obviously was not the reaction he'd expected.

Jennifer raised her chin and blinked at him, unabashed.

At last, he broke eye contact. "I'll be listening to the radio," he said.

Then he, the last of them, was gone, too.

For what seemed a long time, she stood alone and trembling in the empty compartment of the jet.

This is how it feels to send your son to war, she thought.

Although she'd declared boldly to Tyler that she'd stay in Vietnam no matter what, she no longer wanted to be here. She'd felt closer to these soldiers during the long flight to Saigon than she had to any other person in her life. And now they were being wrenched away from her! Especially this peculiar young soldier who'd questioned her motives, refusing to accept her until she'd proven herself.

She wished she hadn't stepped up to that damned red, white, and blue booth on Newbury Street. Did Tyler know her better than she knew herself?

She looked up from folded hands to meet Mel's brown eyes. She had returned after Tyler left. "Coming?"

"Maybe I'm not cut out for any of this," Jennifer said, groaning.

"Or maybe they got the right woman for the job . . . which might be a first." Mel let out a sharp, short laugh. "Come on, you said you're heading downtown. The station will have sent someone for you."

As Jennifer stepped out of the door, behind Mel, she was struck by a staggering wave of heat. The Asian air was oppressive, dense, cloying. The acrid odor of raw sewage pressed into her nostrils. Her gaze drifted across the shimmering tarmac. Row upon row of jets, transports, and helicopters were parked along one side of the field.

The men who'd just come off the Pan Am lined up along a curb. They began to sluggishly march away, already drained by the sun.

"They say it gets worse during the summer monsoons," Mel murmured.

"The jungle must be terrible," Jennifer said. Then a thought struck her. "Where will you be stationed?"

"Here for now. I'll get my assignment within a week or so."

At the foot of the plane's metal stairs, a young man in a three-piece suit stood looking up at them. He smiled a broad, official smile.

"Looks like the Welcome Wagon," Melantha whispered over her shoulder, as she led the way down.

"Jennifer Swanson?" he asked.

"Yes."

"I'm with the ambassador's staff. He's asked me to fetch you. Right this way." He swung an arm at a sleek black Buick Electra sedan parked a couple hundred feet away.

Mel raised an eyebrow. "I'm impressed."

Glancing at Mel, Jennifer hesitated before following the young diplomat. "Good luck," she murmured fervently.

"Hey!" Mel slapped her on the back. "Same to you, Princess."

Feeling a lump rise in her throat, Jennifer followed her driver. Tyler's challenge still rung in her ears. With each step she became more and more determined to prove him wrong.

The attaché opened the rear passenger door for her. "I'm Ambassador Bunker's aide," he said. "Jeffrey Kirk."

She smiled politely and climbed in.

Nestling into the plush interior of the car, she stared at the back of Jeffrey Kirk's head. Her curiosity was piqued. His accent wasn't North Shore, or Long Island, or even genteel Southern. But it was evident from the way he carried himself that he'd been raised in an upper-class family. He certainly didn't consider himself a servant.

He was someone her parents would approve of. Unlike Tyler.

At the thought of the young soldier, she glanced out the window, trying to spot him. But he'd disappeared beyond the shimmering heat devils on the blacktop. She settled back again.

After the hours spent on the crowded plane with too much noise and clutter and cigarette smoke, the cool, silent interior of the embassy car seemed like heaven. She had just begun to relax when an uncomfortable suspicion began gnawing at her stomach. No aide had been sent to whisk Mel off to her job. Wasn't a nurse at least as important as a disk jockey? Scowling as Jeffrey started up the engine, Jennifer sat bolt upright.

"Wait!" she ordered.

Jeffrey's foot remained on the accelerator. "What, miss?"

"I'm getting out. I'll get into town some other way."

Her father had sworn she was on her own, that she'd have no help from him. He'd intended that speech as a threat, but she'd welcomed her independence. She suspected he had broken his pledge.

"Are there any taxis around here?" she demanded.

Shifting the Electra into park, Jeffrey twisted around to look at her. "Did I say something to offend you?"

"Not at all." She spotted a low institutional building with metal-rimmed windows, perhaps the main terminal.

Jennifer pulled on the door handle and stepped out of the car. A scalding wind blasted her in the face, sucking her breath away. She hadn't realized that the short time she'd been in the car the air conditioning had had such an effect on her. Jennifer was tempted to turn and dive back inside the cool, gray cave of the back seat. Remembering Tyler's prediction, she fought against taking the easy way.

"The rest of my luggage?" she asked.

"It's in the pickup area," Jeffrey said, looking worried. "We're headed that way. I'll get it for you. Please, there's no reason to—"

"If you'll just give me my guitar from the trunk," she said crisply, "I'd prefer to arrive like the rest of the passengers from my flight. My father shouldn't have contacted the ambassador. I don't want any special treatment."

"Your father?" He looked confused.

"Max Swanson."

"Sorry, miss, I don't know who that is. Am I supposed to?"

"You mean—" Jennifer hesitated. "You weren't sent to give me the VIP treatment because my father pulled some strings in the State Department?"

He shook his head, looking amused. "The ambassador has a whole fleet of aides. I'm a junior. *Very junior,*" he added pointedly. "We do all sorts of"—he winked at her in a way that was just short of flirting—"odd jobs."

Jennifer swallowed, at last understanding. He was telling her in a nice way that she was at the bottom of the list of notables to be met at the airport.

"I see," she murmured. Her father had kept his word. He hadn't used his clout to throw a protective web around her.

Good! she thought. *That's just the way I want it.*

The embassy was located in the center of Saigon. To reach it, they drove down a long highway Jeffrey referred to as Route 1. The road was clogged with military vehicles, motorcycles, peasants on foot, and flocks of bicycles, but very few civilian cars. There were a few checkpoints, where people were required to stop and show papers. Jennifer saw a Vietnamese being searched.

"To catch VC smuggling weapons and explosives into the city," Jeffrey explained.

Jennifer watched, fascinated and afraid, even a little titillated.

Many of the women wore pajamalike outfits of loose silk pants with patterned blouses. A few opted for long, attractively fitted white dresses. They were split up both sides to the hip and worn over black pants. Jeffrey informed her the traditional garment was called an *ao dai.*

The men favored loose trousers, short-sleeved, buttoned-down shirts, and sandals. Both men and women wore flattened, cone-shaped straw hats tied under the chin, as protection from the scorching sun.

As the car moved through the city, Jennifer wondered if her driver was taking an indirect route, perhaps to avoid the worst areas. She caught glimpses of side streets, crammed with shops, their roofs of overlapping corrugated metal sheets, walls of patched stucco or cardboard. The boulevards on which Jeffrey drove were spacious and tree-lined—although less glamorous than those of New York or London or Paris.

"Your apartment is inside the American compound near the *Song Sai Gon,* the Saigon River," Jeffrey explained.

"Is there fighting in the city?"

"Oh, no. It's not quite as safe as Cleveland. There's a rocket attack now and then, but that's mostly just a nuisance."

More rockets? she thought, amazed at how nonchalant he sounded. "If the city's secure, why is there a compound?"

"Well, it's just a precaution, really," he explained. "Back in '65 there was a rocket attack on the embassy. We lost a handful of marines and some diplomatic personnel as well."

"What's to prevent that from happening again?" She was beginning to wonder if Freck had been completely honest with her parents.

"We built a new embassy, and perimeter security is much tighter now. There's a whole company of marines dedicated to our personal protection."

Jennifer nodded, somewhat reassured. Besides, the city was so exciting. It teemed with life and beautiful mocha-skinned people with lustrous black hair and delicate faces. They watched her car pass with a curiosity that almost equaled her own. She longed to walk through the city's winding alleys. She wanted to talk to these beautiful people and learn everything she could about their lives.

6

Due to the limited space on the grounds for housing, the villas inside the embassy compound were small. Their cheerful red tile roofs reminded Jennifer of the alpine chalets in northern Italy. Her landlady was the wife of an American army officer. Jeffrey followed along as the woman showed Jennifer her rooms, proudly pointing out the luxury appointments: plumbing, air conditioning, a telephone. She informed her that domestic service was cheap and offered to supply references.

Jennifer thanked her, but had no intention of hiring a maid. She'd come halfway around the world to stake a claim on independence. She excused herself from both members of her welcoming committee as soon as politely possible.

The villa had an inexpensively furnished living room with attached efficiency kitchen, complete with basic appliances, Melamine dinnerware, and stainless steel utensils made in Hong Kong. There was a tiny bedroom and a bathroom barely big enough to turn around in. There were just three small windows in the little house. These, like the ones at the airport, were thickly reinforced with layers of curling yellow masking tape.

Thirty minutes later, a Vietnamese delivery crew brought her trunks from the airport. They were just leaving when the telephone rang.

Jennifer hastily tipped the men, locked her door, and breathlessly ran to pick up the receiver.

"Miss Swanson?" a voice at the other end asked.

"Yes?"

"This is Gloria Bates. I'm with American Forces Vietnam Radio. I just wanted to be sure you'd arrived on schedule."

"Arrived, yes," Jennifer said tiredly, surveying the enormous trunks that took up most of her new living room. There were no closets in the villa. A freestanding wardrobe in the bedroom provided her only storage. Never in her wildest dreams could she imagine cramming all those clothes into that little of a space.

"You must be done in," Gloria guessed. "Why don't you rest up? There's a reception for all incoming support people tonight, a sort of get-acquainted party at the embassy. I can pick you up at six."

Jennifer rubbed the bridge of her nose between two fingers. She was exhausted, yes, but she was also eager to see the radio station and get started at her job. She'd waste no time in proving she was serious about staying here. *I'll show you, Tyler!*

"When do I start work?" she asked.

"Well, if you feel up to it, tomorrow you could drop by the station. I'll give you a tour and introduce you to the program manager."

"Great!"

Gloria laughed at her enthusiasm. "Better get some rest. You're going to be a busy girl."

After she'd hung up, Jennifer dragged the heinous trunks into the bedroom, then sat on the bed glaring at them. Maybe half of the contents of one could be crammed into the wardrobe. The rest . . . well, could she live for an entire year out of her luggage?

Jennifer stretched out on the double bed. It seemed narrow and hard compared to her own lovely Empire-style canopied bed at home. This one had a plain pressed-wood headboard, stained maple. There were two chests of drawers with eagle-shaped metal pulls. *It'll do,* she reminded herself, letting her eyelids drift closed. *This is the real world. No pampered princess am I anymore . . . I'm on my own.*

She dozed off with a smile tugging on the corners of her lips.

A steady banging sound woke Jennifer with a jolt. She blinked at the white plaster ceiling above her head, then lifted her wrist in front of her face and stared dumbly at the diamond-ringed crystal of her Piaget. Ten minutes after six.

"Oh my God!"

"Jennifer!" a woman's voice called through the door. "It's me, Gloria. Are you all right?"

Springing off the bed, she glanced with frustration at the mirror over her dresser and groaned. Her hair was a mess. She still wore her travel clothes, which were wrinkled and askew. Yanking her skirt around a quarter-turn, she dashed for the door.

"I'm sorry," Jennifer cried as she fumbled with the lock. "I was out cold."

A plump young woman with short permed hair the nondescript color of shirt cardboard and a friendly smile walked in. She was carrying a sack of groceries. "That's great. I'm sure you needed the sleep."

"Now I'll be awake all night and dozing off all tomorrow."

"Ninety percent of us are night owls. You'll fit right in." Gloria headed straight for the kitchen and set the brown paper shopping bag beside the refrigerator. "I brought you a few staples. OJ. Bread. Instant coffee. Stuff like that."

"Thanks."

"Oh—and bottled water. Don't drink tap water, whatever you do. You'll get dysentery, parasites, or both." Gloria began helping her find a place for everything. "Like your apartment?"

"It's fine," Jennifer said, cheerfully.

"You'll soon make it your own," Gloria assured her. "By the time you're ready to leave Vietnam, you'll have all sorts of wonderful junk to bring home. The station gives you a weight allowance. It's never enough, but you can mail smaller stuff—if you can afford the postage."

Being able to afford anything had never been a problem for Jennifer. Now it seemed an intriguing challenge. She'd already decided to budget her money very carefully so that she'd have extra left at the end of the year. Wouldn't that shock her father?

"I'm terribly sorry to hold you up," Jennifer apologized as she folded the empty bag and shoved it under the sink. "Make yourself comfortable. I'll change quickly." She dashed for the bedroom.

"Take a shower, if you like," Gloria called after her.

The idea of washing off the hours of accumulated perspiration and grit seemed too inviting to pass up. After an intentionally stinging cold shower, she felt fresh and was looking forward to her first night in Saigon. The two young women walked across the compound.

The reception was held in the chancery, an eight-story building shaped like a squat, white marble T with narrow, functional windows. Its harshness was softened by the curved gravel drive, its well-groomed lawn and lovely palm trees. Tropical foliage provided privacy between the villas, the embassy itself, and other official buildings.

A small salon on the first floor had been prepared to welcome the new personnel. Jennifer looked around the roomful of unfamiliar faces, hoping to spot Melantha Benning. Belatedly, it struck her that very few military personnel would be greeted this formally. They came and went in such large numbers that it would be impossible for the ambassador to personally welcome each one.

Gloria introduced her to another person who worked at the radio station, a couple of Red Cross volunteers who'd just arrived, and a handful of embassy staff members. While the growing crowd snacked from silver platters arranged with fresh pineapple and spicy hors d'oeuvres, Gloria pointed out still more people. Jennifer listened politely, sipping champagne poured by a Korean bartender in a short white jacket and black bow tie. She could feel the boredom slipping like a gray sheet over her gaze as she swept the room. This was too much like one of her parents' parties. She wished Mel were here. *She* would liven things up with her booming voice and brash, bold manner. And Tyler. What an intriguing contrast the young soldier's no-nonsense attitude would strike against this stuffy crowd!

Jennifer let her eyes drift across the sea of faces, searching for any of interest.

A number of Asians were included among the guests. One woman in particular stood out. She reminded Jennifer of a satin-kimonoed doll she'd been given when she was very little. Her father had bought it for her on a business trip to Japan.

Every feature of the woman's body seemed to be fashioned in miniature. She wasn't childlike. Rather, she seemed reduced in size and made more perfect. She had widely spaced, bright black eyes that flashed with humor and intelligence, a charming widow's peak, and a tiny nose. Her glossy black hair was pinned neatly into a classic chignon near the nape of her neck. Instead of the traditional Vietnamese woman's *ao dai* that Jennifer had seen in the streets, she wore a Chinese-style dress—a rich ebony brocade with crimson frogs placed diagonally across her breasts and delicate crimson piping outlining the mandarin collar and cap sleeves.

While Jennifer chatted with Gloria and one of the Red Cross volunteers, she watched the beautiful Vietnamese. The woman moved with grace and poise from one guest to another, as if she already knew them all intimately and was being careful to distribute her time equally. Her eyes never failed to sparkle with interest during a conversation, and her smile was radiant and untiring. Jennifer couldn't imagine that face ever frowning.

"How's it going?"

Jennifer spun around. "Oh, Jeffrey!" She was delighted to see a familiar face.

He wore a tuxedo now, looking quite handsome. "Can I get you ladies something?" he asked.

Jennifer was aware that, although he'd spoken to both of them, he was studying *her* with avid interest.

"Not now, thank you," she murmured with a polite smile.

"Gloria?" He cocked his head at the woman beside her who'd been gazing up at him with open admiration.

"No . . . no," she stammered, making a point of not meeting his glance.

Noticing Gloria's uneasiness in front of the suave young diplomat, Jennifer hid a smile behind the rim of her champagne flute. "Jeff," she suggested, "you could choose a plate of assorted goodies, then the three of us can share."

He beamed at her. "Not a bad idea. It is rather cumbersome, balancing glass, napkin, plate, and whatever. Be back in a flash."

Gloria let out a long breath. "I thought he'd never leave." Her soft eyes flickered up at Jennifer. "Where did you meet *him?*"

"He drove me from the airport."

Gloria nodded thoughtfully.

"He is nice looking, isn't he?" Jennifer ventured.

"Oh, he's downright handsome. Dashing even!" Gloria agreed rapturously. "But," she added, leaning toward Jennifer, "he's quite the local playboy."

Jennifer feigned shock. "Is he really?"

"Oh, yes." Gloria gulped down her champagne, then stared at the empty glass with a startled expression. "He's slept with every beautiful woman who's come through Saigon. So they say."

"And how is he?" Jennifer asked pointedly.

Gloria shrugged. "How should I know, I—" She giggled, covering her mouth with one hand. "Oh, you mean *me* and Jeff Kirk?"

Jennifer nodded.

"Frumpy little me? You're sweet." She settled her shoulders back down on her compact torso. "Of course, he'd never bother with me."

"I don't see why not," Jennifer said crisply. "I've only known you a couple hours. I like you. Why shouldn't he?"

Gloria stared at Jennifer, as though trying to decide if she was being teased. At last she said with a perfectly straight face, "You're nice, too. I have a confession. I didn't want to be your sponsor when I heard about how rich you are. But—" She continued quickly when she saw Jennifer's mouth drop open in protest: "I'm awfully glad I'm the one. I wouldn't have wanted to miss knowing you."

Jennifer was touched. Gloria might not dress with the panache of her North Shore friends or have their boarding-school polish, but the feelings she expressed were sincere and uncontrived.

Just then she caught a motion out of the corner of her eye. The Asian woman she'd noticed earlier was moving again, with liquid grace, between clusters of guests.

"Why don't you keep Jeffrey company?" she suggested, hastily. "I'll be right back." Jennifer dashed across the room between tuxedos, sliding to a stop in front of the woman. "Hello," she said, holding out her hand, "I'm Jennifer Swanson. I'll be doing a show for the American radio station."

The soft smile broadened. "I've been looking forward to meeting you, Jennifer," a lyrical voice, tinged with a faint French accent, responded. "Come, come over here to a quieter corner where we can talk."

The two women stepped into an alcove with a velvet-cushioned window seat and they both sat down.

"I am Chau Thi Lian, Cultural Liaison for the USO in Saigon," the woman told her.

"You work for the USO, Chau?"

"My given name is Lian," she explained gently. "Yes. I work for the USO and for the Republic of South Vietnam. I am an advisor as well as the manager. I help to avoid misunderstandings between our two peoples. The USO clubs employ Vietnamese, and many American soldiers visit. There is a lot of room for difficult feelings. I try to make things easier and happier for everyone."

"I see." Lian definitely seemed the most interesting person in the room. She wanted to find out more about her.

74

"You don't look quite like the other women I've seen on the street," she said. "Are your parents both Vietnamese?"

Lian shook her head, seeming not at all put off by her directness. "My mother is Chinese, my father is French-Vietnamese. That is, his family was raised speaking French, as well as Vietnamese. He is an exporter."

"What does he trade in?" Jennifer asked.

"Fine porcelain mostly, from China. He met my mother on one of his purchasing trips. They married and he brought her home with him along with his shipment."

"How romantic." Jennifer let out a long sigh.

Lian smiled. "My mother was so *very* strict with me. I cannot believe she ran away from home with a foreigner. Her family was most distraught. But then they found out how rich my father was and all was forgiven."

"Strange what a little bit of money can accomplish," Jennifer remarked dryly, gazing into the bottom of her empty glass. A waiter passing by with a full tray paused beside them. Jennifer relinquished her empty for two fresh drinks, then held one out to Lian.

"No, thank you," Lian said quietly, "I do not drink."

"No problem."

Jennifer kept both glasses, sipping from one as she glanced across the room to see Gloria and Jeffrey talking. *Good,* she thought with satisfaction. The warm glow of the champagne had helped settle her inevitable attack of restlessness. But, as always after an hour or so at a party, she felt the need to escape to somewhere less suffocating.

"Do you know anything about AFVN?" Jennifer asked.

Lian shook her head. "I'm afraid not. I've driven past the studio, but I've never been inside. I know a few of the Americans who work there."

Jennifer swirled the bubbly contents of her glass. "In some ways, I hope I can start working tomorrow. In another, I'd like to put it off."

"Why?"

"Before I arrived today, I thought I'd be perfectly content to stay close to the embassy, but the ride into the city from the airport was so fascinating."

Lian smiled, looking pleased.

Jennifer continued. "The photographs I've seen of the countryside are lovely. I'd like to go up into the mountains and see some of the beaches and the delta, too," she explained excitedly.

Jennifer glanced up from her glass to see Lian frowning. "I wouldn't suggest leaving the city, Jennifer."

"Why not?"

"The fighting. A few years ago I could have told you safe places for viewing the ruins of ancient temples or the isolated Montagnard villages, which are intriguing. But now . . ." Her voice faded, a cloud passing over her exotic features. "The NVA, the North Vietnamese Army, is unpredictable and desperate. One day a valley is calm. The next, there is shelling and terror. And there are the guerrillas. Better to stay in the city."

But the alcohol made Jennifer stubborn. "I came thousands of miles to spend a whole year confined to one city?"

Lian put on an optimistic smile. "But there is so much to see and do *here*. Wonderful food, and lovely treasures in the museums. The botanical gardens. The people!" Her soft, oval face glowed with love for her city. "They come from the villages and cities, from all over Asia. And there are the French, still here from colonial days, and Australians and Koreans who have come to help us fight the communists."

"I suppose." Jennifer sighed listlessly.

"You'll see," Lian assured her. "Saigon will be more than big enough for you."

That night, when Jennifer lay down, the champagne still buzzing in her ears, she envisioned verdant hillsides, stretches of checkerboard rice paddies, and exotic jungles. And she saw soldiers' faces—*her* soldiers from the plane— playing out life-threatening scenes she'd viewed on the six o'clock news. She owed them more than a voice sifting out of the air. She was determined to give them more!

The next morning, the telephone woke her. Jennifer hid from it, burrowing beneath her pillow.

"Champagne," she grumbled. "Oh God!" Why did it always taste so lovely going down and feel so disastrous the next morning?

At last, she blindly reached toward the persistent jangling and lifted the receiver. "Hello?"

"How about lunch?"

"Jeffrey? What the hell time is it?"

"Almost noon. For a working girl you sure sleep late."

"Oh, no," she groaned.

"Not to worry. I called the station. Gloria said you didn't need to be in right away."

She agreed that eating something would be wise, under the circumstances. And she certainly wasn't up to experimenting in her tiny kitchen. She'd never actually prepared a meal from start to finish on her own. Grilled cheese was the most adventurous recipe she'd ever tackled.

Jeffrey, in short-sleeved madras shirt and smart khaki slacks, met her on the embassy grounds and together they walked out through the main gate where he flagged down a pedicab. Called "cyclos," they were the most common form of transportation in the city, other than bicycles. The rickshawlike vehicle consisted of a canopied passenger seat wide enough for one or two, behind which was a coughing, exhaust-spewing motorbike or a rusty bicycle on which the driver sat.

Jeffrey bartered for a fair price while Jennifer climbed in.

"We'll eat at the USO. They have the only decent burgers in-country," he explained when he joined her.

It was her first chance for a really up-close look at Saigon. The cyclo left the wide commercial boulevards to avoid the worst of the late morning traffic. Soon they were zipping down narrow local streets without sidewalks. Peeling wood-frame shops of one or two stories crushed together, and hand-painted signs on rooftops advertised services, but most of the sales activity seemed to be taking place on the streets themselves.

Vendors displayed their wares on wooden trays arranged on the ground or in portable glass display cases. Cookies, fresh papaya chunks, roasted corn, boiled eggs. Female hawkers carried soup, bean curd custard, or rice in Don Ganh baskets suspended from poles that balanced across their shoulders. Wherever a customer appeared, they stopped and set up shop, serving a portion for a few piasters. Other merchants sold live chickens and ducks, eels, fish, or pigs. Pigs seemed especially popular today.

They continued to weave through streets which grew busier as people left work for lunch. Jennifer took in everything. She was fascinated with the intricate daily rush and rhythm of life. The glimpses of cheerfulness in the people shimmered against the stark reality of life here. Drab bar girls were already trying to drum up business by chatting up passing GIs. Beggars and cripples crouched on street corners. Women seemed to be most actively involved in street selling. Often, what they'd brought to sell couldn't have been worth the time it took to make or set up on the street. One family sold hand-rolled paper straws. Another woman offered slices of fruit she'd bought whole from another vendor. The aggressive Vietnamese pursuit of life in the face of war moved her.

Jennifer turned to Jeffrey on the seat. "Are we very far from the USO now?" she asked. "I'd love to get out and walk."

He looked around to get his bearings. "We could make it there in twenty minutes."

They paid the driver full price and climbed out.

A little ways on, a meat seller had brought a chopping block out onto the street. He used no scale but cut precise sections of meat with an enormous cleaver, then carefully wrapped each piece in banana leaves before handing it to his customer.

They passed an open doorway, and Jennifer wrinkled her nose. "What's that smell?"

"Nuoc mam. Fish sauce. The Vietnamese use it on almost everything, as the Chinese do with soy sauce. Here," he said, stopping in front of a woman who stood beside a small glass case, "you have to try one of these on your first day in Saigon."

"What is it?" she asked suspiciously.

"*Chau gia*. Rice paper rolled around bits of vegetable and meat then fried."

It tasted a lot like egg roll and was delicious. She could have gladly eaten two more and made a full lunch of them. But Jeffrey had his heart set on a hamburger.

At last they reached the USO. More vendors lined the sidewalk outside. Some sold watches, silk scarves, or pottery. One old woman displayed a selection of American-made rifles.

Jeffrey hurried Jennifer past the weapons, but not before a chill of revulsion spiraled down her spine. Where had that woman gotten those guns? Had they been stripped off dead American soldiers?

Even during the middle of the day there seemed to be plenty of soldiers here. A billboard near the door advertised the movie for the day. It starred Clint Eastwood. The menu was all American—hot dogs on buns with chili or sauerkraut, burgers, french fries. Jennifer remembered that she'd have to be careful about spending until she became familiar with the cost of things and arrived at a sensible budget. Still, she'd insist upon paying for her own meal.

They sat at a table and ate enormous, juicy cheeseburgers. She glanced at Jeffrey repeatedly, wondering if he and Gloria had hit it off last night. Jennifer was just about to ask him about the pretty, plump radio-station secretary when she happened to glimpse a familiar face.

"Oh, there's Lian!" She put down her half-finished sandwich. The Vietnamese woman was animatedly talking with two American servicemen. "You just go on eating, Jeff. I'll be right back."

Lian visibly brightened when she saw her approaching. She bid the two men a quick goodbye and met her halfway across the room. "Jennifer! How nice of you to come."

"I'd forgotten that you work here. What was all that about?" She gestured at the two departing soldiers.

Lian lowered her voice as she took Jennifer's arm and walked with her across the room. "The young man in the green shirt, he came to me because he wishes to marry a Vietnamese woman."

"Oh, that's lovely. You're helping them?"

"Unofficially. The paperwork is very confusing and complicated, you see. One has to deal with two governments at once. I can at least direct him to the right offices and help his fiancée fill out the Vietnamese forms."

"Do you have time to sit with us for lunch?"

"I'm afraid I'm very busy at this moment," Lian apologized.

Jennifer was disappointed. She had liked Lian from the first moment she'd spoken to her. They had, surprisingly, a great deal in common. They were about the same age, had grown up in cultured, wealthy families, and were interested in doing something to help other people.

Lian laid her hand on Jennifer's arm. "I'm often here in the evening. Come and see me then. I'll have finished all my paperwork, and you can visit with the soldiers, too. They will be most grateful."

"I will." Jennifer smiled, then hesitated before asking, "You wouldn't have noticed a particular soldier? His name is Tyler, and he has a definite Midwestern accent."

Lian considered for a moment. "No," she said at last. "So many boys come and go. I get to know very few by name."

Jennifer couldn't help letting out a small sigh. "That's too bad."

"Is he someone special?"

"No," she answered quickly. "Just a guy I met on the plane."

Her smile was wistful, though, as she returned to the table where Jeffrey sat watching her.

"Met Mrs. Nguyen, did you?"

"That's her husband's name?" she asked, taking an absent-minded bite of her cold cheeseburger.

"Right. Chau Thi Lian. Chau is her father's family name. It means gem. Thi simply means she's female. Lian means graceful willow . . . I think," added Jeffrey. He'd finished

80

his lunch and sat patiently while she nibbled at hers. "She can be called Mrs. Nguyen, after her husband. Or Mrs. Chau—just to indicate she's married. Either is permissible."

Jennifer was intrigued that names could mean so much. She'd always taken her own name for granted. She had no idea what it meant.

She watched Lian's graceful figure glide across the room. Today, she wore a simple white *ao dai* over silky black pants. "Who is her husband?"

"A colonel with the ARVN, the South Vietnamese Army."

"He must be very proud of her. She's a beautiful woman, and so intelligent."

"I've never met him." Jeffrey glanced remorsefully at Jennifer. "I found out about Nguyen a bit late. I'm afraid I once offended Lian, and she's never quite forgiven me."

"What did you do?" Jennifer asked.

"It was stupid really. There was a big Fourth of July celebration last year out at Tan Son Nhut. The army sponsored it, and all the embassy staff and certain Vietnamese dignitaries were invited—Lian among them, due to her job, but also because her husband is highly respected in Saigon's government circles. Everyone had gallons of beer. And, you see, I have this unquenchable fondness for the backs of pretty necks." He pulled a vampirelike face and Jennifer giggled. "Anyway, I came up behind Lian, wrapped my arms around her, and took a wee nibble."

"That's not so horrible."

Jeffrey shrugged. "One of her husband's commanding officers was standing nearby. She was embarrassed."

"But, certainly, he could see that no harm was meant."

"The Vietnamese are very moral people—Tu Do Street hostesses and prostitutes notwithstanding. Family is terribly important. A wife's fidelity is a matter of honor, and they tend to interpret the slightest gesture between a man and a woman as a threat. I was out of line," he admitted.

"Well," said Jennifer, "I'm sure she'll forgive you one day."

"I hope so. I like her." Jeffrey glanced at his watch. "It's almost two o'clock. I think I'll look in on my office."

"And I should go along to the station. I don't want to lose my job before I do my first show." They parted in front of the USO, Jennifer waving down a cyclo and Jeffrey a cab.

7

Jennifer paid close attention as Gloria escorted her through the various recording rooms in the AFVN studio. Some were very small, with only space for one person to sit facing a table microphone. Others were more elaborate, equipped with multiple turntables, reel-to-reel tape players, shelves of record albums and canned tapes, and their own control board that resembled something out of a science fiction movie. All were lined with acoustical tile and felt carpeting designed to cut extraneous noise.

She was introduced to a score of technicians, news readers, and deejays. Finally she met the program director.

Lieutenant Hugh Metcalf was a short, sharp-eyed man, with a patch of baby pink scalp trapped between two wings of mousy hair. When Jennifer stepped through his office door, he didn't bother to stand up but shook hands with her from behind his cluttered desk.

"I'd better get back to my work," Gloria murmured.

"Thanks, love," Metcalf called after her, motioning Jennifer toward a chair. "Freck raved about you when he called from New York. Bosh! Can sure see why!"

The lieutenant's Cockney accent was unexpected. Wondering if it was authentic, Jennifer gave him a reserved smile. "I only sang for five minutes."

"Yeah?" He grinned. "Well, based on his glowin' recommendation, we've reworked plans for your program." Metcalf picked up a Manila file folder from his desk top. "'A Night with Jennifer,'" he read solemnly, then peered at her over the sheets. "O' course, it won't be a whole night. More like three hours. We'll have to see. You play guitar?"

"And sing."

He laid the folder aside, leaned back in his chair. "What kind of music? Rock? Folk? Hillbilly stuff?"

"A mix. Mostly popular songs—things you hear on the radio."

His grin widened. "That's good, innit? A little bit o' this. A little bit o' that!" Metcalf's eyes flitted across her as if he were a fight promoter sizing up a new contender's chances in the ring, but with an added touch of lewdness. "You're even better in person than the picture New York sent."

With a self-conscious twinge, she remembered having included her graduation photo from Miss Porter's with her résumé. She'd worn a white lace dress and held a red rose demurely in her lap. Her parents loved the picture. She hated it.

Metcalf continued, "We've lined up a bloody crammed-full schedule for you, Jenny-love."

She was disgusted by his overly familiar manner, by the way his office smelled of stale cigar smoke and leftover food and a trace of bug spray, by the habit his fingers had of rolling the fabric of his jacket front as if it were something luxurious and sensual.

But his enthusiasm seemed real, and its contagion overcame her revulsion.

"Wonderful," Jennifer said. "I can't wait to get started."

He nodded. "Friday nights is when we'll run your spot, I figure. Three hours. Plenty o' time for spinning disks, chattin' up the boys and singin' to 'em. Once you get the knack o' it, it'll take one day to tape a full show. In addition, you'll be recordin' some promotional material we're plannin' to use to introduce you and your program."

"That won't keep me very busy," she observed. "A few days' work each week."

"Little Spitfire, aren't we?" He beamed at her, rising to reposition himself on the front corner of his desk. He lit a cigar, then leaned down to speak into her face. "Don't you worry. Most of the time you'll be tied up with personal appearances."

"Personal appearances? You mean like . . . at the USO?" Her heart was racing she was so excited. "Maybe we could do a special live broadcast once in a while."

"Now there's a thought!" Metcalf slapped his knee. "Sure, when you do the USO here in Saigon, it *could* be live. I got a couple crack engineers. They could rig it. Might fly one of 'em along with equipment when you do the bases at Bien Hoa and Da Nang, too."

"My parents were told that I'd be staying in Saigon." Jennifer felt a frisson of excitement and fear.

Metcalf looked puzzled for a moment, before breaking into a sharp laugh. A laugh that clawed at her insides. "Freck say that? Son of a bitch!" He made a show of brushing ashes off his pant leg. "Freck's one of the best government recruiters there is. That's his specialty, see. The military needs a civilian for a special job? Don't have the right contacts? Freck finds him . . . or, in this case, her." He shook his head. "Crazy bloke must've figured they'd bosh the whole deal if he was straight with 'em. Ah well—" He threw up his hands in a defeated gesture, as if Freck were some mischievous toddler run amok. "Sometimes tiptoein' round the truth is what's needed. You don't have no objections to rubbin' shoulders with the grunts, do you, love? Give 'em a teeny peck on the cheek for the cause of God and Country?"

"Well, no—" she began. In fact, this was what she'd hoped for, seeing the boys again. But Metcalf's tone made her job sound cheap, as if she were some whore flown in to satisfy a horny army! The men she'd met weren't like that at all. Whatever bold front they might put up, underneath they were sweet, frightened little boys. "No, of course I don't object."

"Good. Fine then." He jabbed the glowing end of his cigar at her. "I know you'll be a smash." He stood up as if everything had been settled.

Jennifer remained firmly seated, studying his squat physique through narrowed green eyes. "Where, exactly, would I be *personally* appearing?" she asked slowly. "Aside from the places you've already mentioned."

Metcalf's glance drifted toward the office window overlooking the street. From behind the taped glass, she could hear the cries of the vendors, the shrill ring of bicycle bells, the frenzied shrieks of playing children.

"Wherever the grunts need to see a round-eye woman most," he said in an offhand way.

And she didn't care for the way he dropped her into a category. She was a round-eye, because she was white. A Vietnamese women, like Lian, would be a slant-eye because of her own almond-shaped eyes.

"Like where?" she persisted.

"For instance? You want for instances?"

Jennifer gave a sharp nod.

"Let me see." He laid his pink pate on one side and sighed. "We got us a girl band—The Silkettes—scheduled to tour Da Nang, Chu Lai, and about a dozen firebases thereabouts. Probably not as far north as Khe Sanh, though. The stuff's really startin' to fly up there. Wouldn't want to see any o' *my* girls gettin' hurt." He reached out to pat her encouragingly on the shoulder.

Jennifer reflexively slipped out from under his hand and stood up. "Are those very large bases? The firebases?"

As much as she wanted to be with her soldiers, she wouldn't do them much good if she got herself killed her first month in-country. She remembered Lian's warning, and felt a subtle wave of fear ripple through her stomach.

"Sure, they're fine. Think I'd send my girls out into the boonies or something?"

She squinted at him critically. "I don't know."

Metcalf turned serious. "Listen, love. If you're havin' second thoughts, maybe we'd better just ship you home. When I saw your file, to be honest, I had my doubts. I honestly did."

She stiffened, the nerves at the tips of her fingers prickling with irritation. "Doubts about what?" she demanded.

"Well, now. Innit real obvious, love? I mean, here you are—a lovely young girl fresh out of your fancy finishin' school, livin' on pop's estate." He brandished his cigar in the air, tracing putrid smoke trails. "You flit all the way to Asia. 'For what?' I ask myself. 'Is this the girl these soldiers want to hear from? She's pretty enough, sure. But these are simple boys from ord'nary families. If she's goin' to look down her nose on them—'"

"I would *never* look down my nose on them!" Jennifer shouted, suddenly furious that he was making her feel inadequate. But another part of her desperately wanted to prove that she *could* do something worthwhile. And it was her own insecurity that made her the angriest. "I came to do a job, Lieutenant, and I'll damn well do it. I just want to know what to expect!"

Without taking his eyes off of her, he slowly snuffed out his cigar in a tin ashtray. "No problem there," he muttered. "Well, then, let's get this show on the road."

Walking rigidly, Jennifer followed him into a large studio. She expected further explanation from him, some sort of guarantee. Instead, he turned her over to the recording engineer she'd met earlier, Sergeant Dick French, a thin, bashful young man who wore steel-rimmed glasses. Dick took her inside one of three glass-enclosed booths built around his control room and sat her down. He helped her on with earphones and adjusted her mike. Metcalf slipped out before she could stop him.

"Just talk to me for a minute or two once I get back outside," Dick told her, never quite getting up the nerve to meet her eyes, "so I can get a voice level."

She didn't know what to say, but she was still thinking about a number of questions. "Do they send many bands outside Saigon to do shows?"

"Huh? Oh, sure," Dick answered through her earphones.

"Just to the larger bases and big cities?"

"Cities?"

"Where the girls go to perform."

"Oh, that." He twisted a few dials. "Not always. I mean, we sometimes fly entertainers into the highlands to put on a show for a couple platoons. I guess you wouldn't call them cities. Closer to towns."

"Or villages?" she asked.

"Villes, they call them here. Keep talking."

"I don't think I understand," she said. "Isn't that a lot of trouble for a very small audience?"

He shrugged. "Yeah. But out there is where the guys really need to see something from home. Morale's real low. They're out in the jungle for weeks, months. Not even Bob Hope will drop by to shake hands with some poor grunt on LZ Oasis—"

"LZ?"

"Landing Zone."

As she worked through the afternoon with Dick, the fact that Freck and Metcalf hadn't exactly been up front about her job requirements seemed to matter less and less. She'd have to be careful of Metcalf, of course. Careful in more ways than one, if she'd read the leer in his dull little eyes correctly. But, all in all, it looked as if she'd be doing what she'd hoped—singing for the boys! She could hardly wait to start!

The following days were long and busy. Jennifer spent a minimum of twelve hours at the station, most of them with Dick in the recording booth.

Her engineer was a patient teacher. She learned to sit with the microphone at the ideal distance from her lips so that she wouldn't sound as if she were the Jolly Green Giant or as though she were speaking from a closet down the hall. She practiced modulating her voice to avoid reading the army's general information announcements in a monotone. At night, even when she was thoroughly exhausted, she sat on the edge of her bed repeating the obligatory station identification patter:

"This is Jennifer Swanson, coming to you over your Armed Forces Radio Network, station AFVN-Saigon, with music and news around the clock from the Delta to the DMZ."

Interspersed throughout her show, she'd also read announcements for American military and civilian men and women living in Vietnam: "Remember, all 'green' must be exchanged for military scrip when you enter Vietnam." *Green* was U.S. currency. "This is to prevent misuse of our American dollars. We already have enough black markets over here, gang."

And: "At local theaters this week, *Hello, Dolly!,* starring Barbra Streisand, will be showing in Saigon. In Da Nang, *The Graduate* with Dustin Hoffman and Katharine Ross. In Qui Nhon, you can catch *Rosemary's Baby* and Mia Farrow. *Star,* starring Julie Andrews, will be showing in Nha Trang."

The announcements were to the point and never very entertaining. But she realized that they were necessary and served a purpose. It was her own part of the show, though, that she most enjoyed. She sat down with Dick and chose the records she'd play for her first performance. He was a great help advising her about the songs—recent releases and oldies—most popular among the GIs. He helped her find a compromise that would appeal to boys from every part of the U.S. and from every sort of background: The Righteous Brothers, the Ronettes ("Walking in the Rain"), the Beatles, the Beach Boys, Billy J. Kramer ("Little Children"), the Chiffons ("He's So Fine"), the Dave Clark Five, the Hollies ("Look Through Any Window"), Percy Sledge ("When a Man Loves a Woman"), Jonathan King ("Everyone's Gone to the Moon"), the Rolling Stones (anything from their latest album, *Beggar's Banquet),* B. J. Thomas ("I'm So Lonesome I Could Cry"), Otis Redding, Dylan.

They taped each of the songs with Jennifer's personal messages to her listeners tucked like tender love notes in between. Later, Dick told her, she'd be able to do at least this portion of her show live, if she liked. While she was becoming familiar with the studio, it would be better to prerecord everything. That way she wouldn't be so nervous about making mistakes.

She spent three additional days taping her own songs and writing and recording her monologues for the soldiers who'd be tuning her in. At the end of a week, she and Dick finished the final editing of what would be her first show. They both were pleased with the result, and Hugh Metcalf reinforced their feeling that "A Night with Jennifer" would be a popular addition to the weekly programming.

"I know you just got here, love," Hugh said after Dick left them alone in his office, "but I want to start on publicity—getting you seen around the country. Ready for your first personal appearance?"

Jennifer was thrilled. "Where am I going?"

"Fourth Mobile Strike Force Command. They got around two thousand men in three battalions and a couple companies—reconnaissance and airboat, I think. They're headquartered at Can Tho, south of here."

"What will I be doing?"

"Same thing you did on the plane."

She'd told Hugh how much she enjoyed singing for the soldiers on her way across the Pacific. Being a born promoter, he recognized the value of the informal concert and thought they'd be smart to repeat it a few times. A close-up look at Jennifer, then let word of mouth take over. She'd be the hottest thing in Nam within two weeks. By the time her first show aired at the end of the month, every soldier in the country would be listening in.

The day she left for Can Tho, the summer monsoon was peaking. A steady gritty-gray rain fell as the wind whipped it in unpredictable gusts. The pilot who'd been assigned to take her to the Fourth Mobile looked askance at her white leather go-go boots. "They're liable to get pretty mucked up," he commented.

"I don't mind." She climbed cheerfully up into the helicopter and buckled herself into the seat behind him.

90

They flew for almost forty-five minutes, the pilot hardly talking at all. Whenever she asked him a question, he gave her an abrupt reply, not one word more than was necessary. Finally, she leaned forward in her seat and asked through her helmet microphone, "Do you have a problem with my being here?"

He merely snorted. The chopper hovered lower above the tree line.

"Lieutenant," she said clearly, "what have I done to deserve the silent treatment?"

"Listen, honey," he growled. "How *you* want to die is your decision. Leave *me* out of it."

A shudder ripped through her body. "I don't understand. What do you mean?"

He didn't have a chance to explain.

There was a sharp, whizzing sound, then an explosion close by. The helicopter rocked violently. The pilot manipulated the controls, rapidly gaining altitude and reversing their course.

"What's happening?" she demanded, gripping the back of his seat.

"We're getting shot at. That's what happens in a war, sweetheart. They *shoot* at you!"

"Are you turning back?"

"Damn right."

Jennifer drew a jagged breath. She'd been so involved in the excitement of making her first trip out of the city it hadn't occurred to her to be afraid. Now she was shaking uncontrollably.

A second rocket ticked the tail end of the plane and set it wobbling. But somehow they stayed in the air and, a tense hour later, they'd limped back to land at the airbase.

Jennifer climbed down to the pavement and looked up at the pilot. "I'm sorry," she whispered hoarsely, the first words spoken between them since the rocket attack.

The lieutenant didn't respond.

Jennifer watched as he flicked toggle switches, shutting off the powerful rotors. "Look, it wasn't my fault!" she shouted. "You said yourself, in a war people get shot at."

He pulled off his helmet and looked at her tiredly. "Everyone knows Can Tho is hot. Whatever horse's ass ordered this flight ought to be shot. Listen, I don't fuss when they say I gotta lift some poor wounded slobs or drop medical supplies. I'll do it. It's my job, but *this*—"

He glared at her, and now she saw something other than anger in his eyes. *He's terrified,* she thought. He was sure he was going to die delivering a silly teenage singer and her guitar, and it almost happened.

Jennifer touched him on the arm. "I'm sorry," she said. "I had no idea."

He looked away. "Someone should have told you. The guys would have liked to see you, but it's not worth losing more lives over . . . it's not worth losing *my* life over, that's for damn sure." He pushed her aside, jumped down from the cockpit and stomped away.

Jennifer caught a ride straight back to the studio. Her stomach felt hollow, and her knees were shaking as she marched up the steps and along the corridor to Hugh's office.

Of course, she'd hoped to travel some in Vietnam, and to sing for the soldiers—if possible, out in the field. But she'd never imagined she'd be zipping across the country like a duck in a carnival shooting gallery. From what the pilot had told her, Hugh should have known the area wasn't safe to fly into right now. Either he'd been so eager to get her some quick visibility that he'd knowingly risked her life, or he just hadn't bothered to check out the route carefully.

She chastised herself for letting Hugh Metcalf think he could control her, think for even a second that he could do anything he liked with her! Just because she'd signed a piece of paper.

She ran into Dick before she found Hugh.

"Hey, Jenny, what's wrong?" he asked after one glance at her white face and tightly pressed lips.

"Where's Hugh?"

"He's gone for the day. What's up?"

"I was brought here under false pretenses," she snapped. "And on top of that, I never got to Can Tho. My helicopter was hit by enemy fire. My God, Dick, because of me a man was almost killed!"

He steadied her with his hands, gripping her upper arms. "Hey, I'm sure there's no huge conspiracy or anything. Anyone coming over to Nam must know we're not playing games here. The whole damn country's at war. There are going to be risks." He paused. "It probably wasn't as bad as you think."

Jennifer glared at him. *"You* weren't there!"

The softness fell away from his eyes. Dick's voice turned cool. "So maybe this job's not everything you expected. Nobody's forcing you to stay." He released her abruptly. "Pack up, go home."

Jennifer was so shocked that she couldn't manage to squeeze out a single syllable of protest.

Dick shoved his glasses farther up the bridge of his nose before going on, his voice tight. "Maybe at first we all tell ourselves, 'I'll be the one who comes home in one piece . . . because I'll be careful. It's just because the other guys were careless that they got it.'"

Invisible tears fogged the engineer's words, and Jennifer suddenly realized that he must not have spent all of his time in Vietnam in this studio.

"Just answer one question for me, Dick?" she asked quietly.

"What?" His glance dropped to the floor.

"Will my staying here make any difference?"

"It won't save lives," he said dully, "but you might make it easier for some guys to hang in for the duration." He glanced up at her, looking bashful again. Back to his old self. "You have to do what's right for you, Jennifer. Don't let them, or me, talk you into anything."

In her apartment, Jennifer threw herself into a cold shower. She scrubbed and lathered and, for the first time since she was a very little girl, did *not* sing as she washed. It took every bit of her concentration to do what she was doing and think of nothing but that—getting clean.

Once she'd toweled herself off, however, she could no

longer avoid her dilemma. Jennifer stood shivering on the white tile floor. What was she going to do?

In one way she was still thrilled to learn she'd be able to travel outside of Saigon and see other parts of the country. She *did* want to see those boys from the plane again, to sing to them and play an active role in their struggle to do their jobs and survive.

In other ways, she was terrified. Stone-cold-up-to-her-teeth-in-horror of what might happen to her if she left the relatively safe city limits of Saigon again. She'd seen photos on the evening news of marines leaping out of hovering helicopters, squirming on their stomachs for cover as snipers fired at them from the brush. Never in her life had she imagined that she'd be doing *that!*

The trip to Can Tho had changed everything. It had made it all too real.

After a while, her heart stopped racing. She slipped into her favorite robe of baby-blue Swedish terry. Wrapping her hair in a towel, she sat disconsolately on the edge of the bed. She was frightened and felt betrayed.

It seemed so late in the day, although it was only six P.M. Her head thumped with fatigue and confusion. She thought about her promise to return to the USO and visit Lian. She'd been so busy lately she hadn't been able to stop by yet. And now she'd lost all interest in socializing. She considered telling Metcalf and Freck to go to hell. She was quitting, going home.

But there had to be other options. Blinking away the first few tears of disappointment, Jennifer considered the possibilities. If she went home, she'd have to face her father. He'd hold this one mistake over her head forever. She could imagine his voice. "This is what happens when you act on emotions, Jennifer Lynn. You didn't think this through, and people took advantage of you."

Then there were Jeff, Gloria, Lian, and Dick. She liked them all, and had hoped to become their friend. If she left, she'd never see them again.

Most painful of all was the awareness that she'd be giving up—just as Tyler had predicted. She'd be deserting the men she'd flown here with. When they'd said goodbye to her on the plane, every one of them had looked at her with something akin to soul-felt appreciation or respect. She felt as though she'd become one of them. And *they* couldn't just quit and go home.

Sighing, she lay back on her bed. In many ways, those young soldiers had no better idea of what they were getting into than she had. If what Dick had told her was true, they wouldn't understand how random, how utterly impersonal death could be—until they faced combat. Then it might be too late.

If she went home, she'd be hiding behind her sex and denying her obligation to those soldiers. If she didn't leave immediately, she might never get home.

With that last thought in mind, she drifted into a shallow, troubled sleep.

8

The next morning, Jennifer woke without her alarm clock at six o'clock, something she never did. She hadn't turned on the air conditioner, and her window was open. The light through it was a clear amber—a warming, burgeoning glow that promised heat. Already the air was thick, moist, getting thicker.

Jennifer rolled onto her stomach, her chin propped on her fists, scowling at the tops of palm trees visible over the sill. *Do I stay?* she asked herself.

Before she'd left the studio yesterday afternoon, she had stopped by Gloria's desk. She hadn't mentioned any of her misgivings about the job, preferring to give herself time to think. Gloria had read off the next day's schedule.

"At ten, you'll record a promo tape. After lunch, you and Dick will begin planning your second show."

The young woman's voice had been chipper, her optimism temptingly contagious. But however much she might like Gloria, Jennifer felt no loyalty to the radio station. Metcalf and Freck had deceived her, perhaps believing they were doing no harm. What she did feel was an overwhelming drive she couldn't ignore—to rebel against their control over her. Was there any way she could protect herself without packing up and leaving Vietnam?

After almost an hour of tossing and turning in useless deliberation, she decided getting out of bed and moving around might throw her brain into gear.

Jennifer killed another hour sorting through her wardrobe—holding up each outfit, then shoving most of them back into the trunks. Then dragging out another, and another. Tons of too flouncy designer dresses and suits. It was clear from the clothing favored by Saigon women that very little of what she'd brought would be appropriate. Simple, light-weight cotton garb best suited this climate. Assuming she did remain, she'd attend as few embassy functions as possible. She had no interest in becoming chummy with politicians and generals. Her only reason to stay was for the boys whose lives were on the line.

Out of all she'd brought, she chose three outfits that would be relatively comfortable without being too ostentatious. This morning she chose navy-blue camp-style culottes and a white Peter Pan collared blouse. From the bottom of the last trunk, she dredged out a pair of penny loafers. They were custom-made in hand-stitched leather for her by a cobbler in Boston, but their simple quality didn't appear as terribly pretentious as everything else she owned.

Outside the American compound the street was a bustle of early morning activity. In front of the embassy gates a cyclo driver was bartering a fare with a soldier. A minute later, the man moved away, having decided, after all, to walk.

Jennifer approached the wiry driver. His teeth were crooked and yellow. He sported a Hawaiian shirt and dark sunglasses.

"I'd like to ride around for a few hours. See some of the city," she explained. "How much?"

His face grew instantly sly. "Eight hundred piasters—special price for the lady."

She thought that the ten dollars he'd asked in exchange for a couple hours' work wasn't at all exorbitant. But she guessed from the way his eyes flickered sideways at her under the dark lenses that he believed he was asking an outrageous price. She instinctively fought being cheated.

"I will pay you half of that rate," she told him firmly.

The driver nodded, granting her an agreeable, toothy grin. He was undoubtedly still making a killing.

"Where you want to see?" he asked. "Temple of Marshall Van Duyet very popular."

"We'll start there," she agreed, leaning back to absorb the city and, with any luck, clear her head.

At the indoor section of the Central Market, Jennifer climbed out of the cyclo and browsed while her driver lit up a cigarette to wait for her. She bought an exquisite tortoiseshell hair clip and found an amazingly varied selection of primitive textiles. She purchased three pieces of the hand-loomed cloth in sizes just right for shawls. One for her mother, one for Francie, the third for herself.

Returning to the cyclo, she climbed in with her purchases, and they continued on. They rode past large, Western-designed hotels—the Caravelle (in a prime location on a pretty square), the Majestic, the Continental Palace. Her driver, whom she now knew as Phan, pointed out the best restaurants and told her that, in his estimation, they rivaled any in France for their service and menu. He particularly approved of Tour d'Argent, La Cave, Le Gaulois, and Ramuncho.

Jennifer suspected that he'd never set foot in any of them, but she wouldn't hurt his feelings by challenging him.

As they rounded a corner into an alley just south of the Central Market, she glimpsed a young GI. For an instant, her heart stopped beating. Unconsciously, she reached down and gripped the worn edge of her seat.

"Stop!" she cried out to Phan.

With his back to her, the soldier lit a cigarette, then continued browsing through a street merchant's selection of ragged-looking straw hampers and cheap trinkets. His hair was the same dark brown, thick on top, trim on the sides. He had the same cautious, controlled stride. Tyler? She automatically checked his left wrist for the leather thong. It was there!

A lump formed in her throat, and she was seized by panic. When he'd left the plane, he had been furious with her. But she'd been no less furious, for she'd resented his accusations. But try as she might, she hadn't been able to forget him. He was unlike any man she'd ever known. Even as she watched him now, she knew she couldn't let him pass through her life.

"We go now?" Phan asked.

"No, no," she said quickly. "Maybe . . . just move along very slowly. Don't get ahead of that soldier up there."

Jennifer listened to the sing-song litany of the straw vendor as they edged closer. She was shocked to discover that the scrawny old man wasn't tempting Tyler with bargains on baskets after all.

"You want a girl, Joe? Young girl? She very pretty—be nice to you—"

Tyler turned slightly, and Jennifer saw his embarrassed grin as he shook his head.

"Oh, you like boy, then? All right." The man gave him a serpentine smirk. "Can do, can do."

"No!" the young GI answered firmly. He glanced ahead toward a group of four other soldiers who were moving slowly away through the alley. Starting to jog to catch up with them, he was blocked by three little girls who appeared out of nowhere. They cradled bunches of wilted flowers in pitifully grimy arms.

"Got grass! Opium!" the man called after him. "Good stuff, anything you want. Cheap!"

Tyler halted, hemmed in by the forlorn-looking bevy of urchins. "Excuse me, ladies," he said with a smile. "Hey, Morrison!" he called over the little girls' heads. "Wait up."

One of the flower girls held out her dusty bouquet. She approached him with a winning smile. His expression suddenly became wary, and he abruptly pushed the flowers aside.

Jennifer stiffened. *How rude!* she thought. All he had to do was say no thank you.

But the girls didn't seem bothered. In fact, the littlest bravely stepped in front of him, extending her posies while the one closest to her elbow broke into a garbled patois of English and Vietnamese. Jennifer strained to catch any of the meaning and was only vaguely aware of the movements of the third child as she glided silently behind Tyler. He was so busy with the other two, he didn't notice her at all.

With a flash of intuition, Jennifer realized what was about to happen.

"Look out!" she screamed. "Behind you!"

Tyler whipped around. Alerted, his friends took in the situation and launched themselves toward him.

With practiced audacity, a tiny hand whipped into Tyler's back pocket and out again with a brown leather wallet.

"You little monster!" he roared.

But the thief was instantly out of reach. He grabbed for one of her accomplices, missed again as Jennifer jumped out of the pedicab and raced toward the fracas. All three children dodged away and, within seconds, had dissolved down alleys into the market crowd.

The street vendor studiously examined his baskets as Tyler's friends took off in hot pursuit.

"You'll never catch her!" Tyler bellowed. "Hey, guys! Give it up!"

"I don't think they can hear you," Jennifer said.

He swerved around to face her. For an instant, an unguarded warmth and interest sparkled in his blue eyes, then he stifled any sign of pleasure at seeing her. His expression turned frigid.

"What are you doing here?" he demanded.

Jennifer refused to be intimidated. "Shopping. You?" He observed her gravely. "I almost warned you in time. Sorry I wasn't a little faster figuring out the little darlings' game."

"Clever, aren't they?" he commented grimly. "Oh, well."

"You don't seem terribly upset about losing your wallet."

"Didn't have much in it anyway."

Jennifer sighed. "They looked like such sweet little girls."

A tender note that took her by surprise crept into Tyler's speech. "Poor little kids, I'd probably have given them the money if they'd asked."

Jennifer stared at him for a long moment. He was a complex man: compassionate, virile, and principled, as well as ruggedly attractive. Out of the corner of her eye she glimpsed Phan gesturing impatiently. She waved him off.

"They, ummm, seemed so well organized," she ventured at last, hoping to keep Tyler talking.

"Odds are, that's their father or uncle over there." He indicated the basket merchant.

"You mean, he's a Fagin, like in *Oliver Twist?*" Then something worse occurred to her. Maybe one of those "young girls" wouldn't have been too young to rent to a soldier for a night. The thought chilled her to the marrow of her bones.

"Something like that," Tyler mumbled, thrusting his hands into his pants pockets. "Doesn't seem fair, does it? We're over here losing our lives for them, supposedly, and they keep coming up with more ways to con us."

"It isn't fair," she agreed, "but maybe some of them are reduced to stealing in order to survive."

"I know," he said quietly, "that's why I would have given them the money." He glanced down the alley as if concerned about his friends.

"Are you . . ." Jennifer began uncertainly. "Are you stationed in Saigon, Sergeant Tyler?"

He focused sharply on her. "No, not in Saigon."

"Where then?"

"Why do you want to know?" he asked, sounding suspicious.

"I just . . ." She stepped closer, wanting to flirt with him, but feeling awkward. "Well, because we might get together sometime. You know, see a movie or go out dancing or—"

"No!" he snapped with such vehemence that she staggered backward in shock.

"Look," she said gasping, planting her hands on her hips, "I want you to know that I've *never* had to beg for a date. What the hell's wrong with you, Tyler? I told you I'd stay in Saigon—here I am. Do you have a girl? Or don't you find me attractive at all? Or—"

101

"Shut up!" he ground out.

She did, but he must have read the confusion in her eyes.

"I'm sorry," he said almost immediately, making his voice less aggressive for her. "I don't have a girl at present, but I'm not interested in having one either." He looked around uncomfortably. "I just don't want to get too close to anyone over here. It wouldn't be good for me or for her. You understand?"

"Not really."

He groaned. "Listen, men and women get together over here for all sorts of reasons. When it's over, there's a lot of heartbreak because what they had was created by the circumstances, by the war."

"I see," she murmured.

"And that's if both of them make it through the year. That's if one of them doesn't get killed."

Jennifer felt as if she were falling into the depths of his soul through the blue windows of his eyes. He was serious about what he was telling her, and she understood his concerns, but the more she stared, the deeper she tumbled.

"I just want to get to know you a little, that's all." Even as she uttered the words, she knew they were a lie.

"Maybe," he said with emphasis she couldn't possibly misinterpret, "that wouldn't be enough for *me.*"

The words stroked her like velvet, offering encouragement, although he undoubtedly hadn't intended them to do so.

"What's your first name, Tyler?"

For a moment, his lips parted, as if he were about to tell her, then they tightened into a resolved line. "I'm just Tyler." He turned to leave.

"At least tell me where you'll be stationed . . . so I can say 'hi' on the radio and mention your unit!"

He continued walking away from her, shoulders rigid, spine solid and straight as a railroad tie.

"Tyler!" she called, and he broke into a strong, graceful jog.

She soon lost sight of his bobbing, dark head in the crowd.

* * *

Jennifer asked Phan to drop her at the USO.

She walked past the ever-present street vendors, past the guard at his sentry post beside the door. As she looked around inside it was impossible to ignore the feeling of the GIs' eyes catching sight of her and clinging. None of them mattered. She could think only of Tyler. She'd never minded being the center of attention before, but now she felt self-conscious and walked hurriedly over to an American woman behind the reception desk.

"Is Mrs. Nguyen here?" she asked urgently.

The other woman studied Jennifer. "Are you one of the new girls?"

"No. I mean," she corrected herself quickly, "I *am* new. But I don't work for the USO. She asked me to drop by."

The woman smiled pleasantly. "Her office is on the second floor. Go on up."

Jennifer climbed the stairs quickly. At a shellacked wooden door labeled OFFICE, she gently rapped.

A lyrical voice called from inside, and when Jennifer opened the door, Lian looked up from her desk. She wore her hair down today, glisteningly straight, ending somewhere at the middle of her back. The widow's peak centered above her smooth brows softened her already gentle oval face.

"Come in, Jennifer," she invited happily.

"I hope you don't mind my showing up without calling."

Lian shook her head. Whenever she did that, Jennifer noticed, her eyes glittered with any small amount of light that might be in the room.

"Have you started work at the station yet?" Lian asked, waving her to a chair.

"Yes, I . . ." Then Jennifer looked at her and said simply, "I don't know who to talk to."

Lian's pretty smile straightened into a concerned line. "You are in trouble?"

Jennifer shrugged. "In a way."

"May I help?"

She desperately wanted to handle her own life. But she was so confused by Tyler's rejection, by Metcalf's callous attitude toward her life and limb, by so many feelings welling up inside of her that she simply didn't know how to begin to sort everything out.

"I think," Jennifer said at last, "there's a lot in Saigon that I didn't expect to find."

"In what way?"

"Everything seems to be happening so fast. I guess I'm having trouble adjusting. Living in the American compound doesn't help. It's so very different from the rest of Saigon. They're separate worlds."

Lian nodded sagely.

"I guess I'm thinking of going home," Jennifer admitted at last. "I hate seeing poverty and pain, but I can't just shut myself away in the compound and live as if none of this exists."

"Many Americans have no trouble living in the compound," Lian said, noncommittally.

"Well, I'd have a *great deal* of trouble shutting myself off behind sandbags, a barbed-wire fence, and marine guards."

"It really is a wise arrangement. You'll be safest there."

"You don't live there."

"No, but this is my country. You don't speak the language or understand our customs. As in any city, we have crime. An American woman on her own is considered an easy target. You must be practical."

"Where do you live?" Jennifer demanded.

"In the fifth district, on Phu Lac Street."

"Is it a nice part of the city? Do you like it there?"

Lian's hesitation was almost imperceptible. "My husband has given me a beautiful home."

Jennifer sensed the sudden coolness in the other woman's tone. But her dark eyes gave away nothing.

"Your husband is in the South Vietnamese Army?"

"Yes."

"Is he stationed here in Saigon?"

Lian shifted uneasily in her chair.

"I'm sorry," Jennifer said quickly. "Back home, my girlfriend Francie says that I ask too many questions, which is rude. She's probably right."

Lian shook her head. "No. I like talking about my life, my work and family. I find few opportunities to do so." She regarded Jennifer with interest. "Because of my father's trade, my family has lived all over Asia. I attended a Catholic high school in Saigon. But business is much more secure back in Hong Kong, where my mother was born. They returned there. I stayed long enough to finish school. I would have returned to live with them, but I met my husband just before I graduated. That was three years ago."

"You've been married three years? You look like a high school kid!"

Lian smiled, but Jennifer couldn't tell if it was a smile born of pleasure or of politeness. "We were married two years ago. He is in the north, somewhere near Hue. Because of his duties, we've not seen each other in four months. He will come home when he can, but it will be for only a few days." She gazed steadily at Jennifer. "He is a very dedicated man, a very important man in the army."

"I'm sorry," Jennifer said quietly, sensing how hard it would be for two people to love each other while being kept apart.

Lian picked up and played with a tiny crystal dove that had rested on her desk top between them as they'd talked. It was too light to be a paperweight. Jennifer wondered if it had been a gift from her absent husband.

Then Lian looked up abruptly and asked, "Would you like to see my home?"

"I would love to," Jennifer said excitedly.

Lian explained that leaving before the suppertime rush of soldiers would be advisable, so they began walking immediately down the stairs and out to the hot street. There, they soon found a cab.

This drive took longer than the one from the embassy. Some of the main streets were now familiar to Jennifer. They drove away from the Saigon River, but its dank smell followed them. Occasionally she caught a glimpse of a canal on their left between the low shops and tenements.

Lian's home was a simple and elegant white stucco structure. It was sandwiched among other houses that ap-

peared in much poorer condition. Still, it was extremely
modest in comparison to the estates where Jennifer's childhood friends lived.

Inside, there were just four rooms. A living room doubled
as a dining area and two sleeping quarters were partitioned
off by hanging screens. Then there was the kitchen, with
bare floors of dark, polished wood. In the living room was a
beautiful carpet of rich colors: rose, leafy green, and ebony.
"An antique Kayseri of hand-knotted silk fibers," Lian
explained when asked. There were pedestals displaying
Chinese objets d'art arranged in subtly lighted corners. A
small Buddhist altar stood against a side wall. Displayed on
it were black-and-white photographs of men and women
with Asian features—Lian's and her husband's ancestors.

The house possessed an atmosphere of serenity and
separateness from the signs of war outside its walls. Street
sounds drifted away, all but inaudible. Vibrations from
passing traffic were tangible but remote. Jennifer thought
how sad Lian's husband must be to leave this soothing place
and his beautiful, young wife. She was overcome with a
sense of deep remorse that such a thing as war ever had to
be.

"I could die here," Jennifer said at last. "Happily."

Lian laughed. "I wouldn't like that."

"No." Jennifer made a face at her. "I might dirty up your
pretty carpet." She went to the French doors at the far end of
the living room. "Do these open?"

Lian unlatched them for her. Outside was a stone patio
overlooking a carefully tended garden. It was enclosed by a
sturdy, wooden wall. All along it were clusters of fragile,
wild orchids. Between the tall gray boards, Jennifer could
see portions of much smaller houses, tightly packed but
nicely kept. A Saigon white-collar neighborhood.

"Are you hungry?" Lian asked from behind her.

"Starved," Jennifer admitted. "I didn't have lunch." She
thought for a moment. "Or breakfast."

Lian excused herself and disappeared into her kitchen. In
only a few minutes, she brought plates of rice, fish, and

steamed, sliced yams out to the patio. The two women ate and chatted happily for over an hour about their childhood and the places they'd traveled. Jennifer began to feel a little better than she had when Tyler had escaped from her in the market.

The world felt very small and manageable, sitting on Lian's patio, munching sweet yams.

"I'd better return to the USO," Lian said at last with a reluctant sigh. "I've been away too long."

While Jennifer helped Lian wash the dishes, she thought about Gloria. The station receptionist had expected her to show up at around ten A.M., and here it was three in the afternoon. But she had desperately needed time to work things out in her own mind before she tackled Hugh Metcalf. She was better prepared now.

They were on their way out the front door when a Jeep rattled to a stop a few feet from them. Lian glanced up and immediately smiled at the hefty American soldier who swung out of the driver's seat.

"Hello, Sergeant," Lian greeted him.

He snapped his hand up to his forehead in a mock salute. "Afternoon, Mrs. Nguyen."

"Sergeant O'Brien, this is my friend Jennifer Swanson. Jennifer, Norris O'Brien—my husband's aide. He takes care of Nguyen while he is away from me." Her expression was thankful and hopeful at the same time.

Jennifer shook hands with him.

"My husband is in the city?" Lian asked.

"No, ma'am, I'm afraid not. I flew down alone from Hue yesterday." The sergeant smoothed his shirt over his ample belly, tucking the tail into the waistband of his pants.

Jennifer looked at Lian. The other woman's normal composure had slipped. A tiny frown of disbelief tugged at her pretty lips. "He did not return to Saigon with you?"

"No, ma'am. I had a little R-and-R coming to me, and the colonel said I might as well take it." He reached into the passenger seat of the Jeep and pulled out a leather case. "Couldn't say I felt like arguin' with him."

107

Lian's smile was dim. "Of course, you deserve a vacation."

"He asked me to stop by and leave these papers with you for safekeeping. Guess they have something to do with investments the colonel's made."

Lian reached out and stiffly took the case from him. "I'll take care of them." She hesitated, her dark eyes lifting to search his anxiously. "Is there anything else? Did he say when he'd be home?"

"No." O'Brien checked out his shoes for a moment. "You know, I'm always telling him he should take some time off. But he's a hard worker. He won't leave a job half done."

Lian nodded.

"He talks about you, though."

"He does?" she asked softly.

"Sure, all the time." Jennifer thought that the sergeant seemed to be putting a great deal of energy into his assurance. *Was this just the loyal aide's invention to save face for his boss?* "The colonel's always saying how great you cook and how beautiful you keep the house and garden while he's away. And—" He winked. "And about the two of you having a family with lots of little Nguyens after the war."

Lian's face paled. "If it ever is over," she whispered tightly.

"Now, don't you worry," O'Brien assured her. "We're going to bomb the hell out of the North. Won't be a commie standin' between here and China by the time we're through."

"That's very reassuring," Lian said dryly, no longer even trying to smile.

"Well," O'Brien said, turning to Jennifer, "nice meeting you, Miss Swanson."

She nodded at him.

After he'd driven off, she asked, "Are you all right?"

Lian nodded, her eyes glassy. "It's only that I'd thought that *he* might be in the city."

"I'm sorry," Jennifer said, putting an arm around her.

"Maybe he'll come home soon. Maybe now just wasn't the right time."

Lian looked away, down the dusty road, a stoic lift to her chin.

"Come on. I'll go to the club with you," Jennifer suggested, her own troubles temporarily pushed aside. "You can tell me about your handsome husband."

Lian closed up later that night, locking the street door of the USO behind her. The arches of her feet ached, and her head hummed with the noises of the band and loud conversations and clattering dishes. She was lucky to catch a cab at that hour.

It will be better once I'm home, she thought. But once there she felt trapped, inexplicably anxious. After making fresh tea, she sat at her kitchen table and sipped slowly, starting to relax. Her mind floated like a bird supported on an air current, spreading its wings wide to ride an updraft. Taking her back . . . back to a time when she was still a girl. And then to the day she'd met Nguyen at the auction.

At the auction.

She smiled to herself, holding the handleless cup beneath her nose, breathing in the fragrant steam. Nguyen was charming, reassuring, sophisticated. He was a man of great integrity and import in the South Vietnamese government. She, of course, had been impressed with him, and flattered when he'd asked to marry her. That was a happy time. And the year that followed had been happy, too.

At first they made love passionately, often two or more times a day—every day. Well . . . maybe not exactly *passionately!* He was, at least, zealous and she cooperated because she loved him. Nguyen was into her quickly and finished faster than she'd have wished. But the fact that he came to her bed so often seemed proof of his devotion. She, in turn, would do anything for him.

As time went on, though, her husband seemed to grow impatient with her in some secretive male way that she couldn't comprehend. When he was at home, which was less and less often, he would pour himself a glass of American whiskey and brood at his desk, cursing to himself when he thought she wasn't listening.

"What have I done?" she asked him one night when he arrived home very late, offering no explanation for his absence. "Are you angry with me?"

"I am not angry," he replied tightly. "I am disappointed."

She was shocked. "How have I disappointed you?"

He burst into a rage. "How can you be so simple, woman?" he rasped. "What reasons are there for marriage?"

Lian cringed away from his anger. "Love," she answered in a small voice.

He spat on the carpet. "No! It is for children! Why do you suppose we copulate so often?" He sneered at her. "Out of pleasure?"

She stopped herself from nodding. That was certainly what *she* had believed. The cruelty of his words struck her forcefully in the stomach; Lian dropped her eyes in shame. All he wanted from her was an heir.

Now, alone in her kitchen, she set down her cup with shaking hands and buried her face in her palms. He'd hurt her so deeply, yet the fact remained—he was her husband. And she missed the small things that had been good between them.

9

Ducking her head to fit, Mel slowly folded her rangy body onto the bottom bunk in the Bachelor Officers' Quarters at Tan Son Nhut. She stretched out, hands behind her head, and stared up at the springs above, waiting for the other nurses to leave. She was so tired that closing her eyes would take too much effort.

Sometimes she'd thought when she worked the eleven-to-seven shift at Washington General in Surgery Recovery that she'd never be that exhausted again. There was something about being the one to watch over a person whose body had been hastily opened up and rearranged, added to, or taken away from that drew on a person's strength.

Simply being here made her tired. There was the heat. And the bugs: rice beetles so big they reminded her of Chesapeake Bay crabs. And every night blue and red tracers of incoming and outgoing fire arced across the sky just beyond the airfields perimeter, so close Mel swore if she'd only reach out she'd be able to touch their sparkling trails.

The first night they'd fascinated and entertained her—like watching fireworks on the Fourth of July. Then she'd overheard one of the women who'd been in-country six months: "I can't look at them anymore. Every one means someone's dying out there, right this minute."

After that, Mel couldn't see a rocket without imagining Curtis on its receiving end. That very night her nightmares began.

Again and again, she dreamed about working in a hospital recovery room. A gurney was wheeled in. On it was a young black man: Curtis. A doctor came in behind the gurney and looked at her gravely. "I've done all I can for him, nurse," he said. "The rest is up to you." She shook with fear as the man left her alone with her brother. A sheet was pulled up to her brother's chin. His eyes were closed. His black skin looked pale. He didn't seem to be breathing properly. And as she watched his unconscious form beneath the sheet, a red stain soaked through from the area of his chest. She called out for the doctor to come back, but he didn't. She lifted the sheet to try to find out what the problem was.

Curtis's body was in a dozen separate pieces: arms, legs, chest cavity, hands, feet, abdomen. All in a jumble, all oozing blood. And try as she might, she couldn't get them all back together again. She awoke screaming and drenched with sweat after each horrible episode.

Mel made herself think about Washington General and the worst times there. It was reassuring to remember how much she could handle, how good she was at her job.

Mel had a sixth sense about surgical recovery. She'd never assisted in an operation—for some reason the doctors avoided using black nurses—but she observed whenever possible, and after patients were stable it was often her responsibility to watch over them through the night. (She suspected this was because the hospital was so short-handed, especially for the graveyard shift.)

Her sixth sense warned her when a body was not functioning as it should. Twice, she'd actually called a doctor out of bed, overruled her supervisor and insisted he return to the hospital—because she had a *feeling* something wasn't right. Once it had been internal hemorrhaging. Another time infection had seditiously set in and been at work when all

112

had seemed normal. In both cases, the patient would have died before morning.

Soon, the surgical staff at Washington General Hospital considered Melantha Benning more accurate than any electronic monitor. In especially difficult cases, they requested Mel—much as they would have rolled up a machine with bright dials and fancy indicators. She served a valuable purpose, but not once did they acknowledge her value as she wished they would. For Mel yearned to become a surgical nurse, to see if she had it in her to reach that special pinnacle of her profession.

To do that, however, she'd need more training, and there was no way she could afford the tuition. She'd begun thinking about the army even before Curtis had been drafted. After he'd gotten his notice, she quickly enlisted and asked for the earliest entry date possible.

In basic training, the other nurses came from all over the U.S., but she hadn't come to make friends. She didn't care if any of the others even spoke to her. She was going to Vietnam to look after Curtis and learn her profession, not to party. By the time her year was over, Curtis would already be home, and she'd have crossed a crucial professional bridge. With her qualifications, no one could deny her an O.R. job. Race and money would no longer determine her future.

In basic training she had been the tallest and strongest woman in her barracks. Her body thrived on the challenging exercise and regular meals. She grew muscles in the backs of her legs and thighs. She developed a stamina for long marches, so there were times when she bridged the gap of pain and exhaustion and then felt as if she were sailing almost effortlessly through the next mile, then the next . . . and if they'd told her she had another ten to go before she could rest, she'd have done it. There were moments, toward the end of a forced march, when her body wanted to keep on working, churning, pumping even while others around her were gasping for breath and clutching at anything solid to keep from falling on their faces.

Mel was as happy as she'd ever been in her life.

When their assignments came through, some of the other women complained to their COs that there had been an error. A recruiter had fed them a line about preferred duty and choosing stations. They had counted on going to Europe or Japan or remaining stateside near their hometowns. And now they'd been handed orders for Nam. It wasn't fair!

Nobody gave a damn. They went.

But Mel was happy with the army. She'd had a clean bed to sleep on every night since she enlisted—except during the brief survival course. She was fed three meals every day. (There were nights when she and Curtis were growing up when they had only potatoes or cereal for dinner.) She was provided with working clothes (fatigues), and a dress uniform (which she loved to wear). She wore a *butter bar* on her shoulder, a lovely, sparkling gold bar, which meant she was a second lieutenant, an officer. She was *somebody special* with a career and a future—a considerable step up from any other woman she could remember in her entire family.

Problem was, now that she was here in Vietnam, she couldn't shake the terror of her nightmares. She hadn't slept in three nights.

Today, everyone had gotten their final work orders, assigning them to various hospitals or evac units. The other girls wanted to ride the bus into Saigon to celebrate. A couple of the youngest ones invited her along, but when she said she had a headache and wanted to sleep it off, they looked relieved. She knew her size and manner frightened some people, especially white women who'd grown up in places where there weren't many blacks. She could sense it in the way they gave her space and spoke carefully around her, as if afraid of saying the wrong thing and offending her. No one wanted to see what happened when Melantha Benning got angry.

So she let them go off to get drunk while she lay back on the bunk trying to sleep. At last she was able to close her eyes. She told herself, *Life ain't so bad. Life's damn well getting better all the time. You have a future now. Just make it through this year, girl, and you got it made in the shade.*

A squeal from the foot of her bunk sent her rocketing

straight up. She rammed her head into the springs of the bed above.

"What the hell!" she roared.

A wool blanket fell over her face. Struggling inside, she was pulled to her feet and prodded down wooden steps then onto the cinder path.

"What do you think you're doing?" she demanded. But Mel didn't struggle very hard. She knew from the giggles and hoots that this must be some girly prank. They wouldn't hurt her. If she unleashed herself on them, she could do a lot of damage.

"You're coming into Saigon with us," one of them said.

"No one stays behind the last night!" another cried out gleefully, then yipped when Mel inadvertently stomped on her toe.

"I don't want to go," she grumbled into the suffocating wool. Having lived all of her life in a city, she had no desire to see another one.

"Tough, Benning. You're coming! You're coming!" they shouted.

One last push. The steps of the bus banged painfully against her shins. "Lordy, hold your horses! I hope you handle your patients gentler than this! You'll sure as hell kill 'em if the gooks don't."

She stumbled up the stairs. Only when the bus was moving down the highway toward Saigon did they remove the blanket.

She snarled at them and they backed off, only half pretending fear. She must have looked a sight, her uniform skirt and blouse rumpled and untucked, her Afro fuzzed up by the blanket. She wore no makeup, but she rarely did. Someone had brought her purse. She contented herself with forking her hair into the soft black halo around her head and pulling her blouse down inside her skirt. Mel admitted to herself it felt good to be included.

When they arrived at the USO, the nurses split into two groups. Half of them wanted to see some of the city before dark, while the others were dying for real food and went straight inside. Mel joined the eating contingent.

The six nurses were immediately joined by twice as many GIs eager to buy them dinner. The women refused. They let the men know they might like to talk or dance later, but they were going to concentrate on food first. They were temporarily left alone to enjoy their meal.

Ignoring the music and dancing on the room's other side, Mel concentrated on the menu. She ordered steak and fries with a salad. She felt positively spoiled, savoring every juicy bite. She talked as little as possible during the meal, but enjoyed the other women's chatter as more happy background noise.

The plates were being cleared away by a Vietnamese waitress when Mel saw Jennifer walk in with an Asian woman. She couldn't have been more surprised or pleased. She thought how strange her reaction was, because, other than Curtis and her mother, she'd never felt especially close to another person. She'd never let that happen. But this naive white girl from Boston had pulled her in with her music and brought out a mothering instinct she'd never realized was there.

"I'll be back, ladies," she said, leaving them to order their second round of beer.

A group of black soldiers were seated at two tables nearby. Mel was aware of the stares following her across the room—guys probably wondering about their chances of survival if they dared to approach her. She didn't flatter herself that she was a beautiful woman, but men were attracted to her. She'd never bothered to analyze why.

As she moved through the crowded dining area she became aware of a second wave of interest. There were muffled conversations at the tables she passed. Men's eyes were drawn to the slim, blond girl who'd just entered the room.

It wasn't just that Jennifer Lynn Swanson was pretty. Within glowed a special beauty, as if the talent Mel had witnessed on the plane over the Pacific couldn't be contained by flesh: it was bright and strong and undeniable. Mel could hear Jennifer's musical, light laughter in reply to something the Asian woman had said.

"Hey, songbird!" Mel called, booming across the room like a lumberjack.

Jennifer was grinning from ear to ear even before she spotted Mel. "Melantha!" she cried, dragging the other woman by the hand over to her. "What are you doing here?"

"Eating, mostly. How's the radio business?"

A cloud passed over the petite blonde's green eyes. "They want to fly me all over the country—do personal appearances."

Mel thought the news was wonderful. "I'm leaving tomorrow morning for the Seventy-first Evac at Pleiku. Maybe you'll be visiting me!"

"Is that far from here?"

"Eighty miles north and inland. They bring the guys straight out of battle to us, so they tell me. Gets pretty hairy." She laughed uneasily. Even at this distance, her sixth sense was kicking up something fierce, telling her that she'd be dealing with stuff she'd never faced before. The stories she'd already heard were crazy: having to work on guys so torn up there didn't seem enough left to build even half a person, losing patients because there weren't sufficient supplies or a surgeon couldn't break free of another procedure in time.

"I'd like to come to Pleiku," Jennifer said hesitantly. She glanced at Mel, then at the Vietnamese woman who laid a delicate hand on her arm.

"You must be sure," Lian cautioned. "It is very dangerous."

Jennifer met her eyes. "I know, Lian. But I came here to prove something to myself. If I went home now, how could I face the rest of my life?"

Mel glanced at the Vietnamese woman. She didn't much trust any of the locals. She'd decided it was simpler to think of them all as the enemy. But if Jennifer figured this one was okay, she'd give her the benefit of doubt.

She held out her hand. "I'm Second Lieutenant Melantha Benning. Jennifer and I met on the plane coming over. Has she sung for you yet?"

The woman shook her dark head and smiled warmly. "I'm Chau Thi Lian. Very pleased to meet you."

They were headed for a table, Jennifer in the middle of explaining Lian's job, when two air force men approached them. They knew Lian and she greeted each of them with a sisterly hug that surprised Mel. After all, she was no more American than the Emperor of Japan—although her English sounded almost perfect. Then the white boy shyly asked Jennifer to dance, and, to Mel's surprise, the black airman turned to her.

"How 'bout you, sister?"

She stiffened automatically. "I'm not your sister."

His smile fell away. "Sorry. Guess bein' an officer and all, you don't want to be mixin' with us enlisted types."

Mel's hand fell on his shoulder before he could turn away. "You don't have to call me ma'am, either. Just don't patronize me, Airman . . ." She looked at the blue name patch over his left chest pocket. "West." She gave him a hint of a smile, or at least what she imagined a smile might look like on her large, strong face.

He beamed. "All right! C'mon then."

Mel caught an amused smile from Jennifer as he maneuvered her toward the dance floor.

She danced twice with Hank West from Chicago. He was a crew member on a huge C-5A transport that flew between Manila and Tan Son Nhut. Then a few other men worked up their courage.

Tenderness had never been part of her experience where men were concerned, but these boys fell all over themselves to be polite and gentle and beg her attention for as long as the music played. Jennifer, she noticed, was creating quite a stir as soldiers jockeyed for advantageous locations in the room from which to dash onto the floor. One song had barely faded away when a crowd of hopeful new partners swooped down on her.

Fatigue at last overcoming her, Mel begged off and walked over to sit with Lian, while Jennifer tried her diplomacy on another contingent of dance partners. Mel laughed. "Jennifer's sure as hell gonna have her hands full over here."

Lian nodded. "She's so good for them. I wish I had a hundred Jennifers . . . a thousand."

Her street wariness kicking into gear, Mel automatically stiffened and cast Lian a cold, brown-eyed glare. "Someone could make a bundle."

Lian's mouth dropped open in shock. "Oh, no! I didn't mean it that way!"

"It sounded like you did," grumbled Mel. "Why not capitalize on her? That's what you people are so damn good at. Doesn't take but a few days in this place to figure *that* out."

Lian stared at her in silence, then let her glance drift away. "You don't have to protect her from me. I am her friend."

"I am, too," Mel said tightly.

"Lian?" a masculine voice interrupted.

Both women looked up at the same moment. A young man with red hair and freckles, probably no older than Curtis, looked down at the Vietnamese woman with a bashful grin. "You dancin' tonight or working?"

She blinked up at him. "Hello, Bill. I was just talking with our most recent FNG." She smiled sweetly at Mel.

He blushed and reached out to shake her hand. "Welcome to Vietnam, Lieutenant."

Another man stopped awkwardly beside Lian. He looked as if he'd been about to ask her to dance, too, but Bill had beat him to it.

"What's an F-N-G?" Mel asked, as Lian and her flesh-and-blood Howdy Doody danced across the floor between tables.

"Umm, well, sir . . . ma'am. You see it's short for Fucking New Guy."

Mel coughed out a laugh. "No shit!" The chink had a sense of humor, she thought.

"No shit," he said. "Wanna dance?"

Funny thing is, Jennifer mused as she swayed to the music in a young marine's arms, *I'm succeeding just by being here.* Somehow that took off all the pressure. She didn't have to pretend to be someone other than herself, practice her best

119

manners, dress correctly or remember names of people she found boring. All she had to do was listen to these boys, be held like a fragile piece of china in their arms as they danced across the USO floor.

The band soon caught on to the flow of the evening. Although Jennifer never was without a partner—whether the musicians were playing a fast song or a slow one—most of the GIs hung back when a rock number kicked in. If a man managed to be the lucky one to win a dance with her, he wanted it to be a slow one so he could touch her. After the first thirty minutes of the set, the band played slow songs exclusively.

Jennifer met a sailor from Apple Creek, Wisconsin; a marine from Bismarck, North Dakota; and dozens of boys from towns like Moxley, Duluth, Cranston, and St. Paul. After a while, she stopped trying to remember where they came from.

She was amazed that not one of them hit on her, or hardly. Who knew what might be going on in their minds as they held her, or what they'd fantasize about when they lay in their bunks that night, but for the few precious moments they were holding her, they seemed perfectly happy to just dance in silence or tell her about their hometown dreams.

Jennifer wished she could hear Tyler's dreams, wished she could be held in his arms. But, for now, she found solace in being needed by his comrades.

Some were *short*. That meant, she learned, that they had only a matter of weeks remaining in their tour of duty. Then they'd climb aboard a Freedom Bird and wing their way home. Some had more than six months left to serve—but already they looked hard around the eyes and their boyishness was gone. Their hands were often callused and covered with masses of tiny scars from being out in the jungle. Their eyes hid pain, confusion, and experiences they didn't want to talk about.

It was remarkable to her that they treated her so gently. They'd been away from home and women for months. They'd slept, eaten, and cried with men as their only companions—unless they paid a whore in town. Sometimes they teased her, but it was in a harmless way, as they might tease their kid sisters. As time went on and they'd had more beer, some got playful. A couple of them dared to slide a hand very low across the small of her back, but she gave them a tiny chastising frown from the corner of her sparkling green eyes and they were all apologies.

At one o'clock, she was exhausted. Still, she wouldn't have stopped dancing if Lian and Mel hadn't taken charge and pulled her off the floor. Mel stood guard, arms crossed over her chest, her imposing dusky figure in officer's dress warning off the bravest marine while Lian forced her to sit out a couple dances and sip a cup of tea.

"Mel has to leave with the other nurses," Lian told her. "I think it's time you got some rest, too."

Jennifer was torn. She'd gladly let the guys talk her deaf, and she'd dance until she dropped. However, she didn't want Mel to leave without wishing her good luck in Pleiku.

Nodding her agreement, she thanked Lian for a very special night. "May I come again?"

"Anytime," the Vietnamese woman promised. "I would love to have you visit my boys."

Jennifer laughed at her. *"Your* boys!"

Lian shrugged, but looked a little embarrassed. "I cannot think of them in any other way. I work with the enlisted men in the South Vietnamese Army, too. They are mine also. Many of the ARVN are young village boys who have never seen a city before. I try to make them feel at home, just as I do American soldiers."

"I can see that," Jennifer said. "You're such a kind person." She gave Lian a quick hug.

"Come back often," Lian repeated softly. "If you can."

Jennifer nodded. She ran to catch up with the nurses. Mel was one of the few sober women in the bunch. She'd wrapped a long arm around one and was herding the rest out the USO door like a den mother rounding up her rambunctious scouts.

"Mel," Jennifer called, "do you need help?"

"With this bunch of lightweights?" She rolled her dark eyes. "Naw."

"I hope you get to see your brother soon and that he's okay."

"Thanks." The black woman hesitated. "If you hang around . . . well, I'll be listening for your show. Do good, songbird."

"Sure," Jennifer said, and hugged her goodbye.

She caught a ride back to the embassy compound with two MPs. One walked her to the gate and handed her over to the marine guard. She wasn't reassured by their special treatment. Rather, she felt imprisoned.

A cold, impersonal sensation swept over her—erasing the warm glow of the night. Sandbags and barbed wire formed the outermost wall of her new home. She hated the compound and how it separated her from the people she'd, in such a short time, come to care for. People like Lian, Mel, the young GIs, and even the ragged children who daily robbed them.

As she walked down the landscaped paths of the embassy grounds, Jennifer fought hard to talk herself out of the stifling sense of entrapment she'd unsuccessfully tried to explain to Lian.

Even as she lay on her bed that night in the too warm darkness (the air conditioner ineffectively chattering away), she knew she'd remember every one of "her boys." She cherished their gentle expressions of gratitude and wondered why she, Jennifer Lynn Swanson, had been so important to them.

She called up their faces one by one and suddenly saw something she'd never seen in the features of her friends back in Massachusetts: death. These boy-soldiers had seen and faced death. They understood, whereas her friends could not, how terribly precious every minute of life was. To these men, she represented life and a future!

Jennifer curled up in a ball, her vision of the white plaster ceiling fogged by tears. She didn't want to shut herself off from life or death.

Impulsively, she picked up the phone and dialed Jeffrey's residence. He answered after six rings.

"Were you asleep?" she asked.

"Sort of," he grumbled. "It is two in the morning. What's up?"

"I need your help."

"Sure," he said, sounding only marginally more cooperative as he began to wake up. "Anything for the talk of Saigon."

She laughed.

"I'm serious," he insisted. "Even the ambassador has heard about your show. He says he'll be tuning in for your debut. Well?"

"I want to find a soldier," Jennifer told him. "He was on my plane when I came over. He's an enlisted man; his last name is Tyler."

Jeffrey was silent on the other end.

"What's wrong?" she asked at last.

"Look, I know you don't like being told what to do."

"But?" she prompted.

"But I don't think it's a good idea for you to get seriously involved with anyone over here."

Hadn't she heard that before? *"You* wanted to get seriously involved with me when we first met," she teased, "unless I misinterpreted the way you looked at me that first day."

Jeffrey gave an uneasy cough. "Yeah. Well, I'm different. I work an office job in Saigon. I might as well be a Chicago banker, for God's sake."

"You think I'll get attached to someone, then he'll get killed."

"Happens all the time."

"But, it doesn't necessarily happen that way," she argued.

"Jennifer, if you want to take up with someone, choose him from the embassy or support people in Saigon."

Everything he was saying made sense. Unfortunately, Tyler was not a man she could just sit back and let drift out of her life.

"His name is Tyler," she repeated, "and he has a Midwestern accent. I don't know where he was headed. I have a feeling, though, he might be returning to a second tour. Can you find him for me?"

Jeffrey groaned.

"Can you find him?" Her fingers curled urgently around the receiver. She could hear the echo of her heartbeat as she pressed her ear against the plastic.

"I'll try," he promised.

10

The following morning, Jennifer walked to the radio station. It was a long way, through streets that were now becoming familiar to her. The air was stinging hot and humid. By the time she was halfway there, her pink cotton blouse stuck damply to the line of her spine.

During the night she'd been able to put her thoughts into some sort of order. She'd also come up with a strategy for Metcalf. As long as she was in Vietnam, she was determined to be there on her own terms.

She found Gloria in her office. "Good morning!" Jennifer called out briskly.

The dimple-cheeked receptionist shoved away her paperwork. "I can't tell you how glad I am to see you. Dick told me that you were upset about the Can Tho appearance. When you didn't show up yesterday, we were all afraid you'd pulled out on us."

"I almost did," Jennifer admitted solemnly. "I still might."

Gloria's lips had twisted into a tentative smile. Now they spilled downward. "You *are* serious."

"Damn right. You'd better get Hugh in here. We have to talk."

"All right." Gloria stood up, but she hesitated at the doorway. "He's probably in his office. Want to come along?"

"No. Just tell him I'm waiting here."

Gloria gave her a puzzled look, then shrugged and left.

Once, Jennifer had overheard her father discussing power plays with one of his junior partners. Removing the opponent from his home turf put you at an advantage. Perhaps she'd learned more from her father than she liked to admit.

A few minutes later Gloria returned with a scowling Lieutenant Metcalf. "What's the word, love? We can't keep boshing around like this. Got to get this show on the road."

"The word is, Hugh, you fucked me over."

He looked shocked. "Aw, Jenny-love. Old Hugh wouldn't do that."

"Old Hugh most certainly *did!*" she snapped. "And I don't like it one bit." Ignoring Gloria's horrified stare, Jennifer strode over to face the program director.

He was barely her height but made up for it in nervous energy, forever chewing his cigar, knocking ashes onto the floor, tugging on the loosened knot of his tie.

"We never reached Can Tho, Hugh."

He put on a contrite expression. "Sorry 'bout that, love. Dick told me. You musta been scared to death."

"A little publicity nearly cost two lives! Why didn't anyone tell me the truth about this job?" Jennifer demanded.

He stared at her, speechless.

"Never mind. I already know why. Freck had to lie to be sure I'd come." She paused a beat. "But I'll admit, I'm glad I'm here."

He grinned ecstatically. "That-a-girl! A real trooper, hey, Gloria?"

Gloria bobbed her head doubtfully.

"Before we tape the second show or plan any more trips, I have a few requests," Jennifer said.

"Sure. What can we do to make life comfy for our star?"

"First of all, I refuse to live in the compound. I'm going to find an apartment somewhere in the city."

"Oh, Jennifer, I don't know!" Gloria cried, shaking her head.

"No, no." Hugh held up a hand. "If the young lady's going to be here for a year, she should be able to choose where she lives. Mind you, had I the option of takin' a cozy little villa in the compound, I'd grab it. But to each his own." He grinned at her, chomping down on his cigar, his round face placating. "What next?"

"I want to know how many GIs will be hearing my show."

"How many?" He shrugged. "Tough to say. Armed Forces Radio Network has over three hundred stations, but we'll just be using you in Nam. If we put you on all of 'em here, who knows. Tens of thousands of men will be listening in at any given time."

"But," she prompted, anxiously, "will only the guys in the cities, or in the barracks on the big bases, be able to tune in the show? What about our guys at the firebases and in evac hospitals?"

Hugh brightened, possibly seeing where she was headed. "Oh, honey, they'll get you. Every last one of them can pull in our signal, so long as they're not in the middle of a firefight. Maybe even then. Who the hell knows?" His Cockney accent broke over a sharp laugh. "I hear they play Stones tapes on Cobra gunships while they're on strafing runs."

All that was important was that Hugh accede to her demands. "Good," she said, fixing him with her bright green eyes. "You just make sure every station has access to the show."

He grinned around his cigar. "Right. Sure."

"And the last thing is this: I get transportation to *any* base or any other location in the country I want, *when* I want it—no questions asked . . . and I get veto power if I think I shouldn't go some place."

"Now," he said, laughing less happily, "I don't know. I mean, we need someone who'll make the appearances. You could duck out on me. Just take off for a couple months of fun at the beach and refuse to go anywhere else."

"Hugh!" She stood nose-to-nose with him. "I'll *do* the show, goddammit! But if you decide to fly me somewhere and the pilot tells me it's too risky, I want to be able to wait until things cool down a little." She shook a reproving finger in his face. "Remember, little man, it's not just me in that plane or Jeep, it's *the men who are delivering me!* I won't endanger them on my account."

"Oh," he murmured, backing down, "I see. Sure."

"And the transportation?"

He waved his arms grandly. "Whenever, love. You name it. A free ticket."

Jennifer let out a long breath. "Okay. Let's tape."

The second program took two fourteen-hour days to finish. The top-forty songs she announced were interspersed with letters soldiers had written to her. (Faked for the first shows. Hugh predicted that they could expect plenty of mail once the show aired.) She also played her guitar while she sang, and she read new monologues that she wrote during her meal breaks, sometimes with Gloria's help.

When they'd finally finished, Jennifer was exhausted, emotionally drained. She was afraid that she couldn't put herself through this every week, even though both Hugh and Dick assured her she'd cut her recording time as she became more experienced.

Four days after the Can Tho fiasco, Jennifer met with Hugh and Gloria. They listened to eight hours' worth of tape that Dick French had edited out of the rough recordings. Dick wanted to go for a four-hour show, since they had plenty of material for the first two shows. However, the three of them finally came to an agreement that the show should definitely be limited to three hours—to insure quality and save her strength.

It would air on Friday nights, as Hugh had initially wanted. There would be replays of "A Night with Jenny" during the following week, so that those men who'd missed the "live" show because they were on duty would have a chance to catch the taped version later.

For the next few days, Jennifer made short trips out of the city by Jeep to visit soldiers in the peripheral countryside. Although she honestly tried to put Tyler out of her mind, at every stop she found herself scanning for his face in the crowds of uniformed soldiers. Each passing day, her heart ached more rather than less. She badgered Jeffrey constantly. Why couldn't he find one enlisted man? Was that too much to ask with his marvelous diplomatic connections? He explained that it took time for the military to complete a search without a service number. She'd just have to be patient.

By the time she returned to Saigon from her final appearance before the first show was to be aired, Dick had made his final cuts. He'd magically eliminated her hesitations and occasional nervous stuttering.

Everyone at the station was pleased with the final product. The first show was romantic, sentimental, funny, sexy, perfect! It would air at the end of that week. Jennifer took a day off to recuperate.

She slept late, waking at ten-thirty. The rest of the morning she spent tidying up the villa, and during the afternoon, she visited the USO again. Although she enjoyed herself, she felt restless and again constantly searched the young faces around her. Tyler wasn't there. She thought if she never saw him again she might go mad!

The first show, as Hugh had predicted, brought an avalanche of mail. Men wrote wanting to know everything about the woman whose sultry voice they'd heard on their radios. What did Jennifer look like? How about printing a picture of her in *Stars & Stripes?* Was she actually in Nam, or did she prerecord her broadcasts from somewhere in the States?

Hugh's publicity campaign continued but at a saner pace. Jennifer personally checked out each proposed trip with a veteran transport chief at Tan Son Nhut. Publicity photos were taken. She appeared in the military newspaper, along with an interview. She answered as much fan mail as humanly possible, given her busy schedule. The question most frequently asked was "Are you married?"

Two more excruciatingly slow weeks dragged past with no news of Tyler. Jeffrey was definitely on her blacklist. To make matters worse, Jennifer was having no luck at all finding an apartment outside of the compound. Each one she was directed to by Military Housing was in an old Saigon hotel or office building that had been converted for U.S. government use. They were boxlike, sterile. None of them offered the charm and character of Lian's home or the simple closeness to people that Jennifer sought.

She decided to go to Lian for help.

After finishing her recording session one day, she took a cyclo to Lian's house in the Second District and explained what she wanted to do.

"I had hoped you would become discouraged and change your mind," Lian said with a long sigh. "A woman . . . an American woman in particular is not safe living alone."

"Nonsense," Jennifer huffed.

Lian shook her head sadly, then motioned to her. She led Jennifer through the French doors and into her garden. They sat on a stone bench surrounded by pale lavender and creamy yellow orchids. Lian turned to her with a stern expression. "My friend, there are facts you must face. Crime in Saigon is very bad. Prostitution is a way of life here. People steal—kill, if necessary—to feed or protect their families. It is not something I'm proud of, but one cannot ignore reality. There is violence every day on the street."

Jennifer shrugged. "All cities are like that."

"But, for you, an American woman, it will be worse. Saigon boys are wild. When a young man is drafted into the ARVN, his family speaks of him as dead. Our soldiers are not well prepared. They go out to fight, and most die. You may have noticed that it is mostly women, children, and old men you see on the streets. If the boy is not yet of age, he is allowed to run wild. 'Why not let him do as he wishes for today?' say the parents. 'Tomorrow he will be in the army. Tomorrow he will die.'"

"I see," Jennifer said softly. *What a horrid way to raise children*, she thought, *with no hope for the future*.

"And," said Lian, "these boys see how American soldiers treat Vietnamese women." She stopped abruptly, glancing down at the pebbled path beneath her feet.

Jennifer laid a comforting hand on her friend's arm. "If you're worried about offending me, Lian, please don't. I know what men can be like, regardless of their nationality." Jennifer didn't know, not really.

"Vietnamese boys think—if American men treat our women this way, why shouldn't we treat their women so?" Lian lifted her glance and looked levelly at Jennifer. "An American woman on her own in Saigon is regarded as a whore."

However, Lian's distressing words didn't change Jennifer's mind. "I'll have to deal with that if I can't change it." Before Lian could raise further objections, Jennifer rushed on. "Either I live in the city, or I leave Vietnam. And I'm determined to stay!"

Lian's pretty black eyes brightened. "Come live here, in my home!"

Jennifer hesitated for only a moment before shaking her head. "Your husband will be home soon. You'd have no privacy."

Lian sighed. "Then I will help you find a house that is as safe as possible. But it will not be easy, for the little amount of money you want to spend," she said in a scolding voice. "And remember, it is not only the Vietnamese men you must be careful of. American GIs prowl the streets for women. It is not the same as in the USO. There are rules in the club, and I see to it that the boys behave, or they are not welcome back. They know it. But let them loose in the city with booze or drugs in their veins . . ." She turned her hands, palms up, as if to say, *It is beyond my control.*

Jennifer didn't know how seriously to take Lian. After all, she was a woman who'd been raised in a very conservative

131

home by Eastern parents. The catcalls and whistles Jennifer's appearance on the street frequently produced didn't seem threatening.

Nevertheless, she promised to be careful. And Lian reluctantly agreed to help her in her apartment hunting. She had a few promising neighborhoods in mind.

Jennifer already had a sense of Lian's status within Saigon. According to Jeffrey, the young Vietnamese woman was automatically included on all U.S. Embassy party lists and invited to most Vietnamese government functions. When they began making the rounds to different vacant apartments, the landlords always treated her with deference. Lian's husband was apparently an important, well-known man.

Although Jennifer and Lian were the same age, Lian seemed to take an almost motherly interest in Jennifer. She invited her to her home so often during the apartment-hunting process that Jennifer began to feel more comfortable there than within the American compound. She loved the view of the garden from the gracious living room. Even the overpowering aroma from the nearby canal became a familiar and accepted detail of her visits to her friend's home.

One day, after a morning spent on another disappointing round of apartment hunting, Jeffrey telephoned from the embassy.

"I was hoping I'd catch you there," he told Jennifer as soon as she took the receiver from Lian.

"You have word about Tyler?" Her heart was leapfrogging in her chest.

"Yes. At least I think it's him. His name is Christopher Adam Tyler. He's from Missoula, Montana. As you suspected, in Vietnam on his second tour."

Jennifer could hardly contain her excitement. "Go on. Where's he stationed?"

"His unit is out around Cu Chi, west of Saigon."

"Oh, Jeff!" All those nights of envisioning him, cold and alone in a trench, out of her reach.

132

"Jennifer, you're not planning on seeing him next time he rolls into town, are you?"

"No. I'm going out to Cu Chi to visit him."

Jeffrey sounded as if he were choking on something. "You're not serious! Listen, this Tyler isn't some big man on campus. He's here on his second tour in a war zone—which means he *likes* it here. Added to that—he's part of some sort of elite hunter-killer squad. They live out there, halfway between Saigon and the Cambodian border. Their job is to intercept weapons and VC headed for the capital."

With an involuntary shiver, Jennifer remembered the deceptively innocent leather bracelet around Christopher Tyler's muscular wrist. Then she conjured up the deep-set blue eyes that had locked with hers just before they'd parted in the marketplace.

"Hugh has been after me to make more appearances," she said abruptly.

"You've been to most of the major bases—Da Nang, Cam Ranh Bay, Qui Nhon," he reminded her.

"But there hasn't been time to organize trips to any of the more remote ones. Cu Chi can be one of the stops on the next itinerary."

"Jennifer, for God's sake!"

"I'm going, Jeffrey," she said, her voice stretched as taut as a guitar string. Then, softer, "Thanks for finding him. Please don't worry about me, I'll be fine."

She wasted no time setting up her next trip. Hugh commandeered, appropriately, a Huey helicopter and crew to shuttle Jennifer, her guitar, and a sound engineer with equipment. They headed west, out of Tan Son Nhut Airfield. Cu Chi was to be their first stop.

From the air, the army camp appeared in the shape of a five-pointed star. Around it were various levels of defensive rings. The outermost was made up of covered bunkers, each manned by an armed soldier. Inside the bunkers were a circular trench, and inside that a pentagon formed by five low sheds topped with corrugated steel. She supposed that the men slept in some of the sheds when they weren't out on

133

patrol. The land was level, cleared of most trees. Nearby a reddish river twisted lazily.

As soon as the helicopter set down in the clearing, the engineer jumped to the ground and ran for cover. The pilot, a man named Ned Kroopnick, who'd told her he had a little girl named Jennifer at home in Denver, shouted to her over the roar of the engines: "It's daylight, don't worry. The boys have the area under control. They're expecting you."

"Thanks," she said absently. Her attention was riveted on the soldiers clustered eagerly at the edges of the camp. Her heartbeat quickened at a ruffled head of brown hair. . . . But no, this man's shoulders were sloped, not aggressively squared like Tyler's.

"I'll be back to pick you up in four hours," Ned told her.

"Great!" She jumped down to the ground with the helping hand of a soldier who had met the copter. He carried a rifle and wore a helmet. He plunked another helmet down on her head, took her guitar case, and pointed to a space between two of the bunkers.

Jennifer ducked under the swirling blades of the Huey and ran, glancing sideways at him. He wasn't Christopher Tyler either.

The lieutenant in charge of the platoon at Cu Chi was named Johansen. He welcomed her and asked her into the shed labeled Headquarters. He made no attempt to summon the men yet, wanting to chat with her alone first.

She accepted a warm Coke and let him talk for fifteen minutes, all the while thinking of Tyler . . . Christopher. . . .

At last, she pointed out tactfully, "My show runs three hours, Lieutenant, and it'll take a little while to set up. We're taping this today, so I'm afraid time is crucial."

Johansen smiled, reluctant to give her up. "Sure. We'd better get started."

The engineer on this trip wasn't her usual. Dick, as she'd suspected, had spent considerable time as a radio man on reconnaissance missions. He was not at all eager to be anywhere there might be action. The new man required her constant guidance while setting up. She was aware of the soldiers gathering around as she worked, but was too busy to pay them much attention.

Her stage was a level spot of dry ground in the middle of the camp. At last everything was ready and she perched on an empty oil barrel, her guitar resting on her thigh. By now she'd acquired a couple sets of olive-drab fatigues that she wore on trips out of Saigon. They were practical and, surprisingly, not unattractive. The straight-cut pants hugged her slender hips, the shirt fit trimly, accentuating the shape of her breasts. She also had been given a flight jacket by a C-130 navigator. On it she'd sewn a patch representing each of the military detachments she'd performed for. She wore it everywhere and treasured it above all her mementos. This afternoon, though, it was too hot to wear, and she removed it, laying it carefully aside.

Once the show had begun, Jennifer was at last free to study the features of each man in her audience. She sang song after song, peering into face after face. Not one of them belonged to the man she'd longed to see.

Although the show went well and her audience clapped enthusiastically, lining up for autographed photos at the conclusion, she was disappointed that she hadn't spotted Tyler. Perhaps the Christopher Tyler that Jeffrey had discovered was a different man entirely from the young soldier she'd met on the plane.

Finally, she helped her engineer pack up his recording gear, said goodbye to the soldiers and to their captain, and sat down on a pile of spent mortar cases to wait for the Huey to return. Her insides were raw with fatigue and disillusionment. "Tyler," she whispered to herself, "where are you?"

One thing she'd learned about the military, four hours sometimes meant three, or eight, or it just might mean tomorrow. While Jennifer sat numbly waiting behind one of the perimeter bunkers, life in the camp returned to normal. Some men nearby gathered to go out on patrol. A few minutes later, another patrol appeared, approaching the camp from the direction of the river bank.

Jennifer's hand tightened unconsciously on the handle of her guitar case. As the men moved closer, she was able to make out their features, but she first recognized Tyler by his steady, stiff-shouldered walk.

Jennifer sat still, not knowing what to do. She had never before been shy about approaching a man, but this time was different. She sensed tension in the camp. Someone muttered that the patrol was late. Someone else wondered aloud what sort of crap they'd run into and what the men going out would face. She suddenly felt unimportant. Jennifer Lynn had dropped in to make small talk for a few hours. These men were risking their lives.

She was exactly what Tyler had accused her of being: a fair-weather do-gooder. Now, watching him approach, she wasn't sure she had the nerve to face him here, on his own turf.

About ten feet away, he noticed her. The rhythm of his step altered with a jerk, but his expression remained a restrained blank. For a moment she was sure that he was going to walk wide of the bunker to avoid her. Then he seemed to change his mind, and he broke away from the rest of the men and strode straight over to stand in front of her, his rifle cradled across his chest.

"What the hell are you doing here?" he demanded, his eyes flashing blue lightning above charcoal-smeared cheekbones.

She smiled up at him shakily, brushing her long, blond hair back over her shoulders. "Singing."

He looked angry, then puzzled. "Didn't anyone tell you how dangerous it is out here?"

"Repeatedly," she said. Then she dropped her voice to an urgent whisper so that only he would hear her. "I had to find you! I had to see you again."

His eyes melted into hers. She could almost swear that this time she'd reached him, that he somehow understood what had brought her here.

Without warning, he reached down and grabbed her roughly by the hand. "Stay put," he ordered her engineer when he jumped to his feet as if to protect Jennifer from this apparent madman. Tyler pulled her toward the center of the camp.

"Where are we going?" she asked.

"If you're set on dropping in on VC-controlled territory, you'd better know how to take care of yourself."

It didn't matter to her where they were going. Being alone with him for a few minutes was all she'd hoped for and now it was happening.

When they reached a small shed in the middle of the camp, Chris ducked inside, coming out seconds later with another rifle that looked somewhat different from his own. "This is an M-16," he said. "Know how to fire one?"

"No."

"Ever fire *any* gun?"

"No," she admitted. "I don't like guns."

He muttered something unintelligible.

"I think my engineer knows how to shoot," she offered.

"Lot of good that'll do you in an ambush. If he's taken down, what'll *you* do?"

She looked at him, open-mouthed.

"Right," he said. "Come on."

He took her outside of the perimeter fortifications toward the river. A few scruffy trees clung to the bank in a clump. A couple hundred yards from the trees, Chris stopped, scanned the skyline through narrowed eyes before slinging his own weapon over his shoulder.

"The safety's on." He thrust the M-16 into her hands. "Hold it for a minute just to get the feel of it."

The gun was smaller and a lot lighter than she'd imagined —perhaps twenty-four inches, only five or six pounds. Whereas Christopher's rifle had a polished wooden stock, this one was a dull gray-green metal with a plastic stock.

She passed it back to him, then watched while he loaded it, explaining to her everything he did. "It holds a twenty-round clip, but we usually load only eighteen to prevent jamming. It can fire up to two hundred rounds a minute."

Jennifer nodded, transfixed as she watched his hands deftly move over the weapon—throwing the bolt, checking to be sure the chamber was clear, pulling a metal clip from the cloth bandoleer slung over his chest, slapping the ammunition into the gun's underside. True, she didn't like guns and had never harbored the least desire to learn how to use one. But if someone threatened her life, she supposed she'd want to defend herself. So she let him talk, enjoying the coarse masculine sound of his voice, the puissant motions of his body as he manipulated the weapon. She even liked the sweat-salty grass scent on his skin as he moved closer to her to demonstrate.

"If you put it on semiautomatic, it'll fire a single shot each time you pull the trigger, or a burst when you hold the trigger in. Fire in a three- or four-round burst to see where you're shooting. The selector lever is on the left side just above the trigger." He pointed. "Go ahead. Put it on semi."

She obeyed, trying to shut out the sensations of his nearness. If she didn't concentrate on what he was telling her, he'd be furious when she made a mistake. She had to show him she was serious about what she was doing—as serious as she was about him.

"What happens if I put it on full automatic?" she asked, seeing the other marked position.

"There's not a lot of recoil since it's just .22-cal ammo." He put an arm around her shoulders to help her place her hands on the gun. His other arm slipped between her elbow and ribs to adjust her right hand on the trigger mechanism. Jennifer leaned back just a little, pressing her shoulder blades into the muscled curve just below his chest. The earthy, unwashed smell of him hit her full force, but she wasn't repelled. It was natural and male, and she loved it.

Chris tensed momentarily, then seemed to relax. The point of his chin came down to rest on top of her head. "There's a rear and a front sight," he murmured, his lips moving in the wisps of her hair. "Line both up with that first tree."

She lowered her cheek onto the stock.

"Don't rest your face on the gun. The recoil might bruise your cheek."

She obediently lifted her head an inch.

"Squeeze once," he said.

She did.

The gun gave a loud crack and jerked, nudging her backward against Chris's chest. He absorbed the impact easily. "Okay. This time plant your feet. Be ready for it."

And the second time she was. The gun thumped against her upper arm a fraction of a second after she squeezed the trigger, and slivers of bark spit off the side of the tree trunk.

He took the gun from her and fired a short burst. Splinters flew and a white patch of bare wood appeared dead center in the trunk.

"Again," Chris ordered in a quiet voice. "Aim for the target."

After a few minutes, she'd gotten so she could hit within eight inches of Chris's mark almost every time. When the magazine was empty, he made her reload by herself, then fire longer bursts.

She felt a strange exhilaration and power with the gun in her hand. She knew it was deceptive, this almost invincible sensation. It probably made a lot of soldiers falsely confident, and got many killed. She vowed she'd never use a gun unless she absolutely had to, and even then she wasn't sure she could point it at another person and pull that trigger.

But Jennifer didn't tell Christopher Tyler any of this.

She looked up over her shoulder at him after finishing the last cartridges. He'd been watching her face intently, instead of the target. His arms were still loosely linked around her. For a breathless moment, neither of them moved or said anything.

Then a low, beating whir rose up out of the dry Asian plain.

"Your ride's coming in," he whispered. His eyes had darkened nearly to black with only a few sapphire glints.

"I know," she murmured, her heart racing. *Oh, God, Chris—please say something! Tell me you're glad I came. Tell me you feel what I'm feeling right now!*

"Make them give you a gun," he said. "Whenever you leave Saigon, make them give you a gun."

Her throat felt constricted, dry. Her hands were locked on the M-16. And she didn't want to let go of *it*, because then this soldier from Montana would let go of *her*. "I will . . . Chris."

At the sound of his name on her lips, he allowed her a flicker of a smile. "Take care of yourself, Jen."

"I will," she promised breathlessly. "And, please . . . if you can . . . write to me at the embassy. I want to know that you're all right."

Without answering, he released her. Then, taking her hand, he started running back toward the landing area.

Her engineer was frantically waving at her from the open cockpit of the Huey. The equipment was already on board. Lieutenant Johansen stood just out of range of the dust eddies swirling around the base of the copter. He gave Chris a strange look but didn't say anything to him as he rushed past, Jennifer's hand clutched in his, ducking under the blades.

Chris set the M-16 on the ground and, placing his hands on her waist, smoothly lifted her through the opening behind the pilot's seat. As she quickly buckled the web seat belt over her fatigues, she leaned forward slightly, hoping he'd take advantage of this last moment to kiss her.

Instead, he picked up the M-16 and backed off stiffly. The pilot throttled the engine to a high-pitched whine. The landing struts left the ground.

Jennifer couldn't take her eyes off Chris as a cold panic settled over her. So few words had passed between them. And there was so much she wanted to say to him . . . so much she *needed* to know about him. When would she see him again? Would he go out on patrol tomorrow? And, if so, would he come back alive? *Did he want her the way she felt herself wanting him?*

He dropped his eyes to the gun in his hands as the Huey rose slowly, then he shot a glance at Johansen who was waving at Jennifer from some ways back. Suddenly, Chris charged at the copter and tossed the M-16 into the cockpit at her feet. Two metal ammunition clips followed. Then he spun and silently walked away, his shoulders strong and stiff, his gait controlled.

Take care of yourself, Jen.

"Stay low, Chris," she whispered below the beat of the blades.

Later, in a place called Vinh Long, Jennifer lay awake until almost dawn on a canvas cot. She was afraid if she fell asleep she might forget the feeling of his hands guiding hers, his body tight behind her. She might forget the lovely rough sound of his voice coming at her from so near her ear that she'd felt his breath. Perhaps he'd shown her she was important to him in the only way he knew how—by giving her the means to protect herself. Or maybe she was nothing special to him at all. But she *wouldn't* let herself believe that.

Jennifer trembled, imagining his hands on her breasts— where only the crude cloth of the fatigue shirt she was sleeping in rubbed as she tossed. Against her closed lids, she pictured the one hearttrendingly brief smile he'd allowed her. Then she forced her eyes open, to make sure she didn't drift off.

Keeping him close was worth lost sleep.

11

Upon Jennifer's return to Saigon, Lian announced she had found an apartment for her. The good news didn't seem as important as it would have before the trip to Cu Chi. What most mattered to Jennifer now was Chris.

Despite his outward coolness, she was convinced that the physical and emotional sparks she'd felt were not imaginary or one-sided. The war had hardened him, had taught him to withhold his love in order to avoid pain. Somehow she'd have to discover a way to get him to open up to her.

Still, after her recording session, Jennifer accompanied her friend to the place she'd found. The one-room apartment was actually a half-house—a common arrangement in the city—on the outskirts of Cholon, Saigon's Chinatown. There was no electricity, no water, but it was located within easy walking distance of shops and a waterhouse. The rent was cheap—a necessity if her allowance for the year was to last. There were no closets, and the furnishings were sparse: a well-used Montgomery Ward maple kitchen table with two chairs and a twin-size bed behind a curtain. A bamboo mat hung near the back wall. Behind it were water jugs and a charcoal burner for cooking.

But, as common as the interior was, the place was exactly what Jennifer wanted. Living here, she wouldn't feel so guilty when she thought of Chris camping at Cu Chi. Then, too, from her vantage point among the Vietnamese people, she'd be able to learn so much more. Her innate curiosity never left her at peace for long.

"Tell the landlord I'll take it," she instructed Lian impulsively.

"I was hoping you'd change your mind after seeing it," her friend admitted. "Cholon isn't much better than a slum."

"It's perfect," Jennifer assured her.

She was genuinely thrilled. Her father hadn't supplied a penny toward her new home. She used her first paycheck to cover two months' rent. With the little left over, she bought two pretty carved wood chairs from the market, complete with flowered cushions, and a tiny cocktail table to put between them. She shoved Montgomery Ward out onto the street, knowing somebody would adopt the worn, functional set.

As days then weeks passed, no letters arrived from Chris. She wasn't surprised but couldn't help being disappointed. What really shocked her, though, was how difficult it was to put her own feelings for him onto paper. She wrote a dozen letters, then tossed them away, furious with herself because they were inadequate, or sounded insincere. She was afraid that he would read something offensive or embarrassing into her words and that would ruin her chances of ever getting close to him.

Jennifer slowly grew familiar with her neighbors, who were generous, warm-hearted people. She learned the fastest routes between her new apartment, the station, the USO, and Lian's house. Her hours continued to be crammed with work—either taping shows or flying across the country on personal appearances. When in Saigon, she tried to find time to visit the USO, but for days on end she'd be so exhausted it was all she could do to drag herself home to her modest room and collapse into a deep sleep.

And still, she waited to hear from Chris: a letter, a

message passed along through a friend on R-and-R, anything. But after more than a month, there was still nothing. Her own perceptions of the three times they'd been together became muddled in her mind. Those precious moments had been so brief—measured in hurried seconds and minutes rather than long, luxurious hours or days. They hadn't talked about their pasts, their dreams, their favorite songs, colors, or movie stars—any of the things young lovers shared. They hadn't even kissed. He was, she admitted, a stranger.

So why did she feel he was hers, and she his? For weeks on end she was despondent. Then, gradually, memories of Christopher Tyler began to demand less of her thoughts. Even so, a day never passed when she didn't think of him.

It had become her habit to use Ned Kroopnick as her pilot whenever he was available and was granted clearance by his CO. They always sat down together and planned her itinerary. If there was action in the area where Hugh had scheduled a show, Ned warned her so that she wouldn't start out unprepared. If it was particularly heavy or unpredictable due to guerrilla buildup, he'd advise her to wait another month, then reevaluate. She never ignored his advice.

In July, she was planning yet another round of visits to firebases. She and Ned met at Tan Son Nhut that day, and she proposed to return to Cu Chi.

If Chris couldn't, or wouldn't, come to her, she would go to him. For her own sanity, the questions tormenting her had to be answered.

Ned bit his lower lip and looked at her hard. "You just saw those boys not long ago."

"I know," she admitted, her hands knotting in her lap, "but I want to go back. It's a rough station."

"There's a lot of shit duty everywhere."

"Ned!" Her gentle green eyes pleaded, begged, refused to take no for an answer. "Cu Chi is where I want to go."

He shrugged. "Well, from what I hear, the Twenty-fourth Division is busier 'an hell lately. Seems to be some sort of Viet Cong buildup in the works."

"Now may be the best time to go—before conditions get any worse."

He shook his head. "It's too dangerous, Jenny."

Reluctantly, Jennifer stuck to her promise. If the men who put their lives on the line flying her to her shows thought there was too much risk involved, she wouldn't overrule them. Besides, a little voice at the back of her brain warned her that showing up at Cu Chi in the heat of battle wouldn't only endanger her, the pilot, and engineer, it might very well distract Chris to the point where he'd become careless at a crucial moment. That is, if she meant anything to him. And if she did, how could she live with herself if he were wounded or—she wouldn't let herself think of the final possibility.

She chose alternate trips.

By September, Ned's information on the area west of Saigon hadn't improved. Still Jennifer felt she *must* see Chris in person. How to do that safely was the question.

Since that answer seemed to be eluding her, she decided to seek a second opinion on the Cu Chi situation from Jeffrey.

She'd promised to accompany the handsome young diplomat to a reception in honor of General Westmoreland. She had no interest in attending the affair itself, but Jeffrey had begged her to go. If he owed her, she reasoned, he might feel somewhat obligated to pass along information to her. He was typically closemouthed about anything even remotely involving military intelligence.

When he arrived at her little house, she let him in, then excused herself to finish dressing and arranging her hair. While working at the studio or dropping in on remote bases, she wore her long blond hair in an informal ponytail, dangling smooth and straight down the middle of her back. (It seemed to have grown a foot since leaving Boston.) Tonight she'd decided to sweep it up on top of her head in a more formal style that she supposed Jeffrey would appreciate. She fastened the pale golden twist with the silver comb, donned her evening garb, and, at last, stepped out from behind the curtain.

"What do you think?" she asked.

Jeffrey's eyes answered before he found his voice. "I don't think I've ever seen an American woman wear an *ao dai*. You look dazzling, Jenny."

"Thank you," she said, fluttering her lashes at him, just a little. She took his arm, and they walked out to the corner where he'd parked the embassy car. Her own street was too narrow to drive down.

Lian had taken Jennifer to her seamstress to have the *ao dai* made for her. Traditionally, the slim, white silk overdress was slit up the sides almost to the waist and worn over black pajamalike pants. Jennifer had chosen a luscious turquoise brocade for her *ao dai*, white satin for the pants. The fabric felt heavenly next to her skin.

She wore silver kid evening sandals that had been made for her in Paris by Hèrmes and sterling ear clips with a matching necklace. She wasn't sure what sort of impression she'd make on the ambassador or the general, wearing glorified Vietnamese house clothes to a formal party. But she really didn't care. The outfit and her little Cholon house were her way of resisting the establishment. She loved her clothes and home without qualm or apology.

Jeffrey opened the car door. She rose on tiptoe and planted a little kiss on his cheek.

"What's that for?"

"Not lecturing me for the thousandth time on how dangerous it is to live alone."

"I gave that up weeks ago."

"Thank goodness."

Jennifer quickly looked him over. He wore a black tux with a small white flower in his lapel. Jeffrey Kirk was as handsome and nice a man as any woman could wish for. She wondered why her heart didn't race and dodge around in her breast when she stood near him, as it did whenever she thought of Chris.

He bent down, picked up a tissue-wrapped package from the car seat and handed it to her. "You don't have to wear it if it clashes . . ." he mumbled self-consciously.

She'd never seen him less than a hundred-percent sure of himself. His schoolboy jitters touched her.

"Just like going to the prom." She giggled. Inside the tissue was an enormous white orchid with a lavender blush across the petals and a vibrant green center. "Oh, Jeff." She sighed, touching the velvety blossom with one fingertip.

"I thought the middle there . . . it reminded me of your eyes."

She hugged him, thinking how wonderful it would have been to hear those words from Chris. "Now we aren't going to get mushy, are we?" she teased, fighting the moisture that had suddenly formed behind her delicately shadowed eyelids.

"I guess not," he said at last and gave her a friendly smile.

While they drove, she pinned the corsage to her dress. Then she watched the city—so full of life and treachery and beauty—flash by the windows. It was almost eight o'clock in the evening but it wouldn't be dark for hours.

"Has there been especially bad fighting outside the city recently?" she asked offhandedly, still watching the street.

"Hmm?"

"I was wondering why one of my pilots doesn't want to take me to an area west of the city."

"He's probably just being cautious," Jeffrey said, turning down Cong Ly Street, past the U.S. Military Assistance Command.

"Something's going on, isn't it?" She prodded him with an elbow. "Jeffrey, tell me."

"I can't." He set his jaw, glaring straight ahead.

Realizing she was getting nowhere, she let the subject drop for the moment.

Inside the embassy, Jennifer passed along the receiving line and greeted Ambassador Bunker and his wife. Then she met Westmoreland, who, she found, had a charming smile to offset his famous steel-gray hair and dramatic bushy black brows. As she continued into the ballroom on Jeffrey's arm, she dwelled on his unusually taciturn mood. Something very important was in the offing, and he wouldn't even give her a hint of what it was. If it had anything to do with Cu Chi—and therefore with Chris—she must find out.

Not long into the reception, Ambassador Bunker walked over to them. "I want to personally thank you for the work you're doing here," he told her. "I've listened to your show myself. You're giving our soldiers a reason to look forward to the future, Miss Swanson."

"Thank you," she murmured.

"I understand that you've moved out of the compound."

Jennifer sent her escort a deadly look. "Yes, I have."

The ambassador took her hand and patted it. "I hope you won't think I'm a meddling old man, but I believe that was a mistake."

She smiled. "Everyone does."

He studied her expression for a moment. "You resemble your father a great deal. Act like him, too. Stubborn man. Smart."

Jennifer didn't know that she liked being compared to her father. She'd spent much of her life trying to win his affection or avoid him. She'd certainly never imagined herself similar to him in any way.

"I came here to help our GIs," she said. "I've decided that the best way to do that is to be close to them and to learn about the country where they're fighting. I can't do that inside a barricaded fortress."

He seemed to think about that for a while. At last, he nodded. "Your father must be very proud of you," he stated, laying a hand on her arm. "You're a brave young woman."

Their conversation was interrupted a few minutes later by one of his aides who was eager to break him free and shepherd him across the crowded room to several new guests who'd just appeared. Jennifer watched him walk away.

Proud of me, she mused. Her father not only wasn't proud of her, he'd dismissed her as his daughter. As long as she remained in Vietnam, she'd ceased to exist for Max Swanson. An overwhelming sense of bitterness spoiled the effect of the music, the pretty gowns, the twinkling chandeliers, the wine and food. None of it had any impact on her.

Numbly, she circled the room on Jeffrey's arm, chatting mechanically with people. It had been so long since she'd been reminded of her family. This was their milieu, the elite atmosphere of the powerful, the decision makers. It was no longer hers. She felt a stranger here.

After a while, she started paying more attention to some of the things around her. A palpable tension had altered the cordial buzz of voices in the embassy.

At first, she couldn't quite grasp its source. Sometimes, two guests would lower their heads, murmuring only a few words beneath their breath. As soon as she and Jeffrey approached, the polite causerie would begin again—for her benefit she suspected.

Exasperated, she finally pulled Jeffrey into an alcove. "What the hell's going on?" she demanded.

He blinked at her, smiling tightly as a few heads turned their way. "Nothing, Jennifer, absolutely nothing."

"Liar." She crossed her arms over her chest and scowled at him.

"Keep it down, will you?"

"No!"

He groaned, took her by the arm, and drew her out of the room and into the formal garden, brightly lit for the reception. Marine guards stood inconspicuously in the shadows. He glanced at them sideways, then whispered, "It's just gossip."

"You mean it's classified." What had begun as a subtle warning bell tinkling in the back of her mind was now a full-blown alarm.

"No, it's not. Not exactly. There's just . . ." He chewed his lip, making up his mind. "Well, the biggest holiday of the Vietnamese year is Tet, what we call the Chinese New Year. Sort of like Christmas, Fourth of July, and New Year's all rolled into one. It begins the thirty-first of January."

"So?"

"So . . ." He shuffled his feet, lowering his voice still more. "Data has been filtering in over the past couple months. ARVN and U.S. intelligence think that a grand combined assault by the Viet Cong and North Vietnamese can be expected sometime before Tet. We're keeping a close watch on activity in and around all the major cities of the south."

Her stomach tightened into a knot. "You mean, Saigon might be attacked?"

"Maybe. More likely some of the lesser cities would be the targets. Of course, we're ready for them if—" He smiled apologetically, censoring himself. "Whatever might happen will break soon. Once Tet starts, everything should calm down. And, if nothing unusual comes our way before mid-January, we'll know that our intelligence was off. In the meantime, it might not be a bad idea for you to stick close to home."

Jennifer's mind raced. She tried to ignore the clenching fear in her middle. "The military isn't warning the people about this?"

"Why should they? We're taking precautions for them. We're doubling security at all the airfields and ports. There are crack undercover people on the lookout for VC sappers —infiltrators. Extra guards are being placed on duty at checkpoints all over the city. But we must keep this quiet. If we make any sort of general announcement, it would signal the Viet Cong that we're on to them."

Dangerous games, she thought, suspicion folding its black wings around her. These politicians were toying with people's lives, for God's sake! She hated it, but there wasn't a damned thing she could do about it.

"I won't stop going out to do shows no matter what's going on," she told him defiantly.

Jeffrey looked sadly down into her wide, emerald eyes. "I didn't expect you would. Just be choosy about your destinations, Jenny. Promise me that much."

"I will." Her tone was less brittle as she squeezed his hand reassuringly, wishing she felt as certain of herself as she sounded. Every time she left Saigon after that day, she'd wonder if she'd be able to return.

Christopher Tyler lay facedown in the mud of a shallow bunker. It was November. The rainy season had been unusually late leaving the central plains. It had been pouring for five days straight. His platoon was plagued with a growing number of casualties. That, and the fact that not enough new men were rotated into Cu Chi, meant they were severely short-handed.

In order to more effectively thwart the guerrillas who were terrorizing the villages in the area and running arms from the Cambodian border, several recon/combat elements had been formed. More accurately, these were called hunter-killer teams by the men themselves. Each team was composed of six men. They worked independently, leaving the fortified camp beside the river for weeks at a time. They kept in radio communication with their home base if possible.

Being the most experienced of his group, Chris was in command. He shifted his body softly, scanning the distant line of trees, then the ground between himself and the bamboo watchtower they'd built ten days ago. They'd been waiting two hours now. How much longer it would be, he couldn't say. If they were lucky the trap they'd set would draw out the guerrillas. They'd tortured, then killed a farmer and his family for selling rice to the American soldiers. The rain continued to come down in thick gray sheets.

He tried to forget about the rain and the long wait. It seemed as if it had been an eternity since he'd seen her: Jen. Every other guy in Vietnam called her Jenny—because of her show and the way she introduced herself when she signed on. He thought of her as his Jen. Just Jen.

Not that he had any right to her. She was so far beyond his reach that he wouldn't have dared to suppose she'd think of him as anything but just another dirty, horny grunt. Why she'd told him she *had* to see him when she came to Cu Chi was a mystery to him. Maybe she'd singled him out because of the guitar incident. Or maybe she collected a string of soldiers all across Vietnam who were madly in love with her. Some girls fed on that kind of attention. Some girls got turned on by guys in uniform—he knew only too well about that!

But he could let his imagination play around with the

possibility that if he'd been different—had money or been an officer or managed to get a deferment because he was going to medical school—then she might have taken him seriously. Maybe Jen would have picked him from among all the rest and he'd have a chance of keeping her.

It would have been nice. He smiled and let out a silent sigh.

Chris wiped the rain from the tip of his nose with the grimy back of his hand and pulled his helmet forward a bit more. He made sure his view of the tower and the ground running up to it wasn't blocked, then checked out the gray lump midway between him and the tower. He'd planted the lump among low weeds earlier that day. The claymore mine held seven hundred steel ball bearings compressed into C-4 blasting powder. If he pulled the detonation wire beside him, the explosion would be more powerful than twice as much TNT.

He'd eaten nothing but C-rations and rice for almost five months. He hadn't seen a toilet that flushed since he'd left the deployment center at Tan Son Nhut. He carried a razor (which he used sparingly), his gun (a Russian-made AK-47 he'd taken off a dead VC, which he preferred to the army's standard-issue M-16 for dependability), his rucksack, ammo, and one set of camouflage fatigues, which he now wore. When he and his men weren't actively on the hunt and it rained, he took off his clothes and stood naked under the natural shower. It felt like heaven. The fatigues were washed in the river or, if they didn't happen to be near a river, in the largest puddle available. Life was simple.

That was one of the things that had made him come back to Vietnam. After his first tour, he'd gone home on leave. His parents encouraged him to forget the war, to start thinking about the future. They had all sorts of ideas about his future.

They wanted him to return to college. They wanted him to major in computer science—because his father had read an employment forecast in *Time* magazine predicting there would be plenty of high-paying jobs for young people in this new field during the next twenty years. They wanted him to put money down on a house in Missoula that they'd had their eye on for him, marry a local girl and . . . well, life in the States seemed to have gotten very complicated. But, thinking back on it, life on patrol in Nam was pretty clear-cut—all you had to do was stay alive.

His father stopped newspaper delivery to the house because he didn't want his son to come home and read the body counts and articles about campus protests. He was afraid it would upset him. But what really bothered Chris— what absolutely drove him mad—was the fact that he'd left the closest friends he'd ever had back in Vietnam. And they were still over there, trying to survive *without him to watch out for them!* They'd always said Chris Tyler was as good as a soldier got. He could smell a VC booby trap at twenty feet and lug a 60-millimeter mortar for miles, then set it up inside of three minutes. He'd saved a lot of lives. And all he could think of while he was home in Missoula was that he had no God-damned right being here, sitting on his mom's sofa, watching reruns of "I Love Lucy," while his men were over there without him. So he'd volunteered for a second tour.

And here he was back in the mud.

He allowed himself the luxury of letting his mind wander for just another moment, conjuring up *her* face: Jen's face. It was a beautiful, smooth oval that turned up to him sweetly from over her small shoulder as he taught her how to hold an M-16. Her emerald eyes sparkled. Her blond hair felt as delicately soft as his cat's fur when it curled up on his chest for a nap. She smelled of soap and blossoms. If he concentrated, he could taste her—at least imagine the way she'd taste if he ran his tongue up the delicate soft line of her throat.

He'd held her on the pretense of helping her learn to fire the M-16. But it had been clear after the first couple rounds that she was doing just fine without him. Still, he couldn't make himself back away. The curve of her soft bottom hit him at thigh-level. Christ, did she feel good! Did she smell good!

A soft, sliding sound brought him rapidly back to the

present. He realized that he must have lapsed into a semiconscious state. Now he was alert. In one swift, soundless motion he rolled over onto his stomach, aimed the rifle at the invisible noise-maker.

Van Dorf scrambled into the bunker. "Should I check in with the others?"

"Yeah," Chris said, feeling the rhythm of his heart gear down.

Van Dorf radioed each of the other four bunkers. Everyone reported in okay. "You want first watch?" he asked when he was done.

"Sure," Chris answered. "Give me the radio."

"You won't need it. Nothing's going to happen until after dark."

"Give it to me anyway."

Van Dorf handed over the field radio. He rolled himself up in a ball, smacked his rucksack until he'd fashioned a hard pillow. Tugging his cloth boonie hat over his eyes, he settled in.

Chris scrunched down with his back against the dirt wall, his feet pressed into the opposite side. He listened as the evening sounds took over from the day sounds. The crickets *creek-creeked*. The birds grew silent.

Then everything was still—almost. The men knew better than to play tapes or try to get the American radio station out of Saigon for the remainder of the night. They wouldn't even whisper to one another. Hand signals would have to do, unless someone was in trouble. Chris listened so hard his ears began to throb. Every time a cricket hopped from one leaf to another, it sounded like an elephant coming at him. Or the enemy taking a furtive step toward the line of bunkers.

Now, he closed his eyes for a moment, trying to picture Jennifer to make the fear cramps in his stomach subside, trying to bring back the scent of her perfume. Bad idea. His eyes snapped open almost immediately. He couldn't fall asleep, leaving a hole in their defense line at a time he and his men were most vulnerable.

Sometime later, Chris glanced at his watch and was surprised to find it was time to wake Van Dorf. The dark was almost complete. He shook the eighteen-year-old by the shoulder and watched him awaken like a child, slowly, grudgingly. He'd be a lot better off if he learned to wake like a soldier.

"Yer kidding," Van Dorf mumbled.

"I'm not sleepy," Chris told him. "I can take it another couple hours."

"Naw, you'd nod off."

Chris handed back the radio and, without moving any other part of his body, dropped his chin onto his chest and closed his eyes.

This time he allowed himself the luxury of picturing Jennifer, knowing Van Dorf would do his job, for he'd trained him well. And there she was, as lucidly as if she were in the bunker beside him. He smiled in his semiconscious state, feeling warm inside, imagining walking with his arm around her, crossing a sweet Montana field, then lying down with her in the tall, soft grass to make love.

Chris blinked, suddenly awake. He was sweating profusely, although a gentle rain had continued to fall. Something had startled him out of his dream.

"Van Dorf?" he whispered.

"Ho."

"Anything up?"

"Naw. Quiet as a church out there."

Chris sat up, listening. The kid was right. Even the crickets seemed to have stopped chirping.

"Dammit, get on the radio!" he whispered urgently. Chris swung up the AK-47 and shot back the bolt.

"Hey, man. Cool it." Van Dorf laughed. "You were dreaming. You're still half asleep."

This time he didn't bother whispering. "Get on that thing *now*. They're *coming!*"

Shaking his head, Van Dorf humored him by calling through to the other bunkers. Before he'd completed the warning message, a loud crack and a flash came down the

155

line. The earsplitting chatter of weapons fire broke the stillness of the night. Chris pulled the wire on the claymore.

The evac hospital at Pleiku had a reputation for being a "mass-cas" center, a place where they treated heavy loads of American casualties airlifted straight out of battle. It was about two hundred miles north of Saigon in the central highlands.

When Mel had first arrived she was taken around to the various metal Quonset huts that served as wards, and surgery, where she'd soon be working. A number of wounded were being transported out to coastal hospitals during the day. Some preparations were being made to stabilize them for the trip. Strangely, no doctors were in evidence, only a handful of nurses joking with those patients who were awake. On the whole, everything seemed pretty laid back.

When she commented on the atmosphere, the chief nurse laughed. "This is the down side, Lieutenant. We're recovering from a three-day stint in surgery. Those choppers kept coming and coming. Most of the critical patients were flown out this morning, along with the body bags. You take your rest when you can."

As the day wore on, more and more doctors and nurses appeared in the camp, looking only half awake. They greeted each other quietly. By the end of the afternoon, almost everyone had again disappeared.

It didn't take Mel long to discover where they'd all gone. A party was in full swing in a hooch—a shed identical to her own—that belonged to a thoracic surgeon and a bone man. Mel joined the crowd, as there seemed nothing else to do. Somebody handed her a beer.

A tape deck was blaring out Creedence Clearwater Revival, and people were dancing. She met a lot of the staff. They eyed her warily, especially the doctors. She suspected she'd have to prove herself before they felt comfortable working with a black nurse. She was used to that.

Early the next morning, she woke up to find that her sheets were wet. At first she thought someone had played a prank on the newcomer. But by the time she struggled into her uniform she discovered that the problem included much more than just her sheets. All of her uniforms, towels, civvies, underwear, blankets . . . everything was soggy. The humidity was so high that moisture oozed out of the air into anything porous.

She shared her hooch with three other nurses. They were all white. One was friendly, the other two seemed distant. She didn't care. She'd come to nurse, not party. She'd come to look after Curtis. The celebration last night had been truly wild. These people were heathens, treating war like a high school football game.

"Melantha," the friendly one, whose name was Judy, mumbled drowsily from her bed, "what does that mean?"

"What does *what* mean?"

"Your name."

"It's Greek. Means dark flower." She buttoned a fatigue blouse over her khaki T-shirt. Her *damp* khaki T-shirt.

"How unusual."

"My mother read it in a book somewhere." She grinned, picturing Mama's dark, pudgy face and warm eyes that crinkled in the corners when she was pleased. "Must have been while she was still in high school. She never read another one after."

Judy grinned. "I read all the time."

"Why?" Melantha asked.

"Oh, not because I have to. I just like it. Whenever my mom sends me a care package, she always shoves in a couple paperback romances. I just adore Barbara Cartland, don't you?"

"Never heard of her." Mel didn't like talking about unfamiliar things. It embarrassed her. People didn't want to deal with you if they thought you were ignorant. She pulled on her flak jacket and helmet.

Judy giggled.

"What's so funny?" she demanded, spinning around to face the other girl. The two other nurses were awake now and eyeing each other meaningfully.

157

"*No*body wears a flak jacket just out and around," the redhead told her.

"But it's regulation," Melantha pointed out.

"Be my guest, but you'll just weigh yourself down. If we get shelled, everyone gears up. You'd need two to do any good anyway and . . ."

Judy stopped in the middle of her sentence, rolling her eyes toward the ceiling that was tinged red with the peculiar dust Mel had already noted covering just about every surface at Pleiku. "Damn!" she shrieked, stomping her feet down onto the floorboards. "Here we go again!"

That was Mel's first full day in an evac hospital. She later realized she couldn't very well have had a more harried break-in.

The choppers arrived in a black cloud. Surgeons, nurses, and techs emptied out of barracks, shacks, and Quonset huts at a run. Mel stayed with Judy, not knowing which way to turn.

"What do I do first?" she asked, her eyes taking in the endless waves of helicopters. Was it possible that every one of them carried two to four wounded? How would they ever manage to take care of all these men at once?

"You forget everything you ever learned about nursing," Judy advised. "We start by stabilizing the ones that can wait. Drain wounds. Give morphine for pain. The ones that need surgery right fast, we start their IVs and catalog them."

Judy was running from one stretcher to the next, lifting blankets while she spoke, poking and assessing. She was shouting directions to medics and corps men as she went. Amid the barks of doctors and nurses, there were the screams of men in agony, the sobbing of those who were just plain frightened.

"Then there's ones like this," Judy said quietly. Mel had only been able to hear her because she'd bent down, placing her ear within inches of Judy's mouth.

The boy's face didn't even show signs of a beard. His skin was white, his eyes were wide open, and he was breathing in raspy gulps. But under the blood-soaked blanket that Judy lifted, his chest cavity and abdomen lay open. There seemed to be no rib cage at all. His intestines were just lying on the stretcher beside him where the medic had carefully placed them.

Mel caught her breath. She'd learned long ago to contain the normal revulsion one experiences when observing the interior of the human body. This was triage. She'd done triage before. She'd handled enough automobile accident cases, pulled Emergency Room duty in one of the most crime-ridden cities in the country. The Emergency Room, she'd been told, would be good practice for an evac hospital. They were wrong. It was nothing compared to this.

A hand shot out, grabbing Mel by the wrist, dragging her down. She almost pulled free, then changed her mind and let the boy hold on to her while she knelt beside his stretcher.

"Nurse," he begged shakily, "help me."

She couldn't answer for a moment, then the words automatically spilled out: "You're going to be okay, buddy."

"No. No, I won't." He swallowed. "Give me enough morphine to kill me. Please, I ain't gonna make it."

Judy touched her gently from behind. "Come on, Mel. Leave him. He's gone."

Mel was horrified. She wrenched away from the other nurse. "No, he ain't! What do we do? *What do we do?"* she heard herself scream.

Judy pulled out a syringe and primed it before handing it to Mel. "Snow him good, honey. And kiss him good night."

Mel injected the soldier and felt her heart grow numb as if the drug had seeped into her own veins. She watched him just long enough to see a mask of calm spread over his face. He wasn't dead, but he'd succumb to his injuries soon.

Judy was already hovering over another man being taken off the most recent chopper. She was talking to the pilot as she worked, smiling, maybe even flirting a little.

Mel let her body switch to automatic. She tried not to think of the next man as a person when she bent to examine him. He was a thing. She could deal with that. Blood was red liquid. Torn flesh was stuff with no feeling. She checked under the blanket: some shrapnel chest-high and in the shoulder and one arm. He'd live. She gave him a regulation-dose injection then directed two corps men to move him to irrigation. As they started away, the blanket caught under her foot, slipped, and she saw that the shrapnel was just the aftermath of the explosion that had ripped off both his legs at the kneecaps.

"Wait!" she called out.

The corpsmen stopped, glaring at her. "Make up your mind, lady. Where you want him?"

Mel looked around and saw a tent that seemed to be where amputees were being taken. She pointed. "There."

Then she bolted across the yard littered with bodies and blood and crying men and nightmarish mangles of organs to her hooch where she crumpled onto her bed, shrieking because all she could see in each of their faces was Curtis lying wasted like these boys. She'd realized that being here had no impact on whether or not he survived. There was no protecting him.

A doctor who'd spoken to her at the party the night before found her almost an hour later, sitting on her bed, staring at the moldy wall. He sat on the bare mattress beside her and put an arm around her shoulders. She remembered vaguely that he'd introduced himself as Aaron something or other. *Feldman,* she thought.

"Pretty awful," he said in a calm, sure voice.

She didn't have the strength to nod. "I told him he'd . . . he'd make it," she stammered. "I lied to him and he knew it."

Feldman didn't ask who they were talking about. "Next time don't lie. Judy told me about the octopus hold. You've got to shake them loose. You'll have time later to talk to them and hold hands. We have to use our time to save the ones we can, Mel. And we need you in O.R. right now."

She looked up at him. This nice Jewish doctor was being kind to a black woman. Go figure.

"I don't know if I can do it," she said weakly.

"We all feel that way sometimes. Triage is over for this round. But we've still got about forty-eight hours worth of surgery to do. Unless some more show up, then it'll be longer. Either way, that will be plenty of time to teach you to be a surgeon."

She scowled at him, thinking he was kidding. He must be kidding, right?

"Come along," he said, pulling her to her feet until she stood a good six inches over him. "You'll have so much to do you won't have time to freak out. I promise."

12

December 1967

Lian sat at her escritoire. The writing table had been Nguyen's gift to her on their wedding day. He'd bought it in Burma. It was made of padouk wood and inlaid with mother-of-pearl in the shape of a lotus blossom. Four graceful legs ending in delicate claws supported the glossy top with its intricately carved surround. She rolled a gold fountain pen between two fingers, thinking the words across the blank paper—but not writing.

She could no longer tell him she loved him. Where once a glowing gilded ball of hope and devotion rested in her breast, now there was a leaden lump. It weighed heavily against her ribs, reminding her of the coldness that had come between them before he left for the north so many months ago.

She put the pen down and laid her face in her hands. "Lonely," she murmured. "I am so lonely I am sick with it."

But how could she complain to Nguyen about something so common as loneliness? There was a war going on and he was a soldier. Of course, he had to be away from her. It was her duty as a wife to wait. She must be brave enough to at least manage that small task.

She picked up the pen again and forced herself to write. She told him about the bulbs she had planted in the garden last Tuesday. She told him about the preparations she would soon be making for Tet. Carefully, she worded her desire that he might be able to travel south to Saigon for the holiday. (She didn't want to hurt his feelings if his obligations to the military kept him away.)

Lian wished she could write to him that she was pregnant with his child. She longed to give him that gift of joy— then perhaps he would love her after all. But, of course, that was impossible. She was barren, incapable, a shell of a woman.

She wiped a tear from her cheek and dipped the nib of the pen into the ink so many times she lost count. Each time, the fluid dried on the point before she could come up with the right words.

She had intended to tell Nguyen about her job as cultural liaison in this letter. Certainly, she'd put it off long enough. However, they'd spent so little time in each other's company, she hadn't learned to read his moods. His silences and explosions were an enigma to her. She thought, *I'll wait until he comes home.* Then she could be there to see her husband's reaction and reassure him that the only reason she hadn't consulted him before taking the position was because she didn't want to bother him with something so insignificant. And the reason she *had* taken it was because she was so proud of what he was doing for their country, and she believed she must also contribute.

She smiled, recalling again how they'd met, because he'd made her feel so very special that day.

She was sixteen, attending an auction in Saigon with her father. Colonel Nguyen Koa Thuy, who was almost thirty years old and already a respected officer in the South Vietnamese Army, was also there. He was a collector of Chinese artifacts and had been outbid by her father for an enamel snuff bottle of the Kangxi period. She was leaving the auction with her father when Nguyen approached them. He'd introduced himself, explained that his interest in the piece was purely emotional, and offered to pay half again the amount her father had made for his final bid. They struck a deal.

As the two men spoke, Nguyen's dark eyes drifted over Lian much as they had over the Chinese porcelain he'd so coveted for his collection. He really had been very dashing in his uniform. And he hadn't seemed at all old to her, for her parents had been along in years before she was born and both had gray hair now.

She married him six months later. Although the war was on and they saw each other only briefly, now and again, she was content to wait for him, to write regularly and manage his home. When he was able to take leave, they'd traveled together to Tokyo and to Bangkok to purchase additional pieces for his collection. On each trip, he always let her select one item and allowed her to bargain for it. Given his traditional upbringing, she reflected, this was a very modern gesture on his part. It was obviously meant to please her. She felt valuable and cherished.

But, more than anything, each time he came home and each time he left, she felt hopeful. She had agreed to marry young and cut short her education for a reason—she wanted to have children early in life. She longed to lavish them with love and teach them about the beauties of life and art, and travel around the world with them. She loved her parents, but sometimes being around them made her feel ancient. After a time, even being with Nguyen occasionally cast a wispy shadow, like gray strands across glossy ebony hair, across the day-spring of her life. She came to crave her unborn children's youth.

But now that she knew Nguyen didn't love her, and that her children would never draw the sweet breath of life, she'd stopped looking forward to her future. It was a narrow gray road, stretching off forever into an equally gray distance, unwarmed by sunlight, unshared by a man at her side or babies to lullaby to sleep. Still, there was her duty as the wife of a soldier. She wouldn't turn her back on that.

She ended the letter without saying anything more. Signing it respectfully, she folded the creamy sheet of parchment.

There was a festive air as Tet approached. Jeffrey expressed the opinion that it was more intense than usual. "For the past six months everyone's been walking on eggs—afraid of some sort of communist offensive before Tet."

"I'm sure everyone's relieved it hasn't happened," Jennifer said.

He nodded. "There's the isolated siege at Khe Sanh, but apparently that's the most the VC and North Vietnamese can muster. We'll all be able to enjoy the holiday."

It did seem an especially happy time of year. The weather was dry, tolerably mild. There were children in the streets again, young girls bicycling in their beautiful new *ao dais*, newly acquired for their visits to the temple. Jennifer noticed that, while before all she'd smelled was mold, damp dust, rotting straw, and sewage, now when she stepped outside she breathed in the delicious aromas of foods cooking over charcoal and pungent incense.

Only Lian seemed to grow more pensive and spiritless as January drew to an end.

"What's up?" Jennifer asked over a beer at the club.

"Nothing," Lian insisted. She shrugged, her black eyes glittering. Lian was such a private person. Sometimes, Jennifer could only guess what might be going through her friend's mind. She often suspected Lian hid a deep personal tragedy behind her enigmatic smiles.

"The holiday blues?" Jennifer prodded gently.

Lian shook her head. "Tet is the season of great joy. I don't know why I'm acting like this." She broke into sobs.

Jennifer put an arm around her. "Is it because your mother and father are so far away in Hong Kong?"

Lian nodded. "I miss them both very much."

"Can't you visit them?"

Lian shook her head against Jennifer's shoulder. "My husband would not wish me to because of the danger of traveling."

"What about Nguyen?" Jennifer asked. "He'll be able to come home for Tet, won't he?"

Lian didn't answer.

"I'm so sorry," Jennifer said. She had never heard a word of complaint out of Lian, so it was all the more shocking now, when Lian at last showed her vulnerability. "Tell me about Tet . . . what you do . . . how you celebrate." She wanted to be upbeat, to make Lian think about happier times in the past and the future.

Lian straightened up and smiled bleakly. "I should be working now."

"That can wait," Jennifer insisted.

"Well," Lian began in a low voice, "the whole family purchases new clothes for the temple services. The men and boys get haircuts. When I was young, a traveling barber from Da Nang would set a stool near the waterhouse and cut hair all day long. My mother and I spent days cooking." A tiny spark lit her dark eyes. "My favorite was barbecued pork. It's sweet, tender, spicy, and covered with a thick reddish lacquerlike coating. Every household invites many guests to share their hospitality, for as many friends honor you with their visits, you will have that many lucky days during the coming year. My mother, father, and I would go to the Chinese temple, where coils of incense hung from the ceiling. I still visit by myself. Suppliants come to light joss sticks and plant them in urns, or set votive papers afire—hoping for spiritual reward. The air-raid trenches in front of City Hall will be temporarily filled in and planted with flowers."

"Well, then," Jennifer said, "you have plenty of friends to honor and be honored by."

"But they are all—" Lian stopped abruptly as if afraid of offending her.

"American?" Jennifer guessed. She laughed when Lian flushed with embarrassment. "I for one would be honored to come to your home on Tet."

"Would you?" Lian asked.

"Certainly. And I know a couple hundred guys who'd feel the same way."

"Then I shall ask them all." Lian laughed, wiping away tears. "I am a most fortunate woman." She said this looking straight at Jennifer so that her meaning wouldn't be lost on her closest friend. "You will bring someone very special with you. Jeffrey, maybe?"

"If you're asking if I am interested in Jeffrey, forget it," Jennifer said dryly.

"Oh," Lian moaned in disappointment. "He is a very nice young man when he is not chasing other women."

"He is a young man with a big head," Jennifer corrected her. "And a good friend," she added more softly. "Besides, he's not my type."

"He is *exactly* your type."

"All right. He's too much my type and boring."

Lian sighed. "I can't imagine what you are looking for, then. He is young, handsome, rich. And he adores you, anyone can see that."

"Oh, I don't know," Jennifer said. But she wasn't at all surprised when Chris's face surfaced out of her subconscious. "I think I'll know the right man when I see him."

As Tet grew nearer, Lian seemed at last to cheer up. Jennifer made a point of keeping her occupied with holiday preparations. Lian announced through the military and neighborhood grapevines that her home would be open to all guests for Tet.

Two days before the beginning of the holiday, Jennifer moved into Lian's house to help her shop for and cook the food for the celebration. She took only a few outfits with her, including her turquoise *ao dai*. Chris's M-16 lay on the floor under her bed.

Although Lian's modern home had a gas stove, she also possessed several charcoal grills and ovens, which, Jennifer learned, many Vietnamese women preferred to modern gas appliances. A small red clay stove sat on Lian's kitchen table, an American Weber on her patio, and there was even a tiny charcoal burner not much larger than a soup bowl for use on the dining-room table.

Jennifer learned to wake up early, in order to get to the market for the best choices of meats and produce. She and

Lian met in the kitchen to share a pot of tea that Lian brewed each morning. When Lian was alone, she'd drink her first cup of the day right in her kitchen, then keep the tea warm by covering the pot with a British tea cozy. If guests arrived unexpectedly during the day, which wasn't unusual, the beverage could be quickly reheated.

Lian's favorite tea was made from leaves harvested in the central mountain province of Dalat. She called it *Blau* tea and mixed it with crushed, dried lotus blossoms as her father's mother had taught her. During the few days she was with Lian, Jennifer also grew to love the heady, sweet scent of the brewing leaves. After drinking a cup, they shopped for the day's ingredients, then returned to the house for a quick "breakfast."

Her first morning meal at Lian's home came as a shock. Jennifer, who'd survived boarding school on nothing more than buttered toast and coffee to start her day, was presented with a large steaming bowl of soup.

"I don't think I'm ready for this," she muttered, casting Lian an apologetic look.

"It is called Hanoi Soup," Lian explained. "You will find it very nourishing and easy to digest."

Jennifer poked at the hearty chunks of beef with her spoon. Slender, clear noodles swam in a translucent brown broth along with onions, bean sprouts, scallions, and something that looked like parsley.

"Coriander," Lian supplied when asked.

Jennifer sniffed the steam. It smelled of ginger and cinnamon. Lian reached across the table and squeezed a few drops of lime juice into her own bowl.

"You should eat a good breakfast," Lian scolded, as she began eating.

"You sound like my mother, but she never made me sit down to a bowl of soup in the morning."

"Suit yourself."

Not wanting to be rude, Jennifer took a taste of the broth, then a spoonful of vegetables, and at last a slice of the meat.

"This is good," she admitted, surprised. The warm liquid

was soothing, and the vegetables and meat felt as if they'd provide energy throughout the day.

The next morning she asked if they could have the same breakfast, and Lian smilingly agreed that there was enough left over.

Shopping for groceries was a new experience for Jennifer. Back home, their cook had done all that. Cooking was another skill she'd never learned.

Lian ignored her protests of ignorance and quickly enlisted her in picking out both green and ripe coconuts, fresh pineapples, carrots, and a selection of fresh lettuce, coriander, cucumbers, and mint for her fresh raw vegetable platters. Shallots, lemon grass, leeks, little bottles of anchovy sauce, lovely crunchy bamboo shoots, banana leaves, rice sticks, Chinese sausages, bok choy, mung beans, dried and fresh mushrooms were located and purchased.

They bartered with street vendors, ducked into cramped shops where shelves were lined with strangely colored bottles and cellophane sacks full of mystical ingredients. Jennifer loved those two mornings out among the people. By then she'd learned to ignore the American military buses with chicken wire tacked over windows to thwart grenades, the roadside bunkers, even the flares and tracer bullets in the night sky over Saigon. To her, as to the people in the streets, the war's presence had become routine.

She and Lian spent the remainder of the two days before Tet cooking. Jennifer enjoyed feeling the ingredients between her fingertips as she followed Lian's patient instructions. They prepared hundreds of petite spring rolls—crab, noodle, and vegetable fillings bound up in thin rice-paper circles. They made *Banh Chung*, traditional Vietnamese New Year's cakes formed from mung beans, pork, and sweet rice. They also made shrimp pâté and Saigon Soup and dozens of other delicacies, including Lian's beloved glazed pork.

By mid-afternoon of the first day, Jennifer was exhausted, but Lian was still going strong, her delicate fingers working steadily, her humor soaring as she labored in the steamy kitchen, chatting happily, relating the history of each dish to Jennifer. It was clear the activity was good for her, taking her mind off her distant loved ones.

Jennifer couldn't help thinking about her own parents. The month before, they'd sent Christmas gifts that were far too expensive and impractical. Later came a New Year's card, signed by her mother for both of them. Jennifer assumed her father had refused to have anything to do with it.

She felt no bitterness toward him. Coming to Vietnam had set her apart from him. For the first time in her life, she was doing something that had nothing to do with being a Swanson. Perhaps he resented her freedom as much as she gloried in it. But she was neither trying to please nor to provoke him. She was simply following her heart, and she felt stronger, happier than she had for as long as she could remember.

On the afternoon before Tet, Jennifer sat in Lian's kitchen sipping a cup of lotus tea. Lian cleared space at the long table in the middle of the room and announced, "Now, we will make the dish that was served at my wedding."

Hearing the catch in Lian's voice, Jennifer glanced up. "He'll be home soon," she said softly. "The war can't last much longer."

"It has lasted since before I was born. Of course, then the French were here."

Unbidden, an image of Chris standing beneath her helicopter on the landing zone at Cu Chi flashed across Jennifer's mind. She made her decision in that moment. It no longer mattered whether or not he felt anything for her, whether or not she could find the exact words to tell him how she felt. After the holiday, she'd write him a long letter. The worst that could happen was he'd write back informing her that she meant nothing to him. That would hurt, but she had to *know*. Life was too terribly short to keep one's feelings secret.

"Think about next year's Tet," she murmured to Lian. "Nguyen will be home then." *Chris will be back in the States. And so will I.* The thought sent a stinging melancholy wave through her nerves. Would they be together when they went home?

Not wanting to think about that just now, Jennifer jumped down from the stool and asked with forced enthusiasm, "What are we making?"

"It is called 'Jade Hidden in the Mountain.' The dish will take the entire afternoon to make," Lian warned, "but it will be worth it."

By that evening, Jennifer was convinced that all of their hard work had indeed been rewarded. The final dish was truly striking: a mountain of rice studded with bright green peas (symbolizing the hidden jade) was decorated with colorfully prepared bits of chicken, shredded egg pancake, beet, carrot, and boiled ham. At the pinnacle, Lian placed a single fresh chrysanthemum blossom—red, for good luck.

Lian's graceful fingertips plucked the vivid blossom from atop the mountain of rice and vegetables: the signal for the party to begin. Everyone clapped.

The traditional welcome cup of tea had already been served. Several American soldiers in civvies circulated throughout the crowd, passing out glasses of wine. As everyone strolled through the house and garden, conversation was light and happy.

Jennifer was delighted for Lian. Friends from the embassy, from dozens of government and civilian support organizations in the city, had all come. There were American enlisted men and officers, South Vietnamese soldiers with their wives and children, even a few of the Korean officers who served on the international force.

Jennifer helped serve, joking with the soldiers, joining in on conversations about the local horse races and soccer games. Everyone seemed obsessed with soccer. The highest ranked military team was scheduled to play the stevedores. The military team was favored to win.

Second to soccer, Jennifer was the center of interest. Marine recons back from the DMZ, army grunts, special-forces rangers from near Saigon and far away into the highlands, navy SEALS (Sea, Air, and Land specialists) from the Mekong Delta—all passing through Saigon—stopped to pay their respects to Lian. But they also wanted to thank the woman whose voice had soothed and entertained them while they were on duty.

"You're great, Jennifer," one young soldier told her. "I listen to every show. But you should sing more. Anyone can play records. Only you can sing like you do."

"I'll see if the program manager will let me do more," she said.

She wished them all well, signed helmet covers, boonie caps, and anything else they brought that they'd later carry back with them as a good-luck token while they fought. She autographed more than one pair of undershorts.

As the joyous afternoon wore on, some guests left to call at other homes and more replaced them. Several of Lian's most frequent customers at the club showed up. Jennifer immediately recognized Bill Jacobs, the freckled redhead who spent a lot of time at the USO.

For almost an hour he followed Lian around the room, but never seemed to work up enough nerve to speak to her. Jennifer smiled. The young man was clearly entranced by her friend. When she knew no one was close enough to hear, she snuck up behind him.

"Why don't you just tell her, Bill?" she whispered over his shoulder.

He spun around with a horrified expression. "Oh, Jennifer! It's you."

She laughed. "You're being awfully obvious."

"Jeez," he groaned, shaking his head. "Am I that bad?"

"'Fraid so."

His puppy-dog eyes trailed Lian in her white and gold *ao dai*, the back panel of sheer overdress floating out behind her.

"She looks like a beautiful butterfly," murmured Bill, then his eyes dulled. "She's married, huh?"

"Right," Jennifer said, watching his expression.

"Why is she always alone?"

"Her husband's ARVN. Stationed somewhere up north."

172

"If I were him, I'd refuse to stay away so long. I just couldn't do it, ya know." He looked squarely at Jennifer. "I'd be here, taking care of her."

"She told me that he considers it an honor to defend his country. His family lines have been traced back to the last emperors."

"Honor," he said quietly. "It's an excuse for everything: war, murder, deserting someone you love."

Jennifer put a hand on his arm. "Why don't you let her know how you feel?" she suggested. Something told her that Lian would find a way to let him down easily. She dealt with so many young soldiers tactfully.

He drew his tongue over his top lip, staring at Lian as she stepped through the French doors and out to the garden. Without saying another word, he slowly followed.

It was only after Bill had left that Jennifer became aware of someone standing very close beside her, watching. She turned toward him with a prepared smile, ready to chat with yet another young soldier who'd heard her show.

"Hello, Jen," he said, his voice spilling warm ash into her veins. Heat built, swelling, pressing into and through the tiniest furrows of her body until it filled her.

"Chris," she whispered helplessly.

He didn't exactly smile, but his eyes fixed on hers in a way that made it clear he was being rewarded by seeing her. He wore dress khakis and was scrubbed clean and shaved. His short brown hair smelled of a recent shampoo.

"Oh, Chris!" she repeated, in ecstasy.

It was all she could do to keep herself from throwing her arms around his neck and covering him with kisses. But she was aware that only time and her own imagination might have imbued their brief encounters with intimacy. At the firebase, all he'd done to show he cared was to give her a gun. Not exactly your classic token of undying love, she thought ruefully.

"I heard about Lian's Tet bash," he said in a hoarse voice.

"Well, well, great!" What was she supposed to say? She felt giddy, weak-kneed, incapable of rational conversation.

"I'm . . . I'm glad you came." To her own ears, her voice seemed pitched at least an octave higher than normal. Her pulse thudded in her ears like a mortar barrage.

Chris's blue eyes were riveted to her face. "I am, too."

"How did you ever manage to get leave? I heard that Cu Chi has been a hotbed of VC activity for months."

For the first time she could recall, one corner of his lips lifted in a gesture of humor. "Let's just say I took an informal leave."

"Chris!" she gasped, sounding appropriately appalled. She was, in fact, thrilled. "You're not AWOL, are you?"

"It's not AWOL if they don't know I'm gone. A couple guys are covering for me."

His eyes were fixed on her with such force, she might have been the only woman in the room—or the world! They stood without speaking for endless minutes. Jennifer was at a loss to explain why the intensity of his stare had brought on this frustrating attack of mental paralysis. After all, being stared at was part of her job. She *was* the show on her tours to the firebases and landing zones. However, there was something about the tender way Chris's gaze moved over her features, as if memorizing the tiniest detail: the subtlest telling quiver of her mouth, her lashes, even her nostrils betrayed her practiced composure.

At last she managed to break the silence. "How did you manage to get so far without—"

"I hitched rides—military vehicles, donkey carts, walked some."

"You're going to get yourself court-martialed."

"No I won't." He took her fingertips in his hand. His voice was low, even, almost matter-of-fact, as if all that would follow was a simple matter of fate. "The camp was quiet when I left. All anyone wants to do is sleep when it's like that. They won't be going anywhere."

Jennifer's eyes drifted toward the garden. Lian and Bill were standing close together. Lian was smiling softly at him, and he looked delirious with joy.

"Listen," Chris began, his voice tightening another notch,

"can you break away from here for a while? We could take a walk down by the river."

Despite her eagerness to be with him, Jennifer hesitated. She hadn't accepted a date with anyone other than Jeffrey since she'd been in Saigon. She'd sensed early on that she might wind up with more than she could handle if she found herself alone behind closed doors with a GI who'd been away from home—and American women—for six months or more.

Chris gently squeezed her fingers and drew her a little closer to whisper with a hint of urgency. "Come on. A little air won't kill you. And I'll be right there in case of snipers."

"Very encouraging," she murmured dryly.

He wasn't kidding. Only last week an air force major had been killed when somebody in the crowd outside a theater tossed a grenade into his Land-Rover. A few days before that there had been a rash of fatal stabbings. Viet Cong wielding easily concealed hypodermic needles had infiltrated the Central Market and randomly attacked Americans.

Now, gazing up into Chris's blue eyes, she didn't care. More to the point, she simply didn't think about those dangers. She knew he would never let anyone hurt her. It was written in the steadfast expression in his eyes and the unfaltering line of his tightly set lips.

"Okay," she agreed.

They walked hand-in-hand, without speaking, down Chung Quay Street, past the U.S. Embassy and the Majestic Hotel to the river's edge. The docks were quiet and nearly deserted due to the holiday. Sampans floated lazily. The sweet, sooty smell of charcoal burners was everywhere, wafting from the decks of the wooden boats.

"Why are you here, Chris?" she asked, when they finally reached the water.

"You mean, why am I in Vietnam? You *know* why I've come back to Saigon today."

"Yes," she whispered, barely daring to acknowledge the thrill his words sent rippling through her.

He tipped his head to one side. "Coming to Nam seemed the thing to do at the time. And I guess a part of me expected that I could do more good here than at home."

"Have you?"

He shook his head, then seemed belatedly to reconsider. "It depends on what you mean. When I enlisted, I figured I'd come over and sort of help finish up the war—just so it would be over. Once I got here, though, I could see it wasn't going to end. At least, not the way we want it to."

Jennifer was struck with a pang of sorrow. While in Lian's house she'd found respite from the war. Though Jennifer now had Chris to herself at last, a moment she'd dreamed of, she realized his presence could also cause a considerable amount of pain.

He continued, "I feel as if, well—it's hard to say this . . ." He gave her the direct look she'd found so disconcerting on the plane and at the market. "There's a handful of guys who wouldn't be alive now if I hadn't come."

"Do you believe in fate?" she asked softly.

"I don't know."

"Well, I do," she stated. "Maybe you were supposed to come here. Maybe one of those soldiers whose life you saved will one day become president. If you hadn't been here, the course of history would have been altered."

He stared at her as though trying to decide if she were teasing.

Jennifer giggled, feeling intoxicated into playfulness although she'd had just one glass of wine all afternoon. Why did being around this young soldier from Montana turn her inside out? She'd never felt less in control of her emotions.

"Are you saying you and I were fated to meet?" he asked.

She stopped walking and turned to face him.

This time a full, dazzling smile played across his masculine lips. His eyes twinkled with amusement.

"Now you're making fun of me," she accused him.

"Am I?"

She wrinkled her nose. "Are you?"

Chris began walking again, pulling her along before she could give his comment any more thought.

176

"Tell me about yourself," he demanded, slipping an arm behind her. The long muscles of his biceps and forearm pressed through the khaki cloth of his sleeve and around her waist.

Leaning blissfully against his shoulder as they walked, she described her life in Marblehead. Then she asked Chris to tell his story.

He spoke quickly, as if wanting to get it over with. She made him slow down.

"What was your favorite thing to do in Missoula on a Saturday?" she asked.

"Take my motorbike outside town into the scrub," he said without hesitation. "Just ride and ride, until I hadn't seen a soul for an hour or more. Anything to get away from my parents' house and the shop."

"The shop?"

"I worked as a mechanic in a garage." He let out a wry laugh. "Guess your old man would think that was pretty small potatoes."

"Probably," she admitted. Then seeing his face fall, she added quickly, "But I don't give a damn. Are you very good at working on engines?"

His face lit up. "The best," he told her with endearing smugness. "But no matter how great I might be at fixing engines, that's nothing compared to your voice. You'll probably sing professionally when you go home, won't you?"

"I really haven't given it much thought," she admitted. "Maybe I will."

"What kind of singing would you do? You're too good to do clubs and stuff—unless they're very ritzy."

"I'm not above working hard," she said defensively.

"I know. I've heard you." The admiration in his voice made her feel warm inside.

Jennifer smiled, then looked around them. To her surprise, they'd walked well over a mile by now. It was getting dark.

"We'd better turn back," she said reluctantly.

He hasn't even tried to kiss me, she thought, although he'd had plenty of time. And the more she dwelled on that one point, the less she liked the idea of being the one to make the first move. Was it possible he wasn't interested in her in that way?

The fact that his arm was still around her could mean nothing. Many GIs felt a need to touch her, as if to reassure themselves she was real and not just a phantom voice. His protectiveness was sweet, but not particularly unusual either. Her pilots would lay down their lives for her.

Jennifer realized in that moment that her heart simply couldn't withstand another rejection from Chris. She clung to the safety of the small signs of affection he'd already allowed her. She wouldn't push.

"I had no intention of leaving Lian's party for so long," she said as they came to a stop.

"I should be getting back, too." They stopped in front of a shop, simply looking at each other, unaware of the many families passing by on their rounds of visits. Then, with a suddenness that tore the breath from her lungs, Chris pulled her into his arms.

His lips closed warmly over hers. She didn't pull away, sensing that he'd back off with the slightest protest from her. She luxuriated in the rock-hard muscles of his stomach crushing her breasts. He was so much taller than she. She reached her arms up around his neck and smoothed her fingertips over the short hairs at the back of his neck.

Jennifer had kissed boys before. She'd kissed men before. But her head had never spun this way. Liquid fire hadn't shot through her veins as it did now. Time seemed to cease. The war, obligations to Lian, any sense of where she stood, all flew away into the dusk. Her past and her future dissolved into this one dizzy, rapturous moment.

Chris's lips tenderly parted hers. She clung to him shakily, afraid of nothing in the world except the knowledge that his kiss must sometime end. Fiercely she held on to him, willing her body to remember every tingling inch of skin that pressed against his. *Stay with me! Don't let this end!* her soul sang and pleaded.

She never heard the warning whine, only felt the rocket

hit some fifty yards from where they stood. It exploded with an enormous crack, sending glass and splinters flying from a row of shops.

Chris swore, dragging her down onto the pavement. He covered her head and shoulders with his body.

Jennifer was shaking, trying to breathe, trying to talk all at once. "Wh-what's going on?"

"I don't know."

Something that sounded like a mortar hit in the direction of Tu Do Street. There was small arms fire from closer to where they lay on the ground.

"We'd better get you back to your friends," he said, his voice taut.

She reached up, encircling his neck with her arms, keeping him down on the ground with her.

"You're going back to your platoon, aren't you?" she demanded.

"Yeah."

"I wish you didn't have to."

Chris stared into her pleading eyes for at least five of her heartbeats. He lay flush on top of her, saying nothing. She could feel his arousal.

As if finally realizing how vulnerable they were, he shot to his feet, lifted her off the pavement and ran, carrying her toward a nearby ditch. He jumped into it with her still in his arms and immediately sat down with his back to the dirt, cradling her as another shell detonated a few blocks away.

Jennifer took his face in her trembling hands and pulled it down, kissing him on the mouth, squeezing her eyes closed to shut out the wild scene around them. People were running out of shops and houses, shouting and crying. Shells continued hitting randomly, both close and far away, but all Jennifer could think of was Chris. He was so forthright, so handsome and strong and vulnerable, too. She wanted only to stay in this ditch forever with him, and forget about everything else.

"Jen," he said, gasping against her mouth, "it's not safe. Oh, God—I want to stay. But it's too dangerous for you!"

Before she could respond, he'd stood and, with one last

regretful gaze, tugged her to her feet. They leapt out of the ditch and ran, hand-in-hand, in the comparative shelter of shop fronts. People were appearing in crowds now, assessing the damage even as the mortars continued. Sirens shrieked and spotlights scanned the darkening sky. While Chris's hand firmly gripped hers, they flew through the back streets, away from the docks and their precious, stolen moments in each other's arms.

13

Jeeps and cars loaded with guests pulled away from Lian's house. The faces of the men were grim, the holiday mood had evaporated into the air like the early morning vapors above the river.

A thirty-six-hour cease-fire had been planned to honor the lunar New Year, but the Viet Cong had taken advantage of the first stages of the lull in American bombing to infiltrate all the country's major cities.

Jennifer heard two senior officers talking as they awaited their drivers. "Da Nang is being hit hard," one stated. It was the second largest city in the country. She was shocked. If Da Nang was in jeopardy, what about Saigon? But maybe the communists were concentrating their energies to the north. "Guerrillas have mortared the airfield there," the officer continued. "Four F-4 Phantoms and two A-6 Intruders were destroyed, that's all we've heard so far."

A rocket hit close enough to Lian's house to make the walls shake. Jennifer clung to Chris, numbly watching through the front window.

"I have to leave," he said, his voice raspy with emotion.

"I know."

"You're shaking." His arms enclosed her from behind, and she leaned back against his warm, hard chest, closing her eyes, desperately trying to imagine herself far away from here. Back in Marblehead, with Chris on her father's yacht, the *Good Fortune*. But the noise and vibrations of shells impacting on cement and buildings tore at her nerves and made it impossible to forget where they were.

"Go with the others back to the embassy," Chris said in her ear.

She gazed up at him.

"Will it be safe there?"

"Safer than here."

She looked at Lian who was seeing her guests off in much the same manner as she would have under happier circumstances, wishing them health and reunion with their families in the coming year. The scene seemed eerie. Lian, on the surface, so calm, yet everyone around her near hysteria. After all the men had gone would be the hardest time for her dear friend, for reality was bound to set in.

"I can't," she said, suddenly sure of herself. "I have to stay with Lian."

Chris took her by the shoulders. "Jen, she'll be better off without you."

She frowned up at him, not understanding. "What are you talking about?"

"If they find her with an American, what do you suppose they'll do to her?"

Jennifer swallowed around the jagged lump in her throat. "Do?" she murmured.

Chris nodded. "Look. You can't let them find you. If the sappers . . . the infiltrators get into Saigon in any numbers, it won't be the odd grenade tossed under a Jeep anymore. It'll be out-and-out combat in the streets, Jen. Go back to the embassy. Take Lian with you if you must, but go!"

"All right," she promised, tearfully. "Chris?"

"Yeah?" He was walking away from her, into one of the bedrooms.

Jennifer followed him. He began stripping off his crisp uniform, replacing it with fatigues he'd left on the bed, tied in a bundle. He'd apparently worn them into the city, somehow picking up clean clothing before coming to the party.

She shuddered as he strapped on a pistol, cartridge belt, grenades, and other assorted equipment. He pulled out a roll of black tape and secured everything, to keep it from clinking when he moved. His arms were bare below the edge of his T-shirt, the muscles tensed. His blue eyes flashed coldly, and she could almost see the physical transformation taking place between the man who'd held and kissed her so tenderly and a man who could kill as automatically as he'd butter a slice of toast.

"Chris? Will you be all right?" How could she ask for assurances? But she needed to hear him tell her he'd be fine, even if he were lying. Later, she'd remember the words and repeat them in her mind to keep from going mad.

"I'll make it," he said, his voice tight. Then he looked up at her sharply. "Don't wait. Take the first possible car. You still have the M-16?"

She nodded, unable to speak more for fear of tears.

"Keep it with you," he cautioned.

Her fingertips reached up, then trailed down his cheek, and she flung herself into his arms as he started to turn away.

Chris lifted her chin and kissed her so hard the pressure of his lips and teeth hurt. She didn't mind. She wanted to feel his touch for as long as possible after he'd left her.

He released her. And when she opened her eyes, he was gone.

For several minutes, she was so overcome with fear for Chris that she couldn't move. It was ludicrous of him to try to return to his company at Cu Chi. He should have stayed with her! Who would have blamed him? Couldn't he just say he'd been trapped in the city?

But she knew that, even if he'd been able to get away with it, he wouldn't have stayed. He'd have felt as if he were deserting his friends. She both hated and loved him for doing his duty and leaving her. Jennifer sank onto the bed, feeling numb and sick to her stomach.

Why had she let this happen to her? He'd been right, of course, when he told her back in the market that she should let him go his own way. If he were killed and she survived, how could she face going home? Nor was there any guaranteed future for them even if he did make it. Simply because he'd kissed her, he wasn't proclaiming a lasting love. He was just a young man from Montana who took incredible chances to visit a radio singer.

Lian found her sometime later, sitting in the dark on the bed with her face buried in her palms. Jennifer felt her friend's hand on her shoulder and looked up.

"They are all gone," Lian murmured. Her face was white, her lips tinged blue with fear. She had finally run out of strength.

Jennifer sighed and wiped at her eyes. "We can't stay here, Lian."

"There is nowhere to go."

"Chris says we should go to the embassy compound. We'll be safe there."

"If the VC have made it into the city," Lian said quietly, "no place will be safe."

Jennifer grabbed her friend by the shoulders and hugged her. "Don't say that! We're going now." She jumped up and fished Chris's gun out from under the bed. She stuffed spare ammunition clips into the satin pockets of her pants and, dragging a protesting Lian after her, ran outside.

A tank rumbled past. Jeeps and military trucks careened down the road, dodging fresh craters. Jennifer dropped Lian's hand and dashed into the street, waving frantically. The next Jeep stopped with a screech.

"Can you take us to the American compound?" Jennifer asked, gasping, as Lian caught up with her.

The driver scowled. "I'm supposed to pick up General Kelly at the Majestic." In that second, he recognized her and grinned. "Hey, it's *you!* A 'Night with Jennifer,' right?"

She took this as a yes and pushed Lian into the Jeep. "Cut

across Le Loi Boulevard. It'll take five minutes. The general will never know," she promised.

He shoved the Jeep into gear, and they sped through darkened streets. Women scurried through the devastation, pulling away pieces of shattered boarding, crying out names of loved ones.

Jennifer glanced at Lian. Agony was reflected in her pretty eyes, which had turned dull and lifeless. *How horrible it must be to see war in one's own country,* Jennifer thought.

When they reached the embassy, they discovered the Marine guards had shut the gates. Jennifer dragged a limp Lian from the Jeep a second before the driver sped off. The guards recognized her, but refused to allow Lian in. Jennifer argued with them for five tense minutes before a rocket landing somewhere on the next block made the decision for them. They opened the gate in the six-foot-high wall topped with barbed wire.

Once inside, the two women found other civilians running along with them.

"Oh, Jennifer!" Gloria's shrill cry echoed between the sounds of exploding shells and the chatter of automatic fire in the night. "It's so awful. Come this way to the basement shelter."

"Have you seen Jeffrey?" Jennifer shouted as they ducked into an underground shelter.

Gloria shook her head. "Somebody said he was driving a dignitary to the airport."

"In *this?*"

Gloria nodded.

Jennifer looked around the concrete-walled room for the first time. People stood in groups, nervously swapping rumors. Somebody was saying the guerrillas had hit seven major cities throughout the country, and that the city of Hue had virtually been taken over by the communists. Another claimed he'd seen VC officers in the street just behind the embassy.

A girl started crying in a high-pitched keen. Jennifer spun around to see the young American standing with three other teenagers trying to comfort her. They looked close to hysteria themselves. They appeared to be about sixteen years old.

"Are there blankets or mattresses?" she asked Gloria. "It would help if we could make people more comfortable."

"I think there might be some in those lockers over there. I'll check."

Jennifer, Lian, and Gloria busied themselves unrolling thin sleeping pads and calming the most frightened of the twenty-three people in the shelter.

Jennifer glanced at her watch and was surprised to see that it was nearly three A.M. She carried a blanket to the top of the stairs, knowing a Marine guard would be stationed there. When she tried the latch, it was locked. She knocked.

A young man opened the door a crack. All she could see was a pitch-black corridor and the glint from his eyes when the light from below caught them. The sound of small arms fire was loud now. The guerrillas must be close.

"I thought you might be able to use a blanket," she offered uncertainly, then realized the man would be unable to lie down.

He ignored the blanket. "Anyone down there know how to handle a gun?" he asked.

"Me," Jennifer said. "I have an M-16."

"Take this, too . . . in case." He thrust a pistol through the crack, into her hand. "It's a .45-caliber automatic. Loaded and safety's off."

"Thank you."

She shut the door, then said a silent prayer for him before returning to the others.

The shelling continued without pause, and the automatic weapons fire grew so loud that everyone guessed a number of guerrillas must have managed to breach the walls of the embassy grounds.

Jennifer sat to one side of the foot of the stairs, her back pressed against the cement wall, Chris's gun across her lap. One of the men from the embassy leaned against the opposite wall, the .45 propped between two hands. If just one or two guerrillas came down the stairs, they had a chance of picking them off. Gloria and Lian had found some supplies and made instant coffee from jarred water warmed over a heat can. Everything they could possibly do to protect themselves and calm the group had been done.

They sat waiting out the endless minutes that slowly turned to hours. Jennifer thought of Chris. How would he ever make it safely back to Cu Chi in this madness? And what horrors would he have to face once there? It didn't seem fair. She'd at last found someone she cared about, someone who'd awoken a passion she hadn't even known existed, but cruel events were conspiring to keep them apart.

Six hours later, the reports of nearby guns suddenly stopped. Rockets landed only sporadically and at more distant targets.

There was a knock on the door. Everyone jumped to their feet. Jennifer held the M-16 in front of her, flipped the selector lever to semi, and stepped into the stairwell facing the door above.

"It's Lieutenant Kjordski," a voice called out. "The compound is secure."

Jennifer let out a long breath. Others in the room burst into nervous conversation.

Lian ran up the stairs to greet the lieutenant. When he appeared in the shelter beside the Vietnamese woman, Jennifer winced. His face was strained and white. There was a bloody scrape down one side of his lean cheek, and he was holding one arm tightly across his ribs as if a couple might be broken.

"The guards," Jennifer said tensely, "are they . . ."

He was shaking his head. "Two marines were killed, and five MPs. Is everyone here okay?"

Jennifer nodded. The man who'd helped her guard the stairwell thanked the lieutenant and told him they were in excellent shape. Jennifer collapsed on the floor, the M-16 in her lap. Her hands began to shake uncontrollably.

She stared at the weapon, feeling nothing but disgust for it, yet not daring to let it go. Kjordski wasn't the marine who'd given her his pistol. Instinctively, she knew their guard hadn't survived the attack.

"Are we allowed to leave?" Lian asked.

"You can stay or go," the lieutenant said wearily.

Lian looked at Jennifer. "Maybe you would feel safer here, but I cannot stay. I must return to my home."

"Then I'll go with you," Jennifer said quickly.

"If you wait an hour there will be someone to escort you back to your house, ma'am," the Marine officer told Lian. He was being polite, but Jennifer could hear a brittle edge to his voice. Several comrades-in-arms had just been killed by Vietnamese. At that moment, he wasn't particularly trustful of anyone except other Americans.

Two army enlisted men drove them back through streets littered with debris, mortar holes—and, worst of all, corpses. Jennifer had never felt so utterly desolate in her life. The deaths were random: women and children in most cases. They were the ones who had been left at home while their husbands, brothers, and uncles were off fighting.

Military vehicles rumbled urgently through alleys. Small contingents of air force commandos in green fatigues—.45s drawn and belts of shiny cartridges crisscrossing their chests—scuttled from shop to shop, kicking open doors in their hunt for guerrillas. Jennifer spotted one lobbing a grenade blindly into a house before running in with his machine gun firing. She shut her eyes, feeling nauseated. Had there been a child in there, making a suspicious noise? Or a mother hiding her aging parents?

All the way back to Lian's house, she wondered which she hated more: being here or someday having to return to the tidy, ignorant life she'd once lived. Nothing in her life would ever be the same.

The Jeep pulled up in front of Lian's home. One of the soldiers stayed outside with the two women while the other searched the house to make sure guerrillas weren't hiding inside.

When he reappeared, he took Jennifer aside. "You sure you want to stay here with her?" he asked in a low voice.

"I'm sure," Jennifer told him in a clear voice. Then she spoke less sharply, because, she guessed, he and the other GIs were under tremendous pressure and should be forgiven their momentary prejudices. "Thank you for checking the house."

"No problem. By the way, you'd better stay inside. Keep the doors locked until you hear on the radio that the city's secure."

"How long will that be?"

"Probably by tomorrow everything will be under control. Umm—" He grinned suddenly and yanked a folded brochure out of his pocket. She recognized it as one of the advertisements AFVN had distributed the first week she'd been in-country. It had a picture of her in a minidress, her blond hair loose around her shoulders, her smile flirtatious. "Would you mind autographing this?" he asked timidly.

She did, marveling at the insanity of her life in Saigon: so close to death one minute, greeting fans the next.

Jennifer and Lian spent their next few hours doing busy work: anything to take their minds off of the night before, the horrid things they'd seen on the ride back from the compound, their private fears. Jennifer couldn't stop worrying about Chris. And Lian was so uncharacteristically quiet that Jennifer was sure her friend was preoccupied with thoughts of her husband. Lian had told her he'd last been stationed near Hue. If the rumors were true, it was the hardest hit of all South Vietnamese cities, virtually VC territory now.

All the food from the party had been left out and remained untouched since they'd fled to the embassy. It was now ten o'clock on Wednesday morning.

"We'd better throw it all away," Lian said with a sigh.

"No. I'm sure there is some that won't have spoiled." Jennifer tested several items from a fresh vegetable platter that had been set over ice. Although the ice had melted, the carrots were still crisp. "This stuff is okay. And the rice can be reheated."

They spent an hour determining which dishes might be safely kept and which had to be tossed. Lian thought it a good idea to keep as much as possible, since food might be scarce for several days.

Jennifer's legs ached and her eyes burned from lack of

sleep. She longed to lie down, but she was afraid to let her guard down for even a moment. What would prevent a guerrilla from breaking into the house even now? By this time any VC left in the city would be frantically searching for hiding places to elude the patrolling American soldiers. If they could wait out the day, they'd have a better chance of sneaking out of the city under cover of darkness.

Together the two women nailed shut all the windows and both doors in preparation for nightfall. Jennifer pulled Lian's couch in front of the patio doors and stretched out on it, cradling Chris's rifle across her stomach. She realized she didn't know how many bullets were in the clip. Sitting up, she hit the magazine release button, checked to find that the clip held eighteen rounds, then replaced it.

Feeling wired, she had to force herself to lie down again and shut her eyes. Jennifer knew she couldn't possibly sleep.

Sometime later, she slowly raised her eyelids to discover Lian kneeling in front of her with a cup of lotus-scented tea.

Jennifer propped herself up on one elbow and took a sip. "Did I fall asleep?"

"Yes." Lian herself looked ready to drop. Deep black shadows encircled her delicate lashes. The whites of her eyes were an unhealthy pink.

Jennifer glanced at her watch. "Five o'clock? I was out that long?"

"You needed the rest," Lian said. "I watched the door."

"Well, it's my turn now," Jennifer insisted. "I promise, I'll wake you up in six hours."

Lian agreed and disappeared into her bedroom. Almost immediately the telephone rang.

The sound startled Jennifer. She'd assumed they were cut off from the outside world and wondered if she should answer. Finally, she couldn't ignore it.

"Hello?"

"My God, Jennifer! Is that you?"

"Jeffrey!" she cried, sitting heavily on the floor with the telephone in her lap. It was so good to hear his voice. "Are you all right?"

190

"Am *I* all right? I heard you were in the embassy when the VC went over the walls!"

"Yes," she said, and described the terrifying long hours they'd spent huddled in the basement.

"Look, Jennifer, I don't think it's a good idea to be at Lian's house right now."

"Why not?" she demanded stiffly. "She's my friend. She needs me."

He groaned. "Jennifer. Come back to the American compound. You'll be safer here."

"Safer!" she screamed. "Do you realize how easy it was for those sappers to break into the compound? Right outside our door, seven American GIs died. I'm just as safe here as I am in the compound. And besides, the military escort that brought us here said that by tomorrow the city should be secure."

There was a long silence on the other end of the line.

"Jeffrey. He was right, wasn't he?"

"We won't know for a while," he said at last.

"What does that mean?" she demanded. "Is this more of your confidential and secret crap?" She was so nervous and frightened and furious she'd twisted the phone cord in knots around her clenched fist. Her knuckles were turning blue from lack of blood.

Jeffrey sighed long and loud into the telephone. "Can't you just take my advice without all these questions?"

"No! Tell me what's going on."

"Will you come back to the compound?"

"I'll decide after you tell me what's going on," she repeated.

"For the most part, the city's calming down now. The ambassador has been informed that at least eighty percent of Saigon is under U.S. or ARVN control. But several districts, Cholon among them, are still overrun with VC and you're very near there. It's dangerous, Jennifer. Any American is a walking target."

"I'll stay inside."

"You'd damn well better." She could tell by the stifled

sound of his voice that he was gritting his teeth. "Do you two have enough food and water?"

"Yes."

"And you're locked in?"

"Snug as two little bugs," she said, trying to make him laugh. He didn't. "Jeffrey?"

"Yeah?"

"How long before this is over?"

What she'd intended was the siege of Saigon. But his answer could have meant the war.

"There's no telling, Jennifer Lynn. Just, for God's sake, don't go outside!"

14

A curfew was imposed on the city from ten P.M. to six A.M., but few people dared leave their homes at any time of the day or night. There was no electricity; Lian lit candles after dark, using them sparingly to prolong the meager supply. The telephone mysteriously stopped working. During the day the streets outside Lian's window remained deserted, eerily quiet. But, at night, Jennifer and Lian could hear men in the streets, going from door to door.

Sometimes they could hear American voices, cursing the "gooks" they couldn't locate. And sometimes Jennifer would peer out a window into the moonlight and see other men, dressed in black, running and stopping to stealthily try doors and windows. At two in the morning, Jennifer and Lian watched a pair of them drag a man into the street and cold-bloodedly shoot him in the head. Lian suspected the VC had executed him for conspiring with the enemy: the Americans.

Jennifer was shocked, realizing with a numbing chill that because of her work at the USO, Lian would be at the top of any hit list. And she knew that she herself was no less desirable a target. For she not only *was* the enemy, she symbolized the high morale of the American troops. She made the staying and fighting for Americans easier. Executing her would deal U.S. troops a staggering emotional blow.

At other times, they'd hear people shuffling clandestinely through dark streets, like timid mice.

"My neighbors," Lian explained dispassionately. "They are probably going out to find food and water. They chance a trip to a relative's house, or to a shop that will open only to people the owner knows."

"How can you stay so calm?" Jennifer demanded in irritation. She was climbing the walls, shut up like an animal, unable to do anything helpful.

On the third day, they ran out of food. Lian wanted to go out to scavenge that afternoon, but Jennifer wouldn't allow it. That night, Jennifer taught Lian to play poker with cards she'd drawn on cut-up pieces of stationery. Jennifer was dealing, when she heard a soft noise at one of the rear windows.

"Shhhh." She raised a finger to her lips.

Lian froze, wearing a puzzled expression as if she hadn't heard the sound.

Without explaining, Jennifer seized the M-16 from the chair beside her. She quietly slid her own chair away from the table with the backs of her knees and started toward the kitchen. Lian began to follow.

"Stay there!" Jennifer ordered in a hoarse whisper.

If it were the enemy, she wanted to give Lian a chance to run. They'd probably kill an American on the spot, but Lian would be tortured and her body displayed as a lesson to others not to consort with foreigners.

Lian shook her head emphatically at Jennifer and followed anyway.

The kitchen was dark. Two small windows showed only a black sky and a sliver of the white moon.

"I was sure the sound came from here," Jennifer whispered.

She tiptoed toward the nearest window. Standing to one side, she waited. After a moment, the scratching sound came again. Somebody was prying at the window casement.

Jennifer turned and stared helplessly at Lian. Lian's eyes grew wider, blacker in the dark.

With great care, Jennifer moved a wooden chair over to the wall and stood on it so that she could look down on the window. Pressing her cheek to the cool plaster, she stared into the night, her heart thrumming in her ears. Lian hovered behind.

At last she could make out a dark head, and a hand holding what looked like a screwdriver or a knife.

Shutting her eyes briefly, Jennifer fought to steady her breathing. This might be a solitary looter. If so, they could scare him off. But if a guerrilla was breaking in, he probably wasn't alone. If she and Lian tried to escape out the front door, they were bound to be met by his comrades.

But why, she wondered, was he being so careful about getting in? The men she'd seen murder Lian's neighbor could easily break in a door, kill two women, and be gone before anyone realized what had happened.

Jennifer hefted the M-16 and aimed down at the top of the shadowy head. What would happen if she fired the gun with the muzzle angled against the glass? Would the bullet still hit him? Or would it ricochet against the glass and window frame?

In that moment of indecision, a face peered up at her. Blue eyes in the moonlight.

"Chris!" she squealed, dropping the gun.

He smiled from the other side of the window, holding up a warning finger.

Jennifer turned to Lian who'd caught the rifle. "It's Chris. Oh, God! It's okay, Lian." Her heart was pounding crazily, whether it was from relief that she wasn't about to be murdered, or from the joy of seeing him alive again, she couldn't say.

She quickly found a hammer and pried loose the two nails they'd used to secure the window. Chris pulled from the outside. The window slowly slid wide enough for him to squeeze through.

Once inside, he turned and closed it, knocking the nails back into place. That done, he grabbed Jennifer, holding her so tightly to his chest she couldn't breathe. He kissed her fiercely, crushing her cheeks between his palms while she laughed and cried with happiness. He tasted like dust, the Asian brush, and a little like burnt rubber. It was wonderful.

She was sobbing when he pulled back.

"I tried patching a call through from a field phone, but your line was dead," he said. "The embassy told me you'd come back here with Lian. You idiot!"

She kissed him on the mouth. "Oh shut up."

Out of the corner of her eye, she glimpsed Lian slipping discreetly out of the kitchen. Jennifer moved to stop her friend, but Chris held her firmly.

"I said, the telephone is dead."

"I know."

"The city still isn't safe, Jen. Cholon is running with enemy soldiers. You're dangerously close to the worst area."

"So you came all this way to tell me I should go back to the embassy?"

Chris shook his head. "No. I want you to go back to the States."

Jennifer stared at him. "Chris, I can't."

"The hell you can't!" he shouted at her, all softness leaving his eyes.

Until this second, she hadn't realized how weary and worn he looked. In the light of the kitchen candle, she studied him; his face was streaked with charcoal, his camouflage fatigues were smudged with grime. She could feel the side of the AK-47 he'd carried at Cu Chi pressing into her back, for he hadn't put it down since he'd come through the window. His eyes darted around the room, suspicious of the shifting shadows cast by the trees outside in Lian's garden. What had he gone through to reach her?

She felt exultantly grateful that he cared so much for her, while at the same time she felt guilty for causing him such trouble. Jennifer gazed at him lovingly, unable to speak over the tears in her throat.

Seizing her by the arms, Chris shook her. "Jennifer, you can't stay here any longer. You just tell those army bastards you want out. Tell them you've changed your mind."

"How can I do that? Now that I've met you?" she pleaded. Her fingers touched his cheek tenderly. "And I told you I wasn't that kind of person. I don't give up."

Looking desperate and exhausted, he released her. "Jen, forget about what I said when we met. Just get the hell out of this country before it's too late. You're going to get us both killed."

She straightened up indignantly. "I may get myself killed, but that has nothing to do with you, Christopher Tyler."

"Like hell!" he barked at her. "What do you think I've been doing the last three days?"

She shook her head, not understanding.

"I've been *thinking about you!*"

"You have?" she asked softly. Her heart melted like butter on a warm stove top.

"Damn right I have." Suddenly the harshness drifted out of his voice. He enfolded her in his arms again, his lips trembling as they moved over hers. "Jen, I love you."

She surrendered to his embrace, not caring about anything but the fact he was here. He loved her.

"Jen," he murmured between kisses.

"Mmmm?"

"I mean it. I think about you, not myself or the other guys out there. I worry about you. That's not healthy when every sound, every movement in the grass is a warning."

Horrified, she pushed back from him. "You mean it, don't you?"

"Yeah. If I'm not scared out of my mind that some gook's going to shoot a hole in your pretty head, I'm daydreaming about how it felt to kiss you down by the river. And how you . . . you . . ." His hand pressed softly against the side of her breast through her clothes.

An erotic warmth shot through her, leaving her dizzy and breathless.

"Chris," she murmured. "Stay with me."

He tightened. "I came to make sure you were all right, and to get you to the airport."

"I'm not going anywhere," she said stubbornly.

He started to open his mouth as if to say something more,

but she sealed his lips with a hasty kiss. When she pulled away, he gazed at her with hunger.

She whispered, "I can't let you go back out there again without making love to me, Chris. If you're going to dream about me, you might as well have something more than a kiss to inspire you."

"Those lips alone are enough to drive any man crazy," he rasped.

A rocket streaked in, landing just a couple blocks away. She'd learned there was no warning whine when they came straight in on top of you: just the awful sound of it hitting. Jennifer hadn't even flinched at that one.

"Christopher," she said, sighing, "please love me."

He looked uneasily toward the door. "Lian?"

"She understands." *Only too well,* Jennifer thought a little sadly.

His hand came up and stroked her cheek. "I'm dirty. I'm like an animal, Jen, being out there for days. What you're asking for is . . ." His glance dropped away in agony before returning to meet her steady emerald gaze. "You don't know what you're getting into."

"I do know," she lied. How could she tell him now that he was going to be her first? He'd almost certainly leave for fear of hurting her.

They said no more. She picked up a candle and led him to the spare bedroom.

Jennifer started to turn down the bed. Chris's hand stopped her at the sound of another mortar shell striking. He pointed to the floor and she nodded, understanding. It would be safer down low. Another thought struck her: perhaps Chris felt awkward about dirtying Lian's clean sheets with his grimy body.

She pulled a straw mat from a cupboard and spread it on the floor next to the bed. When she turned around, Chris had pulled the doorway curtains closed. At last, he laid down his rifle, unstrapped a side gun from his hip and set it on the floor within arm's reach.

The strangest feeling came over Jennifer. After all the

seductions she'd staged, now that the real thing was here she didn't know what to do. She'd always envisioned being coy and cool, performing a seductive striptease for her lover, driving him wild with passion.

Now she stood in front of Chris, fully clothed, unable to move or even think straight.

His blue eyes sparkled darkly in the candle light. All at once, the intensity of his expression seemed threatening. He was half man, half animal, smeared with dirt to camouflage himself from the night, unbathed and untamed. An involuntary shiver rippled up her spine.

Chris's quick eye spotted her reaction. His hand shot out before she could move away and he gently pushed her down onto the mat.

"Wait," he whispered close to her ear. Then he stood up and disappeared into her bathroom.

Jennifer shut her eyes, nearly weeping in frustration. How could she show even an ounce of revulsion? He'd risked his life to be with her!

She was vaguely aware of the sound of running water. When Chris reappeared a moment later, he was without his fatigues and camouflage makeup. He strode naked across the bedroom toward her. Reddish-brown hair curled across his muscled chest, drifting down into a dense thatch at the top of his powerful thighs.

She stared at him as he knelt beside her, his eyes hard and bright with anticipation, his body rigid with desire. She started to sit up to meet him, but his hands held her down—one slowly slipping inside the bodice of her dress, beneath her bra. He caressed her breast while his other hand clasped softly around her throat. He kissed her until she felt liquid throughout her body.

"I love you, Jen," he growled into her ear, running his tongue along its rim.

She could feel his fingers quickly undoing the rest of her buttons. The callused palm of his hand moved across her soft belly, then inside her panties.

Jennifer closed her eyes, arching her back against the cool

straw as waves of warm sensation washed over her. Somewhere in the back of her mind, she knew she should really be doing something to please and satisfy Chris, yet she felt incapable of exerting herself.

Her arousal was strong, urgent. She could no longer separate her feminine desires from her love for him. The touch of his hands, gentle but persistent, woke every nerve in her body.

"I'm . . . I'm sorry," she stammered. "I don't know—"

His lips silenced her. As he deeply kissed her, he eased down her silk trousers and panties. Chris moved on top of her, steadily gazing into her eyes. She was embarrassed to realize that she had become terribly wet and hoped he wouldn't mind.

He opened the delicate folds of flesh and entered her in one rapid motion. She didn't cry out, but her fingers curled into the knotted muscles in his bare shoulders. Tears of joy mixed with a quick flash of pain welled over her long, pale lashes. A look of surprise crossed Chris's face, then he closed his eyes and came almost immediately with a low shuddering moan. Still inside her, he pulled her flush against his body and rolled onto his side to take his weight from her.

"Oh, Jen, I'm sorry. I'm sorry . . ." he whispered over and over.

He was shaking and so was she. He kissed the tears from her cheeks, holding her tightly, rocking her.

"It's all right," she whispered, blinking the moisture from her eyes so she could see him. "I should have told you. Oh, I feel awful. You needed a woman and all you got was some naive, inexperienced virgin and . . ."

"No!" he said sharply, holding her even tighter. "You were perfect."

He was still hard inside her. Oddly, the pain had gone, and she was left with a sensation of fullness. It was not at all as if her body had been intruded upon. Rather, it was as though she were now complete. Chris had become a precious part of her.

Jennifer gave a self-conscious laugh.

"What's wrong?" he asked.

"I thought it was supposed to, you know, shrink."

"As long as you're in the same room, I doubt it will for more than a minute," he muttered into the damp blond wisps around her forehead.

"And so long as it stays where it is now?" she teased.

"I'm sure it won't," he growled. Then he lifted her chin to look into her eyes. "Does it still hurt?"

She shook her head, then smiled.

"I want to make love to you all night, Jen, but I'll stop if I've hurt you . . . if it's going to hurt you again."

"It won't," she assured him.

"Would you tell me if it did?"

"No," she admitted, "but it won't. I know it won't."

Chris stared down at Jennifer Lynn Swanson. She was the most enticing woman he'd ever known—and out of his league. If it hadn't been for the war, for the bizarre set of circumstances that had landed both of them here, he'd never have even met her.

From the little she'd told him, he knew she was very rich. He'd also heard gossip that her father was an old chum of the ambassador. Everything about Jennifer was so perfect, so exceeded anything he'd ever dreamed of possessing that it made falling in love with her just that much more hopeless.

A suffocating sorrow stole over him, threatening to overshadow the joy of the moment they'd shared. He refused to let it hold him, deciding he'd worry about the future in the morning on his way back to Cu Chi. For now, all he wanted to do was make her forget how clumsy and rushed he'd been that first time and make her understand how potent, invincible, special she made him feel.

He whispered to her again how much he loved her. He took off the rest of her tangled clothing, making a game of it by managing to remove every piece without ever slipping out of her. While she was still giggling at their playfulness, he gently turned her onto her back, supporting himself on his palms above her. He began to move his hips in slow circles until he could feel the tender, pliant muscles around him loosen and moisten again. He could see the pleasure and desire sparkle in her green eyes. By touching his lips to her nipples and to the soft hollow of her throat, running his tongue seductively between her teeth, and moving within her until she clutched him and cried out in ecstasy, he made certain she climaxed no less than five times before he allowed himself to ejaculate again.

Afterward, he lay quietly beside her and watched her drift off to sleep, a blissfully sated smile upon her lips. Her tiny fingers curved over his hard stomach. He tried not to think of tomorrow's long trip back. He'd somehow have to explain his absence. This time, no one would be able to cover for him. Too much was going on and he'd been missing for too long.

Chris let her sleep a couple hours, then softly whispered in her ear. She smiled lazily without opening her eyes.

He pulled her on top of him. They'd needed no sheets to keep them warm. Jennifer nestled into his chest, curling up like a kitten on top of him, plucking playfully at the wiry hairs on his abdomen.

The scent of her skin made him catch his breath. Her hip pressed into his groin. The side of her breast intimately brushed his nipple, sending tremors throughout his body. He lifted her chin on the knuckle of one finger and turned his head to kiss her fully awake.

A part of him that had switched itself off the first few times they'd made love was now working again. While she'd slept, he'd listened to the sounds of an empty house. If Lian was still here, she wasn't moving around at all. But neither was anyone else, which was reassuring.

"I can't stay any longer," he said quietly. "It will be dawn soon."

Pain shot across her features. "Oh, Chris, I—"

"Once more?" he asked. "Then I must go. I don't want to. You know that, Jen, but I can't stay."

"I know." Her voice almost gave way to a quiver. She started to roll off of him, but he held her still, smiling up at her. "What?" she asked, puzzled.

"This," he said, and lifting her hips slightly, he settled her upright on top of him.

She grinned, looking intrigued at this new arrangement.

He didn't say another word. She discovered the rest for herself. He lifted her from him just before they peaked. He stretched over her, sinking deeply and completely into her, needing this one last time—in some inexplicable but basic and masculine way—to dominate and take her for his own.

Jennifer clung to Chris as they stood at the kitchen window. If they'd been in another place, another time, she'd have found a way to keep him there with her. She wanted to learn every possible way to make him happy.

"Where's Lian?" he asked, touching a stray strand of blond hair, then her cheek, then the point of her chin.

He's memorizing me again, she thought. "I expect she's out looking for food. She's been saying she'd go, but I wouldn't let her. She probably took advantage of my preoccupation." She grinned at him naughtily.

"Do you want me to wait until she comes back?" he asked.

"No." She kissed him, draping her arms limply around his neck, dropping her head to his chest. "You'd better leave before it gets light. The MPs catch you and you've had it, right?"

"You got it, babe."

One last sweet kiss, then Chris released her. He climbed on the chair and out through the window. Other than being cleaner than when he'd arrived, he looked the same: fatigues, shirt front open over his bare chest, charcoal smudges beneath his eyes and across his forehead and cheeks. She handed him his rifle through the open window. Reaching back inside, Chris touched her tenderly on the cheek. Then he dropped out of sight into the shrubbery.

Jennifer held her breath, listening in the dark, her heart pounding with fear that she'd hear gunfire or shouts—which might mean he'd been spotted. The night was silent, as frighteningly silent as it ever was these days and nights.

She nailed the window shut and only then realized he

could have left by the garden door, which was undoubtedly the route Lian had chosen, locking it after her but not, of course, able to secure it with nails.

Feeling luxuriously spent, Jennifer stretched out on the couch to wait for Lian. This spot in front of the French doors had become their guard station as they took turns at watch during the night.

After a few minutes, Jennifer heard light steps in the garden. She stood up, ready to click open the lock to let Lian in with whatever groceries she'd been able to scavenge. She was ravenous, having eaten nothing for nearly twenty-four hours.

A shadow rose outside the slatted door, and the realization drifted across her drowsy mind that it was much too tall to be Lian's. A man's voice called out in Vietnamese.

Instantly awake, Jennifer choked back a scream and glanced wildly around the room. The gun! Where had she left Chris's gun?

Finally, she focused on the long dark shape of the M-16 lying on the kitchen table. Inching backward across the living room, she watched the French doors.

The order came again. She recognized the Vietnamese for "Open up!"

She didn't answer.

There was a nerve-shattering crash as a boot splintered through one of the glass panes. A second kick fractured the door frame near the lock. The door swung inward on its hinges. Three men in black burst into the room, weapons raised, ready to fire.

Jennifer dove for the rifle on the table. She spun around with it clutched in her hands. Feeling frantically for the selector on the left side of the gun, she was aware of a dark blur rapidly closing in on her. The button! Where the hell was the . . . there! Jennifer flicked it to full automatic. One of the men threw himself forward, crashing down on top of her before she could get off a shot. She fell painfully to the floor, her breath squashed out of her lungs by the momentum of his body.

He wrestled her for the rifle. Holding on desperately, she

glimpsed a second man out of the corner of her eye, circling them.

Oh, God. Please don't let it end now. Not when I've found Chris! There's too much of life left for me . . . for us.

The second man brought the butt of his own rifle down sharply on her cheekbone. There was an instant of pain. Dazed, Jennifer felt her fingers go numb on the M-16. The gun was pulled from her limp hands. She rolled onto her side with a little moan.

She was distantly aware of a discussion going on above her. One man seemed to be in charge, an officer of sorts. She blearily looked up and saw the teapot.

The squat, flowered porcelain pot was perched near the edge of the kitchen table. Taking advantage of the guerrilla's distraction, she stretched out one hand but her coordination was off. Her fingers failed to grip at the proper moment. The pot toppled over and crashed to the floor beside her.

The officer swung around, his expression dangerous as he reached toward her threateningly.

Jennifer snatched desperately for the nearest shard, her only and last weapon. She slashed at the officer's face. A line of blood surfaced across his jaw, but he didn't react to the wound. Knocking the sharp pottery fragment out of her trembling hand, he reached down and gripped her swollen face between his hard fingers.

"You are American," he said in English.

"I . . . I'm Australian," she answered, attempting an accent. The Aussies were a recent addition to the peace-keeping force, brought in along with a few Koreans and a smattering of other international forces to make the war seem less an American monopoly. They weren't as hated as Americans.

He shook his head. "American," he insisted with finality. He gestured at one of his men and stood up, pressing the back of one hand to his face to stop the bleeding while he rummaged through Lian's writing desk.

The guerrilla pointed his rifle at the bridge of her nose, his finger easing back on the trigger.

Jennifer closed her eyes, steeling herself against the swift, ultimate pain of a bullet slicing into her brain. She stopped breathing. Time seemed to settle into a nightmarish slow motion.

"Stop!" the officer commanded so unexpectedly that her eyes flew open.

He was standing with a USO flier in his hand, one of those that had been printed right after her arrival in Saigon.

The officer strode over to compare the picture of the woman with the guitar to the one lying helplessly at his feet. Finally, he hissed another order at his men then leaned down and, seizing her wrists, pulled her roughly to her feet.

15

Lian had stood silently in her kitchen watching Jennifer and Chris. Adoration and desire were mirrored in the American woman's shining emerald eyes as she clung to the young soldier. And there was no mistaking a man in love.

Lian was overjoyed for them. In the days before Tet, she'd been aware of Jennifer's attempts to distract her from her distant husband and parents. She would always be grateful to her American friend for helping her through that terrible period of depression. Having someone close by had been what she'd needed. But now it was time for her to discreetly retire. Jennifer and Chris needed to be alone.

Quietly, Lian slipped from the room. She went to her own bedroom and lay down, still dressed. She was determined to be happy for Jennifer. She would think of Nguyen, dream of a time when he, too, would come home to her and of the joy they'd share in each other's arms.

With horror, she sat up straight on the bed. "No!" she cried in a choked voice. She didn't move for a long time, her eyes wide with effort, for no matter how hard she tried she couldn't envision her husband's face. All she could remember was the pain she'd suffered when he told her the only reason he'd married her was to produce an heir. Then, without intending to, lanky Bill Jacobs came to mind, with his awkward stance and his quiet hazel eyes that always squinted a little as if they were a bit myopic. She could almost hear the Mississippi drawl that sometimes made it difficult for her to understand him.

Lian buried her face in her hands and hated herself for succumbing to her loneliness. She had, of course, turned Bill away when he'd confessed his feelings for her, but her own heart refused to listen to the advice she'd given him. She cared for the young American in a way, she now realized, she'd never felt for Nguyen, never could feel for him.

Yet her affection for Bill could never be consummated.

When the soft sounds of Chris and Jennifer making love began drifting through her bedroom wall, Lian knew she must leave the house. Their passionate moans and muffled cries drove her wild—summoning vivid images of her in Bill's arms. Oh, what a cruel, impossible fantasy!

Lian rushed through the patio door, gasping for air, leaning against the outside wall to steady herself. After making sure that no one was lurking in the shrubbery, she locked the door behind her.

Walking slowly through the garden, she breathed in the cleansing petal-scented garden air and firmly banished all thoughts of Bill. She stepped through a gate in the wall, slipping silently across the alley to her neighbor's house. No one seemed to have followed. She tapped lightly.

After three more soft knocks failed to arouse anyone, she went to the next door and the next. None of her neighbors answered. She thought that was probably wise.

After over an hour of scampering cautiously in the shadows from doorway to doorway, Lian at last found a merchant who knew her well enough to let her in. She bought rice sticks, a pineapple, one fresh grapefruit, and a killed chicken. It cost her a fortune. He explained that food was very dear, as the enemy had cut off nearly all the highways into the city.

Lian was about to leave his shop by the back door when it

occurred to her that by returning home before dawn she would most likely disturb Chris and Jennifer. The young man had been so wrapped up in his beloved Jennifer that Lian had been able to slip into the night without alarming him. By now his soldier's instincts would again be operating. He'd be alert to anyone entering the house.

She asked Mr. Liu if she might rest in a corner of his shop until sunup. As he was worried about looters discovering his meager hoard, he agreed that might be safer for all concerned.

Her decision proved dangerous, for while she dozed restlessly on Mr. Liu's gritty floor, Lian's rebellious mind drifted again to thoughts of Bill. No longer could she block out his sweet, boyish face.

Bill had told her that he was stationed at the airport. She guessed he was now among the American forces chasing the last of the guerrillas from Saigon. If she chose, she'd be able to see him again.

Then she realized that she *was* somehow going to find a way to contact him. In the garden, she hadn't done a very good job of explaining her feelings. Somehow he'd left encouraged by their conversation. Had she subconsciously intended that to happen?

Bill had to be made to understand that she belonged to another man. There was no hope for them romantically. Even so she couldn't bear the thought of hurting him. She'd have to try again to explain how it must be between them.

When she returned to the garden wall with her groceries, a pink dawn edged the sky over the canal. Enjoying the beautiful sunrise, she strolled through the little iron gate, fishing her house key from the pocket in her black silk pants beneath her *ao dai.* Then she glanced up to see the patio door standing open, the sheer white curtains blowing in the breeze.

Lian's heart leapt into her throat. She dropped the sack of food. Terrified of what she'd find inside, she called from the doorway: "Jennifer?"

No answer.

"Jenny!" she screamed. "Chris!"

Her entire body quaking, she stepped into the living room. Broken glass crunched under her feet. Spinning around, she noticed that the French doors were not just open. The locked frame had been violently shattered. Lamps had been overturned. Papers from Nguyen's desk had been pulled out and strewn across the living room.

Lian ran from room to room, searching the house. In the kitchen, she found her teapot shattered on the floor. Drops of blood were sprinkled like deep red rose petals among the brittle chips.

She shrieked, running from the house into the street. She tore up one sidewalk and down another until she found an American Jeep with four soldiers sitting in it. One of them recognized her.

"My friend—" She gasped. "The communists have her."

"Is she Vietnamese?" he asked.

Lian shook her head, tears spilling over her long dark lashes, trailing down her soft cheeks. "It's Jenny, the radio girl."

The men exchanged disbelieving glances.

"Come on. Get in," one of them said solemnly. "Was she alone?"

Lian hesitated for only a second.

"Yes, she was alone."

Chris, she knew, couldn't possibly have still been with her. If he'd been in the house when the guerrillas broke in, he'd have either fought them off or else she'd have found his body on her floor. He'd never have let them take his Jen.

Jeffrey paced the floor of Ambassador Bunker's office. Lian slumped in a chair, staring blankly at a wall. The ambassador was on his way from his residence. Word of Jenny's disappearance was being relayed to Chris, but it might take days to locate his squad somewhere out in the boonies.

"She'll be all right," Jeffrey repeated for the tenth time. "She's smart. She'll think of a way to make them keep her alive."

Lian didn't respond.

The sound of voices came from the outer office. Jeffrey opened the door and the ambassador strode in, followed by two staff members. He laid a hand on Lian's shoulder. "We'll find her. We'll bring her back."

Gazing up at him through dry eyes, Lian said, "They will kill her."

Jeffrey exploded. "Christ sakes, Lian! Don't say that! Give us a chance to see if we can negotiate her release."

Bunker looked at him patiently. "Son, we have to be realistic. The Viet Cong are using terrorist tactics to make the point that we don't belong in their country. If enough Americans die here, they think the rest of us will go home. It's as simple as that. Jennifer Swanson's death would be an especially powerful blow to American morale." The ambassador sat down heavily behind his desk. "If they handle it carefully, her murder could mean a turning point in the war."

Jeffrey felt dazed. "What do you mean?"

"Public opinion on the home front. Young men getting killed for the cause of democracy—that's a horrible but expected cost of war. A pretty young woman who came to entertain the boys? Her death is unconscionable. It would win a tremendous amount of support for the doves back home."

"So," Jeffrey said slowly, "she's worth more to the communists dead than alive."

Bunker nodded sadly. "I expect they've either killed her already or they'll torture her. For her sake, I hope it's already over."

Jeffrey couldn't believe what he was hearing. He gripped the corner of the desk with two hands, trying to steady himself. He felt like smashing things. "We can't give up until we know for sure. If we act quickly, maybe we can save her. Her father is an influential man. Maybe he can pull some strings."

"Nothing he can do will hold much water over here," the ambassador said tiredly.

Jeffrey turned on the older man. "Stop telling me what *won't* work!" he cried, then blinked, surprised at his own outburst. "I'm sorry, sir. It's just that she's very special to . . . to a lot of us."

Lian rose shakily and stood beside him. "Ambassador," she said with quiet strength, "the fact remains, they didn't kill her at my house. They took her for some reason. Possibly, they'll make an example of her by torturing her and leaving her body to be found somewhere in the city. But if there is a chance we might negotiate her release, I believe we should try."

For a moment the ambassador was silent. "I'll contact Westmoreland. He may have some ideas. And we should notify Max Swanson and his wife. I hate to give them too much to hope for, but if there's a chance of working a deal, the more muscle we have behind it the better."

Lian remained in the office while the ambassador composed a wire to Jennifer's parents. Then she left Jeffrey and the diplomatic corps to do what they could. She took a taxi to the radio station where she told Gloria and Lieutenant Metcalf the news.

"Why did she have to leave the compound?" Gloria sobbed. "Why did she have to insist on doing everything on her own?"

Lian had thought about that, too. "Friendship," she replied. "Jennifer wanted to be friends with the Vietnamese people. Not to merely survive here, shut off from them."

"Bosh it! I *told* her it wasn't smart to move off the embassy grounds." Both women glared at Hugh Metcalf. He took the cigar stub out of his mouth. For a moment, he was silent. "Would it help to spread the word, to let everyone know they've got her?"

Lian glanced at Gloria and saw in the other woman's eyes a tiny flicker of hope. "If her capture is announced on the radio, all the men in the field will be on the lookout for her. I'll clear it with the ambassador."

Chris's return trip to Cu Chi seemed to be over in a matter of seconds.

Jen loved him. *She loved him!*

He hadn't been exaggerating when he'd said she haunted

his every waking minute, that she was a mortal danger to him and his comrades. And she'd been right when she'd told him she would give him something to dream about. Just thinking about her body and the tender, ecstatic, erotic, beautiful gestures they'd shared would keep him happy for a very long time.

The night had been more than he could have ever hoped for. Jen had welcomed him, although he wasn't rich, educated, or finely connected like her family. She'd been willing to let him make love to her even while filthy with a week's worth of dust and sweat. Despite it all, she loved him. Thank God he'd had the self-restraint to tear himself away from her long enough to clean up a bit.

Chris felt invincible as he rode back toward Cu Chi, first in a Land-Rover west along Route 1, then bumping along in a supply truck down the dirt road between marshy rice fields. He watched a few peasants working with their oxen. He had to remind himself that should a mine go off under the truck, he'd end up as dead as anyone else. How could anything like that happen to him? She loved him.

O'Neil spotted him first. He was on watch in the bunker closest to the river and let him slip back into camp with only a raised eyebrow. Chris went directly to his hooch and stretched out with his helmet over his eyes to block the noon sun.

"The old man's hunting for you," a voice said above him a few minutes later.

"So?"

"He's getting a little irritated with your disappearing act. We had action last night."

Chris shoved back the helmet and squinted at the boy in tiger-striped camouflage standing over him. "Anyone buy it?"

"Naw." The young private grinned. "So, how'd it go?"

"What?"

"Ya get any?"

Chris's fingers shot up toward the boy's throat, wrapping around a fistful of T-shirt, pulling him down to his level.

"Hey, it's cool, man! You don't have to tell me." He

looked terrified. "Just thought the little blond canary might be worth telling about."

"How did you know it was her?" demanded Chris. "I never said I was going to see her."

"Hey, man. All you do is listen to her show or wait for it to come on. One of the guys says you met her before somewhere."

Chris shoved him away. He didn't like the idea of them knowing he'd been with her. He didn't want anything to tarnish her or what they had together. The kid made it sound as if he'd sneaked off to pop some whore.

"Don't talk about her like that," he growled.

"No woman's that special," muttered the private, straightening his shirt. "You'd better check in."

"She is so that special," Chris murmured, lying down again. He replayed the night in his mind, recalling every soft curve of her body. When his CO kicked him awake half an hour later, Chris just looked up and grinned at him. Nothing the man could tell him was going to spoil last night.

"You'd better come over to the radio," Johansen said solemnly. "There's something you should hear."

The announcer was unfamiliar. He sounded older than the regular disk jockeys. He had a Cockney accent. Chris squatted beside the radio.

"To repeat that announcement," squeaked the radio, "it's my sad duty to inform all listeners of American Forces Radio in Vietnam that Miss Jennifer Lynn Swanson, the star of 'A Night with Jenny,' has been reported missing."

Chris glanced around the camp, a half grin still lingering on his lips. *This is a joke. I was just with her!* But no one else was smiling.

Soldiers who'd been shaving paused with lather on their faces. Those who were eating out of a container of C-rations froze in the middle of a bite. All talking ceased except for the hasty "shut up" warnings directed at those who hadn't heard what was going on. And every eye gravitated toward Chris.

"We believe that she's been abducted by communist guerrillas still at large in Saigon. She may have been smuggled out of the city. So we're asking everyone to keep an eye out in local villages for her and for vehicles that might be concealing Miss Swanson—anything from ox carts to civilian delivery trucks."

Chris hardly heard the announcer's final words. A tormenting pressure was building in his head. The growl of a wounded animal grew in his throat and, at last, burst between his lips. "NO!" he screamed. "Goddamn fuckin' bastards!"

He grabbed the AK-47 and rocketed to his feet. He was two hundred yards out of camp, with no idea where he was heading, when three guys tackled him from behind.

After wrestling him to the ground, they pinned him while Johansen yelled in his face. "What are you *doing*, Tyler? Tearing off into the bush isn't going to help her! She could be anywhere if she's still alive."

"Jen's alive!" shrieked Chris, tears streaking down his cheeks. "Goddamn you, she's alive!

"Right." The lieutenant exchanged looks with the burly sergeant sitting on Chris's chest. "Listen, we can recon the area—go village to village and cover maybe a hundred square miles inside a week. But who knows where they've got her? And you're no good to her, bursting like a maniac into villages and ripping them apart—which is what you're going to do if we let you up, right?"

Chris didn't answer.

"Cool it just long enough so we can call HQ and get permission to move a team out, okay?"

Chris groaned. He'd left her too soon. He should have waited until dawn. Why the *hell* hadn't he waited?

"Do you hear me, Tyler? If she's out here, we'll find her."

Chris nodded once, slowly. *He* would find her. And God help them if they'd hurt her.

Melantha hadn't been able to get leave to see Curtis. Even if she had been able to swing it, she was told his location was classified and she couldn't locate him. He'd contact her when he could.

One of the doctors who'd been in-country six months

explained the situation to her. "He's gone over the wall, Mel," he said, pouring her a drink while they sat in his hooch.

"Curtis wouldn't go AWOL!" she objected.

"Not AWOL. Over the wall: into Cambodia. We're not supposed to know that's where they are. Chasing guerrillas. The communists have been able to duck across the border to safety until now, but President Johnson has authorized strike forces to follow them so long as the press doesn't catch wind."

Mel shivered, took a stiff belt from her glass. "That's dangerous."

"Hey!" He laughed. "Living's dangerous here, haven't you noticed?"

She had. There were times at the Pleiku Evac Hospital when the shelling came so close they had to lower the operating tables and work on their knees wearing two flak jackets. There were nights when the mortar bursts crept in on them and she slept beneath her bed, clutching a can of Coke and bag of squashed Fritos her cousin had sent from D.C. After a while, she got to prefer the mat under her bed to the soggy, mildewed sheets above.

Then one night, when she'd already been in O.R. for sixteen hours straight, a medic came in and whispered in her ear. The blood drained from her head, and she felt suddenly dizzy.

"Curtis?" she moaned.

"He's all right, Mel," the guy told her hastily. "He hitched a ride with a medevac chopper."

She'd darted a look at the surgeon she'd been assisting, and he winked at her. "Almost done with this one. Take twenty minutes, huh? You're due a break."

Knowing that's all the time he could give her since they were so short-handed, Mel yanked off her gloves and threw them into the overflowing bin of bloody rubber. She grabbed two paper cups of coffee from the urn outside O.R. and ran into the daylight. She hadn't realized the sun had risen.

Curtis sat on an overturned oil drum, his helmet in his

hands. When he saw her approaching, he leapt up and scooped her off the ground—a physical feat very few men ever attempted. Mel hugged him tightly, tears of joy rolling down her cheeks.

"You idiot!" she scolded. "What you doing scaring me half to death? I thought they'd brought you here in pieces!"

"I'm all together," he said, letting go of her with a grin. Then he glanced down at the pile of bloody fatigues, knapsacks, rifles, and hand grenades outside the surgical hut.

Melantha followed his gaze. "We have to take their weapons away from them at triage. Some of them don't want to let go of their stuff."

Curtis nodded, understanding. She could see that he too had learned to never surrender his weapon. Even as he'd embraced her, he'd clutched a grease gun in one hand. She remembered the coffee and handed him a cup that was now only half full. She'd lost some of it in their hug.

"Hot coffee." He sighed with satisfaction, and downed it in one swallow.

She handed him her own cup and ran for refills.

They sat outside O.R. with their backs to the long corrugated metal wall, sipping coffee. She'd been chugging Cokes and coffee all night long, trying to stay awake. One of the nurses had had to be carried off and dumped in the scrub room. She'd fallen asleep on top of a patient. They'd given her an hour, then woke her to relieve another nurse near collapse.

"I tried reaching you when I first got here," Mel began, "but they said your platoon's location was classified."

Curtis nodded. "If you need me, ask one of the medevac pilots. He'll pass the word. Most of the wounded you got today are from over the wall. They're pickin' 'em up like dead flies over there."

Mel swallowed the last of her coffee. The caffeine had lost its kick. Her head was ringing like a church bell, her eyes burning with fatigue. "Dammit, Curt, why you have to come over here?"

He shrugged. "Don't know. Ain't all that bad if you know

how to look after yourself. There are regular meals. They airlift us all the free Cokes we can drink. I haven't had a real bath in six weeks, but that makes me think fondly of the old days." He grinned at her.

She smiled, jabbing him in the ribs with her elbow. "You'd do anything to get out of a bath when you were a little boy."

"Yeah, don't know how you an' Momma ever put up with me."

"I don't think Momma ever let you go six weeks, Curt." She wrinkled her nose, then turned serious. "You all right? You're not sick or anything, are you?"

He shook his head. "How's Amelia?" he asked.

"I saw her the day I left for basic," Mel said. "She looked real good, Curt. She found herself a little apartment of her own with the money you been sending home. I wish I could see the baby. The pictures she's been sending are beautiful."

His eyes shone with pride. "Ain't he something?"

Curtis stayed long enough to clean up. But he didn't have a change of clothes with him, so he put his dirty fatigues back on. Melantha thought he looked better anyway for the washing.

They stood holding each other while medics pulled wounded off of a helicopter. Then Curtis climbed aboard. He gave her a cocky salute as the chopper grumbled into the sky.

Mel returned to O.R. to relieve two nurses on separate tables, alternating duties as scrub nurse on one, surgical assistant on the other. She tried not to think about Curtis. Her work—that's all that she could control.

She'd learned to make incisions, remove shrapnel, resection bowel, and do a hundred other jobs that were normally reserved for the surgeon. In Nam you did what was required at the moment. Traditional rules for surgical etiquette no longer applied.

It was almost noon before the choppers stopped coming. Mel lost the last two patients at her tables. She was furious with herself and heartbroken. Both boys had been in bad shape, but not as bad as some others that had made it. She couldn't help wondering if chance had brought these boys in six hours sooner, when the doctors and nurses could still function through their fatigue, would they be alive now?

She walked back to her hooch with two other nurses. No one spoke. She lay down on her bed, without undressing, closed her eyes. She couldn't sleep. She'd reached the point where exhaustion thwarted the body's ability to relax. Her brain replayed each casualty that had crossed her table, hearing a boy pleading with her to save his leg, his arm, his penis, hearing her own reassuring words. Almost a third of them didn't make it.

Somebody shook her shoulder.

She looked up blankly.

"Lieutenant," the corps man said. "Sorry. There's a call for you at Communications."

She frowned, her heartbeat faltering. It couldn't be Curtis, he'd just left. Had something happened to Amelia or the baby?

Mel stumbled across the compound, her olive T-shirt still smeared with blood, sticking to her body with her own sweat. She clutched the receiver and croaked into it: "Hello?"

"Melantha?" came a soft voice.

"Who is this? Over."

There was a pause while Communications switched over to receive. "Melantha? This is Lian Nguyen, in Saigon."

Christ, thought Mel, *this is really what I need.* She pulled out the scalpel she always carried in her pocket and flipped it idly in one hand. *The Vietnamese bomb the shit out of my boys and drive me to the edge of my grave. And when I have a couple hours to sleep, they want to rap.*

"Listen, Lian, I'm beat. We had a lot of casualties the last two days. I have to sack out." She started to hand the receiver back to the R/T man when she heard a terrified squeak from the other end.

"Mel, no!"

She pressed her ear to the receiver.

"It's Jennifer. The guerrillas took over parts of the city. They've kidnapped her. Over."

Mel closed her eyes, gritting her teeth so hard they creaked. Of all the unfair things. Death and rotten conditions were part of war. Soldiers—even the young ones—knew that was part of the deal. But that naive pipsqueak of a girl from Boston had just wanted to make the guys happy. She had nothing to do with politics! She wasn't trying to be patriotic or subversive or any of that shit.

"Are you sure?" she asked, her voice unnaturally weak.

"Yes. I only called you because I thought you'd want to know."

"Yeah," Mel said, thrusting the scalpel back into her pocket. "Thanks. Tell me if they . . . when they find her. Over."

Mel hung up and walked numbly across the compound toward her hooch, then straight past it into the nurses' latrine. She vomited her last four cups of coffee. There was no food left in her stomach and she had dry heaves for another ten minutes before she could stop. After all the blood and dismembered bodies she'd learned to tolerate, the thought of Jennifer Lynn Swanson being tortured to death in this stinking, foreign country was just too much.

16

At home, Lian picked up the pieces of broken teapot from her floor, wiped the bloodstains from the floor, put Nguyen's desk back in order, and, after finding a second pot she rarely used, made herself a very small amount of tea. She drank it, with measured sips.

She didn't feel like eating, but made herself munch on a few dry rice crackers so that she could think more clearly.

The ambassador had made it clear that, although every man in Vietnam would keep an eye out for Jennifer during his assigned duties, a war was on. Large numbers of troops could not be spared to hunt for one woman. Still, there was, he claimed, every chance they'd find her if she was alive.

Lian was well aware of the many ways a person might be concealed in the vast countryside. The VC could shuffle Jennifer from village to village for weeks, even months—just ahead of any American platoon.

Then there were the tunnels. Some had been built twenty or more years ago. They were extensive, covering hundreds of miles between supply depots, villages, camps, and bunkers. Some had been widened and fortified into subterranean *villes*. Not long ago, a two-hundred-bed underground hospital was discovered by American Marines.

If Jennifer was being hidden in any of them, her captors could keep her alive and out of sight for months, years if necessary. Or maybe just for a handful of hours before they executed her.

Simply watching for her was no solution.

With trembling fingers, Lian picked up a pen and started to make a list of organizations with which she had frequent contact. Some were strictly humanitarian with no political or military ties. Totally impartial, they were respected by the communists. The American Friends Service Committee, The Red Cross, The International Voluntary Services, and Catholic Relief Services. Maybe . . . just maybe.

She spent the day visiting one organization headquarters after another. The IVS was the most promising-sounding, and Betty Madison, an officer there, promised she would begin a dialogue with her North Vietnamese contact.

"Perhaps," Betty said, "unofficial word can be passed to Hanoi. They might be able to locate Jennifer."

"Thank you," Lian said gratefully.

At dusk, Lian returned home, drained and disconsolate. A Marine guard was stationed at her front door, and all her windows, as well as the patio door, had been boarded over.

She lay on her bed and gravely stared at her ceiling. What could she do but wait and pray?

Lian decided then that she must return to work the next day. The USO would be open during noncurfew hours. If she remained at home any longer she'd go insane thinking of Jennifer.

Then, she heard a door creaking softly open.

"Who is it?" she called, sitting up.

Lian assumed it was the guard coming to ask to use her bathroom. She should have offered its use earlier. She rose to meet him and found herself standing face-to-face with her husband.

Nguyen's small, bright black eyes stared down at her.

"Oh," she murmured uncertainly.

He was thinner than she recalled, and his dark hair was

sparse, combed to one side, and shaved in a sharp line around the ears. He looked markedly older than when she'd last seen him seven months ago. *Has he changed so much?* she wondered frantically, *or have I?*

Although she'd been educated in modern schools in the city, she dropped her glance in a traditional sign of wifely obedience.

Nguyen laid a hand on her head, clearly pleased by the respectful gesture. "It has been difficult for you here, I see," he said, observing the boarded windows. He must have already spoken to the guard outside.

"Yes," she answered in her native tongue. "There has been a lot of violence in the city. They say it will soon be safe again."

"And you have kept my home. I am proud of you."

"I am humble, husband," she returned in a traditional greeting.

Nguyen gave a short nod, reassured that everything in his life was as it should be.

He preceded her into the bedroom and Lian followed. She felt a dry wedding-night fluttering in the pit of her stomach. Only, this time, after she'd removed her clothing and he touched her, it didn't disappear as it had on their honeymoon. Lian felt as if she were with a stranger.

Her husband's hard soldier's hands moved over her flesh raising goose bumps. She responded with silent compliance. And after he had left her to sleep, she moved onto her side and pulled up the soft quilt and cried because the loneliness she'd lived with for half a year hadn't left with his return. She dreamed uneasily of Bill lying in her husband's place on her bed, and she was ashamed.

The next morning, Lian awoke to the sound of songbirds. They hadn't serenaded the dawn since Tet. Their return to her garden must be a good omen, she decided. Today would be better.

For Nguyen's breakfast, she made Saigon Soup, which consisted of a richer, heartier broth than the one she'd made Jennifer.

He asked her about various neighbors and affairs in the

city, about repairs that might be necessary to the house. His eyes focused on her with an alert expression as he spoke, as if he were afraid of missing something. At last he asked the question he'd asked every time he returned home.

"You are not yet with child?"

"No," she said, surprised, and a little perturbed as well. Since he'd been home last, seven months ago, she'd have been due to deliver in two months. Anyway, didn't he realize she would have written to him about a matter so important to both of them? *Stupid man!* She looked down into her bowl of cooling soup. "I am not."

"It isn't, of course, all your fault," he allowed. "I would be with you more often, if it weren't for the war."

"Yes." But she knew he was, at least in his own mind, being generous. He really *did* blame her for not giving him an heir.

She bitterly glanced at the slender streaks of sunlight seeping in around the boards over her window. She hated being here with him, resented how little he cared about her concerns, how he didn't even view her as a woman. The sun was rising high in the morning sky. As Nguyen noiselessly ate, his spoon moving in precise circles between bowl and mouth, her mind wandered, and she thought again of returning to the USO. It had been almost a week since she'd been there. She knew she was needed, and the streets had at last been proclaimed safe during the daylight hours. But she couldn't very well leave without some explanation.

Lian stood up, then drifted around the kitchen, tidying, moving dishes around. Nguyen retired to his desk, where he took out some paperwork. Several times, she started to approach him with an announcement of her job on her lips, but she changed her mind each time. Never before had she been so afraid of him, though he hadn't ever so much as raised his voice to her. All the same, the fear was as real as her growing resentment. She kept both shut inside of her, fermenting like a bottle of *nuoc mam:* fish sauce, growing stronger with waiting.

She prepared a noonday dish of pineapple, rice, and tiny

slivers of chicken. For the late meal of the day, she went out to buy a small piece of pork and several sweet potatoes.

When she returned she found that Sergeant O'Brien, Nguyen's aide, had arrived with still more papers for Nguyen. The American stiffened and looked up with an odd expression when she entered the room with her groceries.

"Will you stay for dinner, Sergeant?" she asked.

O'Brien glanced briefly at Nguyen as if for permission. Her husband only gave him a dry quiver of a glance. "No, ma'am, but thank you," he answered politely. "There's too much to get caught up with since the colonel's back in the city."

Isn't that the truth, she thought spitefully.

By the end of the day, she and Nguyen had spoken only a dozen words to each other. Her husband walked wordlessly into their bedroom and she followed, as much out of habit as out of deference to his will. He bedded her quickly, efficiently. And as soon as he'd planted his seed, he left the room without a tender word or unnecessary touch. She heard the front door open and close. Very late that night, he returned, slipping onto the bed beside her, being careful not to let their bodies touch.

By the next morning, Lian felt more strained and frustrated than she had during her long months of abstinence. Nothing had changed! Nguyen was using her, insensitive to whether or not she received any satisfaction from their intercourse.

But she couldn't make herself confide any of her frustrations to her husband, for she sensed that he was incapable of understanding them. To bring her concerns out into the open would only make matters worse. The tension between them was like a ripe melon ready to burst.

They sat, without speaking, over their morning soup. At last she couldn't stand being in the house any longer.

"Nguyen," she said.

"Yes?"

"I will need to go out today."

He looked across the table at her and nodded. "I will give you money for food."

"I'm not going to buy groceries. And, besides, I have money of my own," she said quickly, her pride overruling her head. She bit her lip, realizing she'd spoken too soon.

"What money is this? Have your parents sent money, thinking I cannot support you?" Anger crept over his words like a flickering-tongued lizard.

"Oh, no," she said quickly. "I have earned it at the USO."

He put down his spoon. "You have a job?"

Wanting him to be proud of her, she straightened her shoulders and smiled at Nguyen. "Yes. You are risking your life for our country. I cannot remain idly at home. This is my way of helping."

His head jerked forward, a shock of straight black hair falling over one eye. The lines around his mouth congealed. "You have one job already. If you cannot do that properly, you should not take on another!"

Lian shot to her feet, the blood draining from her face. "Whether or not I can produce a child has nothing to do with my other abilities!" she shouted.

"'A barren woman is a burden to her family,'" he said, bitterly quoting an ancient proverb.

"Nguyen! How dare you—"

"Sit down at my table!" he roared, his eyes bright and black as a winter night sky. "You are a disrespectful woman!"

Lian's mouth dropped open. She sucked in a steadying breath and sat to give him a chance to calm down. She would not allow him to force her to rash words or actions!

After a while, he spoke stiffly. "This place where you work, the USO, you are a secretary?"

"No," she said. "I serve as a manager. I hire hostesses, waitresses, and kitchen help. Sometimes I counsel the American soldiers about their problems. They need to know who to see in the Vietnamese government to adopt a child or to marry a Vietnamese woman."

Nguyen's expression was unreadable. "You talk to these men a great deal?"

"That's my job," she said carefully.

226

He looked away from her and was silent for several minutes. "I have heard from a man whom I trust, who is loyal to me, that you do *more* than talk to these soldiers."

One glance at the disgusted twist of his lips told Lian everything. "Nguyen!" she said, gasping, "I have been faithful."

He glared morosely at her.

"Sergeant O'Brien told you I was working there, didn't he?" she demanded. "What did he say about me?"

Without another word, Nguyen stood up from the table and marched out of the room. A second later, the street door slammed.

He was gone all of that day while Lian seethed, furious at all men. They were all self-centered, jealous little boys! But, as angry as she was with Nguyen, something warned her to tread cautiously. She didn't dare leave the house for fear he'd return and find her gone. Her absence would make his suspicions seem real and she didn't trust his moods.

The telephone lines were working again. She called the central business office that oversaw the seventeen USOs located in Vietnam and spoke to her boss, explaining that her husband was home on leave. He told her to take whatever time she needed. He'd send the Saigon USO a temporary to fill in until her return. He wished the colonel his best.

"I will tell him," Lian said impassively.

Next she called the merchant she'd visited on the night Jennifer had disappeared and ordered a duck with an assortment of fresh vegetables for delivery. She cooked Nguyen a special meal hoping it would mellow him, so he'd listen to her explanation, because she couldn't bear to leave her job and her friends. She waited.

It was almost eleven o'clock, an hour after official curfew, when he stumbled through the front door clutching a nearly empty bottle of Scotch.

Lian backed away from him as he lurched blindly across her path and into the bathroom. She could hear him urinating. She could tell by the sound that he was failing to reach the toilet most of the time. That was something she hadn't missed, cleaning up after a man who couldn't hit the target when he was drunk. Nguyen drank when he wasn't soldiering. She'd forgotten.

Hoping to avoid him until he was sober, Lian returned to the kitchen, redolent with the smell of overcooked duck. Nguyen came looking for her. He didn't have the bottle anymore. He grinned at her with such effort that his eyes became black slits.

"Come, my pretty Lian who waits for her husband so devotedly," he lisped in Vietnamese.

"Nguyen, I will make you tea," she offered, backing away.

"Is that what you serve the American soldiers you lie with?" he asked in a wily tone, as if he were tricking her into admitting a sin.

"I do not sleep with them!" she protested.

He seized her around the waist, pulling her to him. His breath was thick with liquor, and she turned away from its stench. He trapped her face between his callused thumb and forefinger, and forced his lips down over hers.

At first she didn't try to pull away, but he was displeased with her lack of response. He glared at her furiously.

"Kiss me, whore!" he ordered.

She pried his fingers off of her and slipped out of his grip. He was her husband. According to law, she owed him her life and obedience, but she wouldn't tolerate his abusiveness.

"You will speak to me with honor as your wife!" Lian demanded, stomping her foot at him as if he were a child who'd overstepped his mother's good nature.

Unfortunately, this approach seemed to anger Nguyen more. He lashed out with one arm, knocking a kitchen chair aside, lunging for her. She wasn't fast enough. He slapped her hard across the face with the flat of his palm.

"No!" she shrieked, falling to the floor.

The pain stunned her. She was disoriented, unable to follow his motions. Then she felt her *ao dai* being ripped downward from the throat. With a scream, she covered her bared breasts.

"Shut up, whore! You service foreign soldiers, you'll receive your husband!"

"No, please!" she said, sobbing. She couldn't stand the thought of him touching her.

Nguyen struck her in the stomach with his clenched fist. She doubled over in agony, rolling on the tile floor, gasping.

She hated herself for not being able to defend herself. As she nursed the pain in her belly, a red welt blossomed across her cheek. She wanted only to be left alone, but his sandpaper hands pawed away the last scraps of fabric from her skin.

Lian struggled weakly, squeezing her eyes shut to block out his looming face. "Please don't . . . please don't . . . please, Nguyen," she pleaded as if the rhythm of the chanted words might deter him.

He ignored her cries of anguish, forcing her legs apart, thrusting himself inside of her.

After an eternity of pain and humiliation, he was done and withdrew. Then she heard him fumbling through her cupboards. Peering through tear-swollen eyes, she watched him take down a bottle of rice wine and stagger from the room, his fly open, penis dangling limply.

He left her sobbing and aching on the kitchen floor. It was some time before she managed to hobble slowly to her bed.

The next morning, Lian woke to the sounds of Nguyen washing himself. The muscles across her stomach still hurt. She felt raw and ripped inside. Studying herself in the mirror, she was surprised to find only a slight puffiness across her left cheek. If she met neighbors on the street, they probably wouldn't notice anything different about her. *At least Nguyen's honor will prevail,* she thought indignantly. Besides, according to the law it was impossible for a man to rape his own wife. She dressed and went into the kitchen.

When Nguyen joined her, she stiffly set a bowl of soup at his place, refusing to look at him. He nodded in acknowledgment of the meal and ate without speaking. She waited until he was done and had departed before she breakfasted alone.

When she was done, she sat for half an hour, staring into her empty bowl. "What am I going to do?" she moaned aloud.

Three days had passed since Jennifer's disappearance. Now, all Lian had for company were her fears for her friend and confusion over her disastrous marriage. She desperately wanted to stay out of Nguyen's way. If she went to the USO and threw herself into her work, she wondered, would she stop thinking about Jennifer? Would she forget about Nguyen's rage and brutality? She'd be safe there among the soldiers. Hopefully, Nguyen's jealousy had been spent in that one violent outburst.

But what if she were wrong? Recalling the horrid details of his unexpected assault, Lian trembled. If he were so displeased with her, perhaps he'd divorce her. By law, a husband could do so merely by saying the words: *I divorce you.* He could legally throw her out of his home because she was barren. Anything would be better than suffering another humiliation like last night's.

Lian took a cab to the USO. Her temporary replacement had collected the mail from the post office and drawn up the week's employee schedule. Lian thanked her and sent her back to her regular job. Then she caught up on calls to local merchants for supplies, bartering with government and military offices for those in shortest supply. She paid all the bills and didn't stop for lunch. During the afternoon, she reviewed the pile of personal messages from GIs who'd been concerned when they heard that guerrillas had broken into her house. It was the first happy moment in many days. Their solicitude deeply touched her.

By late afternoon, Lian was satisfied that things were on their way back to normal. She sat down and composed the first letter she'd ever written to a man other than her father or husband. She wrote to Bill Jacobs at an address he'd pressed into her hand on the day of her party. She told him about the assaults on the embassy and her home, and of Jennifer's disappearance. She was certain that by now he would have heard most of the news, but something compelled her to put the terrifying particulars on paper. Bill seemed the only person who would really understand her grief over everything that had happened. If he came into the club before she had a chance to mail the note, maybe she'd just give it to him.

The one thing she didn't mention was Nguyen's preposterous behavior. She sensed that she must keep that to herself. If Bill found out that she'd been beaten, he might do something foolhardy. She'd never forgive herself if he came to harm because of her.

That evening was particularly busy. Few men had been given any leave immediately after Tet, due to the need to secure the city. Tonight, for the first time, GIs were beginning to be seen off-duty in the streets. Lian was in constant motion, running from the USO kitchen to the dining area to the lounge, where a Vietnamese rock band played. Every inch of the club required careful supervision, especially since she was short on help. She closed at nine forty-five, because of curfew, and flagged down a cab. All the way home, she prayed that she wouldn't have to suffer through another confrontation with Nguyen. Thankfully, she found him asleep on the couch, another bottle lying beside him.

She took it and threw it into the trash, then cleaned up his muddy boot tracks in the hall and across her beautiful living-room carpet. She wiped the sticky yellow splashes from around the toilet bowl before retiring, exhausted, to her bedroom.

The door to her bedroom slammed open.

Lian had been sound asleep. Startled, she sat up in bed. She remembered the nightmare she'd had sometime in the early morning—about the guerrillas taking Jennifer. She imagined they'd come back for her, too, but it was Nguyen.

He stood uncertainly in her bedroom doorway for a moment, his face sallow from too much drink, his thinning black hair mussed. His eyes were bloodshot and watery, and he looked as if he might be sick at any minute.

"You were away last night," he rasped softly.

"I was working." Lian threw back her sheet and rose from the bed. In the bathroom, she splashed cool water on her face. She was afraid of him but didn't want him to see. And she couldn't remain lying down while he was in the room, for fear of giving him ideas. She still wasn't healed from the last time. The mere thought of him touching her made her flesh crawl and her stomach turn sour.

"Do you often work so late?" he asked.

"That is when I'm most needed. In the evenings more clients come. The staff needs supervision."

When she straightened up from the sink, her cheeks dripping cool water, she could see his face reflected in the mirror. He looked strangely passive.

"I am asking you to stop going there," he said with almost childlike supplication.

"Oh, Nguyen," she murmured, spinning around to face him. Had he had a change of heart? Perhaps now was an opportunity to clear the air between them. "Please understand," she began, "I find it very difficult to remain in an empty house for months at a time when I can be doing some good for people."

The muscles along his narrow jaw tightened. "I do not wish to discuss your excuses," he said. "I am willing to forgive your infidelity, if the last time has passed."

"My infidelity!" she cried. "Have you heard a word I have said?"

"Women cannot admit to sin," he said placidly. "I understand the shame you must feel. Denial is understandable."

"Nguyen!"

He looked at her with a puzzled stare, and suddenly she realized what the real problem was. She wasn't even a *person* to him.

"I have remained faithful to you, and I shall in the future," she said firmly. "I am your wife before all else. But I will continue to do my job, because I am needed and because I enjoy it. You must accept this much."

A look of abhorrence flashed across his black eyes. His lip curled, and she cringed, expecting another blow. Instead, he simply cursed her and left the house.

She dressed, furious and bewildered and heavy of heart.

Was she doing the right thing by defying him? In the back of her mind, even after all that had happened, was the languishing hope that he might surprise her by adjusting to her needs. But even if she agreed to all he demanded, what was her future likely to be? She couldn't try any harder to have a baby. If she didn't become pregnant in the next year, there was a good chance he would divorce her. Escaping from him, she realized, would be a relief.

But, if he did divorce her, what then? A woman known by the community to be cast off for infertility wasn't a valued commodity in her society. She'd probably live husbandless for the rest of her life if she remained in Saigon.

At the USO that day, Lian dwelled uncomfortably on Nguyen, but she was also preoccupied with Jennifer. She telephoned the embassy twice. Jeffrey reported there was no word from Hanoi on her location or condition. She thought sadly about two young lovers: Jennifer and Chris. They'd had just one night together. It seemed so unfair.

Lian worked for three hours in her office, letting the secretary know she didn't wish to be disturbed. Part of her job entailed locating impossible items, such as tubs of ice cream for an ice-cream-eating contest, or movies that weren't five years old, or red paper napkins for Valentine's Day. And all of this required a fine hand at bartering, using medical or mechanical supplies that had been mistakenly delivered to the club in trade for what she needed. Tonight, she handled the most outrageous deals first, hoping to lose herself in her work.

Later, Lian made a conscious decision to stay away from the dance floor. If her husband sent O'Brien to spy on her, she didn't want to be found in some soldier's arms. A Korean band was playing Beatles songs. "I want to hode your 'and!"

She knew the switchboard girls on the second floor had been working six hours straight. She went up to relieve one of them.

This was where GIs could come to call home to talk to their mothers, dads, siblings, or girlfriends. There were dozens of booths, each with its own telephone. A boy wrote down the phone number and handed it to a receptionist who logged it then took it to an operator when his number reached the top of her list. He sat waiting for his name and booth number to be called. The process might take hours, since each call had to be patched through by way of Hawaii and a series of ham radio operators, but they were all patient.

A lot of them cried, or got angry and swore, or kicked at the walls when their line was accidentally disconnected. It unfortunately happened all the time because of the intricate network involved. It was an emotional place to be. Many young men, Lian knew, were thinking that this might be the last time they spoke to the people they loved. Some would be right.

Lian stayed for most of the evening, placing calls, reconnecting those cut off, reassuring others who were frantic when their wives weren't at home.

"She'll be out buying groceries at this hour in Kansas," Lian told one young private. "She would be heartbroken if she knew you'd called and she missed you." The prospect that his wife would be upset somehow made him feel better.

Acting as a bridge to carry love between people: that was what she enjoyed.

Lian often listened in on conversations because she had to cut off each call after five minutes in order to let others have their turns. She tried to do it as gently as possible, at an opportune moment.

Lian looked down as the girl from the front desk handed her another number. "Mississippi," she said to herself, then saw the name.

Lian lifted her gaze up over the counter to see Bill standing on the other side, smiling at her. She smiled back, reassured that he seemed to be in good spirits. Maybe her letter had helped him, too.

His call went through relatively quickly. An older woman's voice with the same lazy twang as Bill's came on the line. Lian smiled to herself. "Your son is calling from Saigon," she said into the receiver. "Will you hold, please, Mrs. Jacobs?"

234

She looked up, signaled Bill with three fingers held up. Booth number three.

Starting to pick up the next slip in front of her, Lian hesitated. She wanted to be sure he really was all right. She listened in.

At first there was a great deal of confusion from the U.S. end of the line. Bill's mother was shouting at someone in the room with her, perhaps his father.

"Hi, Mom!" Bill's voice. "Hey, listen, before you say anything, there's a system here. You have to wait till I finish talking and say 'stop.' Then you talk and say 'stop' when you're done. That way we don't get cut off. Stop."

After a short pause of dead air the woman's voice came back on the line. "Military nonsense, boy? Stop."

"Yeah, right, Ma. Listen, I'm calling to let you know I'm okay. The food's lousy. You ask for steak in a restaurant, and they give you water buffalo. It's tough as leather, can't even cut it with a knife. But I'm not complaining 'cause we just got orders that we're being split up and sent out to different platoons in the boonies."

Horrified, Lian shot a look at Bill's back. Although being a soldier in the city wasn't without danger, here he was relatively safe. Men assigned to the city were called Saigon warriors. They walked the streets in starched fatigues with spit-shined boots and had relatively plush jobs. But if he were sent out on reconnaissance missions . . .

His mother was talking, asking about the weather, asking if he was glad to be able to get to see some of the countryside instead of being cooped up in the city.

My God! She doesn't know. She has no idea what it's like over here, Lian thought wildly.

"I still have more than half a year to go, so I'm not exactly short. But I have big plans for when I get out of the army."

Lian gripped her headset now, feeling guilty for intruding but unable to switch off. She glanced at the clock. One minute left.

"I'm getting married, Ma."

A sick sensation settled in her stomach. Lian dropped her forehead into one hand and closed her eyes. *Stop it! You should be happy for him!* Then she glanced up to meet Bill's twinkling hazel eyes. He'd known she was listening.

"She's a gorgeous girl, Ma. You'll love her. She's Vietnamese. Her name is Lian."

Her throat tightened until she could barely breathe. Lian shook her head at Bill. What was he thinking of? He knew she was married!

Bill just grinned and winked at her.

Breaking in on the line, Lian managed to croak out, "Your time is almost up!" She wrenched off the headset, tossed it onto the desk, and ran from the switchboard room.

17

Lian slammed the office door behind her. She pressed her back against it, gasping for breath.

Almost immediately, there was a knock.

"Go away!" she cried. "That wasn't funny!"

The knob turned, and gradually the door opened in spite of the pressure she exerted from the inside. Without a word, Bill reached out, gently entrapping her in his long arms while tears brimmed, then spilled over her long dark lashes. He shoved the door closed with his heel.

Lian pounded him furiously with her fists, but the young soldier still held her. He didn't try to kiss her or touch her in any intimate way, willing to simply contain her turbulent emotions.

Bill wasn't much taller than she. He was built more like a Vietnamese: small boned with no body fat. His hair was curly, short, and red, and his freckles gave his face a sweet boyish innocence. She looked up at him, no longer capable of struggling.

"Lian," he drawled, "I'm not stupid. I know it's not that easy."

"It's *impossible,*" she moaned.

"No, not impossible."

Bill blotted her tears with the pad of his thumb as they trickled down her cheeks. He smelled like Old Spice and vanilla ice cream.

After a while he spoke again. "Nguyen doesn't love you, Lian, and you don't love him. I could see that in your eyes, hear it in your voice when you talked about him at the Tet party. You think you owe him something. I don't know what went on between the two of you at the start. But you don't owe him your life, not if you have to pay with your happiness."

She gazed up at him through beaded lashes. Did he guess how frightened she was of Nguyen? She hadn't said a word about his hurting her, or the coldness with which he treated her.

"A wife has certain obligations," she stated, although with less assurance than she'd intended.

"So does a husband." Bill's eyes deepened to a rusty olive as he slowly bent toward her. His lips touched hers softly, and she felt nervous excitement in his embrace. Like so many Vietnamese boys, this American was too young to fight, and certainly too young to die. In a way, though, his predicament was far more tragic. This wasn't his country and he didn't want to be here. Feeling sorry for him, she softly kissed him back. Then, liking the feeling of his lips on hers, she kissed him again.

"Lian," he whispered, "I've never had a girl. Not really. I went out with a couple girls in high school, but we didn't even go steady."

"Why?" she asked, mesmerized by the soft southern wash of his words.

"I always figured when I met the right girl, we'd both know it. We wouldn't bother going together. We'd just get engaged, set a date, you know. Listen, Lian," he said, his soft eyes suddenly darkening. "None of them were right for me. I knew that. But the very first day I saw you—"

"No!" she protested, terrified of what he was about to say.

"Yes! Anything's possible, Lian. Believe me. You *can* leave him. You can divorce him. We could start filing papers so that when I go home, you'd be able to come with me as my wife. We can do it."

It was as if his speaking the words made them real. Yes. She could see how it might work! She'd never considered that she could divorce Nguyen. For a brief, blissful moment, her heart soared.

But Nguyen was not the type of man who'd surrender his wife to another, even if he himself was dissatisfied with her. He'd divorce her for his own reasons, but if he found out about Bill he'd hold on to her as a matter of pride.

Lian trailed her fingertips delicately across Bill's cheek. A fine, soft stubble of blond-red beard peppered the skin. As his arms folded more tightly around her, she felt the firmness of his thighs against hers, his arousal against the flat muscles of her stomach. A warm sensation answered from inside of her. She clung to him. *It's never been like this!* she mused, thoroughly amazed.

When he kissed her this time, she accepted his mouth on hers, feeling the thrill of his body reacting to hers. She closed her eyes, savoring him.

His hand stroked down the long black fall of her hair to the small hollow of her back. With a shudder of desire, Lian forced herself back to reality. "Bill," she murmured. "Please. Let me speak."

With reluctance, he released her and moved back a couple inches. His expression was hopeful.

"I need time to think about all of this. And," she said quickly before his expectations rose too high, "I must be sure that any decision is right for all of us. And I will not sleep with you."

His smile teetered.

"Not until Nguyen is no longer my husband. I have disgraced him by not giving him a son, which is something you should know about. I will not be able to give you a child, either."

Bill smiled at her, looking amused. "I think a baby would be great. But I love you, Lian. If it's just the two of us forever, I'd be in bayou heaven."

"And what about our not sleeping together?"

"Is this a test? You think if I can't get you into the sack within the next twenty-four hours, I won't want to hang around?" He looked hurt.

"Of course I don't think that of you," she said, shaking her head. If he only knew how much she needed his love. She kissed him lightly on the mouth. "Now you must go. I have work to do."

"Will you be here tomorrow night?"

"Yes," she promised. "But I won't have an answer that soon."

"All right. You just take your time. We have lots of it. But Lian, I don't want to go home if I can't go home with you."

Her heart leapt with joy. Understanding how much Bill must miss his home and family in Mississippi, his vow meant a great deal. She kissed him goodbye and gently closed the door behind him.

The rest of the night, she dwelt on those last precious words. What would it be like to live in the United States? She might never have a chance to return to Saigon. She might never see her parents again. A part of her was terrified by that prospect. Regardless, she thought only about Bill and being his wife. She accomplished almost no work that night.

On her way home in the cab, she was still thinking about Bill: how sweet and naive and genuine and affectionate he was. She imagined how much he'd appreciate the little things she'd do, the things Nguyen seemed to take so much for granted. Bill made her feel like a young girl again, and it was with an odd sense of shock that she remembered she actually was *only nineteen!* Nguyen had robbed her of her youth and her pride and ability to be passionate. Bill returned these gifts to her. She could feel the difference being with him for only a few minutes had made.

Lian opened the door with her key and, hearing no movement in the house, went straight to her room. Still glowing with happiness, she undressed and slipped under her sheet.

As she lay on her bed in the dark, she again thought of Jennifer and wondered helplessly what had happened to her. Finding one woman, dead or alive, in a country where hundreds perished every day and others simply disappeared never to be seen again seemed impossible.

Without knowing it, Bill had helped her face this problem, too. If there was a way for her life to take a turn toward joy and hope during this time of war, pain, and hatred, then surely there must be a way to find Jennifer. Lian simply would not accept the possibility that her friend was dead. If necessary, she'd travel from village to village herself until she found her.

Closing her eyes, Lian drifted off to a comforting sleep.

It was the feeling of a more substantial presence in the room than the Bill of her dreams that awakened her. She slowly opened her eyes without moving. A shadow knelt over her bed. Lian tensed, catching her breath. She could smell stale Scotch.

As her eyes adjusted to the darkness, she recognized Nguyen. His fists were clenched around the hem of her nightgown. He was silently weeping into the fabric.

Lian blinked, stupefied. Could it be he really did love her in some obscure way she hadn't understood?

"Nguyen," she said.

His head snapped up with a start.

"My husband," she said in Vietnamese, "I am sorry you are in pain. I wish there was something I could do to make your burden lighter."

He snatched at something in the sheets and staggered to his feet. "Dishonorable woman," he choked out. "I went to To Do Street tonight. I saw for myself!"

She stiffened.

"I saw how you talked to soldiers. They touched you! You treated them like lovers."

What has he seen? she wondered hysterically. Not Bill embracing her—that had been in her office, behind a closed door. Then she remembered passing through the lounge at one time during the night and greeting two young American soldiers. They were both returning to their homes in the States the next day and had stopped in to say goodbye. She'd given them each a motherly hug.

"They are my family," she objected. "I treat them like brothers." Although she was tense and alert to his gestures, she was still lying down. There was nowhere to go as long as he stood directly over her. Lian's glance was attracted by something shiny in his right hand. It had been resting on her bed a moment ago. Now he was trying to hide it behind his body.

"Family!" He spat on her nightgown. "You who cannot produce a son would spend your time with foreign men instead of your husband!" His voice was shaking. "I am the last son of my family. If I should die in battle, my family perishes as well. We are no more! My mother weeps every night for the lack of a child to carry her husband's name. A name that began with a great and ancient emperor!" He began to sob.

"It's not my fault!" Lian cried out. Something about his sorrowful drunkenness combined with the clarity of his accusations alarmed her. Why had he come into her room? To mourn his unborn family? To rape her again in punishment?

He pushed off of the side of her bed, but she lifted herself on one elbow and, covering her breasts, called out to him, unable to restrain herself any longer. "Nguyen, I wasn't raised to believe that a woman should do only her husband's bidding, to believe she was worthless if she could not produce a baby every time he lay with her. I don't agree with the old ways. You knew that when you married me!"

A sad light crossed his eyes as he turned to observe her. He looked as if he wanted to come to her. She held her breath, praying he would not, dreading his touch. The only man she'd ever wanted to be with, she realized in a flash of intuition, was Bill Jacobs.

In a tender motion, Nguyen reached down, caressing the soft curve of her shoulder before he left her room.

18

First came the faint, soothing sound of water buffaloes as they were herded past. Then the crickets began their dusk serenade. Monkeys chattered in the banana trees, a glimpse of which Jennifer could see through the cracks in the walls of the hut although night was again falling.

Her ankles were bound, her hands secured to a wooden post. They'd taken away her shoes days ago. She knew that even if she were able to loosen the ropes and escape the camp, she wouldn't survive for long barefoot in the jungle.

Sometimes she could estimate the size of the jungle's wildlife by the sounds animals made moving through the undergrowth—darting, furtive scurries or predatorial howls and thrashings when the chase was on. Her pilots had warned her about the little, green vipers that clung to blades of grass, their bites delivering almost instantaneous death. Then there were the mines and booby traps. On several of her visits to firebases, the men had warned her about strolling outside of the secured area.

Now she had no idea at all where she was, or in which direction to head for help.

The guerrillas and she had arrived at the abandoned *ville* nearly a week before. Two men stayed with her while their commander took the rest into the jungle. Twice each day, one of her guards would push a tin plate of food through the doorway at her. At nightfall, a soldier would rap on the door post to retrieve the pottery bowl she used for her toilet. Soon after, he brought it back emptied.

Jennifer was embarrassed by this last detail of her simple daily routine. It helped if she fantasized that her guards were not people but creatures devoid of intellect or emotions. They were, she thought, robots in pajamas, queer sorts of servants, and she was their mistress. Only somehow, as in most dreams, the logic of things had become mixed up, and they wouldn't allow her to leave when she pleased.

In more lucid moments, she tried to evaluate her situation logically. Why were they holding her? Why hadn't they already killed her? She suspected they might be hoping to trade her for a ransom, but she doubted AFVN would cough up very much for a rookie radio announcer.

Jennifer survived the long, languid days alternating dozing and waking. Time meant only daylight or darkness. She supposed she wasn't far from Saigon, although she had no memory of the trip to the camp. One of the men had struck her on the head before they'd taken her from Lian's. Because the climate here wasn't much different from that of the city, she believed they were not as far north as the highlands where Mel was stationed. She thought they might be just a dozen or so miles into the country, yet the jungle seemed quite dense.

The nights were unbearably long. She rarely slept then. To keep herself from going mad she devised ways she might escape—all of which were impractical and foolhardy on reconsideration the next morning. She wondered if anyone had figured out what had happened to her, if they even knew she was missing. Perhaps Lian would think she'd gone off with Chris.

Sometimes she broke down in tears and cursed her own stupidity for ever having come to Vietnam. She'd been so naive, thinking she could do any good. This was where such idiotic idealism had gotten her.

Then she thought of her friends and she knew she'd made the right decision. If she hadn't come to Nam, she'd never have met any of them. She'd still be at Radcliffe, probably marching in a student protest. She'd be listening to the evening news and hearing Walter Cronkite give the body count.

She hated the men who'd captured her. They'd taken her from her job and the people she loved. But most of all she hated them because of the control they exerted over her. She felt herself becoming dependent upon them. She came to look forward to the twice-daily platters of bananas and vegetables, and even the small portions of minced water buffalo meat. She hoped for their early arrival to dump her toilet bowl, because even in the mild warmth of a February day the smell quickly became nauseating and she couldn't push it far enough away from her. After the first week, she began trying to hold back from eliminating until it was closer to the time they usually retrieved the bowl, just before dark.

No one spoke English to her, although she suspected the guards might understand at least a little if she tried to communicate with them. She did listen to their conversations outside the hut and was surprised at how much she was able to understand. She'd picked up a fair amount of the language just by living in Saigon and bartering for her groceries with local merchants.

As mild as the weather was, it could still get chilly, especially at night. Sometimes she thought she couldn't stand sitting on the damp ground any longer, but she did not complain until the ninth evening. When her meal was shoved into the hut, she called out in Vietnamese, "Do you have a blanket?"

Silence from the other side.

"I'm cold every night. May I please have a blanket or a coat . . . *anything?*" She added the last word wistfully in English.

Jennifer heard footsteps retreat. Her heart sank. Of course, if they were keeping her for the purpose of torturing her as an example, they certainly wouldn't care one way or another whether she were comfortable.

But a few minutes later, she picked out the tread of several sets of boots coming closer. They stopped in front of her hut.

Two voices discussed the fact that she could speak Vietnamese—apparently a surprise. Very few Americans bothered to learn the language.

Jennifer called out in Vietnamese. "I do appreciate the food and water, but I'm very cold at night."

After another minute, a head poked through the opening.

A young guerrilla whose features looked as if they might belong to a twelve-year-old child looked solemnly at her. "No blankets," he told her firmly in his own language. "Major says maybe warmer clothes."

Although he didn't sound especially friendly, she was encouraged. If they talked to her and were willing to make even small concessions, maybe they didn't consider her a doomed woman.

A few minutes later, the young guerrilla returned carrying a flight suit with a U.S. Air Force insignia.

Jennifer reached for it, then automatically drew back her hand. The outfit had belonged to an American pilot, undoubtedly shot down. She looked at the guerrilla, and he must have understood her unvoiced objection.

"He is in a prison camp in the north," he said sharply. "He wears clothing we've generously provided."

She didn't know if it was the truth. She stared at the flight suit. Finally, the man tossed it on the ground and left. As darkness fell and the packed dirt under her hips cooled, eating at her bones, she eyed the suit longingly.

An hour after sunset, Jennifer decided that, whether or not the pilot was still alive, she must keep *herself* alive. She grimaced at the ropes pinching her wrists and ankles. Tied up like this, she probably wasn't going to be able to do much more than wrap the garment around her shoulders anyway.

"Guard!" Jennifer called out. Almost immediately, he appeared in the opening, but she couldn't come up with the word for untie. "I want to change clothes," she said, extending her bound wrists.

He muttered something and disappeared again. Unsure whether he'd gone to ask permission to untie her or had simply dismissed her request as ludicrous, she waited. The officer who'd commanded the raid on Lian's house returned in his place.

He hadn't spoken to her since that horrible day, nor had he taken any direct part in her care, leaving that to his men. Now, she looked up at him apprehensively, afraid of being hurt again.

"We will untie you," he told her in careful English, "but you must not try to run into the jungle. It is very dangerous."

"It's no piece of cake in here," she mumbled, as he loosened the knots at her wrists.

He didn't seem to hear her. "You are still hungry?"

She shook her head.

Her wrists at last free, Jennifer rubbed them, bringing back the circulation while he worked on her ankles. For days she'd feared they'd rape her before killing her. Visions of being forced to accommodate an entire company of communist guerrillas had terrorized her. She'd heard stories about the atrocities committed by the North Vietnamese, the torture and brainwashing of American POWs, the slaughter of whole villages when the VC learned that the inhabitants had cooperated with Americans. She wasn't about to trust this man on the basis of one compassionate act.

"I won't try to run away," she said, meeting his dark eyes. Her glance shifted uneasily to the jagged four-inch scar along his jaw, marking the place where she'd slashed him with a piece of Lian's teapot. "May I change my clothes in private?"

The major bowed. "I will talk to you when you're done," he said, backing out of her hut.

The goose bumps on her limbs rejoiced at the motion of her body as she pulled off the cotton minidress. It felt so good to stretch and bend. Although she'd been able to hobble around a very small area inside the hut while tied, any real exercise was impossible. Moreover, there hadn't seemed much point to it, since she'd believed that at any moment they were going to kill her. But now, for the first time since her capture, Jennifer felt hope. This man in charge did not seem unreasonable or especially cruel.

Jennifer stepped into the flight suit and pulled it up over her bra and panties. She felt dirty, not having bathed for days, but much warmer. The closely woven fabric had been designed to protect against the cold of high altitudes. She heard steps pacing outside her hut, thought fleetingly of trying to dart past the VC officer, then dismissed that idea for the time being. With him so near, how far would she get?

Before calling out to the officer, Jennifer jogged in place until the blood coursed freely through her limbs and she felt somewhat revived from the sluggishness of her days of inactivity.

"Ready," she called out in English.

The major returned with a cup of hot tea for her. She smiled to let him know she was pleased and sat down on the ground near the center post. After taking a quick sip of the steaming liquid, she held the tin cup in both hands, extending her wrists toward him.

Standing over her, he tilted his head to one side and observed her. "I've heard you on the radio," he said quickly.

She frowned, for a moment surprised, before realizing that anyone with a receiver could pick up an unscrambled radio frequency.

"Do you like American music?" she asked.

"Some of it. British music usually more."

"The Beatles?"

"Ah." His eyes lit up, and he squatted on the ground in front of her. "Paul McCartney. John Lennon. Very fine poets."

Jennifer laughed. She'd never thought of McCartney and Lennon as poets. However, in this land of poetry she guessed that might make sense.

"I like the Beatles, too," she said. "And the Dave Clark Five."

"Dusty Springfield, Moody Blues, Peter and Gordon," he added.

"'A World Without Love,'" she whispered, remembering one of the duo's first songs, which seemed so appropriate to this time and place.

He sat, staring at his hands. His hair was thick and black, similar to Lian's. It was raggedly trimmed, as if by someone unaccustomed to cutting hair. He was tall for a Vietnamese man, lean without appearing undernourished. His hands looked strong.

It occurred to her that he wasn't watching her very diligently. She sat, sipped the hot tea, wondering when he would tie her up again.

"You have a beautiful voice," he said without preface.

Was he asking her to sing for him? She suspected so. What she now perceived as his natural sensitivity to her situation kept him from coming straight out and requesting a song. He didn't want her to think it was a demand because she was his prisoner.

She began in her lightest, softest soprano, to sing the melancholy Peter and Gordon tune about preferring solitude to a peopled life without love.

When she finished, he smiled, and the half-healed cut along his jaw twisted. It still looked sore and raised. She felt a sting of regret and, oddly, of gladness that she hadn't struck a few inches lower at his throat. His men would have captured her anyway and she'd have killed this man who was not the evil monster she'd first imagined.

"Of course," she said, "it doesn't sound quite the same without the harmony."

"But, it is beautiful. A world without love." He shook his head sadly, then glanced up to see that her cup was empty. "Would you like more?"

"Yes, please."

From outside she could hear the sound of a soft rain beginning to fall, though this was Vietnam's dry season. A few words passed between the man standing guard and the major. He returned with another cup of steaming tea, his hair dripping wet. He sat while she drank—as if hoping she'd volunteer another song. She sang some of the ones she now considered her favorites, because she had sung them so often for her GIs.

The night grew deep and even the rain didn't sound as dismal after a while. It must have been very late when he at last stood up and stretched.

"I must sleep," he said, still in English for her benefit. He glanced down at the pieces of rope on the ground. "I won't tie you up this time, but do not try to escape. This is for your own protection."

Impulsively, she reached up, grasping his arm. "What is going to happen to me?"

"My name is Major Thieu," he said as if he hadn't heard her question. "Tell the guard to fetch me if you have a problem."

Her grip on his arm tightened, her nails unintentionally digging into his bare skin. "Tell me. I want to know what you're planning to do with me."

He looked down at her, and, to her dismay, she noticed a flash of regret in his dark eyes. "I do not know."

19

Since Nguyen wouldn't speak to her and was absolutely unconvinced of her innocence, Lian stopped trying to force any communication with him or explain herself. He disappeared for days at a time. She refused to sit at home waiting for him. She went on with her life.

Bill was patient when he learned she'd put off asking Nguyen for a divorce. He was, however, charmingly persistent in other ways. He asked her to meet him at a hotel in town. She refused. He begged her sweetly to spend a day alone with him at the beach. Again she refused. If there was any chance for them at all, they must do it right. That meant divorcing Nguyen before they allowed intimacy to become a part of their relationship. And broaching the subject of divorce had to wait until she could catch the colonel when he was sober. This was turning out to be quite a challenge.

When Lian wasn't at the USO, she was at the embassy, trying to help Jeffrey trace the elusive trail of the guerrillas who had taken Jennifer. Even before Cholon was totally secured, she visited a number of her parents' old friends in the district, asking for names of families who might know a way of getting through to the VC. Younger sons who hadn't been drafted by the ARVN might themselves be guerrillas. She had to be discreet, of course, merely drop by for tea and, as was the custom, share a poem or neighborhood news. Only then would she casually mention her missing American friend. She could only hope to pick up a stray word, reassuring her that Jennifer was all right. But day after day passed, and she heard nothing.

For five days, no casualties arrived at the hospital at Pleiku. The last wave of injured had all been shipped out to the Eighty-fifth Evac Hospital on the coast at Qui Nhon. The staff slept and ate and watched the empty sky in disbelief. No one dared remark on the silence, the hated missing choppers, the empty operating room. Then doctors, nurses, and med-techs alike spent the next two days in delirious celebration of the previous five.

The party began informally with a few friends that Mel's roommate Judy invited to their hooch. After ten hours, it had spread to include most of the hospital personnel. Judy, Mel, and two doctors took a bottle out behind the latrines somewhere around the forty-sixth hour of revelry and settled into the brush for a little privacy.

"Feels good," Mel said, leaning back into the scratchy grass after a full swig of Jim Beam. She gazed up at the moon poking out of a crisp cold mountain night.

"Wha' feels good?" slurred Webster Chaseborn, one of the surgeons.

"Doin' nothin'," she replied with a long satisfied smile. Her head spun, rotating the sky a full circle. Mel reached out and grabbed Chaseborn's shirt front to steady herself. "Better," she said.

Judy snuggled up to the other doctor. "What does tonight remind you of?" she asked, gazing dreamily into his eyes.

He kissed her long and hard instead of answering.

"I know what this reminds me of," Mel murmured happily. "Nights at home on the stoop. The stars. A big old orange moon. Cool, sweet winter air. But then . . ." She struggled with the concept, which seemed difficult to wrap her reeling mind around while so thoroughly under the effects of the booze. "But back then, I used to wish a time would come when I'd never be bored, when there'd always be something important, real important to do. I hated just hanging out, you know."

"I understand perfectly." Chaseborn hiccuped. "Excuse me."

"Certainly," Mel allowed with a gracious wave of her hand as she reached for the bottle.

"You realize," Chaseborn said, concentrating on pronouncing each word accurately, "that if you'd been clever you'd have wished for a mini . . . mini . . . minimum of eight hours' sleep in the bargain."

There was a sudden movement in the brush.

Fearing infiltrators, Mel twisted around, as alert as possible considering the quantity of liquor she'd consumed in the past two days.

"Up and at 'em, folks!" came a voice, followed by a young med-tech. "The radio's buzzing up a storm. There's been a napalm incident, plenty of casualties on their way."

"Damn!" Judy groaned, loosening her arms from around her doctor's neck. "More VC. It's not fair we gotta treat the other side, too. Not after what they've been doing to our guys."

"No," the med-tech explained, "there was a miscalculation. Our planes hit a whole squad of our own."

Mel shot to her feet, her heart shriveling up protectively in her breast. "Near here?" Her head was clearing remarkably fast.

"Naw. Close to the border, almost due west."

Before he'd finished, Mel was running headlong for the copter pad, with Chaseborn close behind her. She beat the first choppers, stood breathing in the cold night air, swallowing it into her lungs in long shuddering gulps until she could feel its icy fingers clear down to her toes. She slapped her own face with the flat of her hands, desperately trying to counteract the lingering fog in her head.

"Mel," Chaseborn said over her shoulder, "you don't know that it's Curtis's group."

She scanned the dark sky, straining to hear the whir of

rotors. At her sides, her fingers pinched the seams of her fatigue pants as if crimping pie crusts, the way her mama used to do. Then somebody thrust triage supplies at her. She automatically caught them.

The helicopters landed three at a time, like glowing-eyed dragonflies coming down out of the night. Mel raced from one to another, performing her duties. These were the worst burn cases she'd ever seen. She'd heard other nurses refer to patients such as these as Crispy Critters. It had seemed a cruel joke. But now she understood that the horror of facing these charred, screaming human bodies was more easily dealt with by grisly humor.

She raced to another chopper. One of the boys on this one was so badly burnt she couldn't tell if he were black or white. His hair was singed off, his face a mass of crackled black and red flesh. He was naked, his clothes either having been burned off of him or torn off in a futile effort to stop the scorching chemical from reaching his skin.

He wasn't going to make it. There was nothing she could do but set him aside with the other hopeless cases.

"Put him there, medic," she instructed, struggling to keep the revulsion out of her voice.

The sickeningly sugary smell of burnt flesh drifted up, making her gag. She crammed a fist into her mouth. Just as she turned away, the soldier's hand shot out. It closed in a jerking spasm around her wrist.

"Let me go, soldier!" she cried, anxious to tend to the others who might still be saved, as well as to reassure herself that Curtis wasn't among this tragic group. "I have work to do. You just . . . just rest."

"N-n-n-no," he managed through cracked lips. His eyes, swollen nearly shut, squinted up at her. "Mel. Mel, h-help me."

For a fraction of a second, she froze, her eyes widening with horror. Then she let out a strangled scream. It felt as if every bone in her body was snapping into little chalky chunks, disintegrating into fine powder, sifting uselessly down through her body.

"Oh, God! Curtis. No, no it's not you, baby."

Chaseborn and Judy appeared from nowhere. Judy grabbed her around the waist, struggling to pull her away.

"Let him be, Mel," Chaseborn commanded in her ear. "There's nothing you can do."

"Curt! Oh, Curt!" she wailed.

The surgeon took a syringe from the tray Judy had set on the ground and injected Curtis with a long, slow dose of oblivion. "He's a brave boy," he murmured. "Not even crying." He turned to Judy. "Let her stay with him. It won't be long."

The young nurse nodded and released her roommate, backing away.

Mel knelt beside her brother's stretcher, tears streaking down her face. "I . . . I don't want to touch you. It'll hurt," she told him.

He loosened his grip on her wrist and held out his hand anyway. She took it in hers.

"Tell me if there's anything you want me . . . anything I should do for you, or . . ." She couldn't go on.

"Amelia," he whispered so softly she could barely hear him above the chaos of the agonized cries of the injured and the frenetic shouts of the medical teams.

"Amelia," she repeated. "I'll look out for her . . . and the baby."

"Good," he breathed. Then the pitiful black parchment rolls that were all that was left of his fingers seemed to relax, becoming unnaturally light in her hand. She knew he was gone.

For a long moment, Mel sat there, unable to move, unable to absorb what had just happened. Her stomach drew up into a knot and her head began to spin again. But this time it was not the Jim Beam.

"Jesus Christ!" she screamed. "What the fuck do you think you're doing?" She shot to her feet, shrieking at the heavens, shaking a clenched fist. "You took my little brother, you bastard!"

Then she was tearing across the field, dodging stretchers and nurses, running blindly. She found herself in her hooch, the world closing in dense and black. "Oh, Mama," she said, sobbing, falling to her knees. "I tried. I tried so hard to keep him safe for you. I just . . . just couldn't do it."

As she doubled over, rocking herself, holding the pain in with her arms wrapped around her body, something sharp bit into her side. Sniffling, Mel straightened slightly, reached into her pocket. Her hand came out with the scalpel.

For a moment, she held it loosely in her palm. The lights from the helipad caught on the steel and sparkled dully. With careful precision, she leveled the short, sharp blade along her left wrist then made a deep incision.

Blood spurted from the gash. She didn't cry out. Curtis hadn't cried. Neither would she.

Because she'd severed nerves and muscle tissue along with the pulsing vein, it was difficult for her to hold the scalpel steady with her left hand. But somehow she managed to cut the other wrist.

Lian was at the club when the call came from the evac hospital at Pleiku.

"Mel?" she asked breathlessly. "Have they brought Jennifer in?"

"This is Dr. Webster Chaseborn," an unfamiliar voice announced.

Lian clutched the receiver, her heart thudding in her ears. "Mrs. Nguyen?"

"Yes, I'm here," she said shakily, confused. "Go on."

"I'm calling about Melantha Benning, a nurse here." *Why isn't Mel herself on the line?* The doctor continued. "I'm Mel's CO, and I'm authorizing leave for her. I want her to go home for a couple weeks, to get herself together. Unfortunately, she's not cooperating. You see, her brother was brought in a few days ago—"

"Oh, no!" Lian gasped.

"He didn't make it."

Poor Mel. Perhaps they hadn't gotten along perfectly at the start, but Lian respected the reason Mel had come to her country. She herself had no brothers or sisters, but if she'd had any, it would be difficult to be separated from them.

"She refuses to go home with the body?" she guessed.

"Yes. I'm sure her parents will need her at home. And Mel has to get out of here, at least for a while. She's breaking."

"I don't think her parents are still alive."

"That makes things more difficult." Chaseborn paused. "Perhaps there are relatives who'd take her in? I'm afraid she's been drinking rather heavily, ever since she heard of Jennifer Swanson's disappearance. We all drink, of course. It passes the time between heavy casualty dumps, but in Mel's case . . ."

His voice drifted off. She could hear commotion in the background, what might have been helicopters landing.

"But that's not what concerns me most," he added. "After her brother came in, she lost all control, just went to pieces. I sent one of the other nurses to check on her. In the few minutes she was alone, she had an accident with a scalpel."

"She tried to kill herself?" cried Lian.

"Mel won't admit it, but I'm sure that was the intention. There was a clean, penetrating slice in her left wrist. A less serious one in the right. Someone has to keep an eye on her."

"If she won't go home, she can stay with me," Lian offered quickly.

"I was hoping you'd suggest that. From what little I know of Mel, she has only two friends in-country: Jennifer and you. It would help if you'd come and fetch her. Are you willing to do that?"

"Yes," Lian said immediately.

"I'll arrange for a dust-off pilot to pick you up in Qui Nhon. You can get a lift out of Tan Son Nhut to there. The authorizations will be cleared by the time you reach the airport. Meanwhile, I won't allow her in O.R. She's at such loose ends, she's not fit for duty."

Lian hung up.

She wondered where her husband was. She hadn't seen him in two days. Perhaps, she thought with mixed feelings, he'd returned to his company in the north. If he were gone, she'd feel safer. But then she couldn't talk to him about the divorce. However, she suspected he was still in the city since Norris O'Brien continued to leave messages for him at the house.

She decided not to leave a note to explain where she'd gone. The mere idea that she was flying north to pick up a black American nurse was bound to irritate him, like everything else she did. She'd be back late that same night anyway.

The pilot of the Huey who took her on the second leg of her journey to Pleiku was a boy from Kansas with a crew cut. He smoked a cigar and played tapes by a group called The Association on a reel-to-reel recorder wedged under his seat. He flew like a madman—buzzing low over tree tops, shooting straight up into the sky to avoid pockets of snipers. His music was strangely gentle, with songs called "Cherish" and "Windy" and "Never, My Love." And one very bouncy tune she'd heard often in the club—"Along Comes Mary."

"I can't wait for you," he told her when she climbed out on the dusty red landing pad at Pleiku. "Another chopper will pick you up for the return trip."

"Fine," she said. "Thank you."

She found Mel's hooch with the help of a nurse she ran into a minute later. Ducking under the flap, Lian waited while her eyes adjusted to the comparative darkness. Mel, in a dirty olive-colored T-shirt, fatigue pants, and boots, was lying on a cot not two feet away.

Gently, Lian laid a hand on her arm. "Mel. Mel? It's Lian."

The black woman slowly opened her eyes. They were glazed yellow and shot through with red veins. For a moment, she seemed not to recognize Lian.

"He's dead," she muttered. "They shot my baby brother."

"I know, I know," Lian whispered, sitting on the cot beside her. "But there's nothing you can do, Mel. Come with me for a few days. You can't deal with this anymore—not without some rest."

"Jennifer's dead," she said in a wooden voice.

"What?"

"She's dead. They took her away. Your fuckin' comrades murdered her."

An icy chill raced through Lian's nerves. It wasn't the fact

Mel blamed her countrymen that rocketed her heart into her throat. It was the absolute certainty with which she spoke.

She gripped Mel by the shoulders and shook her. "How do you *know?*" she demanded.

Mel's glance slipped away. Tears nestled under black lashes. "They kill and kill and kill. All anybody knows anymore," she mumbled, becoming less coherent with each word. "Pretty, innocent little thing. She never had a chance. They raped her, tortured her. Never had a chance in hell . . ."

Beside herself with fear, Lian shook Mel even harder. "How do you *know?*" she rasped. "Mel, what have you heard?"

Mel threw back her head and laughed as tears rolled down her cheeks.

Lian gave up. She released the nurse and ran out of the tent. Where was Chaseborn? She scanned the rows of metal hangers, the canvas-and-wood shacks. Medics, nurses, army officers, and enlisted men darted from one structure to another as a bevy of helicopters descended upon them.

Lian grabbed a passing nurse. "Dr. Chaseborn," she demanded.

"He's busy, honey." The blunt bite of the woman's voice was familiar. She didn't trust Lian, a slant-eye.

"I'm Mel Benning's friend," she explained breathlessly. "Dr. Chaseborn called me to take her back with me to Saigon. I have to ask him something important."

The nurse's expression changed immediately. "Oh sure. He's in surgery. But I can get you in unscrubbed, as long as you stay beyond the sterile circle."

They ran to a long, low building surrounded by piles of sandbags.

"Dr. Chaseborn," the nurse called from an interior doorway not far from an operating table. "This woman has a question for you."

A tall man in surgical mask and gown turned just enough to see who it was. Then his eyes flickered back to his patient.

"Is she going?" he asked.

"I think so. I don't know." Lian swallowed, not wanting to hear his answer to her next question. "But does she know anything about Jennifer? She says she's dead."

Chaseborn shook his head. "She's been rattling on like that since she heard the news that Jennifer Swanson disappeared. She's seen too much death and . . ." His hand swept the operating room. Blood was everywhere.

Until that moment, Lian hadn't noticed her surroundings. Now she looked away, nearly gagging before forcing herself to continue. "Then you've heard no word of Jennifer?"

"Nothing."

Every ounce of energy remaining in Lian seemed to seep away. She leaned against the door jamb, closing her eyes. Her emotions had been tugged and twisted from every possible angle for what seemed like forever. Bill—Nguyen. Jennifer—the VC—Chris. Her instinctive need for independence—her desire to please her husband. And the war, always the war. Would life ever be simple again?

"Are you all right?" a woman's voice asked.

Lian looked up and nodded. "I may need some help getting Mel on a helicopter. Do you have time?"

The nurse, who'd been scrubbing up, shook her head. "Look, I barely got off an eighteen-hour shift in there, had three hours' sleep, now here we go again. Besides, every dust-off available for miles around is on its way in with casualties. You'd better forget about getting out of here tonight."

Lian sighed. Already she could feel the thrum-thrum-thrum of another wave of whirring blades vibrating in her chest.

She returned to Mel's hooch to find her asleep, tossing feverishly every few seconds. She sponged Mel's sweat-soaked brow, removed the scalpel from the pocket of her fatigues and laid it on a footlocker that had been propped up on end. On top of everything else, there was a rocket attack that night. Flying out of Pleiku became even less feasible. When Mel woke up, Lian sat with her to make sure she didn't drink or do anything to hurt herself. And when she finally slept again, Lian helped the less seriously wounded men in the yard outside.

Some of the Marines and soldiers wouldn't let her near them. She was the enemy. Soft words and reassurances couldn't convince them otherwise. But she tried to treat those who would let her with the same gentle attention she'd have given her own husband had he been brought in wounded. As she comforted and spoke to each of the men, she realized something. She cared as much for each of them as for Nguyen—no more, but no less either. She didn't love him anymore.

An hour before dawn, the rocket attack ended. The quiet was unnerving. Lian was physically drained but gratified when Mel awoke in a calmer frame of mind.

Lian brought them both coffee from the mess hall, and they sat together on Mel's cot, sipping the strong, black brew.

"He's going home," Mel said abruptly.

"Your brother?" At first Lian was worried that the other woman believed Curtis was still alive.

Mel nodded. "Home to Mama in heaven."

"Yes," Lian said softly.

"I came here to keep Curt out of trouble. I promised Mama. Great job I done, huh?"

"You couldn't protect him. No one expected you to," Lian whispered into the steam over her cup.

"*I* expected me to," Mel said morbidly.

"You did more than most sisters. You risked your life to be near him." She couldn't help thinking of Bill, the man she loved. He might very well be assigned the same sort of duty as Mel's brother. And what had she done up to this point to prove her devotion to him? She'd turned down every chance he'd given her to be with him. Now that realization burned bitterly inside her.

Lian watched as Mel finished her coffee with one gulp, crumpled the paper cup and threw it across the floor boards of her hooch. She glared at it in disgust.

"I want you to spend a few weeks in Saigon with me," Lian said firmly.

"Why the hell would I want to do that?" Standing up, Mel felt around in her pockets.

"Because you can't keep driving yourself like this. Especially now, since Curtis . . ."

"That's why I have to keep working!" Mel insisted. "You know how many guys we save here? If I go home, they'll be another nurse short. How many lives will that cost?"

"But you need to get away for at least a while."

Mel bent over her cot and started pulling off the sheets.

"What are you looking for?" Lian at last asked.

"My scalpel. I feel naked without it. I need it on me."

"I donated it to the O.R. in your name," Lian said without so much as a blink.

Mel swung around, brown eyes blazing. "You what?"

"They know how to use them in there, for saving lives instead of ending them," she said pointedly. Then her tone softened. "You're determined to kill yourself, one way or another. The work . . . the liquor . . . slashing your wrist."

Mel was silent.

"We're not going to let you do it."

"We?"

"Dr. Chaseborn called me to come and get you."

"That prick!" Mel bellowed.

Lian stood up, tossing her empty cup on top of a trash can already overflowing. She retrieved Mel's squashed cup and threw that away, too.

"I'm taking you to Saigon. You'll stay at my house. If you want to be useful, you can help me at the USO or in other ways. Maybe by working together we can get more information about where Jennifer is. Nobody's been able to come up with anything so far."

Towering a good fifteen inches over Lian's petite five-feet-two, Mel continued to glare down at her. "You damn slant-eyed bitch. Who gave you the right to move in on my life and start giving orders?"

Lian stood her ground. "You gave up your right to make decisions for yourself when you stopped caring whether you lived or died. Keep punishing yourself and you'll kill as many patients as you save in the operating room."

Mel looked away. After a long while, she said in a quiet voice, "I'm sorry, Lian."

"I know."

"I'll go crazy thinking about Curt, worrying about Jennifer if I'm not busy or drunk."

"I'll keep you busy and won't let you drink," Lian promised, "and when you come back here, you'll save twice as many lives because you'll be back on your feet again."

Mel nodded solemnly. "Right."

20

As Jennifer had suspected it would, eating the guerrillas' scavenged food and drinking untreated water took its toll. She suffered from stomach cramps, the runs, and felt increasingly weak. There was no medicine available. The best she could do was to drink as much liquid as possible to keep from becoming dehydrated, though she suspected that treatment would eventually worsen her condition since she was ingesting more of the bacteria that had made her sick in the first place.

Major Thieu also was a source of worry. He'd started allowing her to wander unfettered within the camp, and in doing so she'd spent more time talking with him. She discovered that he was a complex man of odd contrasts. While in camp, he was the perfect gentleman. He would share tea with her, ask perceptive questions about growing up in America and listen with rapt attention to her answers. He'd politely ask for a song or two each time they were together and lavish glowing praise on her voice. He was, she thought, a very good-looking man with warm, expressive eyes and a gentle side. He'd make a great headmaster, or a doctor, because he listened so well. But she never lost sight of the fact that he was a communist guerrilla.

When he left her at dark to go off with his men, *he* became one of those who hunted down and killed other Vietnamese whom he considered traitors to his country. Because they collaborated with a foreign military presence, he felt justified in anything he might do to them. If they lived in Saigon, his men bombed their houses or shops. In the country, he'd set fire to their homes, or entire villages, and watch them burn to the ground. He ordered the mining of roads with special explosive charges affectionately dubbed Bouncing Betties by American GIs for their ability to jump hip-high into the air and explode with a slight delay. The effect was to blow off the legs of their victim and emasculate him, yet leave him alive: a great deflator of morale.

She never forgot that cruel side of Thieu. And as charming as he could be, she never totally let down her guard around him. Because he expected his men to follow his orders without question, she sensed that he too would follow his superiors' orders. If he were ordered to kill her, he might genuinely regret doing so, but he would do it.

A half dozen times during the next two weeks, the guerrillas broke camp and moved to another location. Jennifer trekked along with them on trails increasingly more rugged into higher altitudes. A grass coolie hat was now added to her less-than-chic ensemble. They never covered more than five or ten miles at a time. Just enough, she guessed, to avoid being found by American patrols. That was another reason she was sure they couldn't be very far north. She'd simply have been dumped in a prison camp.

On one particularly cool morning, she was snuggled up close to the remnants of their campfire when one of Thieu's men woke her roughly. "Up, get up!" he commanded.

She struggled to her feet, still half asleep. "What's wrong?" she asked in Vietnamese.

"We go," he said, stepping up from behind and pushing her. A second man stood slightly in the background, tensely surveying the surrounding brush.

Jennifer began to move sluggishly in the direction he pointed. Her stomach dully ached. She wondered if the dysentery would kill her before the guerrillas got around to it.

Giving herself a chance to wake up, Jennifer looked around, taking in the weather and terrain. She was surprised to see the sun shining down through the tree tops. There was a feeling of frost in the air. Last night, they'd camped just outside a remote village on a river bank. They'd been here less than twenty-four hours. She wondered if an American platoon might be tracking them, getting closer. For the thousandth time she mused, *If I were able to wander a little ways from these two guys, just enough to get a head start* . . .

Pausing, she let her eyes drift up the hillside. None of the villagers were in sight. An eerie stillness filled the air. She could hear her heart singing in her ears: *Run—run—run!* It rose to a heady drumming sound until her whole body felt filled with the rhythm and the drive to break free. She resisted, knowing it wasn't the right time.

Without warning, one of the guerrillas struck her solidly between her shoulder blades with the butt of his carbine. She gasped, falling to her knees at the unexpected impact.

"Move!" he barked at her.

Struggling to her feet, she looked about frantically for Thieu. Where was he?

Then a horrible thought occurred to her. He had gone away with the rest of his men for the night and now it was morning. What if he'd been killed? What if he wasn't coming back and she was left here alone, unprotected, with these men who hated her?

"Where is the major?" she asked.

"No talk. Move!" he demanded this time in English, as if to be sure she understood. Taking a step forward with the carbine held out at an angle across his body, he shoved it against her chest.

She stumbled backward, catching herself against the side of a palm frond lean-to. There was nothing she could do but start to walk, hoping he was under strict orders to deliver her to the new rendezvous point in one piece and breathing.

They plodded northward for nearly three hours before the guerrillas gave any sign of slowing. Another half mile along, they entered an area of defoliated trees, burned leafless and lifeless by napalm. The remains of a village stood nearby: scorched walls of huts, a mud-brick cooking stove, strewn clothing and cooking utensils.

"I have to rest," she said finally, the only words she'd uttered since they'd left their last campsite. Although her feet throbbed and itched with fatigue, she didn't dare to stop walking until the guards gave her permission. She mechanically placed one foot in front of the other.

Behind her, the two men discussed her request in lowered voices before ordering, "Stop!"

She stopped.

"Sit."

She sat exactly where she stood, on the charred ground. She was shaking inside, but refused to let them see her fear. Or was the trembling another effect of the dysentery? Her stomach felt worse now. Jennifer stared down at her hands. Her palms were covered with tiny cuts and sores from the razor-sharp jungle leaves. Each day she acquired more and the ones she already had never seemed to heal. She expected they were infected, but there was nothing she could do.

One of the men went off into the burnt brush, the other remained with her.

Jennifer hummed softly, as if bored, while covertly studying her new surroundings. What she needed was an escape route and a place to hide where they wouldn't find her. It occurred to her that if Thieu were dead, she might no longer have a choice but to risk a desperate dash into the jungle.

After fifteen or twenty minutes, a soft crunching sound approached. Her captor reacted without alarm, as though he'd been expecting someone. Thieu emerged from the charred landscape, followed by the second guerrilla who'd marched her here and six other men, all in black pajamas— less than half of those who'd left with him the night before.

The major looked exhausted, his face strained, his eyes sunken with lack of sleep. When he saw her, not a glimmer of a smile creased his face. She ran up to him.

"What's happened?" she asked.

He didn't look at her or respond to her question. Instead, he snapped out a string of orders to his men, and they dashed off in different directions, leaving Thieu alone with her.

He sat cross-legged on the fallen trunk of a banana palm. She lowered herself beside him and brushed the dirt from the legs of her flight suit, her bare ankles, and her toes. They'd given her Ho Chi Minh sandals—homemade shoes fashioned from the tire treads of American Jeeps. Nevertheless, vicious-looking jungle sores covered the delicate skin of her feet. She winced when she accidentally touched one still bleeding. But she didn't complain; the major's men suffered from worse wounds.

"You should know what is happening as it concerns you," Thieu said in a quiet voice.

A chill sliced down her spine. "Yes?"

"Hanoi has been contacted by the American embassy and . . ."

"Thank God!"

But Thieu was shaking his head gravely. "We have asked for a prisoner exchange. Seventeen of our men held by the Americans in exchange for you."

Seventeen for one. Already her heart began to sink. The price was too high.

"They've refused?"

"The American ambassador would agree, but Prime Minister Phan Huy Quat and the ARVN commander-in-chief, Major General Minh, want to barter." Thieu's voice was bitter. "They argue for your unconditional release, as a nonpolitical civilian."

"And Hanoi?"

"They want our men back."

"What will happen next?" she asked softly, her fists clenched tensely on her knees.

"We will wait a day or two, in case some compromise can be reached."

Jennifer swallowed, feeling the life seep out of her. "Then what?"

He faced her for the first time, his black eyes sorrowful but unwavering. "If the exchange is not approved by Quat and Minh, I will have no further means of bargaining for your life."

She'd been right. Thieu might easily have killed her in Lian's home, or let his men do it, but he'd argued that she was worth more alive. It seemed he had been wrong. And now there was nothing more he could do for her.

"I will be killed," she said, her voice sounding bizarrely strong in her own ears.

"Yes." He paused. "There is an ancient Vietnamese proverb from one of my favorite poems. It is called the 'Ballad of the Scented Slipper.' 'Nothing occurs that fate has not ordained.'" Thieu's black eyes fixed on her green ones. "'Let no fair look distract from Heaven's will.'"

Jennifer felt surges of terror, anger, and disbelief wash over her in turn. "You're telling me that if the South Vietnamese government refuses to buy my freedom, my death is meant to be?"

Thieu observed her tranquilly. He gave a brief nod, pressed his lips together.

"You can't have me killed," she said in a low voice. "We are friends."

He reached out, taking her hands gently in his. "And for that reason, I will not allow my men to touch you. I will do it myself, my friend. I promise, you will not suffer."

The following days passed with excruciating slowness. Sometimes Chris thought he couldn't bear another hour of worrying about Jennifer. He slept little, two hours at a time. Then he was wide awake, wondering how far away she might be, how frustratingly close. Or if she were still alive at all.

Something inside of him refused to believe Jennifer was dead. She was most certainly in extreme jeopardy, but she could not be dead.

He discovered he'd been right when he heard she was being held for exchange with VC prisoners. Johansen came to him with the news.

"It's just a matter of time before she's back in Saigon," the lieutenant said, slapping Chris on the back.

A few days later, Chris managed to get a call through to Jeffrey Kirk, the young diplomat at the embassy whom Jennifer had once mentioned as an emergency contact. He learned that Johansen had jumped to an optimistic conclusion.

"I'm sorry, Chris," Jeffrey shouted over a staticky line. "I can't believe the bureaucratic mess that's being made of this. Jenny's father flew in. He's rallied half of Washington to help get her freed, but because the South Vietnamese think that releasing known VC would be setting a bad precedent, everything's come to a screeching halt."

Chris couldn't believe his ears. His gut churned. "You mean they've refused to make the swap?"

"Not exactly. The idiots are haggling. Playing power politics with her life."

Kirk didn't sound in great shape himself, Chris thought. He wondered how close he had been to Jennifer. He sounded as if she were special to him, too. It was no time, however, to succumb to jealousy.

"What are the chances something will eventually be worked out?" Chris asked.

There was a long pause. "I don't know what to tell you. Fifty-fifty? Maybe less. I'm afraid that if the politicians hold out too long, the VC will decide they're not being taken seriously."

"The only way to save face will be to carry through their threat and kill her."

"Right."

Chris took a deep breath. "Do me a favor. Let me know as soon as you hear anything either way."

"Of course," Kirk promised.

Chris's platoon had spent most of the time during the past few weeks marching from village to village. They asked people if they'd seen a blond American woman, showed her photo around. The answer was always the same. No.

He couldn't tell if they were lying; it was impossibly

maddening. He knew the almost imperceptible flickers in the eyes of the peasants had subtle meanings. Perhaps they had actually seen her but were afraid to admit it. Or maybe they were calculating what they would or wouldn't say if she did suddenly turn up. The risk was great. Even to point the American soldiers in a certain direction might result in their entire village being torched.

The Cu Chi group also kept in touch with other nearby units. One day, just after dawn, a message crackled over the R/T man's receiver. "We may have something here on Operation Songbird."

Overhearing the transmission, Chris nearly knocked Van Dorf over as he grabbed for the field phone. "Did you find her?"

"Naw. But we hit two villages in a row where little kids told us they'd seen an American woman. They don't know if she was a blonde. She wore a grass coolie hat and kept her head down. She was dressed in an American pilot's flight suit."

Chris frowned. "Was she injured? Was she tied up like a prisoner?"

"No. She was just walking along with the men. The kids thought she might be one of the local missionaries or a woman from Catholic Relief."

Chris closed his eyes, gritting his teeth. She could be anywhere, of course, but this was as close to a lead as they'd come. "Thanks." He handed the phone back to Van Dorf.

"Better than no news," the radio man said.

"Where's Johansen?"

"Last I saw, over by bunker three."

A group of six men were huddled near the bunker. Johansen stood a little way apart. A couple of the soldiers were shaving, four were playing poker. The lieutenant looked up expectantly when he saw Chris coming.

"What's up?"

"I want a transfer," Chris said. "Effective immediately."

Johansen lowered the clipboard he'd been writing on. "Why?"

"We just got a call from a company in Two Corps. Jennifer may have been spotted in a couple villages in their quadrant. That's just twenty-five miles north of here."

"If she's there, they'll find her."

"I can't wait for them to stumble on her. I have to be there, dammit!"

Johansen sighed. "I can't just send you up there without orders. Cutting them will take headquarters four or five days."

Chris whipped off his helmet, throwing it on the ground. "Christ, Rick! I've saved your ass and most every man's in this outfit at least once. I'm begging you for this one favor. Okay," he added in desperation when the lieutenant motioned helplessly with one hand, "forget the transfer. Just turn your back."

"You know I can't do that. Stay put until we can make it official." Johansen reached out to put a hand on Chris's shoulder. "Run off one more time, and I'll have to report you."

"Shit!"

"It's for your own good, Tyler." Making a final check mark on his clipboard, he turned and started across camp.

Chris scooped up his helmet. *What now? What the hell now?*

"Hey, Chris," a soldier named Rogers said quietly. He was looking into the little piece of reflective tin he used to shave by, scraping the razor up the curve of his throat. "If you need a backup—I'm yours, man."

Wilson and Palmer glanced up from their cards. They each gave a subtle nod.

"Count me in, too, Tyler," another soldier named Meeko said. "I raise you a bill." He placed a sheet of military scrip on the ground beside his boot. "Just say when, Tyler."

It was only five hours later when Jeffrey called back. The R/T man summoned Chris to the communications center.

"It's been a nightmare here. Negotiations have broken off," Jeffrey said breathlessly. "There won't be any trade."

"Have the guerrillas holding Jen been told there will be no exchange?"

272

"If they don't know already, it's only a matter of hours until word trickles down to them."

Chris gripped the receiver, his knuckles turning white. A booming sound not unlike that of an artillery barrage filled his head. He'd never been so consumed with rage in his life. "They'll kill her the moment they know."

"Probably." Jeffrey sounded as if he hadn't quite given up.

"But you think there's a chance they won't?"

"In any kidnapping case, there's the possibility that an emotional bond may have been formed. Jennifer's a smart girl. If there's a way she can protect herself, she'll do it. Maybe they'll be reluctant to kill her right away.

"There's one other thing," Jeffrey began again hesitantly. "Lian told me you know your way around out there pretty well."

"I've already thought about that. We received a message from a unit north of here. They may be closing in on a group of VC traveling with a woman who might or might not be Jen. But I can't get cleared by my CO for a transfer."

Jeffrey paused. "Look, Chris, if I could tell an M-16 from a bazooka, I'd be out there myself right now. I'm not trying to talk you into anything. However, the next few hours are crucial. If you gentlemen have a lead to work at all—"

"I want to take a couple friends up there," Chris interrupted. "Can you get me one or two choppers?"

"Give me coordinates."

Within thirty minutes, the whir of helicopter blades filled the air with their familiar pulsing beat.

"What the hell's going on?" Johansen barked, ducking out of the headquarters to stare up at the incoming Cobra gunship and Huey.

Palmer stepped up behind his CO. "Nothing personal, sir," he said, touching the muzzle of his gun to the back of the lieutenant's neck as a small group of men dashed across camp.

"Chris!" bellowed Johansen. "Don't do it!"

"Gotta, sir. Palmer will keep you company till we get

back." He was hustling around, taping as much ammo to his body as possible, gathering gear and extra weapons. He had no idea what their chances might be of finding Jen, but this was a hell of a lot better than sitting and doing nothing.

Chris hauled himself up into the Cobra after the rest of his team boarded the larger of the two helicopters. They shot up into the air, flying just above the tree line. The broad plains of the area north of Cu Chi gave way to a mountain range sliced through by a steep river valley. The land was first covered by dense forest, then they flew over a section that had been napalmed into scorched desolation. A twisting dirt road was visible below, as well as an occasional primitive dwelling.

"There's the bunch that rang us this morning," Van Dorf shouted through Chris's earphones. He was pointing out the open side of the Huey to a string of American infantrymen moving slowly off the edge of the road.

They spotted the helicopters, looked up, and waved.

"We'll set down in that clearing just ahead," the Cobra pilot said. "Keep in touch. I'll circle the area in case you flush them out. We might have a better chance of spotting them from the air."

"Right." Chris cast the men in the other helicopter a silent look of thanks. No one had forced them to come. Maybe they considered this fair payback for all the times he'd saved their hides. He hoped to God all of them made it through this trip.

While the two planes hovered a few feet above the ground, they jumped out and ran, zigzagging toward a stand of charred trees. They split into two groups to more efficiently cover ground. Chris tried not to think about the possibility that the woman who'd been spotted might not be Jen at all.

Jennifer huddled in front of a simple mud hut, her arms wrapped around her pulled-up knees. The sun was still out but a chill permeated her bones.

The thought of being blown apart by a mine or shot in the back as she tried to escape no longer seemed the worst of her alternatives. The worst would be lying down to sleep one night and never waking the next morning after Thieu leveled a gun at her head. How much better it would be to take a chance and run.

All of the men were in camp now, eating their last meal before going out on a night raid. She waited, her stomach clenched in a knot, while Thieu's men became involved in their rice and the day's news. They talked of supplies being delivered soon. Food was running low, as was ammunition. Thieu himself was conversing with his first sergeant in front of the next hut.

Jennifer slowly rose to her feet and started moving across the courtyard of the *ville*. The villagers themselves were absent, most having taken to their huts while the guerrillas were around. She walked as if she were coming to join the men in their circle for a bite of food, a moment in the flames' warmth. Several eyes darted automatically to take in her movement, then settled back on their rice bowls after deciding she was staying within an acceptable distance.

When she was almost equally near the group and the surrounding stubble of blackened forest, Jennifer started backing away from the men. She stooped now and then to pick up a tiny stone or piece of grain on the ground, as if to study it leisurely. She held her breath, her heart thudding erratically in her chest. None of the men seemed to notice how close she stood to the edge of the trees. Suddenly she spun around and dashed into the undergrowth.

A shout went up almost at once. Jennifer didn't stop.

Bullets spit against burnt tree trunks. Darting behind one, she left the footpath. Her sandals slipped on soggy leaves, and she fell. Picking herself up, she tore off the crude rubber shoes and straw hat, then plunged on, her breath coming in short painful spasms.

She could hear men crashing through the jungle after her. "Jennifer, stop!" It was Thieu, not far behind.

Thieu was no longer her friend. What did it matter, if he saved her from a mine or a deadly viper? He would kill her as soon as he'd caught her. This wasn't hysteria speaking.

She dodged on still faster. Her loose blond hair stuck in thick ropes to her sweaty brow and cheeks. Her bare feet were torn by sharp roots and the knifelike leaves that had grown back since the chemical sprays had destroyed the original foliage. Suddenly, her ankle wrenched to one side, and she went down hard.

"Oh!" she groaned, rolling headlong down a slope that led to a river bank. She must have tumbled twenty feet, almost straight down before coming to rest in the mud at the river's edge.

Hearing brush rustle, feeling the vibration of running feet, she looked around desperately for something to use as a weapon. She glimpsed the top of a rock lodged in mud, dug it up with her bare hands. It was smooth from the river's flow, about the size of a croquet ball.

Dragging herself behind an uprooted tree trunk, Jennifer waited, trying to quiet her breathing. She might take down one man with the rock. If she could get his weapon away from him, she might even eliminate a few more of her pursuers. She shut her eyes briefly. *Then what, Jennifer Lynn?*

Chris and half of his men circled one village while keeping in touch with the rest of the Cu Chi volunteers by radio. When he reached the clearing in the center of the village, there were only children and a couple old people around. They looked up in fright as the soldiers broke through the undergrowth.

Chris's buddy Meeko hustled them into the center of the village. Chris and Rogers searched each of the huts.

"Nothing," Rogers reported, coming out of the last.

Chris's heart fell. "Ask them about the American woman," he ordered Meeko, who had learned some of the language while living with a Vietnamese woman in Saigon.

"Already did. They say no." He threw Chris a sympathetic glance.

The radio strapped to Chris's hip crackled: "Hey, something's going down!" It was Van Dorf, with the other half of the men.

Chris pressed the send button. "What?"

276

"We're just outside a village. The forest is swarming with VC. They're crashing around like damn water buffalo!"

"We're coming." Chris took off at a run, his friends following.

Before long, Chris could see the cooking smoke of a second village above the black line of trees. Ahead lay a river. Chris jumped in, boots first. He held his AK-47 above his head, wading deeper, moving as fast as the flow of water allowed.

By now he was able to hear shouts. He couldn't tell above the sound of the rushing water if they were from his own men, VC, or peasants. He was too far ahead of his group to communicate without stopping to radio, and he didn't want to waste precious seconds.

Chris headed for the voices. He wasn't thinking about his own jeopardy, his mind and heart were full of Jennifer. But the soldier in him shifted into automatic, combat boots lifting high, plunging straight down to best avoid trip wires, staying clear of any area that looked too well traveled—for fear of booby traps. He ran like hell.

Jennifer held her breath and stood up, her back pressed against the rough, charred trunk, the heavy rock braced in two hands at chin level. Footsteps approached.

No longer running, their owner seemed to sense her proximity. With shaky hands, she slowly raised the rock above her head.

Then—"Jennifer? Come out. We won't hurt you. You'll only injure yourself."

She could almost believe Thieu. He sounded sincere. For a second, she hesitated. Then the tip of his carbine came into view around the tree, followed by a hand, his strong face in profile.

She drove the boulder downward at the same moment that he must have caught her in his peripheral vision. Thieu was so close to her when he swung around that the barrel of his gun smacked against her ribs. She dropped the rock, and it glanced off the side of his head.

Crying out in pain, the VC commander brought his hand automatically up to the bloody gash in his forehead. She lunged for the gun barrel, but he saw her coming and swung it out of reach. Thrashing through the jungle not far away, his men could be heard closing in on them.

"No!" she rasped out, shaking her head. "You can't kill me."

He looked at her with deep regret and, to her surprise, laid down his carbine. Did he mean to let her go?

Then she glimpsed his hands, steady and strong as they rose toward her throat. Staggering backward, she felt her way along the rugged ground. Another step. He followed. She turned and bolted.

After only three strides, he caught up with her. Thieu tackled her, and Jennifer went down hard under his body. She struggled futilely. He turned her over so that they were facing each other, his black eyes and rigid mouth inches from her face. His fingers locked around her throat.

She tore at his wrists, his fingers, his shirt, but nothing she did had the least effect.

"Goodbye, my friend," he whispered, his fingers tightening. A thick black haze descended over her eyes.

21

She was worlds away. Neither light nor sound penetrated death's cold shadow, but she felt through the violent vibrations in the ground an explosion very close by, then a chatter of smaller, more distant ones. Almost at once, the pressure around Jennifer's throat eased up. A gray light seeped between her lashes. Blurring shadows swam before her eyes.

The first image she saw with any clarity was the side of Thieu's face—one eye staring at her—as it rested on her chest. His body lay heavily on top of her.

Screaming, she struggled to push him off. *Run!* her brain demanded, not bothering to question what had stopped Thieu at the last second from finishing her off. All she could think of was that his men must be close by now. *Run, run, run—for God's sake!* But she was overcome by a terrible lethargy. Her body ached with the strain of having fought a man whose natural strength was at least twice her own. Her feet and limbs had been shredded by vicious undergrowth, her insides hurt terribly, her heart battered her ribs. Brain commanded, *Flee!* Body argued, *Lie still and rest . . . rest . . . rest. Let what happens happen.*

She had never been able to ignore her brain.

Jennifer shoved Thieu's head to one side. It lolled off her shoulder. Then, without any effort on her part, the remaining weight of his body was removed from her. And she stared with wonder up into Chris's mud-streaked face.

For a moment, she couldn't react. In the next, a flood of emotions overcame her. Tears streamed down her cheeks as he bent over her, pulling her close, cradling her against his chest.

"He-he-he's dead?" she managed over a train of hiccups.

"Yeah, babe."

She could feel Chris shaking, too, as if he also realized how close they'd come to losing each other forever. But when she pulled back to take a look at his face, his alert blue eyes were scanning the brush around them.

There was a sharp crack, then another burst of weapons fire, shouts from not far away. Chris pushed her down, covering her with his body while he fired into the jungle.

It seemed an eternity before the firefight ended. When it did, Jennifer felt as if every muscle in her body had been tied in knots, every nerve overloaded. It struck her that she was unsure whether she was glad to have survived or not.

A man with a radio strapped over one shoulder ran up to Chris. "There's three dead, four including this *gook,*" he said, indicating Thieu.

Chris turned his back to the other soldier. "Any of our guys hurt?"

"Meeko took a couple in the leg. Rogers is a bit messed up, but I think he's repairable. You?"

"I'm okay," Chris said tightly. He looked down at Jennifer. "Can you walk?"

"I think so."

"There's a chopper coming. He'll put down about a quarter mile from here."

She nodded and started staggering away without regard to direction. She had to get away from this place. She was confused, stunned, felt an inexplicable sense of mourning for the deaths of the men who had been her captors for nearly a month, and a special sense of loss for Thieu—the man who would have killed her. *I must be going crazy,* she thought. But she was almost certain the major would have felt this same emptiness for her loss, had he been successful.

Chris gently pulled her around to face the opposite direction. They moved in silence for a hundred feet. She stumbled more than walked. Then Chris hitched his gun over one shoulder and wordlessly lifted her into his arms. He carried her the rest of the way to the helicopter.

Jennifer lay curled up on a pile of canvas as the chopper lifted off. She was aware of hushed masculine voices all around her, conversation somewhere up front between the pilot and his gunman.

The canvas shifted slightly as somebody sat down next to her.

"Jen?" Chris asked softly. "Did he . . . did they—"

"No!" she answered with a sharpness she hadn't anticipated. "Nobody raped me."

Chris was silent for a while. "It's all right to not know who the good guys are. Sometimes it gets damn confusing. But there wasn't time to ask questions. I had to kill him, Jen. It was you or him."

"I know," she said, loving Chris for understanding a little of what she'd gone through. She put her head in his lap and fell asleep.

Lian's house was overflowing with guests, so many that it made her Tet party look like a flop. They came from the embassy, from the bases surrounding Saigon, from as far away as Hue to the north and the lower reaches of the delta to the south. This celebration was in honor of Jennifer's homecoming.

Her father was there. Since the hunter-killer squad from Cu Chi had rescued her and she'd arrived back in the city, Max had stayed close at hand. Jennifer spent three days in the Third Field Hospital in Saigon while the doctors checked her out for injuries, treated her jungle sores, and started her on ampicillin and a liquid diet for the dysentery. Max had set up camp in the hospital for the duration.

This morning she'd been released on the condition that she stay with someone to ensure she took her medicine and didn't overtax herself. Lian insisted that she come to her house. Both she and Mel would be there to watch over her.

The day was bright and warm and the sky was a periwinkle blue. Jennifer sat in the garden with Chris. Max had interceded on the young soldier's behalf. Instead of facing court-martialing for disobeying his CO, he'd been given a week's leave with a possibility of more. Chris was also staying at Lian's house—sharing Jennifer's room. It was heaven.

The GIs, embassy staff, and people from the radio station hugged her and, many with tears in their eyes or foggy voices, told her how overjoyed they were that she was with them again. She was moved by their warmth and affection. All she had done to deserve it was sing a few songs. She marveled at how little it often took to make people happy.

Max was staying at the embassy and planned to fly back to the States the next day. Father and daughter had already suffered through a number of one-way discussions on that topic. He'd informed her he had a ticket for her and she would accompany him.

Jennifer hadn't actually refused. The little girl in her wanted desperately to return to the life of quiet comfort at her parents' home. However, the less emotional part understood she could never return to the carefree, frivolous life she'd lived before Nam. Marblehead would never be the same.

"The flight leaves at six A.M.," her father reminded her as he walked into the garden. "Have you finished packing?"

"No," she said quietly, watching his concerned gray eyes. They'd never observed her in quite the same way as they had in the moment when he'd rushed into her hospital room. She'd been cleaned up and put into a hospital gown, but her eyes must have reflected the terror and vulnerability of her weeks in captivity. He came to her, sitting on the edge of her bed, and held her. Then Maxwell Swanson wept.

"Lian says she'll help you when you're ready to pack," he said.

She looked across at Chris, who was trying to appear impartial. "I don't know if I'll be leaving," she said at last.

Other than slightly narrowing his eyes, Chris allowed no reaction to show in his face. "Jen, your father just wants you to be safe."

"I know," she said. *"Safe* isn't what I want." She looked meaningfully at Chris.

Her father must have understood. "Look, honey," he began cautiously, "if you and Chris have an understanding, he'll want you to go back with me." He waited for support. When none came he continued. "Chris told me he's on his second tour. He's done his duty. I'm sure I could arrange an early release from the army for him. Then you can both come back to the States and have time to work things out—see if what you have is a lasting relationship."

It was clear by his tone that he accepted Chris only because he'd saved his daughter's life. Undoubtedly, Max hoped that once she was back among her own crowd—North Shore society—a simple soldier from the Midwest would have considerably less appeal.

Chris must have sensed this, too. His jaw grew rigid, but his voice remained in control. "Jen, he's right. You should go back where you belong."

"And what about you? Where do you belong?"

"I don't know," he answered her solemnly, "but Nam is as close as it gets for now."

She nodded. "I'm staying."

Both men looked at her in shock.

With a jerk, Chris shot to his feet. "Not because of me you aren't. If you stay it's for your own reasons. I haven't made you any promises. Just because I pulled you out of the jungle doesn't . . ."

"Shut up, Christopher," she said.

He stared down at her as she took a sip of her Coke.

"I'm not *only* staying to be near you. I'm staying because I have work to do. I'm not leaving here until I've done what I'd promised."

Her father's ears burned red. "That bastard Freck tricked you into coming over here. You don't owe him or his people a thing."

"Oh, Daddy." She sighed. "This is my decision, not an

obligation based on some contract. I *want* to stay. It's going to take the rest of my year to figure out what kind of life I want for myself, where, and"—she looked straight at Chris —"with whom."

Her father shook his head, baffled. "I don't know what to say to your mother," he said softly.

"Tell her I love her."

The next week was one of readjustment and rest, both of which Jennifer needed desperately. And so did Mel and Lian—and especially Chris, who'd lost fifteen pounds since Tet. He looked as if he hadn't slept much.

While in the hospital, Jennifer had dozed off for brief naps, but was unable to sleep through an entire night. The bed felt too soft after weeks of sleeping on the ground, cushioned only by palm boughs. The ward was hushed, lacking the night sounds of the jungle that had lulled her into shallow slumbers during her captive days.

Once she was again established in Lian's home, she reverted to something closer to her old pattern of falling deeply unconscious for a full six hours, waking briefly to check on her surroundings, then drifting off again for another hour or so. Chris lay beside her, waking when she did. He reached over, drew her close, touched her softly. Reassured, she closed her eyes and slept.

Jennifer had never been so content as during those early days and nights. She and Chris were like newlyweds. Oftentimes, whether there were other people in the house or not, their eyes might meet across the parlor, kitchen, or garden. Jennifer would smile. Chris would glance toward the bedroom door, his brow quirked seductively. With hastily murmured excuses, they'd disappear into the guest room for an hour or more.

Jennifer had prepared herself for a letdown. After their first night together during the Tet invasion, what could possibly be so exhilarating? Their lovemaking had been charged with the eroticism of two near-strangers discovering each other's bodies. That rapture could surely not be duplicated.

If anything, though, their intimacy after her rescue exceeded her memories. Chris was a tender and passionate lover, by turns recipient and aggressor. He encouraged her to touch, to tantalize him in any way she chose, and she was thrilled at finding new ways to arouse him. And, when she most needed him to take charge, he always seemed to sense the subtle change in her sexual tempo—something even she didn't understand. Chris caressed and kissed her until she was breathless with anticipation and nearly mad with desire. Then he would enter her and they would cling to each other wildly, joyfully for the duration of their climaxes.

Since her body and emotions still required additional healing time, she often napped in the afternoons. Jennifer often had vivid dreams, saw the guerrillas again and again, heard their kind words as well as their frightening chatter and hate-filled curses. Every time her brain replayed these scenes she felt saddened, then somehow reassured that that tragic part of her life was over. She could move on, look forward to a future. But she still had no idea what that future might hold. She and Chris never spoke of marriage. She sensed this was forbidden territory as far as he was concerned, and for now it was enough to love him and be loved by him each day as it came.

On her third day at Lian's home, she became less preoccupied with her experience as a hostage and began noticing her friends again. She learned that Mel's brother had been killed and she'd reacted by trying to commit suicide. Jennifer tried talking to Mel about it. Her friend was unwilling to discuss Curtis at all or admit that her slashed wrists were anything but an accident. Jennifer also became aware of Mel's drinking problem. After Jennifer's welcome-home party, Lian systematically removed all alcohol from the house and she never let Mel go anywhere in town alone. The black nurse was at first furious and abusive toward Lian, but after a few days she seemed to accept the house rules.

Lian was the strong one these days. In addition to keeping a sharp eye on Mel, she protected the privacy of Jennifer and Chris with unflagging energy, turning away well-wishers and reporters alike who wanted Jen to tell her story for the hundredth time. Lian instinctively understood Jennifer's need for quiet, for slow-paced days and time alone with Chris. She prepared meals for everyone, kept the house scrupulously neat, working with inconspicuous diligence, and gave the young couple the run of her property.

Regardless of Lian's calm exterior, Jennifer sensed a consuming despair in her friend. Lian might try to mask whatever secret sorrow she held inside with gentle smiles, but it was clear something was terribly wrong.

One day when they were alone in the garden, Jennifer asked Lian if she'd heard from Nguyen. "He must be able to take leave soon," Jennifer said, sipping her morning soup.

"He has been in Saigon for several weeks on temporary assignment," Lian said all in one breath, avoiding her eyes.

Jennifer was shocked. "Why isn't he staying here?" Then she bit her lip when she saw Lian's pained expression. "It's not because of us, is it?"

Lian ran a finger around the lip of her porcelain soup bowl. "He is a troubled man," she said simply.

Jennifer stood up. "It *is* us, isn't it? He found out you'd filled his house with American guests and there was no room for him. This is awful. Why didn't you say something?"

"No, no," Lian quickly denied.

Jennifer stared at her. What had happened to change Lian since she'd been gone? Her delicate oval face was ravaged by worry. "Can you talk about it?" she whispered.

"Yes," Lian said. "I would like to, if only to reassure you that Nguyen's leaving has nothing to do with you." She paused. "My husband came home soon after Tet. It's strange. In his absence, I remembered all the good, strong things about him. Some of the bad I'd forgotten. Some I just didn't want to dwell on. When he returned, he started drinking again . . . much worse than Mel ever did . . . and that is my fault."

Jennifer's mouth dropped open. "Your fault!" She laughed. "Listen, lady, if a guy hits the bottle because you dumped him, maybe it's your fault. If he does it after you've waited faithfully for him for almost a year, he's got a major hang-up."

Lian smiled weakly. "Nguyen has a major hang-up."

"Which is . . ."

"He wants a son."

Jennifer threw her hands into the air. "My God, are we back in the Middle Ages or something? He's ticked off at you because you haven't gotten pregnant?"

Lian flushed, nodding shyly. "He is of a very old and distinguished family. The Nguyens are directly descended from rulers of the sixteenth century. He is the last male of his particular line. There is only his mother, himself, and his older sister, who is a widow. Her two sons were killed by communist guerrillas before they found wives."

Jennifer paced the garden path in front of her friend. "Has he left you? I mean, for good?"

"I don't know," Lian said thoughtfully. "At first, he came back every few days to . . ." Her voice drifted off and her shining dark eyes shifted away from Jennifer's in embarrassment. ". . . to visit," she finished at last.

How could he treat Lian like chattel? She was so sweet, so trusting and beautiful. Jennifer had so hoped Lian would be rewarded for her long wait by the arrival of her alive and loving husband. It had never occurred to her that the man might not be worth the dust on Lian's slippers.

"Divorce him, Lian," she said suddenly.

The Vietnamese woman looked up at her through huge eyes. "I've thought about that a great deal," she said softly. "I have wondered if it would be best for Nguyen, too. He could find a woman who would do her duty by his family."

Inside, Jennifer was raging. But for Lian's sake alone, she controlled her temper. "Did it ever occur to either of you that it might not be your fault for failing to conceive?" she asked mildly.

Lian looked puzzled, then frightened. "Oh, you mean that *he*—oh, no! That would be terrible. Nguyen could not bear it if he were sterile. Then his family would have died and he'd have no one to blame but himself."

Jennifer gave a dry laugh. "This is insane!" She paused, thinking. "You don't love him, do you?"

"No," Lian admitted so quickly that Jennifer realized

she'd given the question a great deal of consideration. Then her face lit up. "There is another reason for my wanting a divorce. I am in love with Bill Jacobs."

"Oh, Lian! That's wonderful!" Jennifer hugged her happily. "I hope everything works out. It must! You deserve some joy in your life."

In the days that followed, Nguyen never set foot in the house, but his steadfast American aide stopped by a number of times to retrieve various papers and files. The colonel, he informed Lian in a cold tone, was staying downtown. His attitude left no doubt as to where his loyalty lay.

Chris managed to have his leave extended and they all spent the following week at the beach. The four of them lay on the sand for hours, playing cards with the radio turned up much too loud. Hearing the other AFVN deejays sometimes made Jennifer anxious to get back to work, but for the most part she was blissfully content to doze in the sun, dreaming up new patter to accompany her records. She'd brought her guitar along and played for Chris. He was captivated by her voice. She'd lean into his body, his arm slung around her protectively as she strummed and sang in her light soprano.

They were never alone for long. Although it was only March, the weather was mild and the country's lovely beaches were a popular respite from the war. Soldiers on leave appeared, drawing close to listen, often clustering around Chris and Jennifer's blanket for an hour or more to request favorite songs.

As callous to death and killing as some of the soldiers may have become—even the Marines with their shaved heads and steady, dangerous eyes—they mellowed out, and the muscles in their bare shoulders lengthened and relaxed after a couple songs. She believed her music, as much as the blue-green ocean and warm sun, was a vital part of their recuperation.

Chris was generally good-natured about sharing her with other GIs during the day. At night, however, the foursome retired to their rented bungalow, and he wanted no one else around. It was just Mel, Lian, Jennifer, and him.

Then, around eleven o'clock, Chris would silently gather a

couple blankets, take Jennifer by the hand, and they'd walk across the sand to a sheltered cove. There they slept in each other's arms, naked beneath the blankets.

The fresh salt air and the sound of waves lapping up over the pale tan grains below their feet composed a lullaby so irresistible that Jennifer drifted into a deep, dreamless sleep. She awoke cradled in Chris's arms, to the morning cries of sea birds and the laughter of young couples—often American soldiers with Asian women—strolling the unblemished sand.

On the fourth day of their stay, Jennifer took a break from her singing and maneuvered Chris away from the others for a long walk down the beach.

"I need your help," she said as they strolled, holding hands.

It was wonderful to see how he'd opened up to her since they'd first made love. Chris seemed a different person when she got him away from combat and could work the magic of her tenderness on him. She hoped that he'd never again close himself off from her.

"What you need, babe?" he asked, nuzzling the base of her neck playfully.

"Do you think you could find someone for me? A soldier named Bill Jacobs. Lian has fallen in love with him, but she's waiting for her divorce before she and Bill make it official."

"What do you have in mind?" he asked, glancing at her in amusement.

Jennifer sighed. "I'm not sure, yet. I just want to see Lian happy. Her husband is the only man she's ever been with, and it's been a rotten experience for her. I suspect a lot has happened between them that she won't talk about. Bill sounds like a sweet guy. I'll bet having a lover would do her a world of good."

"Has it done *you* a world of good?" he asked, with a devilish glint in his rich blue eyes.

Jennifer felt herself go liquid inside. It seemed, these days, all he had to do was look at her and she'd feel that glow within. She'd have loved to give Lian that gift.

"I'll send word out along the beach," he promised. "We'll find him."

As they'd talked, Chris had been opening a pack of Lucky Strike cigarettes. She hadn't thought much about what he was doing at first, then an odd realization struck her.

"You don't smoke."

"No. What about you?"

"I think it's a ghastly habit."

He grinned, sat down in the sand, dumped out all the cigarettes into his lap, and began redesigning the packet with the aid of his knife and material he'd produced from a small brown bag tucked into a pocket.

Jennifer sat and watched him work.

When he was done, he said, "Since you're set on going back to work, I want you to carry these with you."

"You want me to play practical jokes on my friends? What do they do, make sooty black smoke when you light them?"

"No." He was no longer smiling. "This is an old VC trick, but hopefully they won't expect it from you. If you ever find yourself in a desperate situation again, pass around the pack, or ask for a last smoke before execution . . . then try like hell to get out of the way."

"It's a bomb?" she gasped.

Chris nodded. "If any one of the cigarettes are pulled out, a drop of acid will be released onto a membrane. The membrane dissolves, detonates a powder charge—the same principle as the beer-can mines the VC leave for thirsty GIs."

Jennifer frowned at him. "Isn't it a little dangerous to be carrying something like that around in my pocket?"

"Not unless someone tries to bum a cigarette," he said, with a grin.

Chris did something else very special during that week. He took Mel aside for a couple hours each day while Jennifer sang to her impromptu audience. They sat apart from everyone else and spoke quietly.

Lian was watching them one afternoon when she and Jennifer had a few minutes to themselves. "Christopher is a wonderful man," she told Jennifer. "Mel talks to him about

Curtis when no one else can get through to her. He's really helping her."

"I hope so," Jennifer whispered.

Lian looked at her. "You love him very much."

"Yes." The word seemed to catch in her throat. "I love him beyond words, Lian."

They were silent for a long while. At last Lian spoke.

"Will you marry him?"

"He hasn't asked."

"Has he told you that he loves you?"

"Yes, but not since Tet."

Lian winced.

"It's all right," Jennifer assured her. "I know that he loves me, although he has trouble saying it. I think it's because he's afraid he'll lose me or that something will happen to one of us before we can return to the States. We both have a few months left."

"Maybe," Lian added, "he's even afraid of losing you after you go home."

Jennifer thought for a moment. "You think so? Yes, I suppose you're right." She let out a dry laugh. "After all, he met my father."

And, through her father, Chris had learned a great deal about her family background. He'd seemed surprised at some of the things Max had intentionally let drop: the size of their home in Marblehead, the fact that they had servants, that Jennifer had never seen the inside of a public school, and that she had been ten years old before she first ventured into an everyday department store.

Jennifer's growing uneasiness about her future with or— she couldn't imagine it—without Chris cast a shadow over the final days of their idyllic retreat on the South China Sea.

22

When the week was up, the group reluctantly returned to Saigon. Then Mel returned north to her duties, stronger than ever. Chris helped Jennifer move back into her own apartment on the outskirts of Cholon. It had been broken into during her absence and had to be cleaned up, a task requiring half a day's work. She'd kept nothing of much value there. Most of her beautiful designer clothes were in storage since she had no use for them. Miraculously, she still had furniture, but most of her cooking utensils and knick-knacks she'd bought in the Central Market had been stolen. She and Chris went shopping together and replaced them.

If we can just get through the next few months, she kept telling herself, *then, whatever happens, we'll be together.*

She'd said as much when she accompanied Chris to the airport. He was silent, refusing to speak about the future as if to do so would bring them bad luck.

"I'll always love you, Jen," he murmured, kissing her softly on the lips just before he climbed into the helicopter that would take him back to his unit. "No matter what happens, I'll always love you. Promise me that you'll remember that."

"I will," she gulped, her eyes overflowing with tears. "I love you too, Chris, with all my heart."

But he was already busy talking to the pilot, strapping himself in, adjusting his earphones.

She was disturbed by his strange preoccupation in their last moments together. But then she assumed that he must be refocusing his mind to combat weariness. She wanted him to be careful and keep his mind on staying alive, didn't she?

With Chris gone she felt compelled to immerse herself in work. The long days of rest at the beach had done much to restore her health. She'd finished her medication and, although she sometimes felt a bit rocky, was able to function quite well. She added another hour to each of her new shows and taped service advertisements to be broadcast throughout the day.

"That was Tommy James and the Shondells with 'I Think We're Alone Now.'" Jennifer leaned toward the microphone. Smiling at her engineer on the other side of the glass, she whispered, "Just imagine—you and me alone, soldier." Dick pretended to swoon.

She picked up the next announcement and started reading: "When you're out in the boonies, do what you can to keep your feet in good condition. Change your socks daily and air out those boots. Remember—take care of your feet and they'll take care of you.

"Now let's hear from Leslie Gore, who says, 'It's My Party and I'll Cry if I Want To!'"

She cued Dick, then used the time while the song played to tune her guitar. She'd get the rest of the ads out of the way, then sing for the last twenty minutes. So many men had told her they liked when she sang without interruption for the final segment of the show.

Leslie finished with maudlin panache.

"All right, men, listen up!" she crowed cheerfully as she picked up the next ad on the pile. "Maintenance of the M-16 in the field is affected by weather and geographical conditions. In the upper altitudes, only a light lube should be applied. In areas of plenty of water, be extra sure your lubrication doesn't get contaminated. Take care of your weapon and your weapon will take care of you!"

She rolled her eyes at Dick. *Who writes this stuff?* she mouthed.

Laughing, he shrugged.

"How're the two most beautiful women in Saigon?" Jeffrey asked as he pulled an embassy car alongside Jennifer and Lian. They stood in front of the USO, unable to catch a cab.

"Dead on their feet," Jennifer said, groaning, but she smiled anyway.

After working the entire day at the station, she'd joined Lian at the USO. The night had been fun, a whirl of dancing, hearing guys' stories about home, sharing their dreams for the future and quite a lot of beer. By one A.M., though, she couldn't have remained standing for another minute. She and Lian had hoped for a quick cab ride home.

"Hop in," Jeffrey invited.

Jennifer went first, sliding over next to the young diplomat who wore a tuxedo. She assumed there had been some sort of reception at the chancery.

"Heard from Chris?" he asked, as they pulled away from the curb.

"Yes." Jennifer grinned. "I write to him every evening and, somehow, he finds time to dash off at least a few lines every day." Often she'd receive nothing from him for three or four days, due to the difficulty in transporting mail into the city from remote areas. Then a flurry of notes would arrive and she'd spend the night in ecstasy, reading each one over and over again.

"Too bad. I keep hoping he'll wear thin on you. Then I'll catch you on the rebound."

Jennifer laughed. "Not likely."

"I'm wounded."

"That's not likely either." She kissed him lightly on the cheek. "You have the heart of a rhinoceros."

They turned into Lian's street and pulled up in front of the low white house.

"Come in for a nightcap, Jeffrey?" Lian asked.

"No. I have an early morning tomorrow. In a few hours, actually," he amended, glancing at the gold watch on his wrist.

"Jennifer?"

"Thanks, but I think I'll take advantage of Jeffrey's wheels," she answered, wiggling her bare toes. Her shoes rested in her lap. Her feet felt two sizes larger than they had been at the beginning of the evening.

"Good night, then," Lian said as she closed the car door.

Jennifer turned to Jeffrey as soon as Lian disappeared behind her door. "What's up? Given the hour and those black circles under your eyes, something made you come looking for me." She thought, *It can't be Chris. He wouldn't have been joking about him if something happened to him.*

Jennifer watched Jeffrey's aristocratic profile as they moved into the light, late-hour flow of pedicabs interspersed with the odd taxi or bicycle.

"I didn't want to talk in front of Lian."

The nerves in the back of Jennifer's neck prickled. "What's wrong? Has something happened to her husband?"

"Worse. It's Bill."

"But he's just stationed out at the airport! It's been quiet out there."

After Chris had learned where Bill Jacobs was stationed, he told Jennifer, who in turn contacted Jeffrey. He had developed a network to keep track of friends in-country. Sometimes tracking people down involved use of intelligence communiqués, and when he'd first come to Vietnam, he'd never have dreamed of breaching security codes by leaking news to people outside the embassy staff. Over the course of many months, he'd mellowed.

Today's news, however, was general knowledge. "Bill won't be at Tan Son Nhut for long," he explained. "Some dick-faced general has decided to rotate certain clerical and combat personnel. Share the hardship, that's his idea."

Jennifer shook her head. All GIs, except special combat

troops like SEALS, Marines, and special forces troops, went through the same basic training which included some combat situations. But the most dangerous moment for any of them would come the first time they hit the field: when they had no experience to back them. She couldn't imagine the gentle redheaded clerk from Mississippi in hand-to-hand combat.

"Are you sure Bill's involved?"

"Afraid so."

Jennifer thought for a moment. "Lian hasn't seen or heard from him in days. I wonder why he didn't call to tell her."

"I wouldn't be surprised if he intended to leave without saying anything to her."

"Without even saying goodbye!" Jennifer said, gasping.

"He probably thinks it'll be easier on her that way."

Jeffrey braked to a stop in front of her door.

They sat in silence for several minutes before Jennifer asked, "Where is Bill headed?"

"North of Pleiku somewhere."

Jennifer had been up to that area, but only twice. For weeks at a time, landing a Huey would be next to impossible. Enemy fire was too unpredictable and casualties were high.

"We can't let him leave without seeing her one last time. It would break her heart." She paused, unsure of how many of Lian's confidences she could, in good conscience, share with Jeffrey. "She told me that she refused to sleep with him until she was properly divorced, but her husband's disappeared. If anything happens to Bill, she'll never forgive herself for putting him off."

"He'll probably come back fine," he said in a quiet voice.

"But he might not. Is there some way you can arrange a short leave for him? Just do it, without his having any say in it?"

"Well, yeah. If he's needed for special duty—for instance, if he had important information to hand-deliver to the embassy, they'd temporarily reassign him. But under the circumstances, it would be for no more than twenty-four hours."

She grinned. "That should be enough."

Jennifer had learned that the most important chain of command when dealing with the military was not always the one with the generals at the top. If you needed a Jeep or a Huey and no vehicles were officially available, there was always something sitting around that no one would miss if the right person turned his back. Mel had told her that surgical supplies often had to be obtained through a series of complex trades. Bartering was a way of life in the military and sometimes the only means of survival in Vietnam. Although the U.S. government was willing enough to foot the bill for moving thousands of young men halfway around the world to fight communists, it often cut corners on purchasing sufficient supplies to keep them comfortable or even alive.

In two days' time, she was able to gather crepe-paper streamers, a white-frosted cake from the commissary for which she paid a Vietnamese woman to fashion candy roses, one pair of pale blue silk pajamas, champagne, caviar, and—her *pièce de résistance*—silk sheets.

Jennifer knew that Lian would never entertain Bill alone in her husband's house. She also suspected that nothing could coax her into one of the shabby hotel rooms that catered to GIs and prostitutes. Even a nice suite, which Jennifer would have gladly paid for, wouldn't have struck Lian as quite right. But she sensed that her friend would feel at ease and discreet in the little two-room apartment she'd helped Jennifer pick out and furnish.

When she was finished with her preparations, Jennifer took a cyclo to Lian's house, arriving there just in time to see her step through her front door and turn to lock it.

Lian smiled. "I thought you were working today. Are you going to walk with me to the club?"

She shook her head. "I just came from there. I arranged for you to take the night off."

"But they need me!"

"There were plenty of volunteers to fill in. You need a break worse than they need you. You haven't had a night free in ages."

Lian gave her a suspicious look. "You want to talk about something important, don't you?" She turned back toward her own door, as if to unlock it again.

Jennifer put out her hand to stop her. "Let's go to my place."

They walked the ten blocks easily, without discussing the reason for Jennifer's sudden insistence that Lian take the night off. But as they rounded the corner, Lian slowed down. One of the embassy Electras was parked in the unpaved alley in front of Jennifer's door.

Lian looked delighted. "It's a surprise party!" She laughed, her tiny body lifting into the air on her toes as if she were about to take flight.

"Aw, Jeffrey spoiled it. Look, just act like you don't know what's going on, okay? That way no one will be disappointed."

"I will," Lian promised, stifling a conspiratorial smile.

Jennifer opened the door and held it. Lian stepped through. Bill and Jeffrey were sitting at the square table in the middle of the room, and they stood up immediately.

As soon as Lian saw Bill, she jerked to a stop. Her eyes widened, filling with heavy tears. The lanky redhead wore his army dress uniform, pressed to perfection. His cap was crushed between his hands. Her heart swelled with love, and it was all she could do to not throw herself into his arms.

Bill looked helplessly from Jeffrey to Jennifer, and back to Lian. "I'm sorry I didn't come to see you sooner, Lian," he whispered.

She nodded.

"I thought it would be easier."

"Easier?" Lian repeated in a choked voice. "You were going to leave me for another woman?"

"Oh, no, Lian!" he shouted, dashing forward to enfold her in his arms. "Is that what you thought? There ain't ever gonna be another woman for me. I'm being transferred. They didn't tell you?" He cast a puzzled look at Jennifer.

"I thought it would be best if Lian heard it from you," she explained.

"Yeah," he said, swallowing hard. "I'm headed north with a combat unit."

"I may never see you again," Lian whispered, resting her head on the American's chest.

"Naw. I'll be back. I was just being selfish, see?" Bill touched her damp cheek tenderly, with his long fingers. "I thought I couldn't stand saying so long, knowing it'd be months before we could be together. And then I thought—well hang it, maybe it's just as well. After all, in a couple of months, maybe you'll have squared things with your husband, and you'll be free to marry me."

Lian smiled softly, then stiffened. For the first time, she noticed the table with its sumptuous feast for two and ornate cake. Streamers draped in corkscrews from one corner of the little room to the other.

"Are you angry?" Jennifer asked.

"No, not angry." Lian held Bill tightly, as if she'd never let him go again. "In fact, I am most grateful. But now," she said with a self-conscious smile, "I ask you and Jeffrey to leave."

Outside in the street, women were scrubbing clothing in tubs; others were carrying water in square tin cans or selling meat, live ducks, rice, or bean-curd custard. The air was full of spring and promise. Repairs to reinforce the outer wall of a house were being made with flattened-out beer cans. One woman was hammering together a few pieces of scrap lumber to fashion a step outside her front door. Home improvements, although they might be simple and seem insignificant in the middle of the squalor, were signs of hope. The Vietnamese were ever optimists.

Jennifer smiled and took Jeffrey's arm as they approached the embassy car.

"Happy, Little Miss Matchmaker?" he asked.

"Quite." She sighed.

* * *

Lian and Bill held each other. Neither spoke. The soft sounds of their breathing filled the room while street noises drifted through the parchment-thin walls.

Lian looked into Bill's eyes. She saw in his gentle hazel gaze none of the insistence upon subservience so familiar to her husband's intense glare. Bill's desire for her was undemanding. Nguyen's lust was purposeful, malicious, demeaning, and always unsatisfied.

With total and blissful surrender, she reached up around the American soldier's neck and pulled him toward her until their lips touched, warm and tender.

Bill bent down, easily lifting her. He carried her to the single wooden bed at the back of the room, releasing the curtains to fall around it. He laid Lian down then undressed her as if she were a precious flower. He was peeling the velvety petals away in search of its nectar, its essence of life. And for him Lian glowed with love, with a passion she'd never before experienced. She was love made flesh, tenderness made woman. By claiming her, he was releasing her. She would never again feel as if she were a possession to be passed from her father's house to another man's bed. She was free to give herself and she chose to give herself to Bill.

When she was naked before him on the sheets, she turned on her side and patted a spot near her hip. Still clothed, Bill sat. She fixed him with her shining black eyes and, reaching up, slowly unfastened the buttons of his shirt in descending order. His chest was smooth and hairless like a little boy's. She was reminded of how very young he was. With mounting anticipation, she unclasped the buckle of his belt, lowered the zipper of his pants.

Sliding her small, cool hands into the dark nest within his underwear, she stroked him tenderly for several long minutes. The pleasure in his heated gaze intensified, smoldered, rewarded her. He bent and, maneuvering out of his pants, stretched out beside her.

She was prepared to give herself to him immediately, but he took his time, caressing her with his hands and mouth until her breasts tingled with his touch and she was moist and pleasantly swollen.

"Who taught you to love a woman this way?" she asked foggily as she skimmed her nails lightly over his buttocks.

He smiled at her. "There's lots you can learn in the back of a pickup truck on a hot Mississippi night."

"Mmmm." She sighed, feeling him ready against the soft flesh of her stomach. "I will like to see your Mississippi in the summer . . ."

They'd never spoken in detail about their future. Now it seemed so real to both. They *were* going to be married as soon as she dealt with Nguyen. Their love would be forever. And the idea that she must leave her own country didn't seem so horrible when she thought about being with Bill. The world seemed a very small, cozy place. She could be happy anywhere as long as Bill was with her.

"I love you, Lian," he whispered from above her.

She blinked up at him, tracing a finger the length of his freckled nose. "I love you, Private Jacobs."

The joy in his eyes was as bright as the stars glittering through the crack that separated the roof from the walls of Jennifer's house. Their world spun away in a golden haze of passion and heat, and the night passed slowly as they pledged their love again and again, treating each other to the exotic, flawless ardor only possible when lovers have longed for, waited for, and finally found each other.

Lian felt limp, wonderfully tired. She woke early, leaving Bill to sleep a few extra minutes while she ran out to buy soup from the nearest breakfast kitchen. When she returned, he made her put the bowls down and come back to bed with him.

Although she had thought she was satisfied, as soon as his palms cradled her breasts and his warm mouth covered her nipples, she hungered again. They made love, long and gentle, then more wildly for over an hour before sinking together onto the straw mattress, luxuriously entwined in each other's arms. At last, Bill allowed her to slip from his grasp long enough to fetch their breakfast from the table. They sat in bed, happily conversing while they sipped and ate the cool soup.

Returning to her own house in the late morning after Bill had left, Lian felt at peace. She passed the custard seller, also on her way home, her empty baskets at the ends of a long pole, swinging in the warm breeze. The tailor's door was propped open to catch the mild spring air. Sewing machines chattered from inside. And farther down the block, women water carriers made their stooped way from the pump house. Even though Bill's company was leaving tomorrow for the north, she was not truly sad. They'd talked so much about their plans for the future that she believed in them entirely. All of Saigon seemed to embrace her, rejoicing in her joy.

Lian smiled at everything. Holding her head high, she unashamedly greeted each of her neighbors. For the first time in her young-old life, she felt truly fulfilled, and she prolonged the route home by circling around to the back of her property to enter through the garden gate.

She decided she'd go back to bed for a couple hours. It would keep Bill with her longer, at least in memory. But first, a cup of tea. Inside her kitchen, she lit the portable charcoal stove and set it on the table top. Then she scooped water from the stone jug on the floor, poured it into the teapot and placed it over the coals.

Humming to herself, Lian reached behind her to select the dried tea leaves she'd use from the nearby shelf—but her hand brushed against something unexpected. Startled, Lian let out an involuntary whimper and spun around.

Nguyen's sharp features glowered down at her, his expression black and damning, his nostrils flaring intimidatingly.

For a moment, Lian's heart seemed to stop beating altogether. Her mouth turned as dry as straw. "Nguyen!" she managed.

His lips twisted into a vicious snarl. "You have betrayed me," he growled.

She couldn't deny it, for this time his accusation was true. But she felt remorseless, and some sign of her defiance must have flashed across her face.

Nguyen cursed her and slashed at her with his open hand. She felt strangely incapable of avoiding it.

The blow knocked her to her knees with such force that for several moments she couldn't breathe. The second slap knocked her head against the stone floor.

"Please!" she said, sobbing. Her thoughts were muddled and at odds. Bill. Divorce. She had to make Nguyen understand that as long as they were together, neither of them would be happy. He must understand that much!

Lian looked up to see a blurry form hunkering toward her. She blinked. He swam in and out of focus. Then she glimpsed the short ceremonial dagger in his hand. Another scene flashed across her mind's eye: Nguyen in her room one night, the gleam of metal hidden behind his back. *He meant to kill me that night!* Fortunately, then, she'd woken and he hadn't found the strength to carry out his revenge. Apparently, he'd been brooding for weeks, trying to work himself up to the task again. This time he meant not to be deterred.

"NO!" she shrieked. Lian kicked fiercely at his groin, but she only succeeded in striking the muscled part of his thigh.

"Whore!" he bellowed, lunging at her.

She rolled to one side, kicking blindly, her foot connecting with the side of the blade. The sword flew out of Nguyen's grip, clattering along the stones. Lian's hand lashed out and grasped the dagger. She braced the hilt against her stomach, pointing the tip toward Nguyen as a warning.

"Get away from me. Get away!" she screamed.

His eyes, wild with rage, locked with hers. Ignoring Lian's cries, he launched himself at her.

Whether or not Nguyen ever saw that she held the knife in front of her, she never knew. A shattering weight crashed down upon her. She cried out in pain as the blunt hilt drove into her diaphragm. The sword twisted once, gruesomely, in her grasp as Nguyen thrashed. Then he lay unmoving.

23

Lian wandered in a daze: out her back door, through the garden bright with blossoms, into the busy Saigon street. Plodding blindly, with no concept of who she passed or where she was headed, she cried silent tears.

Her mind ceased functioning. The sole sensation cutting through the glaze of horror was one of great loss. Something fine and beautiful and right had been sacrificed and could now never be part of her life. Oh, yes, it had been wrong to kill Nguyen, but it was the forfeiture of Bill and their future together that choked her with despair.

Stumbling along a narrow alley, Lian lifted clenched fists in front of her eyes. A sticky dampness glued her fingers together. When she forced them open, they resembled bright red poppy petals. Blood on her hands, as damning as the guilt she felt closing in around her heart.

She was vaguely aware of bumping into someone. An old woman screeched, staring in horror at Lian's *ao dai*, and Lian followed her shocked eyes. The delicate white fabric of her dress was splotched with fresh blood.

Starting to run, Lian thrust herself through the morning crowd of shoppers, desperate to put distance between herself and the house where her husband lay dead by her hand. A Vietnamese woman who slew her husband was dealt with severely. She would be locked away in prison for the rest of her life if her judge was lenient. More likely, she'd be executed.

The farther she ran, the less she thought of escape, which was, after all, impossible. People had seen her leave the house, had stared at her blood-spattered clothing, and Nguyen would soon be found. Hadn't Sergeant O'Brien called yesterday to say he'd be by at noon for another of her husband's files? Escape was out of the question. The force driving her on came from another source.

A blur of faces, an agitated hum of voices seemed to follow her, but no one stopped her until she reached the radio station. One of the Marine guards in his snappy dress uniform and white, stiff-brimmed cap thrust out his rifle, blocking the entrance. "Halt. State your business," he ordered.

Lian leaned wearily against a pile of sandbags. "Jennifer," she croaked. "I need to see Jennifer Swanson."

The guard's narrowed eyes took in her stained *ao dai*. He laughed. "What happened, dragon lady? Your slaughter pig get away from you?"

"I must see Jennifer Swanson," Lian insisted dully. By now she could barely exert the energy to lift her head. Her vision drifted off of his face. She heard him summon another guard. There was some discussion while she wavered on unsteady legs. Limply, she sank to the ground beside the sandbags.

A moment later, they were half carrying, half dragging her out of the glare of the sun and into the building.

"Let her rest there for a few minutes," one said.

Lian's head cleared enough to focus on the two men. One seemed to be returning to his post outside, the other stepped over to an office door, knocked, spoke to someone inside.

"Jenny's on the air now," came a woman's voice. Lian recognized it as Gloria's.

Lian covered her face with her hands. Already the shame was beginning. She wished her own breast, rather than

Nguyen's, had been pierced. No one would believe she'd killed him accidentally. They would discover that she'd slept the night before with an American soldier and that she desperately wanted to be free of her husband. The reasoning would follow; her husband had refused to agree to a divorce. Suddenly, she knew why she had to see Jennifer. She must tell her friend the truth before the ugly stories reached her. *I never meant to hurt Nguyen!*

Lian pulled herself shakily to her feet, lurching off across the lobby toward the door leading to the broadcast studios. The guard was too occupied to notice her as she sagged against the swinging door, pushing it open.

As she wove her way down the corridor, Lian peered into large glass panes. In the third studio, she spotted Jennifer. The slender blonde sat in front of a microphone with her guitar in her lap, earphones in place. Her mouth was gently parted as if she was holding a long note when her eyes met Lian's pleading gaze through the glass.

It took Jennifer a moment to recognize Lian. Her friend's face was as white as freshly steamed rice, and her clothes were wrenched out of shape, streaked with what at first appeared to be paint. She realized something terrible had happened.

It was blood smeared down the front of Lian's *ao dai* and dried on her hands that pressed against the glass separating the two women.

Jennifer deftly flicked a couple controls and placed a record on each of the two turntables to her right. She stabbed a finger at Dick French in the control booth, thankful he couldn't see Lian from his angle. She bolted from the studio.

Jennifer caught Lian under the arms and supported her. "What happened?"

"I've killed him."

Jennifer swallowed.

"Who have you killed?" she demanded, walking and dragging Lian along toward her office at the end of the hall.

"My husband," Lian blurted out. "I did not mean to. Oh, Jennifer, I swear I did not mean—"

"Hush. Let's get out of the hall first."

Once she had Lian inside the small office, she closed and locked the door. When she turned around, Lian had sunk into the swivel chair behind the military-issue desk.

Jennifer knelt in front of her. "Are you hurt?" she asked.

Lian shook her head. "I wanted you to know. I wanted to say goodbye to you, Jennifer, before the police come."

"Stop it. Don't say that." Tears welled in Jennifer's eyes. She brushed them away.

"Please," Lian continued, her voice trembling, "tell Bill that I love him and I'm sorry. I've been so foolish. I have spoiled everything for us."

"Tell me what happened," Jennifer demanded.

Lian described how Nguyen had been waiting for her when she'd returned home that morning, and their struggle.

"Did you call the police?" Jennifer asked.

Lian shook her head.

Jennifer had learned enough about Vietnamese law since she'd been in Saigon to understand one thing. Lian wouldn't stand a chance of being released once the police got hold of her. In Vietnam, women's rights were a low priority. The best lawyer Max Swanson's money could buy would do Lian absolutely no good.

"Did any of your neighbors see what happened or come in afterward? Did anyone call the police, as far as you know?"

Lian moved her head tiredly from side to side.

A ray of hope broke through the darkness. Jennifer squeezed her friend's hands encouragingly. She stood up and paced the floor. With the help of a few trustworthy friends, she might have time to . . . to do what? To hide Lian? To spirit her off to her parents' home in Hong Kong? But how? She wasn't even sure that Lian would cooperate. She might be so ravaged by guilt, that she'd insist upon turning herself in. But Jennifer couldn't bear to think of Lian, the gentle, almond-eyed woman she'd loved like a sister, wasting away in a prison.

She went to Lian and gripped her by the shoulders. "Don't give up. Not yet. We can get you out of this, my friend."

Lian looked up at her bleakly.

"We *can!*" Jennifer insisted. "You want to be with Bill, don't you? If you let them take you away, you'll destroy him, as well as yourself. And what good will it do? Lian, don't you realize you were acting in self-defense? That bastard would have killed you if you hadn't stopped him. You didn't mean to murder him—*just stop him!*"

Something in what she'd said must have penetrated. Lian's dark eyes seemed to clear a fraction, and she nodded.

"We have to get you out of Saigon before the police discover his body."

"Yes."

"Where do you want to go?"

"With Bill," she said simply.

Jennifer groaned. "That's impossible right now. How about your parents' home?"

"I would need a new visa. To get one would be difficult. . . . The police—"

"Right," Jennifer agreed. Then a thought occurred to her. A risky and dangerous but utterly perfect plan. "I have it," she said, giving Lian a quick smile.

"Tell me."

"First I have to see some people and make a few calls," Jennifer told her breathlessly. "I want you to stay here. Lock the door after me and don't answer for anyone. I'll be back in a couple hours. With any luck, we'll have your escape arranged by then."

Jennifer ran down the hall, back to the broadcast booth. She poked her head around the corner to Dick French's side.

"An emergency's come up," she said. "I have to leave for the rest of the day."

"We haven't finished taping tonight's show," he pointed out. "What do you want me to do?"

"Dub in one of the prerecorded tapes to fill the dead space."

"Right."

She dashed down the hallway, found an empty office, ducked inside, and sat down in front of the telephone. She had to make dozens of calls fast. Everything had to be arranged within the next hour. Once Nguyen's body was discovered, the police would start their search for this important man's murderer. Guards at checkpoints on all the major roads leading out of the city would be looking for suspect travelers. Police would screen the airports and stop taxis leaving the city. They might initially suspect a VC terrorist, but once they discovered that Nguyen's wife was missing and witnesses who'd seen Lian on the street related their stories, the search would focus on her.

She dialed Gloria's desk in the reception area. Making herself take slow, even breaths, she asked, "Can you get me an outside line?"

"Sure, hon. Something wrong? You sound terrible."

"Tell you about it later, Gloria. For now, I need an outside line—a clear line."

"You mean a secure line? Can't do. Station calls are always monitored."

"Damn!"

"Jeffrey could handle it, if it's important. The embassy has protected lines."

"Thanks, Gloria."

She caught a cyclo a block from the station. "Please hurry," she told the driver, waving double his usual fare as she threw herself into the little canopied seat.

He pedaled furiously, weaving with expertise around pedestrians, bicycles, and cars stopped at lights. In front of the embassy stood two stalwart Marines, weapons at the ready. Would they let her past without buzzing security? Clearing her would take precious minutes.

She recognized the taller marine as one of those who'd held off the Tet attack on the embassy. He grinned as soon as he spotted her.

"Did you catch last night's show?" she called out with forced cheerfulness as she ran toward him.

"Never miss it, Jenny."

"All right if I run up to the ambassador's office? They just called the station. Some big wig's flying in and they want him to get the royal treatment. I have to plan a show around him."

"Probably the secretary of defense. He's coming next month."

"No doubt," she sang out as he motioned her through.

Her heart pounding, she made her way quickly to Jeffrey's floor. Throwing open a frosted-glass door, she plowed past the receptionist with barely a wave, then straight into the junior diplomat's office, letting the door slam behind her.

Jeffrey sat at his desk, bent over a thick sheaf of papers. He looked up at her, surprised, then clearly irritated.

"Thank God you're here!" she said, moaning, dropping into the leather chair across from his desk.

He closed the folder in front of him. "Something wrong?"

She nodded, trying unsuccessfully to catch her breath. "Lian. She's in trouble."

"But she and Bill just—"

"Not *that* kind of trouble," she wailed. Then, lowering her voice, she said, "Her husband was waiting for her when she got home this morning."

"Oh, no."

"He attacked her. She tried to defend herself. There must have been a terrible struggle, and he fell on his own dagger and—"

Jeffrey shot out of his chair. "He's *dead?*"

Jennifer nodded, watching his expression, unable to tell what he might be thinking. If he refused to help them, Lian was lost. If he did and was caught, his diplomatic career would be over.

Jeffrey came around the side of his desk. Putting his hands on the arms of her chair, he looked down at her solemnly. "What have you got in mind?"

"We have to get Lian out of the country, and we obviously can't arrange it through official channels."

"Right," he agreed. "But smuggling a Vietnamese national out of the country is risky for everyone involved."

"I know."

Jeffrey straightened, but his eyes never left her clear green gaze. "You know I'd do anything for you." He cracked a smile. "Guess I just don't know where to draw the line. What do you want me to do?"

"Oh, thank you, Jeffrey!" She hugged him fiercely around the neck. "Is your telephone on a secure line?" she asked.

"Yes."

"Good. Then all you have to do is leave me here with it. I'll arrange everything." She reached out, pulling his phone over in front of her. "And don't worry. If I get caught, I'll say it was my idea. You left the office to get some coffee, and I used the phone without your permission."

"No," he said firmly. "I'd better speak to the switchboard operator, to make certain your calls are put through."

"You're a dream, Jeffrey." She touched his cheek gently. "First, contact Mel at Pleiku. The rest of the calls depend upon what she can tell us."

Jeffrey had no difficulty reaching the evac hospital in the highlands, but there was a long wait while someone went looking for Mel. Jennifer was frantic. Every second wasted seemed as if it were an hour. At last Mel came on the line, and she sounded exhausted.

"We've been in the O.R. since sometime yesterday. No one can remember when the first chopper came in."

Jennifer told her about Lian's plight. After a moment of silence, Mel asked, "Where do you want to send her?"

"The States," Jennifer said quickly. "We can get word to Bill and set up a place and time for them to meet after he's discharged. But we can't possibly get her on a commercial flight."

"If she were posing as a nurse, she could get on an evac jet. There's a flight leaving Qui Nhon at six A.M. tomorrow and flying into San Francisco by way of Hawaii. I'll call a friend who'll meet her at Qui Nhon with a uniform. She can be in the States in less than twenty-four hours."

Jennifer smiled to herself. "Thanks, Mel."

"Wish her good luck for me."

Jennifer turned to Jeffrey as soon as she hung up. "We

311

have a way to fly her to San Francisco on a medevac jet. Now all we have to do is get her to Qui Nhon and call in some favors with the flight crew."

"She'll need a visa and passport. I'll start working on them," he told her.

At Tan Son Nhut airbase, Jennifer reached Ned Kroopnick, the daring young chopper pilot who'd taxied her to dozens of firebases from the delta to the DMZ.

"No sweat," he told her, when she explained to him that her friend needed an emergency lift. "Next to what you and me've seen, Jenny, this'll be smooth duty. When you want the pickup?"

"In one hour," she said quickly. "I'll be with Lian on Route 1, east of the base. We'll park just off the road, midway between the two military checkpoints. You know the spot?"

"Sure."

"Is there enough room for you to land?"

"Only need a dime," he bragged good-naturedly.

"Thanks, Ned."

"Anytime, babe."

Next she called the flight sergeant at Qui Nhon. She asked for the names of the flight crew for tomorrow's evac.

"One of the nurses wants to dedicate a song to them, and she doesn't know their names. It would be much more personal if I could . . ."

Lieutenant Ralph Anderson was slated to pilot the C-5A transport that had been rebuilt to serve as a hospital ward during its flights back and forth across the Pacific. She'd done a show at Qui Nhon and only hoped he'd seen it, or at least was one of her fans. When Jennifer finally had him on the line, she dropped her voice to her on-the-air intimate murmur.

"Hello, there, Lieutenant Anderson! You're talking with Jennifer Lynn tonight. Any messages for the folks at home?"

Jeffrey, at her side, raised his eyebrows questioningly. She smiled at him and held up crossed fingers.

"Oh, sure," Anderson said, sounding a little groggy, as if he had just woken up or was hung over. "Mom, hi! Uncle

Pat, Barbara, Freddy, and Nancy—and, oh, yeah, hope your operation went okay, Aunt Felicia!"

"Stay on the line for a moment, Ralph," she said cheerfully. "We need to take down your mailing address to send you an autographed photo. Okay?"

"Oh, sure," he said, a little more coherently. Then he went silent, as if unsure whether he was supposed to keep talking or not.

Jennifer put him on hold for a moment. "Here," she said, thrusting the receiver at Jeffrey, "write down his address. Then tell him I want to say goodbye."

Jennifer glanced at her watch. Eleven-thirty. Lian had to be at the pickup spot in forty-five minutes to meet Ned, but it would do her no good to reach Qui Nhon if she couldn't board that evac.

When Jeffrey passed the phone back to her, Jennifer told the lieutenant what a wonderful job he was doing, flying her boys home. He was modest, but clearly pleased. "I have a favor to ask," Jennifer said at last, her heart in her throat.

"What's that?" he asked magnanimously.

"I have a nurse friend who'll be accompanying a few patients back to the World, and, well, you see, she's Asian. At least she *looks* Asian. Actually she was born in California, but you know how some guys are: a slant-eye is a slant-eye is a gook over here."

He sounded understanding. "Ain't that the way. Bet she takes a lot of crap from the lifers."

"A lot," Jennifer said with a loud sigh. "I just thought that maybe there was a way you could sort of watch out for her. You know, make sure no one hassles her."

"You got it," he promised.

"And, maybe, when you get to customs and immigration—"

"Hey, those jerks could hang her up for hours. I'll look out for her. Leave it to me, Jenny."

"Wonderful, I feel better already." She winked at Jeffrey.

He handed her a snifter of bronze-colored Remy-Martin after she'd hung up. "I'd hate to ever be on your bad side, Jenny," he said, clinking glasses with her.

"You never will," she promised.

He looked down at his hands encircling the crystal. "I have a confession. When you first came to Saigon, I decided you were going to be my mistress." He winced nervously. "I thought it would be easy. Thought you'd be swept off your feet by my suave manner and exalted status in the diplomatic corps." He let out a self-deprecating laugh, shaking his head. "It didn't matter whether you liked me in any other way. I just wanted to impress you and get you into bed."

"I'm sorry it didn't work out," Jennifer said with a soft smile. Jeffrey was a handsome man with a lot to offer the right woman. Jennifer wasn't that woman.

"I don't think you really are, Jenny, but I am. Believe me, I am." His glance drifted teasingly down her petite figure, then rose again to meet her smiling green eyes. "You're more beautiful now than you were that first day at the airport. If I thought I ever had a chance of getting you away from that damn bush fighter, I'd . . ."

"Don't," she said softly, touching her fingertips to his lips. "I like you a lot, Jeff."

He wrapped his arms around her and rested his chin on the top of her soft, blond head. "If he ever leaves you, Jen. If things just don't work out, I'll be around."

"I know," she whispered, tears in her eyes. She felt so fortunate to be loved by so many wonderful people in so many ways.

"I'll get a car," he said quietly. "We'd better pick up Lian."

24

The Huey spun down out of the midday sky, its blades stirring up a cloud of gray dust. Jennifer squinted to protect her eyes from the grit that whipped through the open window and into the back seat of the embassy car. Jeffrey had already climbed out to flag down Ned Kroopnick.

"Drink up quick," she said, pouring the last of the cognac Jeffrey had brought from his office into Lian's glass. Jennifer had made Lian drink three glasses of the heady liquor to calm her nerves as they sped west on the road out of Saigon.

"It's time!" Jeffrey shouted from outside the car.

Lian's hand was shaking when she gave Jennifer back the empty glass. "Oh, Jennifer, I'm so frightened. What if this doesn't work? What if the police stop me before I get on the transport?"

"It'll be fine," she assured her. "*You* will be fine. Really."

"Come on!" Jeffrey shouted. "The pilot can't stay on the ground this close to the highway for long. Someone will ask questions."

"I know . . . I know," Jennifer muttered. She turned to Lian after they'd both climbed out of the Electra. "Here, take this."

315

Lian looked at the white envelope that Jennifer jammed into her hand along with the visa and passport Jeffrey had somehow produced at the last moment. "What is it?"

"You'll need a little cash to tide yourself over until you find a job." Jennifer had withdrawn all but two hundred dollars from her account at the American Express office. The little she had left would have to see her through the final weeks of her stay in Nam.

Lian shook her head. "I can't take—"

"No arguments!" Jennifer yelled above the roar of the chopper as they ran toward it. "You can pay me back in a couple months. Just don't forget to write to tell me where you are. I'll pass the news along to Bill." Tears she'd struggled to hold back sprang into her eyes. "Now—go!"

With a last emotion-charged hug, the two women parted. Lian clambered up into the seat beside Ned. He gave Jennifer one of his cocky salutes, then the powerful machine rose straight up into the air.

Jennifer stood watching the camouflaged silhouette, like a metallic dragonfly shrinking against the bright aquamarine sky. "Oh, God," she murmured tearfully. "I hope she makes it."

Jeffrey put an arm around her shoulders. "She'll be okay, Jenny. You did everything you possibly could."

As it turned out, less was made of the colonel's death than she'd expected. In fact, there was nothing at all in the English-language papers. A couple days after Lian left, a pair of Vietnamese police officers showed up at the radio station. They asked Jennifer if she knew where Chau Thi Lian, wife of Colonel Nguyen Koa Thuy, might be. They did not explain why they wanted to know and she made a point of not asking. The less volunteered, she sensed, the better. She might make a careless slip if the conversation continued. She told them she hadn't seen Lian for three days, and they left.

As the days passed, she could almost forget the horror of Nguyen's death, almost believe it had never happened. Jennifer didn't write to Mel or Chris about Lian's departure.

She was afraid of her notes getting into the wrong hands. Could the Vietnamese government insist upon Lian's extradition if they discovered she'd escaped to the States? Jeffrey thought not, but to be safe she spoke to no one about the colonel's death. And when soldiers at the USO asked about Lian's disappearance, she pretended to be as puzzled as they were.

The only problem was Bill Jacobs. She wondered if the police knew about him. If they did, he'd be an immediate suspect. He couldn't have returned to his unit by the time Nguyen died, so he very well might not have an alibi.

Jeffrey kept a quiet watch through his contacts. Apparently, the police investigation never extended beyond the immediate area of the city, and Nguyen's death became a minor piece of news buried under larger, more pressing ones.

Jeffrey sent a message to Bill at his new post warning him not to write to Lian. He'd explain why later. Jennifer was sure he hadn't risked writing to her before. Her husband might have intercepted the letters. So perhaps the police didn't know about him. She prayed this was true.

Everything seemed to be under control. Jennifer began thinking about her own future, and going home with Chris.

She wrote to him every day, becoming more and more excited as her remaining time in-country grew shorter. They could live in Missoula if he wished. Or they could live anywhere else he liked. Anywhere in the world! She didn't care. Being with Chris was all that mattered.

He wrote back asking what she wanted to do, really *do* with her life. Wasn't she going to keep singing? She wanted to, but wasn't exactly sure how she'd do it, and where didn't seem important. But they had time, lots of time to think about things like that.

At first she could feel the mounting anticipation in his letters, too. Then they grew less frequent, dropping off to just one each week. His unit had come under prolonged and heavy fire recently, he explained. He'd lost Meeko, one of his closest friends and one of the men who'd volunteered to help free Jennifer from the VC.

She tried to pour all her love and sympathy into each note she sent off to him, but she knew that words would have little power. She needed to be near him to soothe the emotional wounds of the war, to reassure him that something good had come out of Vietnam: their love.

Then Chris's letters stopped.

"You have to find out if he's all right!" she begged Jeffrey one day, only a little more than a week before she was due to fly home.

It took him almost twenty-four hours to reach Chris's recon group by phone and radio link. When Jeffrey met her that night at the dining room of the Caravelle Hotel, his expression was blank. She seized his hands across the table. "Tell me," she demanded, "has he been killed?"

He shook his head, but still looked miserable. "God, I wish I wasn't the one to tell you this, Jenny." Jeffrey looked away from her. "Chris doesn't want to see you again."

The words struck Jennifer like a physical blow in the stomach. She felt dizzy, and for a moment she was positive she hadn't heard him correctly.

"What do you mean? He loves me!"

Jeffrey shifted uncomfortably in the velvet upholstered chair. "I think I understand what he's doing, Jenny. He's cutting the tie for your benefit."

"What?" she shrieked. Heads turned in every corner of the sumptuous restaurant.

"He thinks he's not good enough for you." He looked at her levelly across the table. "And I agree. He's not your type, never was and—"

"You're making this up," she accused, her eyes filling with angry tears. "Jeffrey, don't lie to me!"

"I am not inventing this. He thinks you have a great future with your voice and your father's money. You'll have a very successful career." He laid a warm hand over her fingers, which were trembling, clutching the white damask cloth. "He'll only hold you back. He knows that, Jenny."

She shoved the chair back from the table, threw her napkin down, and, racing between tables, tore out of the room.

318

Jeffrey caught up with her on the street two blocks from the hotel. He grabbed her by the arms and spun her around to face him.

"I'm going to Cu Chi to see him," she managed between sobs. "Let him tell me to my face he doesn't want me!"

He glared at her sternly, but there was concern and fear in his expression, too. "You can't."

"Ned will take me—"

"No, Jenny. You don't understand. He's not at Cu Chi anymore. I never actually talked to him. Two of his buddies filled me in. Chris applied for an early out from the army. It was his second tour, so he got it. He left Vietnam a week ago."

As if a razor-sharp bayonet had plunged into her heart, Jennifer crossed her hands over her breast. Piercing, execrable, inescapable pain; the life seeped out of her. She broke the young diplomat's grip and staggered backward in disbelief.

"You must be lying."

"It's the best thing he could have done," Jeffrey said soothingly, taking a step toward her.

But Jennifer couldn't bear to listen to any more. "I'll find him!" she shouted over her shoulder as she ran down the street.

For the next six days, she did everything she could to track down Chris. But she always came to a dead end. He had processed out of the army while still in Saigon. His flight back to San Francisco had been another Pan Am, but he hadn't shown up in Missoula. Even his parents claimed to have no idea where he was.

Mel called her from Tan Son Nhut. She had another ten days left before she, too, would be able to fly home. Jennifer told her about Chris.

"Wait for me in Saigon, then we can fly home together," Mel suggested.

"But I have to find Chris," Jennifer insisted.

"Honey, if a man doesn't want to be found, you ain't gonna find him."

And so, what she'd anticipated as being one of the

happiest days of her life became the saddest. Jennifer prepared to leave Saigon with a heavy load of memories: some so full of joy it was hard to believe a year at war had given them to her, others bitter and soul-shattering. She'd found love, only to lose it because of who she'd been born. It seemed she'd never be able to escape that curse.

25

Jennifer was free to leave for home but decided to wait for Mel. They'd come to Vietnam together, they'd leave together. She spent her final days visiting all of her friends, saying tearful, heartfelt goodbyes.

"I'll miss everyone so much," she told Gloria, "even sleazy old Hugh."

"You'll be glad to be home again," the young woman assured her.

Jennifer shook her head. "There's nothing for me in Marblehead. They're all strangers."

"Stay here then. Do the show for another year."

"I could," she mused. But Chris was gone, as was Lian and soon Mel. Perhaps she should just return to the States and start looking for Chris. She could convince him to come back to her and give their relationship another chance.

In her heart, though, she knew that talking him out of his doubts wasn't the solution. If he really believed he couldn't be a part of her life and she part of his, no amount of reassurance would help. The choice had to be his and he'd made his decision. She felt desolate, empty—knowing she'd lost Chris forever.

Jennifer helped out at the studio for a few hours each day. In Lian's absence, she manned the nighttime phone lines at the USO, danced with GIs as she had so many times before, even waited on tables—anything to keep busy. She counted the hours until Mel's tour would end. She thought that maybe she'd stay with Mel and Lian in D.C., at least for a while. Mel was being placed on inactive duty for the remainder of her enlistment and intended to go back to school. Lian was staying with elderly friends of Mel's mother until Mel herself returned. Bill would complete his enlistment in the fall of that year. Until then, the three women could share an apartment.

On the day Mel was due back at Tan Son Nhut, Jennifer was given an emotional farewell party at the radio station. Afterward, waving and choking back the tears, she climbed into a Jeep borrowed by her long-time friend and broadcast engineer Dick French. She was glad she wasn't riding with a stranger. Dick would understand her silence during the trip to the airfield.

As they drove along Route 1 in the dusk, the sunset's glow deepened from pink to maroon on the horizon ahead of them. Jennifer touched the guitar case on the seat beside her and drifted back over the past year. So much had happened. So much . . . too much . . .

Subconsciously, she became aware of another vehicle coming up behind them, its engine racing. She didn't bother looking until it pulled up alongside, matching Dick's speed.

Indifferently, she glanced to her left and, for a moment, failed to recognize the driver, who was alone in a second Jeep. His identity registered belatedly, and she remembered smiling a second before he jerked his wheel to the right, ramming his bumper so violently against the side panel of her Jeep that it skidded off the road, rolling down the steep incline before groaning to a stop in a ditch.

Chris had loose ends to tie. He had processed out of the U.S. Army in-country so that he could finish what he'd started—training a couple of the new grunts in his platoon at Cu Chi so they'd stand a chance of surviving after he left for good. He called Meeko's mother in Houston to tell her how sorry he was about her son and to ask if he might drop by her house to talk. He also planned to stop in at the embassy to thank Jeffrey Kirk in person for engineering his parting with Jen. Now that her year was up and her final show had aired, she'd undoubtedly returned to Massachusetts. He then felt safe about reentering Saigon.

The ambassador's assistant wasn't in his office when Chris first arrived. He made himself comfortable in a leather armchair and looked around the walls at a prominently displayed diploma from Yale, oil paintings tastefully framed in dark woods, a gleaming rosewood desk, a rich blue Oriental carpet, and fully stocked liquor cart.

This was Jennifer's class of man: polished, tasteful, affluent. Chris had thought a lot about their possible future before making his final decision. He'd have her for a while, but she'd inevitably grow disenchanted with an ordinary guy like him, restless for a glitzier life. She might even pretend to be happy, stay with him out of the goodness of her heart. He couldn't bear that.

Jeffrey walked in, with a grim look on his face that turned grimmer when he noticed Chris. "What are you doing here? I thought you'd left the country."

The diplomat had always been skeptical of him. Chris suspected that Jeffrey had only agreed to deliver his parting message to Jen out of his own motives. That Jeffrey was in love with her cut Chris up inside, but he knew she'd be better off marrying a career diplomat. Jeffrey would look after her, treat her right. She'd be safe, comfortably supported, and . . . he ached just thinking about them together. But there was no other way.

Chris blinked away the annoying mist that clouded his vision. Jeffrey was pouring himself a bourbon and held up the bottle as an offering to Chris.

"No, thanks. To answer your question, I out-processed two weeks ago, but had some unfinished business hereabouts. Jen thought I'd left, right?"

Jeffrey nodded. "She telephoned your parents, hoping to reach you in Montana."

"I haven't told them I'm coming home yet. Guess I'd better call so they don't worry."

"You're sure about leaving her?"

Chris winced. Being sure that leaving was the best for both of them wasn't quite the same as not having any regrets. "Yeah, I'm sure. Was she okay?"

"She'll be fine." Jeffrey's voice was unusually firm, as if he was concerned Chris might, even now, change his mind about letting her go. "Actually . . ." He took a healthy swig of his drink. "Her plane's due to take off in less than an hour."

"You mean she hasn't left already?"

"I just came from her bon-voyage party. She stayed around a couple extra weeks in Saigon waiting for Mel. Don't worry, I'll keep in touch with her."

"I bet you will," Chris muttered, then gave Jeffrey a half smile to let him know that, in his place, he'd be doing the exact same thing, courting Jen. No other woman could compete with her flash and exuberance, the joyous talent and beauty she'd shared with him. She'd dazzled him from the moment they'd met on the plane headed for Nam, and she continued to every time he heard her name mentioned. Years from now when he made love to another woman, he'd imagine Jennifer Lynn Swanson, looking up at him from a creaky wooden slat bed in Saigon, her green eyes shining with love and a desire so intense and breathtakingly pure he'd never be able to shut them out of his memory.

Chris planned to concentrate his energies on setting up a little auto-parts shop into which he'd invest the service pay he'd carefully saved. The store would cater to guys like him who'd grown up tinkering with their bikes and cars. In time he might be able to parley it into a modest chain. Maybe he'd marry a local girl—decent, down-to-earth, attractive in a simple way. He'd always wanted to have a family. It might work out. But, oh, how Jen had spoiled him for other women.

"So, what can I do for you now, old man?" Jeffrey asked, bursting through Chris's melancholy haze.

Chris looked at him solemnly. "I just wanted to say

324

thanks for everything: pulling strings and all when Jen was being held by the VC, covering for me when I couldn't say goodbye to her." He hesitated, swallowing over a lump in his throat. "Tomorrow morning I'll be heading out to Tan Son Nhut myself, taking the Freedom Bird back to the States."

Jeffrey set down his drink, looking relieved, and held out a hand. "I wish you the best, Chris."

"Thanks." They shook, parting with a wary respect for each other. Each man had done, and would do, what he had to for his country, and for Jennifer. Their country might or might not reward them for their loyalty, but Jennifer Swanson would never know of their masculine conspiracy.

Chris stood outside the embassy, looking up and down the busy Saigon street. Damn Jeffrey. Damn his smooth Eastern prep school veneer, and his family's money, and his diplomas, and his silky smooth bourbon, and his rosewood desk. And damn that plane that would be taking Jen away from him in less than an hour.

No! he thought, suddenly confused. Don't damn the plane. God speed her jet over the Pacific and across the States and back to her safe haven of Marblehead. God speed it, and God bless Jen.

He looked up from the dusty pavement at the wheezing sound of a shuttle bus pulling up in front of the embassy gates. It ran a regular route between the city and airbase. He thought, *I might as well head out now as in the morning. This way I can watch her plane take off.* He stepped up onto the bus, feeling as if this was the first step of a thousand he'd have to force himself to take to leave her. *One step farther from Jen,* he thought. *I can do this. I just have to keep taking these damn steps, just like that day in the market. Get on this bus, get off, cross a runway, walk away from a plane twenty-four hours later in Frisco. Walk away from her . . . one agonizing step at a time. I can do it.*

The ride back to the airbase seemed to take an eternity. Chris watched through the window as darkness fell, wondering if he really would make it before her flight took off. The land was flat and the sun had left a crimson stain low in the sky. After passing the second checkpoint and continuing about a mile down the highway, the bus slowed to avoid something in the road. Curious, Chris looked out the window and spotted an abandoned Jeep pulled partially off the road.

Instantly, his soldier's intuition kicked in, and he leaned forward in his seat to tap the driver on the shoulder. "Pull over."

"Doesn't look like anyone's around. Probably just a flat."

"Probably." But it didn't look right to him.

Chris climbed down to the road and looked around while those left on the bus grumbled at the delay. He had reluctantly surrendered his AK-47, but held onto a .45 automatic and his field knife. Until he was stateside, he wouldn't feel at ease without a weapon. Now his hand slipped into the waistband of his trousers and pulled out the pistol.

He checked the Jeep; there didn't seem to be any damage except for a superficial scrape along the right front bumper. The motor was still running. He squinted into the gloom. Had the Jeep's driver been picked off by a sniper? Or had he just stopped to take a leak?

Leaning toward caution, Chris decided not to call out, and a moment later he spotted a second vehicle overturned in a ditch below the level of the highway. Behind it in the thickening darkness, a shadowy figure moved.

"Anything wrong?" came a shout from the bus. The figure stiffened, then quickly ducked out of sight.

"No," Chris answered loudly, as he headed back toward the road. "Just an abandoned set of wheels. I'll turn in a report so the MPs can come for it in the morning." On his way past the first Jeep, he reached in and shut off the engine. Too bad these things didn't require keys to start up, he'd have pocketed them for sure.

A dozen or more men were on board the bus, mostly green grunts heading back to the base from a day in town. He wanted to get them clear of here. It seemed reasonable that if someone had stopped to aid accident victims, the good Samaritan would have hailed a passing vehicle for assistance. Instead, whoever was out there was trying to avoid detection, and that worried Chris.

As the door closed behind him, Chris gave up his hope of seeing Jen off if only from a distance. He directed the driver, "Go on ahead a quarter mile or so, then slow down. I'm jumping ship. Soon as you reach the airfield tell the gate guard to send some men back here. I think somebody's in trouble."

Jennifer never lost consciousness. She heard herself scream as the Jeep was forced from the road and flipped, throwing her clear. For a while she held her breath, touching herself at sore spots, assessing her condition. Nothing seemed to be broken, although her legs were painfully scraped and a cut was oozing blood from somewhere behind her hairline. She was afraid to move and give away her position, for she had no doubt that the man had been trying to kill her when he ran her car off the road. She listened in the darkness, heard footsteps coming closer. Then nothing.

Jennifer breathed shallowly, prickles crept up her spine. Still no movement in the brush around her. Yet she knew he was here, somewhere.

A gun fired from close range. She jumped, her heart thumping wildly in her chest. And it took only a fraction of a second for the horrible truth to hit her. *Oh, God, he's shot Dick!*

Unable to do anything to help her poor engineer, Jennifer forced herself to think about what she should do next. The footsteps were again approaching. Automatically, she reached for her M-16, always beside her on earlier trips, only to realize it was no longer there. She'd given it to Gloria as a parting gift.

Just then, she heard a deep rumbling, a truck or bus approaching. The headlights stopped by the edge of the road and her heart leapt with hope. If she could somehow signal that she needed help . . . but to do so would guarantee that her attacker would locate her. She remained quiet, praying someone would come to investigate without an invitation, and someone did—thank God!—step off the bus. She could see his silhouette against the headlights. Unfortunately, whoever it was reboarded almost immediately, and all she could do was watch in desperation as the red taillights faded.

Jennifer hadn't had a chance to consider her remaining options when a hand came down hard on her shoulder and yanked her brutally to her feet.

"Hello, Sergeant O'Brien," she whispered.

"Bitch!"

"Not a nice way to greet an old friend."

"You're no friend, lady. You helped Nguyen's wife escape from the police."

"Yes."

"And so did that nigger nurse."

She narrowed her eyes at him. Had the colonel's loyal aide already hunted Mel down? "You didn't—"

"No," he interrupted, guessing what she was about to ask. "But I'll find her, too. And one of you will tell me where the colonel's wife is. You'll all be punished."

"Lian was only trying to defend herself."

"Liar!" He growled in her face, gripping her arms so tightly she lost sensation in her fingertips. "That woman was a whore. He told me all about her . . . cuckolding him with GIs while he defended his country. She even did it while he was in Saigon on leave. He had to move out of his own house, he was so shamed by her behavior!"

"She was faithful to her husband," Jennifer stated. "All she wanted from him was a divorce."

"Shut up!" he screeched in her face.

But Jennifer had no defense except words. "Nguyen was a drunkard. He beat and abused her."

"I told you to shut the hell up!" he yelled. Then a smile of satisfaction spread across his lips, slowly, like sweet molasses pouring from a jar. He raised a pistol to her temple.

The cool, hard metal muzzle touched Jennifer's temple.

"Please," she pleaded.

The gun pressed into the soft crescent of flesh in front of her ear. She swallowed as a few possible defenses flashed through her mind. She might slip free of his hand, run a few paces before he shot. But at such close range he didn't have to be particularly accurate. Or she might twist her body just enough to knee him in the groin. Would the pistol go off as soon as he sensed an aggressive move on her part?

Then she remembered the cigarettes. She still carried them in her blouse pocket—less for their usefulness than as a reminder of Chris.

Jennifer had little hope that O'Brien would fall for a last-smoke-before-execution plea, conveniently pulling one from the pack for her. But perhaps there was another way. If *she* were to contrive another reason for taking them from her pocket and pull one out while he was still holding her . . . at least he would no longer be around to harm Mel or Lian. And she had no doubt that he'd keep his promise to hunt them down unless she stopped him here and now.

Oh, God, give me the strength.

"Please!" she gasped. "I'll pay you! I'm rich, let me go and you can live your life in comfort."

A vague light of interest crossed his fury-swollen face.

"Look, I have jewelry." She gingerly moved her arm out of his loosened grip. "This watch—it has diamonds around the crystal. It's worth several thousand dollars."

His eyes flickered, taking in the delicate Swiss timepiece as she unclasped it from her wrist and handed it to him. "Anything else?" he asked. He might not be willing to exchange her life for valuables, but apparently he wasn't so principled he'd turn down funds that would help him avenge Nguyen's death.

Slowly, Jennifer reached into her breast pocket. Her fingertips brushed against the crisp cellophane wrapper, then the filter end of one of the primed cigarettes.

"No!" O'Brien barked.

She froze.

"Drop your hands. I don't trust you, bitch."

Jennifer shut her eyes, shuddering as his knuckles slipped inside her pocket. Her heart throbbed in her ears. *Oh, Chris, what would it have taken to make it work for us? A miracle, I guess. No less than a miracle.*

She felt the cigarette pack rise out of her pocket.

"Huh," the sergeant snorted. "It figures, a sneaky cunt like you would try to smuggle jewelry past customs. Well, now that you've paid me, I'll pay you back. How's that, little lady? Not with your life, though . . . only with a quick death, more than a traitor deserves."

As he spoke, he raised the pistol to her forehead again, delaying only long enough before pulling the trigger to dip his head forward as he lifted the red-and-white Lucky Strike package. Using his lips, he plucked a cigarette free.

Chris was crouching in the ditch beside the crashed Jeep. He checked the driver's pulse. The man was dead but not from the effects of the accident—a bullet hole pierced the center of his forehead. He checked the back seat. No passengers. However, as his glance scoured the ground nearby, he spotted a dark shape, and when he stepped closer, he could see it was a guitar case.

Cold lightning streaked through his veins. *Jen! Oh, God!* She was here, at least she had been here. Just then a shot echoed through the darkness, followed almost immediately by an ear-ringing explosion.

Instinctively, Chris threw himself down in the dirt, covering his head, and a sick feeling filled his stomach. Both sounds—a gunshot and a mine?—had come from the same direction, and all he could think about was *her!*

Without regard for possible VC trip wires, Chris scrambled out of the ditch and tore across the field. He felt dizzy and hot with helpless rage as he scanned the dark landscape. Not a soul was in sight.

"Jen!" he roared.

Silence. Godawful, terror-filled silence.

"Jen! Please answer. It's Chris!"

A soft moan came from a tangle of branches to his left. He spun, aiming his pistol, and a small, white tennis shoe caught his eye, then he was running with his heart jammed up into his throat.

She was crumpled in the brush, one arm hanging limply at her side, a shoulder clutched with her opposite hand, blood trickling between her fingers.

She was alive, for the moment. But what about the other person, the one with the gun who might still be a threat? Chris's practiced eyes swept the clearing once more as he stood protectively over her, and gradually he became aware of the pungent stench of burnt powder and flesh. At last he saw the man, almost indistinguishable from the dirt where he lay, his olive-drab fatigues charred and bloody. There seemed to be nothing left of a face, no hand on the left arm.

"I feel awful," she mumbled.

"I'll bet you do, darling," Chris whispered, with tears streaming down his face as he knelt beside her. On examination, it seemed to Chris that the bullet had entered near her right shoulder blade and had exited cleanly out the front. "It's all right, Jen. You'll live to sing another day."

He scooped her up off the ground and started walking toward the road with her in his arms.

"I love you, Jen," he murmured. He said it again and again, on every alternate step until he reached the road, knowing he'd be looking for ways to prove his words for many years to come. He had no intention of leaving this extraordinary woman again.

Epilogue

The sweltering kitchen of Melantha Benning's simple apartment in southeast D.C. was a far cry from Swanson House's elaborate, air-conditioned dining salon. The day had been one of the hottest of the summer, reaching 103 degrees by one o'clock. The dripping humidity reminded them all of the jungle.

Jennifer stood with her back to the others, her gaze fixed on a distant place beyond the open window, beyond Washington, beyond the sprawling great land mass that was the United States, and still farther beyond to an Asian country. Chris came up behind her, put his arms around her. These days he was always there when she needed him, always aware of the moments when the past slipped back to haunt her. This time, it had been a radio playing from an open window across the street. The disk jockey had been a woman.

It had been a year since they'd left Nam, yet the months spent there, the friends she'd made, the men she'd sung to—the ones she'd seen smile, then go off to fight and, sometimes, more often than she could bear to think of, to die—still lived within her. That year had changed her entire life, and brought her a love so satisfying she couldn't imagine being without it. Or without Chris.

"Are you back yet?" her husband whispered in her ear, squeezing her tenderly.

"Almost." She smiled over her shoulder at him.

"It seems like a long time ago, but just like yesterday, too."

"That's exactly how it seems," she agreed.

"Break it up, lovebirds!" Mel crowed.

Her face aglow, Jennifer turned to her friend. "When will Lian be here?"

"She gets off work at five. Bill's due back in the city around six."

Instead of Jennifer moving in with Mel, Lian shared the apartment with Mel. Bill had joined them six months later when his enlistment was up. Lian worked as an interpreter for a manufacturer that exported throughout Asia. Bill spent much of his time traveling up and down the East Coast, job hunting. So far he'd found nothing but poorly paying construction jobs.

"How is school going?" Chris asked Mel.

"Great, but it's tough as hell. I have to study every waking hour and then some. Still, it's pretty cool to have performed surgical techniques these green-ass medical students are just reading about."

Mel had applied to and had been accepted by Georgetown University's highly respected School of Medicine. Discarding her dream of becoming a surgical nurse for the reality of becoming a surgeon was a step she'd never have taken if it hadn't been for Jennifer's badgering.

"And what about your own classes?" Mel asked Jennifer.

"I love them. And I love New York, but as soon as I finish my vocal training at Juilliard, we're moving out to Montana to start Chris's business and establish a home base."

"Luckily, Jen fell in love with the Montana wilderness when I took her out there last fall. If she's going to pursue her singing career, she'll have to spend a lot of time on the road, and I'll travel with her whenever I can. But she'll have a quiet retreat to come home to," Chris said.

"We're building a cabin about fifteen miles outside of Missoula," Jennifer said with a contented smile. "It's heaven."

For his part, Chris couldn't have been happier. He would be able to open Tyler's Auto Parts with modest local financing added to his own savings. Max Swanson had offered start-up funds, but Chris had turned him down. Just as important to him, Jennifer would be doing what she loved most: singing, bringing joy into people's lives. She was training with one of the best classical voice coaches in the country, with the idea that she might try her hand at opera. Her teachers had already told her she showed great promise. There were times when they'd have to be apart, but the absences would only make their moments together that much sweeter.

Jennifer squeezed his hand. "Now who's drifting?"

"I was just thinking that I'd never have believed anything good could come out of this war."

Jennifer nodded. There had been so much tragedy. Mel had lost Curtis. Lian had suffered immeasurably at the hands of a cold husband and nearly lost everything as a result of his final assault. It still remained to be seen whether she'd ever see her parents again. Now Lian had a new life with Bill. However, the young couple were under a lot of pressure, for despite Lian's yearning for independence, she was having difficulty adjusting to American culture. They were poor as could be, but would accept no help, wanting to work things out for themselves.

The war still raged in Asia, but there were signs it wouldn't last forever. The U.S. military was getting less public support, and looked as if it might eventually have to pull out of Vietnam entirely. She hated to think what would happen to the thousands of Vietnamese who'd supported the American forces. Reprisals were chillingly likely.

Jennifer had decided to make no judgments about the war—whether America's being there was right or wrong. She couldn't believe the boys who'd died had given their lives for no good cause or that the killing had been justified.

It had happened, that was all. She wished with all her heart that it wouldn't happen again.

She gazed into Chris's face, feeling the chill of life's terrors warm out of her bones under the sun of his smile. All she knew was that she wouldn't be the person she was now if it hadn't been for those days and nights in Nam. She wouldn't have Chris or her new-found dedication to her music. For the present, that was all she wished from life.

Printed in the United States
By Bookmasters